DEADLY ENCOUNTER

The boy swam closer to the center of the river. New voices joined in the droning along the shore, swelling like a Gregorian wind. A series of mocking cries rose over the building din; and then, finally, one long scream.

"Howlers," the boy muttered. He dove, and swam underwater. When he surfaced, the warbling ululations were diminished. He left the water, once again entering the vegetation.

Almost instantly he was jumped by three Howler sentries who set upon him with glee and drooling. He crumpled to the ground. As he lay in the ferns, struggling for air, the three guards licked his body all over with their long, prehensile tongues—preparatory to the kill.

It was a kill they never enjoyed . . .

Also by James Kahn
Published by Ballantine Books:

WORLD ENOUGH, AND TIME

TIME'S DARK LAUGHTER

JAMES KAHN

A DEL REY BOOK

BALLANTINE BOOKS • NEW YORK

A Del Rey Book
Published by Ballantine Books

Library of Congress Catalog Card Number: 82-3938

ISBN 0-345-29248-0

Manufactured in the United States of America

First Edition: July 1982

Cover art by Laurence Schwinger

GRATEFULLY DEDICATED TO
MATTHEW MEISTERHEIM

That which is in disorder
Has neither rule nor rhyme,
Like the stars at Heaven's border
And the troubled laughter of Time.

—Francis Carlin,
The Raveled Edge

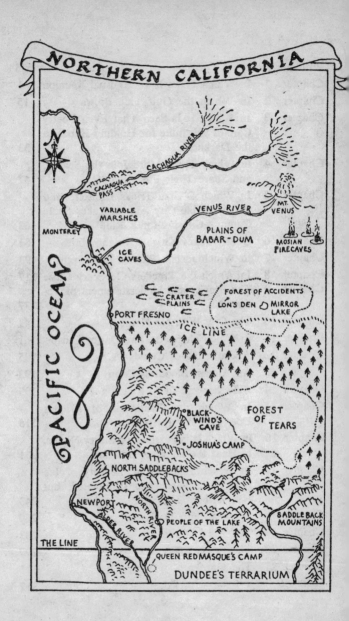

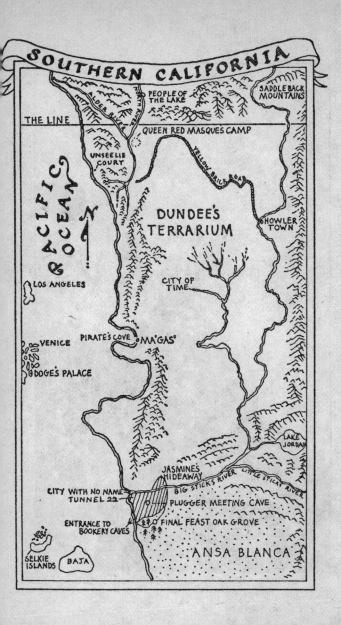

PROLOGUE

DRAGON eggs.

Tuberous, knobbly, soft; they sat in a warm, shallow pool where water from a hot spring trickled down the cold stone of the tunnel. Dark and warm.

An attenuated species, Dragons. Once grand, flaming, they were now almost extinct; yet a small clutch had found these tunnels, and proliferated. Their wings stunted, reflexes dulled, they wormed stiffly through the dank corridors that laced the cliffs beneath the City—living on the refuse of the people above, or on the smaller sewer creatures that cohabited their subterranean domain. Their mating habits, once directed by the stars, now knew only the season of the cave.

So, softly, the scrabble of talons on wet stone, scales grating against cavern wall, the rut and bellow of Dragon lust.

While in a warm, shallow pool not twenty feet away, still only half-incubated from the last mating, and still quite oblivious to the writhing lizards in the cul-de-sac beyond—

Dragon eggs.

Tuberous, tantalizing . . . from behind the lip of a narrow chasm, down the shelf of rock that abutted the pool, something studied these eggs.

A shape, without form, without motion; a blackness in the blackness—it crouched, staring at the eggs, sniffing the air, watching the nearby Dragons circle and couple. As the giant reptiles neared their frenzy, the formless shape crept swiftly from its shelter, padded up the slippery channel to the warm pool, looked left and right, paused. Its pupils constricted in the weak light from a side tunnel not seen from the earlier vantage. The light was feeble but gave the creature a silhouette. It had the outline of a Cat. Its name was Isis.

Warily Isis watched the clambering shadows of the Dragons in heat—clawing each other and the endless night in extremities of passion. They roared thunder. In that moment, Isis snagged the nearest egg with her forepaw, rolled it down the stony slope, over the ledge to her hidden ravine—then tore it open with two quick yanks.

She lapped voraciously at the congealing yolk; chewed the few cartilaginous bits that had begun to form. This was a rare treat.

When she had done, she sat; licked her paw, drew it across her face, repeating this many times. In this, she was meticulous.

Suddenly, in mid-stroke, she stopped: the crashing above—the mounting—had ceased. The mother Dragon could be heard scraping, step after slow step, back to its nest.

In complete silence, Isis backed through her ravine to its other end, down a three-foot drop into a twisty fast-water canal. Cannily, she swam several rough turns, paddling out finally at a dry, cool cross tunnel, where she sat only long enough to shake herself out; then trotted calmly off into the dark.

CHAPTER 1

In Which There Is an Unusual Reunion

THE boy ran silently down the limestone path that twisted through the jungle. He was barely fifteen years old, yet muscled like a tiger. Feline were his feet, too, calloused as footpads; and his eyes, which registered all movement even in these dark mists; and his instinct. Into the flesh of his chest a large ruby was sewn, glinting every time his pectorals flexed. He burned bright, this tiger of a boy.

It was night in the rain forest, steamy and dense. Everything was suffused with a red glow cast by the phosphorescent algae that covered the ground, filled the pools. The foliage so closely surrounded the path down which the boy ran that he had to crouch to avoid getting tangled. Like as not, he would have crouched in any case: he had crouching ways.

Presently he came to the Alder River. The Alder ran backward. That is, it made a white-water plunge from the Pacific Ocean into the depths of the rain forest—quickly at first, then winding down to a subdued saline flow. Not much vegetation grew along the banks here, due to the brininess of the soil, but bleached bones were strewn everywhere, like the broken stalks of death.

The shoreline was the gray-white of a dirty salt lick, and just beyond it, the jungle encroached as closely as it dared. Invisible birds chirped, insects buzzed. Steam—the real substance of the jungle—hovered in the air as animals screamed or were silent, according to their sense. And the deeper the boy weaved his way into the dense matrix of the rain forest, the more inexorably he became part of the jungle itself, a cell in the organism.

He lowered himself into the river from the chalky bank,

1

taking rest as the gentle current bore him south and east. Once, a Gator approached his backside, showing its teeth; but the boy warned it off with a select phrase in its own language; and it quickly disappeared into the depths. Most animals knew by scent or sense: it was well not to make sudden moves near this boy.

Others approached. Eyes, recessed into the foliage, like dark jewels buried in thought, kept silent pace for a time. Then they, too, withdrew.

The boy seemed calm, but alert. He assumed the world was hostile, but took this as such a basic premise that it neither upset nor surprised him. Things were as they were. He had always endured; he would endure.

A giant Lizard stood on the shore munching palm leaves, balefully eying the boy who floated past him. The boy saw the Lizard but ignored it, for it posed no danger.

A quiet rain began to fall—fat, soft drops plopped heavily all around, partially clearing the hot vapor that filled the air. In the undergrowth, jungle eyes glittered.

The boy didn't know what to expect from the tribe whose Queen he sought—it was spoken of only in rumor. Some said it comprised the misfits of a dozen other groups: creatures who had banded together to seek utopian values after having been exiled from their own peoples. Others swore it was a penal colony that had overthrown its keepers and now lived at the expense of unsuspecting travelers. He was ready for whatever he found—as a Human in a largely animal world, he felt at ease with outcasts.

In the distance, the main fork of the Alder was approaching. The boy brushed a cobweb from his face. From the trees, suddenly, a sound: a continuous humming of voices in the lower registers, almost a groaning. It rose and fell, in pitch and volume, as if it were the jungle's own erratic pulse, as if the beast were stirring from deep sleep.

The boy swam closer to the center of the river, automatically, without expending any energy in the decision or the effort. His energy was focused on his senses. His actions were unclouded by fear or ambivalence or strain. His mind was ever clear.

New voices joined in the droning along the shore, swelling like a Gregorian wind. The boy pulled a spider web from his nose, then dipped his hand into the river to wipe off the sticky shreds.

A series of mocking cries rose over the building din; and then, finally, one long howl.

"Howlers," the boy muttered. He dove, and swam underwater for nearly five minutes. When he surfaced, the warbling ululations were diminished. He left the water, once again entering the vegetation.

Almost instantly he was jumped by three Howler sentries, who set upon him with glee and drooling. One held his legs, one his arms, while the third heaved a club into his belly. He crumpled to the ground. As he lay in the ferns, struggling for air, the three guards licked his body all over with their long, prehensile tongues—preparatory to the kill.

It was a kill they never enjoyed.

He blinded two simultaneously with precise stabs of his clawed fingernails. The third he killed in the same moment with a kick to the throat. Then he stood and dispatched the first two with his knife before they could howl. He stood only a minute longer, catching his breath, then went on.

Great, furry, melon-sized Spiders lived in this area of the river, and Spider packs attacked him twice. But each time, at the first hint of a web sticking to him, he would quickly follow the thread back to the Spider who had spit it—they were not, for all their treachery, nimble beasts—and kill the creature with a swift knife thrust or a heavy rock. A few such encounters, and the Spiders desisted.

The boy moved like a vapor toward the tribe's encampment. It was their Queen he wanted; he had to get her. For seven days, he had been stalking, seeking the way with a careful, thoughtful urgency that characterized the two sides of his personality: calculation, and fettered passion. It gave him a hunted look.

One step at a time, he neared his destination, closing like an elusive suspicion. If a creature got in his way, he would kill it with little feeling. A step, a kill—it was all one to him.

Until the Vampire swooped out of the tuli tree to clamp

its icy fangs in his neck. This was no witless engagement; for the boy loved to kill Vampires.

Ignoring the electrical pain in his neck, the boy thrust toughened fingers into the demon's mouth and, with two twisting, violent tugs, nearly tore off the Vampire's jaw.

It shrieked and jumped back in amazement, its bleeding mandible dangling curiously to the left, unhinged. One of its fangs had broken off in the boy's neck. They regarded each other with malice, and circled.

Again, the Vampire lunged, wings spread. But his timing was off, the boy had unnerved him so. The young Human side-stepped the attack and stabbed the Vampire above the right kidney—twice, in and out with such speed that he could have struck twice more before the Vampire turned; but he wanted the death to be slow. He was never cruel this way, except with Vampires.

The wounded creature staggered off into a moss grove. The boy let him leave, and returned to stalking the Queen's camp.

The rain stopped, the steam returned. Morning was only an hour away, as he crawled meticulously under a thicket of barbed orchids. Finally, through a matting of vines, he saw the bivouac. Tents, fires, a stream. An altar. Howlers, Frangols, Spiders, Vampires, Harpies, a couple of Neuromans, probably Cidons, Snakes, Cats, some Griffins.

The boy watched from his protected position, absolutely motionless, drawing barely two silent breaths each minute. In the clearing, activities went undisturbed. Some creatures slept, some kept watch. In one corner, Spiders were laying eggs in a ragged hole they had chewed in the belly of a dying Gorilla. Near the main fire, a mother Sphinx suckled her baby.

The boy's attention was drawn to a far tent, from which two Vampires dragged a weakly struggling Human. They pulled him to the stone altar at the center of the camp; then each gnashed one of the Human's wrists and began sucking from the wounds. The Human passed out, and with his bloody wrists the two Vampires drew ritual designs on the stone. The boy, who watched from the bushes, clenched his teeth—it was all he could do to keep from running into the clearing and cutting them.

Suddenly a figure leapt out of a larger tent, a creature so overwhelming that all the others seemed to shrink. It was a woman.

A tall, naked woman, red of skin and hair, with kohl-black eyes, and a crown of jewels framing her head. The Howlers fell face-down on the earth before her; the Spiders quivered.

This, in the carmine darkness, was the Red Queen.

The Vampires at the altar faced her. They were visibly shaken.

The red woman screamed: "Gos! Vhu! You have broken my law!"

"We had our own laws before we had yours," spat the Vampire named Gos, his anger overwhelming fear.

The Red Queen raised her hand, and green flame shot from her fingertips. Like a liquid nightmare, the flames engulfed the head of the Vampire who had spoken. He ran, screaming, into the jungle, his face on fire.

The other Vampire fell to his knees and bared his neck to the red woman. "My Queen, forgive me."

"You dare indulge in these ancient rites," she hissed. "I have forbidden them." The bleeding Human on the altar stirred. The boy in the bushes watched.

"I wallow in the black dreams of my ancestors," said the kneeling Vampire.

"You must pay penance," said the Red Queen, somewhat subdued. Two young Harpies tumbled over each other with a ball, and this further broke the tension of the scene. Someone rattled a pot. A Lizard barked.

Before he heard another sound, the boy was grabbed by five creatures. No fewer could have held him. The Python wrapped his legs while the others dragged him into the clearing. All other movement stopped.

They pulled him to the feet of the Red Queen and held him there for her to view, to decide, to pronounce. He looked up at her mighty figure, her head in the steam, her muscles taut with purpose.

"Release him," she said quietly.

They hesitated fractionally, then obeyed their ruler. The boy stood and faced the magnificent woman, her powerful body glistening in the heavy night.

"Ollie," she whispered.

"Jasmine," he replied.

Before the astonished eyes of the jungle camp, they fell together and hugged each other until they couldn't breathe.

They sat alone in Jasmine's royal hut trading stories the rest of the night and the following day.

"Where have you been?" she demanded. "How *are* you? Where's Josh? What are you doing here?"

"I'm . . . fine." Ollie smiled. He had a slight hesitation to his speech, and hoarded his words like a miser his money. "And you?"

Jasmine—now Queen Redmasque—had never been stingy of syllables, and launched immediately into a rambling narrative.

" 'I'm fine. And you?' That's a response after two years? That's Joshua's influence, the taciturn Scriptic. Me? Of course I'm fine, I'm Queen of the Jungle, here since, oh, two years ago almost—right after I saw you last, in fact. Let's see," she continued, "last I heard of you all, you and Josh were trapping Rat around Ma'gas', fur-trading with the Ice Countries; Rose and Beauty were trying to farm olive trees east of Port Fresno; and Humbelly had died of natural causes in the Flutterby migration of '25. We were having a reunion, as I recall, near Newport; and a grand one it was. Then I went over and spent some time up at the Mosian Firecaves." She was aware she was babbling a bit, but she was uninterested in stopping herself—here was an old friend from a distant past, and Jasmine felt effervescent with words.

Ollie knotted his brow. "Near Mount Venus? That's all in ice by now."

"That part of the country has been in ice for years now. There's a city there, anyway, though—under the ice. A city of Neuroman scientists, mostly bioengineers. They use the Firecaves as the city's energy source. There are a number of interesting projects going on there, I found out, including the one I took advantage of—they do bodywork on old Neuromans like me. Tuned up all my parts, rewired my circuits, filled me up with Hemolube that almost never needs to be replaced. I'm telling you, I felt like a new woman. But that wasn't all, they added some special features—I couldn't resist. Look, I've got a hidden abdominal compartment now . . ."

A small door opened out of the plastic skin of her left flank, revealing a dark, empty space in Jasmine's belly. She closed it again quickly, and its margins were instantly lost in skin folds.

"For special secrets," she went on, with a wink. "Then they modified my fingers—some have magnesium napalm flares in them, some explosives, some potions. Anyway, with so many new toys, I needed a special playground—so I came right on down here, to the Terrarium."

Ollie smiled nostalgically at his old tutor-friend-nanny. In spite of her fearsome appearance, she had changed not an iota—still a garrulous, warm madwoman. After the daring rescue from the castle five years before, she had taken him under her guidance for a time—tried to teach him how to live and act in a world sparkling with danger. He had learned to be hard and cold as a jewel on ice—not the lesson she taught, but what he took away: in such ways we give credit to our teachers for things they never did, or even intended; but such is the nature of students and teachers.

Ollie envied Jasmine her ease in the hostile world, her power to be touched without being weak. His strength lay in his ability to remain untouched. That is, her nerve endings registered awe when most people's would register pain or fear; Ollie's nerve endings were usually just numb.

Still, he smiled now to see her so happy to see him. In some ways, she was still his teacher, though they both knew he had left school long ago.

She continued speaking. "Most creatures down here never heard of high-tech, see, so they just thought I was magic. Got quite a following. Howlers mostly at first—they're very impressionable—then the Spiders and Snakes.

The more powerful I got, the more animals joined up. Even some other Neuromans—they knew what I was; they just wanted a piece of it."

"Piece of what?" Ollie queried.

"The action, child, the action. The Ice has been moving south so fast the last few years, animals don't know what's going on. Migrations, strange behavior—everyone's moving south, and lots are coming into Dundee's Terrarium. And when they wander into this part of the jungle, brother, I run it.

"Animal wants to live here, he works for me, Queen Redmasque—that's me. We mine jewels, we process herbs, we smuggle, and we guide. We've got a religion and an arsenal, and we take care of our own. Anyone breaks the tribe laws, we eat 'em. Anyone violates the jungle around here, we do worse than that. We're a scary bunch, and that's all there is to it." She smiled broadly, the unscariest smile Ollie had seen in many a long day. He rarely smiled himself, but now felt such a warm glow from the grin of this wily Neuroman that he was moved to embrace her again.

"The world was always a grand wonder to you," he marveled.

He spoke with affection, though he would never admit to such a feeling—he was much too proud, scared, and protected, Jasmine knew, ever to betray so soft an emotion. She couldn't, she knew, read actual love into his voice, because Ollie was still too hollow, after his experiences in the Vampire harem, to be capable of that helpless condition. Too vulnerable to expose himself through that most vulnerable of states.

He sat back again and took up his own recent history. "I left Josh soon after this reunion you mentioned. Hunting with him, trapping—it was me in the trap, not those sorry Ice Rats. And I hated Scribery—which was very upsetting to Josh."

Ollie came from a family of Scribes, but he had forsaken the religion the day he escaped from the Vampire harem: words had neither saved him nor given him solace—his friends had saved him, through cunning and force. The holy written word, he had decided, was as flimsy as the paper it was written on.

"So I left. Joined a pirate ship in Ma'gas' and sailed for a year. Learned speed and trickery. Had a pirate woman for a while, but I lost her in a BASS fight off the Baja coast. Guess I should have known better."

Jasmine wondered if he meant he should have known better than to fight Born Again 'Seidon Soldiers in their own waters or known better than to get close to someone.

He paused briefly at this sensitive memory. "I left the sea after that. Did a little smuggling on my own. Took some vigilantes into the southeast Terrarium, burned out some of the Vampire colonies. You can't burn them all out, though—there's too many, you know. One way or the other, you end up with blood fever, so what's the point."

It was the febrility of a killing frenzy that, Jasmine suspected, had begun to affect Ollie, not the hepatitis endemic in Vampire colonies. She was soothed to see he had been conscious of—and dissatisfied with—the vertigo of blood heat.

"So I went back to living with Josh," he continued. "At his camp in the Saddlebacks. We hunted some. Evenings he wrote in his journal. I played my flute. Then last week Rose came to visit." He pursed his lip.

"Rose!" Jasmine laughed. "And how is she?"

"She was living with Beauty—moving farther south each year, of course. As you said, the Ice pushes us all. Beauty was off scouting the eastern face of the Saddlebacks—he was going to join us when he found a good place to settle. Josh was very happy to see Rose. I can't remember him so happy. She didn't seem right to me, though."

"How not?" Jasmine was suddenly aware of a somber undercurrent in the boy's narrative.

"Kind of distant, not like she used to be. Upset. And then, one night, she met someone. I don't know who—it was too dark, and when I got to the place, they were both gone, and Rose showed up at camp later without a word about it. But I went back to that spot the next morning, the spot where they'd been . . . and I found this."

He handed Jasmine a small square plastic object. It was

flat, like a lid, and had a rim all around its edge, and nine
short prongs sticking from its face.

"It's a plug," she said gravely. It was more than just a
plug, though; it was a sign. And in a flash, Jasmine had a
premonition of things to come.

"What's that?"

"Go on with your story. I'll tell you in a minute."

"Well, I got back to camp, and Rose was gone again.
Only this time she didn't come back. But that's not all that
was gone—you remember the wire helmet Josh always
wore to protect against the spells?"

"I remember," she nodded. Rose was gone again, and
the helmet too. And here, a plug. Jasmine was definitely
uneasy. "And what of Josh?"

"That's why I came. He had seven seizures that day.
Most of the time between them he was in a trance. He
couldn't speak. I would have tracked Rose, but I was afraid
to leave Josh alone. I stayed awake as long as I could, but I
finally nodded off. That's when Josh went away. I'd have
followed him, but he left me this note. Here, it's for you,
too. I'm no Scribe, but I can read."

He handed her a folded piece of paper he had pulled out
of his belt. She could see this was all very upsetting to him,
though he would never readily admit that. After hatred of
Vampires, Ollie's strongest emotion was protectiveness toward Josh; despite their differences, they were brothers,
members of a dying race. And when Ollie had been captive
in a harem in the City, Josh had saved his life.

Jasmine took the paper from him, unfolded it, and read:

> Ollie—spells again, must return
> to City, must sleep, must must Queen must
> will meet Rose in City. Find Jasmine fork of
> the Alder, she will know, go now, help.
> Jasmine—Rose unplugged, outlet below
> the Sticks
> Queen calls me, must go must
> Final Decon Nirvana Limbo Communion
> Rose knows
> Pluggers flew
> into Tunnel Twenty-two

as in remember sanitation maps
Queen calling again
Help us

Ollie watched Jasmine as she read the message over twice. "Explain to me about plugs," he said quietly. They had never told him completely what went on in The City With No Name, because he never really wanted to know. It was a period of his life he had managed, by and large, to repress successfully. Now he needed to know.

"When we rescued you and Rose from the City," Jasmine spoke thoughtfully, "you were in Bal's harem, in the Outer City. But Rose was in the castle proper, in a section of the labs beyond the Final Decontamination Room, in a room labeled Communion. Josh found her there among rows and rows of other Humans. They'd all had brain surgery, they'd been left with permanent electrical outlets in their skulls—and all of them had cords plugged into their heads. The cords led back to a central computer bank, which integrated all the information coming from the plugged-in brains. Josh unplugged Rose, and just before they escaped, they unplugged all the others in that room of horrors—and showed them the escape hatch, as well. This" —she held up the small plastic lid Ollie had found—"is a blind plug. An outlet cap. There was a shelf of them in the Communion Room. It snapped onto the open outlet at the back of Rose's head—to keep her connections clean, and impenetrable. To keep extraneous wires out of her brain. To keep her connections private. To keep her outlet closed."

Jasmine's voice was trailing off; she was speaking, increasingly, to herself.

"What?" whispered Ollie.

Jasmine pulled herself out of her spinning reverie. "This blind plug. As far as I know, Rose has kept it in place ever since the escape."

"So what does this mean?"

"I don't know," she shook her head. "This person you saw Rose meet, maybe he uncapped her. Maybe he took Joshua's helmet, to induce the spells again, to get him back to the City. Maybe Rose took the helmet, I don't know why. And this letter is confusing. First, these references to the Queen—there never was a queen, we found out. It was just the computer, programmed by a cadre of Neuroman genetic engineers to integrate all the information from the captured Human brains, probably to use the brains for information storage as well. No queen, just a lot of complicated circuitry—and Josh knew that. So what's this now about a queen?

"Then the part to me. *Rose unplugged*, I understand. *Outlet below the Sticks.* What outlet? Does *below* mean *under*, or *south of*? Then the list of rooms. Is that where he's going? *Rose knows*, he says. And she's going to the City. *Pluggers flew into Tunnel Twenty-two.* I drew a blank on that. I don't remember the tunnels under the City being numbered. And the sanitation maps he mentions— the ones that detailed the tunnel system under the City— we left those in my jungle cave hideout after the escape, over five years ago, what there was left of them. Not much left now, I imagine."

"His last line is clear."

Help us. Jasmine reread it with a sense of grim completion. Quite clear, and yet quite murky. Like déjà vu. Like a recurrent dream. She folded the paper and wrote the word *Beauty* on it, then drew a picture of a Centaur. "We'll stop by Joshua's mountain camp on our way. I can look for other clues, and we can leave this note for Beauty, who, I expect, will track Rose there as soon as he decides she's missing—he'll come to the City, too, after that; I've no doubt we'll meet up with him sooner or later in this operation."

"You'll help, then," Ollie said tentatively. He was too relieved to inflect it as a question, too unsure to make it a conclusion.

"I'll help." She smiled; and he allowed himself a smile in return.

She called her tribe together that night and told them she had to leave for an indefinite period of time, on a crusade to destroy dangerous animals in the south. She left her sceptre in the willing hands of Eng, a swarthy Vampire who had been her first lieutenant and second lover for the better part of a year. Then, with a great deal of smoke and flash, she disappeared into a passage hidden in the trees, emerging a mile upriver, where Ollie was waiting with a boat.

They took the east fork of the Alder, going north—it flowed that way, paradoxically, into the Saddlebacks—toward the place in the mountains where Joshua's trail began.

CHAPTER 2

In Which the Gulf Tide Brews

TIME seemed out of joint to Joshua. He wandered the winter alleys of Ma'gas' with that peculiar clarity common to mystics and psychotics, a certain vivid grasp of some internally cohesive set of images, largely unrelated to our world of Earth and its coordinates. So though Joshua didn't know exactly where he was, or how he got there, he knew everything there was to know about the way the sun glinted on a particular piece of glass; the way the water in the harbor sounded exactly like what it sounded like; the way he knew this place, but did not know it, as if it were the dream of a place he had once been. Joshua was, in fact, post-ictal.

That is, he was between seizures. He had been having five or ten a day for a week—ever since he had lost his helmet—and somehow had stumbled along from his camp in the mountains down to this woolly port town that he knew had meaning for him, but did not know what. He had just finished convulsing behind a bar, and probably wouldn't do so again for a few more hours. So now he was post-ictal. It was a state of special perceptions.

For example, time seemed out of joint. Moment did not follow moment with any sense of pace or pattern. Each second had its own design to be sent singing into the universe or held back and examined in detail as seemed fit.

Yet nothing quite seemed to fit.

His head was too big for his body; his feet, too small for his boots. The docks entered the water at the wrong angle, the sky was too blue. The January air had the fragrance not of air but of a pungent mix of the various odors of its component ethers: oxygen, nitrogen, salt, death, opium,

15

laughter. Josh smelled them all distinctly—individually and in combination—with a sort of giddy fatigue.

The city clanged around him as he made his way up and down its cluttered boulevards. Street life abounded: beggars, vendors, musicians, whores, pirates, smugglers, zealots, and cutthroats of every cut. Joshua stared at some, stared through others. At one point, he gave all his money to a legless sailor for a piece of taffy, which he presently threw up.

Only a week before, Joshua was a proud Human, hunter and Scribe. Now he didn't recognize the quill pen in his boot, the sound of his own name, or the direction he was headed. He felt vaguely like a cork in a typhoon: drowning when he wasn't flying.

He walked along the wharf in the afternoon. Ships were being loaded and unloaded. Fishermen drank jungle rum, creatures gambled their lives for a lark. The waterfront clattered with noise and sun. It all seemed terribly gay.

The bars and brothels along the docks were fairly new in one long section that Joshua kept nosing around. Only a few years old, as if rebuilt after a fire. Josh stared intensely at one new structure, a barnlike fish warehouse, when suddenly, before his eyes, it burst into flame.

Great foaming flames lapped up the sides of the building like rare silks in a high wind. Creatures ran out screaming, burning, falling: Harpies, Satyrs, Humans, Vampires, Centaurs. A centaur. It was Beauty.

Joshua's heart paused. Beauty, his dearest friend, graceful Centaur, comrade of a hundred campaigns: Beauty rearing, his mane on fire; Beauty wailing for breath; Beauty calling for strength from his ancestors! Josh ran toward him tearfully, arms extended—and he vanished. Simply disappeared, along with the fire and its orphans. Nothing left, except the new fish barn, the scurrying sailors. The present, material world.

The fire isn't now, thought Josh. *It was then.*

He sat, with a small thud, on the pier, his legs dangling over the water, and looked at his reflection, torn into jumping strips by the choppy surface. *This is me*, he thought. *This is now. No fires, and Beauty isn't here, and I'm alone.*

The liquid broken face in the water below seemed to laugh at him.

"Why am I here?" he asked the Face.

The Queen calls, the Face answered, dancing.

"Where are my friends?" Josh demanded, suddenly truculent. And sleepy, he was getting sleepy.

The Queen is your friend, said the Face, only now it was speaking in slow motion.

Josh opened his mouth to speak again, but his tongue had become a huge, unwieldy slug.

Time was running down.

But Josh was uneasy. He wanted Time to speed up, to spin, he wanted Time to dance. He wanted to dance with time.

He stood up on the dock and began to dance. Slowly, at first, for he wasn't too steady. A jig. Hop on the left foot, right foot out, cross right leg over left knee, hop again. Change feet. Do it again. There, he felt better already.

A few animals paused to watch him briefly, then went on. Humans were usually rather gross, and always erratic; and generally speaking, best to avoid.

Up the deck and down, he danced like a palsied sprite. In his mind, Joshua waltzed with a voluminous procession of memories and fantasies, characters who had lived and died, or lived still, or never lived at all. One and all jumped out of his head to the dock now, to dance: Beauty, and Jasmine, Ollie and Rose. Now Jarl, the Bear-King dos-à-dossed; now a Cyclops bartender kicked the cancan.

Now Dicey bowed and poised. Josh took her in his arms, and slowly they turned. Dicey was his cousin, his young bride, his dear love, killed by Vampires five years before; but now, in Joshua's arms, she was graceful as air.

Faster they whirled, unencumbered by gravity, and as they flew, they made the rest of the world—the bloody world, full of pain, full of incomplete rewards and blank denials—disappear. Josh tried to hold the moment, tried to keep it pressed within him, that it might never go; or that he might reclaim it, all the smells and feelings, on an instant's recollection.

The dance was over. Dicey curtsied, Joshua bowed. Dicey giggled and ran up the dock, behind the ship that slowly rocked at anchor near the slip. Josh followed her, though now he felt slow on his feet, even a little dizzy. When he reached the blind side of the schooner, he stopped short. Dicey was gone; but a grim scene arrested him.

Hanging from a boom swung out over the wharf was a pendulous fishnet. And tangled in the net, struggling and swinging to no avail, was a Mermaid. A beautiful creature, her Human torso lithe and coffee-colored, flowing sinuously into a muscled seal tail of light-brown fur. Both arms were thrust akimbo through holes in the netting, preventing constructive movement, keeping her just more firmly trapped in the mesh, suspended and swinging over the docks.

Josh stared at her face. Was it Dicey? his mind raced. It almost could have been. More weathered than he remembered Dicey's face being, certainly; more wise, perhaps. But the lines were there, and the spirit. Could Dicey's spirit have entered this desperate, delicate creature's body? Josh approached, hesitantly.

Others got there first. Two Vampires, a Sphinx, an antlered Monkey—all pirates, they jumped down from the deck of the ship to the wharf and coarsely began to abuse their catch.

The Vampires each grabbed one of the Mermaid's wrists—helplessly entwined in the net—and slashed them horribly, then lapped at the blood that flowed to the wooden planks.

The Monkey jumped on the poor thing's back, rubbing itself on the exquisitely soft sealskin of her backside as it reached around to her chest in the grossest manner to squeeze and pinch her.

The Sphinx only watched, and chuckled.

Joshua trembled with rage. The sight of these grotesques mutilating this rare beauty, this incarnation of his lost love, was more than he could stand. He rushed forward.

When five feet from the scene, he leapt at the hanging Mermaid. He clung to her, and his momentum swung the boom around, over the ship's deck, and then out over the water of the harbor. The Vampires and Sphinx were left in total surprise on the dock, while the Monkey on the netting barely realized what was happening. With a single blow, Josh slammed the antlered primate in the head, knocking him into the water.

For a moment, Josh clutched the Mermaid through the twine of the fishnet. They stared deeply into each other's face. Josh saw, with transient clarity, that this was not Dicey—only a lovely creature, caught and quivering in one of life's horrors. She looked back into his eyes, and saw something similar.

He took the knife from his belt and with a few quick cuts, opened the net enough for the Mermaid to wriggle free. She dove into the bay, and vanished from sight.

In a second the others were alert again. Pirates on the deck swung the boom back over the pier, and the Vampires pulled Josh out of the net. They would have knocked him senseless on the spot, but there was no need—he was having another seizure. Instead, they wrapped his twitching body in a canvas bag, tied it up at the mouth, and tossed it carelessly into the hold of the ship.

Paula sat in the bar and watched the young man who kept nodding off on the pier. He looked familiar. She was certain she knew him from somewhere. She watched him through the window, across the docks, drinking her beer.

She was a tough, wiry woman—a Human, a Scribe; pretty, but without softness. She sat alone. She watched the young man on the pier talking to himself. She ordered another beer.

Where had she seen him before, she wondered. Years ago, it must have been. She had an eye for Human faces, though; she arranged every one she had ever seen, like a display of flowers, in her mind. It was only a matter of finding that flower again in the arrangement. She stared at the addled man on the dock, and thought, *Petals of night, closed in fear, never see moonbeams or shadow men.*

Poetry was the highest form of Scribery, as far as Paula was concerned. She had read all the old poetry books she could find—they were her closest friends. Of all writing, poems held the most meaning in the fewest words. Every word, then, contained the maximum power—and this was what the religion was all about: the power of the written word. Of course, most other Scribes felt poetic words were too ambiguous; their information value was diminished, hence their power dissipated. But then, Paula wasn't like most other Scribes.

Scribes were generally a cliquish bunch, the militant Scribes of the secret society known as the Bookery even more so; but among them, though she was one of them, Paula was considered a loner. Bright, able, respected, even liked, she nonetheless shunned the company of others, preferring to it that of herself or her books. She particularly hated getting involved in heated theological arguments over the power of poetry versus that of fiction or essays—an argument popular among the clergy of the sect. She was interested only in reading her poems, being left alone, and scouting the animal cities for signs of organized hostile activities against Humans.

She watched the man on the dock get up and begin to dance. It struck her as ridiculous at first; it even shamed her to see a member of her race make such an obvious fool of himself, dancing on the jetty as if it were a grand ballroom, a ghost for a partner. A shame for the other animals to see.

Yet the man seemed so entranced, so internally beguiled, it was hard for Paula to grudge him. He was just doing what he wanted to do, after all, because it pleased him to do so, no matter what others thought, be they Human or Hydra. Paula smiled at her own mixed feelings, raised her glass to the complexities of being Human, and took another sip.

Suddenly the man stopped dancing to stare at a Mermaid, squirming in a hanging net, being tormented by some of the ship's crew. Paula saw the expression on the man's face turn from bliss to horror as he watched the abuse of the beautiful sea creature. She tensed as he ran across the dock, jumped into the net, and swung it over the water. And when he cut the Mermaid free, Paula's heart sprang free as well, to witness such a heroic act!

Her admiration turned instantly to quiet fury, though, as

the gallant Human was swung back around over the docks. And then fury to outrage as the poor, brave man began having seizures where he lay—and instead of helping him, the others kicked him, urinated on him, stuffed his still clonic body into a canvas sack, and threw him into the hold of the ship.

Paula's eyes became narrow slits. She knew the largest of the pirates involved, a well-known Sphinx, a contract-slaver who worked primarily for the Queen of The City With No Name.

She finished her beer in a gulp and ambled down the dock as the pirate ship was weighing anchor.

Paula sat at the tiller of the sloop, her eye firmly fixed on the pirate ship in the distance. Ellen sat beside her, and Michael stood up front, fiddling with the foresail. All were Scribes; all, Bookery spies.

Ellen shouted lightly to Michael, "Careful, you fop, you'll fall in."

"Just trying to catch a little more wind, sport," he mumbled to no one in particular. "I believe the villains are pulling away."

"We're just following, you know. We're not trying to catch them," Ellen replied too quietly for Michael to hear. Then, to Paula: "Anyway, we don't want to get too close. We don't want them to *see* us, do we?"

Paula shrugged. "I don't see that it matters. I doubt if they care, and they couldn't catch us if they wanted to. I hope they *do* see us." She hoisted her middle finger at the distant ship, a symbol that had survived many ages and wars.

Michael finished fussing the sail and came back to join them. "So what's the scoop, sport? This bloke a renegade archivist, or what? The ANGELS going to torture him to find out all the new words he's discovered? A lexicographer, that's what he is, a lexicographer." He pointed a finger in mock triumph.

Ellen found this patter tiresome, and made a thing of ignoring him. With more motion than was needed, she opened a book, rustling the pages to find her place. *Deer-*

slayer. Michael settled down and read over her shoulder.

Paula continued staring after the captive Human in the long ship. "I *know* him," she whispered. It was a visceral feeling more than anything else. Deep, resonant. Almost as if she had known him in a different life. Some Scribes believed in reincarnation, but Paula wasn't sure. It was said that some people were reborn *in* their favorite books; or that two people deeply in love could be reborn as beloved characters, joined to the page forever in a well-preserved leather-bound edition. Some even said that rare and gifted Scribes could write the characters they wanted to be—write entire life histories, whole novels—and when dead, he or she would be reborn as the person in the book, to live until the book crumbled to ash.

Paula wasn't sure about any of this. She was certain only that somehow, somewhere, she had known this Human she now pursued.

Paula steered past the City, going south, several miles out. She watched the pirate ship anchor at harbor; the tiny figures appeared to be unloading their cargo of prisoners. Paula sailed on.

"What now?" Michael asked, staring at the activity in the cove.

"Home," said Paula.

She wondered if she would ever have a home—if any of them would. They lived in caves, now: a dark underworld of dreams and fears; a waiting world. It was a place where they worked on their lexicons, and planned for the day the Human spirit would be revitalized, grow again. Later, not now. For how could they flower if they couldn't yet put down roots?

Paula looked at Ellen and Michael, sitting quietly near the bow. She thought of them as her younger siblings—harmless children growing up in a time full of harm. She had taught them the craft of survival, doling her lessons to them out of a half-empty heart. For this, and all her other dour affections, they loved her, this childlike pair. And when she could catch the glimmer of that feeling, she knew her heart was at least half full.

She called up to them. "I'm thinking of a seven-letter word beginning with the letter *A*."

Michael perked up immediately. "Animal, vegetable, or mineral?" he asked.

"Does it *haaave* to be one of the three?" Ellen stretched the word for effect.

"It's a pretty good place to start, sport."

"Well what about *fire*? That's none of the above." Ellen arched her voice.

"That doesn't have seven letters, sport."

"It's vegetable," Paula interjected with a smile. "And that's your first question."

They struck a course south-southwest until they were long beyond viewing range of the castle, then tacked slowly back until dusk, when they bore in on the cliffs some five miles south of the City, and out of sight of it due to a bend in the shoreline. As night fell, they floated silently on the tide to the base of the sheer cliffs jutting out of the sheltered water. These were not solid white like those on which the City was built, though; for honeycombing this cliff face was a myriad of large and small cave openings.

The sloop carrying the three Scribes glided, smooth as a yawn, into an oblong cave whose mouth was lapped by the night-black water with an echo that sounded like the hollow gasp of a dying animal.

It was evening outside The City With No Name. Out on the water, past the harbor, the waves rose and fell in stately procession toward the shore. The wind was low, as was the moon. Blue-tailed Egrans circled high overhead, alert to traces of movement below the surface, searching for supper on the fin.

There was a quiver below the surface. One of the Egrans poised against the wind, then dove . . . then swerved up just before he hit the water. The glint of the low-lying moon had tricked him—this was no dinner fish; this was something a bit bigger; this was a creature that waited at its leisure, just beneath the gentle rippling of the sea.

The Egran flew away to likelier pickings. Below the surface, outside the City, there was no trace of movement.

* * *

Josh slept on his feet as the tumbrel carried him unceremoniously through the streets of the Outer City. He opened his eyes once: Vampires and Neuromans bustled and milled. This was an old dream, Josh decided; he had been here years ago—not now. He closed his eyes again.

The tumbrel rolled past a second set of gates, into the Inner City, and finally into the castle. Joshua felt every turn, saw every hallway reflected against the interior of his closed eyelids, through a lens of dark memories.

In time, he was put into a private cell. Still semiconscious, he felt himself washed, dressed, probed, and examined by dozens of hands over the course of many hours—perhaps days. There were periods of light, dark; confusion. And then, finally, he woke up.

He found himself in a small, dirty, windowless room. He had no idea where he was, though his head felt clear for the first time since . . . since the night Rose left.

What was the fantastic story she had told him? She was going back to The City With No Name! To find something she had lost there, she had said. No, Beauty didn't know—he would only have stopped her. She wanted Josh to come.

He had told her he couldn't possibly—he himself had already lost too much there ever to dare returning. That was why he always wore the mesh helmet she had given him, to block out the transmissions from the City.

It was gone. His helmet was gone.

He crawled all around the floor of his cell looking for the helmet, but knew it wasn't here. Rose had taken it that night, and almost immediately he had begun having spells. Tunnel Twenty-two, she had told him. Below the City. That's how the Pluggers escaped; Twenty-two on the sanitation maps.

Who are the Pluggers? he had wanted to know.

My comrades-in-circuit, she had said with a laugh. The Humans she and Josh had freed, the ones who had been plugged into the Queen, with Rose.

There is no Queen, he had told her. She had parted her hair, showed him her outlet. Where's your outlet cap? he had asked, alarmed.

We uncapped it, she had said defiantly. Join us, she had said.

She had removed his helmet as he slept. He awoke hearing her say "Forgive me, I want you there." Then the spells began.

And now he was here. Where was that? He tried the door. Locked. Could he be in the City now? He had dreamed he was in the City, he knew . . . or was it a dream? His heartbeat quickened in fear and uncertainty.

Ollie would worry, he knew. He wished Jasmine were here to help—she always had a plan. He flexed all his muscles. Everything seemed to be in working order.

It was a disorienting situation, and Josh searched his mind for something to get a grip on. *The Word is great, the Word is One*, he thought—the chant of Scribes for generations. However strong was the necromancy that had brought him here, he should be able to find words to write that would counteract it. A good Scribe could write his way out of the gravest danger, and Josh marked himself a pretty mean scribbler.

He wasn't pious, the way some Scribes were—making a big thing about how many words he knew, or how extravagant were the flourishes of his calligraphy—but he believed with simple faith in the power of the written word, and read every chance he got, and wrote when he could.

So he tried to think of words now—to steady himself; to transport him to safety. *Sesame. Madrigal. Rocket fuel.* If only he had something to write them down with. He reached for the quill he kept in his boot, but he was barefoot now, his clothes were not his own. He had read a book once about a prisoner who tunneled his way to freedom from his cell, but Josh didn't hold much hope for that here. He would need implements for that, and he had none. He tried to think of more powerful words. Suddenly, behind him a door opened.

He turned to find a Vampire watching him curiously. Reflexively the hairs on Joshua's neck bristled, and he crouched, ready to fight.

"So, you're awake," the Vampire said quietly.

"What do you want?" Josh growled in monotone.

"You are fortunate," said the Vampire with great tranquility. "It is said you will have an audience with the Queen." Whereupon he closed the door again.

Josh relaxed his muscles, but not his resolve; wherever he was, he had to escape.

The Queen . . . Joshua's fists opened and closed as he tried to think. What was happening to him? What was happening?

He spit into a pile of greasy dirt and mixed it with his finger into a viscous ink. Next he tore a long piece of straw from the mat on the floor; and then a square of canvas from his bedding. And finally, using the straw as a pen, with the calming satisfaction of a lifelong ritual, he set down the record of what had befallen him.

Jasmine and Ollie made good time to Joshua's camp, found nothing of interest; then hitched a ride on a mailboat they helped repair, from where it had beached some miles north of Newport, all the way down to Ma'gas'. Once there, they split up: Jasmine took the bars to the north of the main pier; Ollie, those to the south.

The first tavern on the wharf was called the Thirsty Bones. The building itself was only a few years old, and Jasmine well knew why. The last time she had been to this town, over five years before, there had been a fire that destroyed half the waterfront. It had been started by Joshua, in the bar run by Jasmine's friend Sum-Thin; while Jasmine was dueling the Priest of Hoods. It was quite a time—a turning point, even.

She settled herself now into a chair in a corner of the Thirsty Bones and let her mind roll around the times in her life that had in some way seemed pivotal since her birth, in the middle decades of the twenty-first century, three hundred years before. Her conversion to Neuromanity, certainly; only her brain and nervous system remained of her original Human self. Everything else about her—from the nuclear heart to the viscous, oxygen-carrying Hemolube that simultaneously oiled her parts and fed her nerves—was a synthetic creation of what in those old days was called Western Technology.

She could still die, of course: the Hemolube could be drained from the valve at the back of her head; she could drown, given enough time. But barring unforeseen trauma, her brain was expected to senesce at a vanishingly slow rate. No Neuroman had yet expired of natural causes.

There were other turning points, though, in her history; in the world's history, too. The Bacteriological War, the Nuclear War; the Clone Wars, which ended in the death of most Humans. The Great Quake, and the Coming of Ice. The Age of Ice, when Jasmine first explored Dundee's Terrarium with her Vampire lover, Lon. Her quest five years ago with Josh and Beauty. Lon's death, and Sum-Thin's. Her return to the Terrarium, to rule as Queen Redmasque over the children of the jungle. And now, here, back in Ma'gas', with Ollie, on this new journey.

It had been a wild and tumbling life, but somehow Jasmine sensed that the biggest tumble was still to come. There was a simmering feeling in the air, like a pot ready to boil. She smiled at her mood: quiet excitement, as before a great battle. She noted her fear, but didn't let it consume her; rather, she used it as a weathervane of the moment, or as a tool to hone her perceptions. Yes, this was quite a time, too.

She stood and got a beer at the bar, then sat down near the front window. Ma'gas' was always a wide-open town, but Jasmine sensed an even greater undercurrent of frenzy than usual. The sexual bartering that ordinarily took place in the alleys and below the docks had spilled out onto the main thoroughfares. Jasmine watched two brawls within fifty yards of her window, and both left dead bodies that no one bothered to clear away. The quays were crowded beyond belief, swollen with animals Jasmine had never seen so far south—Ponies, Otters, Snow Leopards, Wongs, Ursumen. It was as if they were all massing for some event.

They weren't, though. It was just the Ice Madness: displaced by the encroaching glaciers, or often just by the *thought* of the encroaching glaciers, they crammed into the port town, dizzy with abandon and droll with fear. They had the smell of hopeless high rollers. Jasmine watched them through the window as she considered her next step.

A cargo of slaves was being off-loaded from one of the ships at the dock. Humans and Centaurs, mostly; a few mixed breeds. One of them bolted, but the guard—a Basilisk—swooped down and tore out the prisoner's belly before he had run ten steps. Scavengers sniffed the entrails; backed away, fearing a trap, grew bold, and dragged the carcass into an alley.

A band of jugglers drew a crowd for a little while, tossing torches among themselves. A crew of laughing pirates passed. There was a contest of some kind. A small troupe of musicians got thrown into the harbor after a dispute, presumably over money. Two Hermaphrodites approached a Vampire, and after some discussion, he picked them up and flew them to a ship in the bay.

Jasmine watched it all, sipping her drink. When she felt she had a sense of the current temperament of the place, she began to circulate, asking questions.

Had anyone seen a dark-haired Human having convulsions? Acting strange?

"All Humans act strange," she was told.

"Convulsions of conscience, perhaps."

"Why waste time looking at Humans?"

"Yes, there was one, last year, heading north."

"Yes, I saw three, and killed them all."

"Yes, but it's none of your business."

"No, but Georgio spoke of such a thing. He'll be back next month."

"A dark-haired Human having convulsions? What an amusing idea."

Not a particularly fruitful line of questioning, Jasmine decided. Humans were not held in high regard, even as a commodity on the slave market.

Jasmine went looking for Ollie to suggest they provision themselves and leave Ma'gas' quickly. Josh and Rose were certainly on their way to The City With No Name, if not already there. Little was to be gained in Ma'gas' beyond the general information she had already obtained—namely, that the Queen of the City was still paying top price for Humans; and that no one else wanted them, except Vampires—and Queen Redmasque. The story went that the magical Queen of the demented jungle tribe planted the Humans in charmed soil, where they grew into trees that guarded the tribal camp, and strangled all intruders with their aggrieved, remorseless vines. Only after a Human-tree had consumed a thousand invaders, it was said, would Queen Redmasque allow it to seed—for the flowers of these seeds then grew into Humans who were identical to the Human the Queen had originally planted; and these flowers were allowed to run free, or serve in the Queen's army, as they desired.

It amused Jasmine to hear such apocrypha about herself. The fact was, she did buy Humans from slave traders—to take them off the market. Still, she was well pleased with the rumors her little cult was beginning to generate. So Jasmine laughed silently now, at the ornate illusion that was her past, and at the imponderable design of her future.

She figured the best plan was to go directly to her hiding-cave upriver from the City and see if the sanitation maps they had left years ago were still readable. Maybe they would shed some light on Joshua's cryptic note. So she walked the wharf, in the direction Ollie had gone, and poked her head in each bar along the way.

In the fourth tavern on the south side of the docks, her attention was drawn by a large noisy crowd ringing some kind of demonstration in the center of the floor. She wormed her way to the front row of spectators and stopped cold. There in the clearing, Ollie was toying with a Vampire.

The boy had a bloody dagger in his hand and a cold fire in his face. The Vampire was staggering blindly—both eyes cut by Ollie's knife. One of the creature's hands lay, imploring, on the floor. He swung his oozing stump in great unseeing arcs, trying to club the Human devil. The crowd bellowed, made bets, hooted suggestions, and spat. Ollie stayed behind the circling Vampire, occasionally poking at him coolly with the knife, like a heartless picador.

Jasmine took two steps into the killing circle, tore the knife from the hand of her startled companion, and quickly slit the Vampire's throat: he died in a moment. The crowd cheered. Jasmine turned back to Ollie and spoke to him in an icy, restrained fury: "Don't ever let me see you behave like that again." She threw the knife to the floor, burying the point an inch in the wood.

He pulled the knife from the plank and faced her, his eyes twisted with hidden pain. "I hate Vampires," he whispered.

Jasmine turned and pushed her way through the dispersing crowd to the door. On her way out, she heard one of the spectators say, "I've never seen a Human that fast."

In the street, Ollie caught up with her. He pulled her around by the arm. "They made me this way. They've brought it on themselves," he rasped.

"That Vampire may have brought something on himself," she said quietly. "But nobody made you the way you are. We all make ourselves, in our own images. It's useless to speak further of it. I don't know how he provoked you, but I saw your response—and I don't permit such loveless, gratuitous displays in my friends."

They stared at each other for a long, strained moment. Finally Ollie spoke, in his slow, guarded way. "I don't need your friendship. I don't even want it if it demands apologies. But I need your help to get Josh. So if it's what you require—I'm sorry for what you saw."

Jasmine's feelings were mixed. She was appalled by Ollie's cavalier torture of the wounded Vampire; yet she knew the source of his hatred, and shrank from that memory. And now he was being totally honest with her—he wanted her assistance, so he apologized for giving offense. His motive was simply to save his dear brother, who had once saved him. Jasmine smiled, shook her head, put her arm around Ollie's shoulder. "I think maybe we're all a little crazy with Ice these days."

Ollie said nothing, though he disagreed with her flatly: he felt not the slightest bit crazy. He felt calm, clear, and directed. He simply hated Vampires beyond all reasoning. His hatred was pure; it didn't bollix him or confound his other senses or create internal conflicts. He felt his hatred was justified—Vampires had murdered his family, tortured and bonded him at the age of ten, done things to him and his cousin he could never speak of. Vampires were hateful.

They had sewn jewels into his skin to identify the harem he belonged to: he still kept the ruby in his chest, as a reminder—if he needed one.

He couldn't explain this feeling to Jasmine; nor did he want to. This was simply the way he was. This feeling kept him strong; alive, even. He felt great warmth for Jasmine—she had helped save him, back then—and he knew she felt charity for all creatures. For that reason, he decided to make an effort to keep his feelings to himself in her presence—though he certainly didn't make a habit, he knew, of sharing his feelings. Still, he would not test her softness now; he would be a mask. But neither would he ever relinquish his hate, even though Jasmine begged him: this hatred he held too dear, like a deformed child.

He walked with Jasmine now to the end of the pier, and they dangled their legs over the edge. Ollie took from his belt a bamboo flute which he had cut during their trip through the jungle. He put his lips to it and played, on the early evening air, the saddest, strangest melody Jasmine had ever heard. It struck her to the soul, and had she been Human, she would have cried.

It was a sixteen-note refrain, silver and somber as the wind in a lonely place. It made Jasmine's heart quicken, then hush. In a way, the melancholy of the keening strains unsettled her almost as much as Ollie's earlier flagrant sadism. But she was tired, so let such considerations go, and watched the gulf tide brew in the gathering darkness as the boy's music whispered to the stars.

CHAPTER 3

In Which It Is Seen That Even Poetry Cannot Substitute for Holding Hands in the Darkness

THE rear walls of the cavern winked orange and black in the light of two fish-oil lamps. Its farther limits could not be seen at all, but only intimated by the sloshing gurgles that reverberated off the high recesses. It was a chill place.

A river cut along the center of the cave, running into another, larger cave at one end, and then directly into the ocean. This water was fed by a dozen tributaries that entered through dark openings in the rock, some small, some large, many indefinable. One branch of the river sidetracked abruptly into a deep, still pool that occupied a thousand square feet of one of the cave's hidden corners. Boats were anchored there.

Scores of tunnels opened off the nether reaches, half of them dry. None were visible in the dense lightlessness. One of these led, twisting, to a series of connecting chambers and, finally, to a small, well-lit room where dozens of people sat writing. Bookery people, militant Scribes dedicated to the mystical aspects of the written word, to the supremacy of writing as a power source, and, most recently, to the overthrow of the Queen of The City With No Name.

The Queen and her cohorts had been abducting Humans for years, using them in vile experiments. To the Books—so these Scribes called themselves—this was untenable: Humans were the bedrock of Scribery, of writing itself. To a Human, one day (it was written), would be revealed the original Word—the powerful force contained in that primordial amalgam of letters from which all later words derived. It was this great, elemental power, a function of the first key letters and their magical relation to one another,

33

that the Book people so devoutly sought—and that they now sought to protect from the Queen's machinations.

Row upon row of them worked here now, hunched over long low tables, writing additions to the Great Lexicon. The G.L. was the lifework of the Bookery; its goal was no less than to learn and define every Human word. Every rediscovered book or journal was pored over by these Scribes. Any new word found was set down on multiple record sheets, its definition derived from context, or cross-referenced. Older members of the clan were sometimes hypnotized, their early memories searched for clues to a specific definition—some long-forgotten remark a parent had made, or a magazine article they had glimpsed in their youth.

Everyone had to take a turn setting down the G.L. record. Several rooms were set aside for it, the long tables covered with quills, inkwells, and reams of blank paper; and several more rooms were set aside for storing the records, along with their indexes.

People could always be found writing in the Lexicon— either laying down new words or adding shades of meaning to old ones. When they weren't in the caves doing that, they were out looking for long-hidden volumes, or recruiting new Scribes to their cause, or spying in the animal cities on enemies of the Word, or tending their prized winery or their mushroom gardens. But mostly they just stayed in the caves and wrote, and plotted the Queen's overthrow, and read, and wrote some more.

Beside the main writing room was a smaller cave, used primarily for conferences. Here Paula, Michael, and Ellen sat, speaking with Addie and David.

Addie was an old, old woman. Her hair was thin; her skin, the texture of a dried apple. She was almost blind, and quite powerful: her written vocabulary was greater than that of any other living Scribe.

David was a young, intense man with wire-rimmed glasses and a large writing-callus, which he constantly picked at, on the middle finger of his left hand. He tightened his eyes on Paula as she quietly spoke.

". . . So the word in Ma'gas' is the Queen's put a high

bounty on any Human having spells. I'm certain that's what this kidnapping was. Otherwise, they'd just have killed him."

"But you said you knew him." David squinted. He was trying to put the event in perspective.

"Yes, but I can't think of how." It annoyed more than perplexed her—she didn't like not knowing things. Only savages were ignorant.

"You could describe him to the Pluggers," Ellen suggested. "Some of them used to have spells—before they got plugged in, anyway."

David bit at his callus. "Look, I think our major concern should be with the fact that after a long quiet period, the Queen has begun putting the net out for Humans again. In a big way. Whether Paula knows this guy is neither here nor there."

"I don't agree, sport," said Michael. "If Paula knows him, the boy's a good Book."

"So?" David retorted peevishly.

"So maybe we should move on the City now, before they operate on him."

"We're not ready." David was emphatic.

"I'm ready," said Michael. "Ellen is ready. Half the Pluggers are ready. The word-poor fish I caught for bloody supper was ready. So what do you mean *we're* not ready?"

It was an old fight brewing. David always wanted to plan more, prepare further, consider options; Michael wanted to act. Generally Paula had to come between them to prevent it coming to blows—for her alone would they desist in their bickering. For her part, Paula felt rather neutral—about David and Michael, as well as the issues that inflamed them. David was so obsessed with clauses and modifications, he could never make a decision of any kind; Michael would read about a subject until he was bored or tired, then make his decision based on some feeling or whim totally unrelated to the words he had just read. Paula could relate to neither mode.

She made decisions quickly—based on feelings, yes, but feelings engendered by her readings. To Paula, that was one of the greatest powers of words—to create feelings. That was one reason poetry was such a powerful word form. So she couldn't understand this endless debate among David, Michael, and the others. To raid the City; to storm the castle; to wait and see . . . such wasted energy. It seemed clear to her they should simply read what could be read, make a quick decision, and act on it. If the action proved ill-conceived, they could try something else. But all this talk talk talk drove her to distraction. She couldn't understand it. And the fact that everyone else did it so much made her feel, often, quite alone. It was the caves, she thought—the caves somehow created this aloneness in her, this twisting loss of direction in her friends. David and Michael were starting to go at it again, but before it could flare, Paula closed her eyes, to shut them out.

Michael made a face and sat in the corner, where he opened a book and began to read.

David picked at his callus. "Try to think where you know him from, Paula. It might help."

Josh sat nervously in the large, intimidating room: intimidating because of all the incomprehensible machinery that lined the walls, and because of the five empty chairs that faced him.

He had been back to normal for two days. He knew who and where he was, and that he must somehow get out. This was the City he had raided years earlier to liberate his people; there was no love for him here—though he didn't think anyone could possibly know what his role had been then.

He had been moved to a larger, cleaner cell the day before, been given a bath, some clothes, some meals. And now this room of machines. The door opened.

Five creatures walked in—three Neuromans, two Vampires—and sat in the chairs facing Josh. The Vampires looked large, dark, and potent. The Neuromans were quite distinctive: one was thin, pinkish, with an almost see-through body; the second was horribly misshapen, like an Accident; the third was short, tense, and covered *in toto* with reptilian scales. The only way Josh spotted them right off as Neuromans was that each had the small protruding

spigot valve at the back of the head through which all Neuromans refilled their bodies with Hemolube.

They sat without moving for five minutes, when finally
the reptile-Neuroman spoke in a gravelly voice.

"Welcome, Human. I am Bishop Ninjus. I am the Chief
Security ANGEL. This is the Security Council, and we are
here to evaluate you—because for whatever reasons, our
Queen has demanded to speak with you in private. We
wish to know why, and by Quark's Charm, we will know
why."

The others sat in rocky silence, waiting for Josh to respond.

Josh was mystified. "What do you want me to say?" he
questioned, straining for meaning in the unreadable faces.

"We want you to say why you are here," said the
translucent-pink Neuroman. "I am Fleur, Chief Genetic
Engineer. You must tell us why our lady, the Queen,
wishes to see you."

"I'm Joshua, Human and Scribe," replied Josh, extending trust for trust. "And I'd also like to know why I'm
here."

The Accidentish Neuroman spoke softly to the frosty
clear one who had identified himself as Fleur. *"Uman
danang Gueen zologlu."*

Fleur nodded and spoke to Josh again. "My colleague,
Elspeth, suggests we be frank with you. Very well. For five
years the Queen has been seeking a Human who was involved in the senseless vandalism of these premises. Wan-
ton destruction of property, the deaths of the ANGEL
Gabriel and others . . ."

They knew! How did they know? Could he deny it?
Could he run? A dozen lightning calculations ran through
Joshua's mind as Fleur continued speaking.

". . . So the question remains: are you that Human?
And if so, why have you come back now?"

Josh felt on such shaky ground that he decided limited
truth was the safest recourse. "It wasn't senseless vandalism at all—we were freeing our people who didn't want to
be here."

There was a great murmuring among the inquisitors.

Bishop Ninjus, the Neuroman with the reptilian armor plates, blurted out, "Quark's Charm, you mean to say it *was* you?"

"Besides," went on Josh, emboldened a bit by the stir he had created, "what's all this about a queen? There never was a queen. That was a lie—it was just the kidnapped Human brains you wired together into your computer that you called the Queen." Josh didn't really even understand exactly what a computer was but that was how Jasmine had explained it. He was unsure now, though, for his questioners quieted down so quickly.

"Who told you this?" growled Ninjus.

"Gabriel," Josh returned. He tried to keep his voice cool, but he was getting scared again. Gabriel was the ANGEL Josh had surprised next to the Communion Room five years earlier, just after he had unplugged Rose from the cable in her head. Gabriel had said there was no queen— the new intelligence that ruled the City was simply the potentiation of all the captive Human brains, integrated by a computer.

He recalled now, too, that Rose had always remained rather quiet on the matter, never saying much one way or the other. Josh assumed her reticence was akin to Ollie's— a desire to forget the entire episode—until her last visit to Josh. Suddenly she had been full of the Queen this and the Queen that—as if there really were a queen, a real person, and not just a roomful of connected brains.

What had she said that night? "Josh, I need you. Come with me to the City."

"I can't. There's nothing for me there."

"I am there," she had said. "I am there waiting for you now. Come with me, come to me."

It was strange. Josh recalled thinking even then how odd she sounded, almost as if she weren't Rose at all. And then that night she had taken his helmet, and then the spells began. Josh blinked at his inquisitors.

After conferring briefly, the five stood. The Vampires still had not spoken. They walked up to Joshua and remained on either side of him, while Fleur put a metal cap on the Human's head and took measurements of some kind. Josh sat quite still, afraid almost to breathe. He thought to himself: *The Word is great, the Word is One.*

After thirty minutes of this, they all left, and before Josh knew what was happening, he was taken back to his cell.

Fleur and Elspeth left the meeting in low spirits. Of all the ANGELs in The City With No Name, Fleur was the most delicate. He was Neuroman, of course, and had taken pains to engineer the most elegant detail into his own construction. Willow-thin, he moved like a cool breeze in a dark place. His skin was a translucent pink, so that light from the sun or moon would glow directly through his body, casting subtle shadows off the fine network of nerves that laced his limbs like the veins of a leaf. This was Fleur.

Elspeth was quite another matter. She was the senior Associate Neuroman Genetic Engineer, Liege, et Sage—and almost disarmingly gross. Her external body parts had been built specifically out of proportion to one another—one huge hand, one stunted; asymmetric eyes and a malformed nose in a misshapen head. That is to say, she had had herself built to resemble an Accident, in order to instill fear and loathing in those she met, as well as to give them cause to underestimate her intelligence. It was a successful mask. It had served her well through many wars and intrigues, moving her, over two centuries, up and down the corridors of power. Until finally she had come to rest here—as chief adviser to the Queen of The City With No Name, directing the future of the world. In her long life, she had had few friends.

Fleur was her friend. An unlikely combination, by all accounts, yet it was so. They traded hopes, impressions, and glances just like the oldest, or youngest, lovers. And the grandest dream they shared was of the new world they were creating.

"Queen *ologlu dor*," Elspeth muttered as they reached their rooms. She's acquired, over the years, a patois of English mixed with Accident—partly to fill out her façade, partly because she felt it was more expressive. "*Olionto rorog.*"

Fleur nodded his head. "Ever since the breach in security five years ago, I agree. All those Humans escaping, it unhinged her, somehow."

"Hindsight *ras,* okay *nog noras*?" Elspeth spoke softly, tentative in her implications.

"She seems to've lost sight of her goals, is the problem," Fleur answered, circling the question. "Of *our* goals."

Elspeth held out her hand, gently touched the smoky skin of Fleur's cheek. "*Tog Lomper*; Fleur, we must. *Nef gluaka.*" She turned her head and averted her eyes to express more formally her reluctance.

Fleur kissed Elspeth's hand. "No, I quite agree, my dear. It's time to speak plainly. This Human must be made to talk. I think, perhaps, Ugo's services will be invaluable in this regard."

Josh was awakened by a feeling more than a sound, as such, and looked up to find a vampire standing over him, studying him. It was one of the dark Vampires who had been present at his interrogation.

"I am Ugo," he said when he saw Josh was awake. Josh focused his eyes. Ugo was large and powerful; his hair was filthy, matted, stringy; across the left side of his face a horrible scar from an old burn pulled the skin into glossy, twisted, designs. "You can trust me," he said.

"Let me go," Josh whispered.

"I cannot," replied the Vampire with great regret. "But if you tell me what you know, I can help you."

"How?"

"First, what." Ugo's voice acquired an edge.

"Nothing," Josh shook his head. "I've told everything I—"

Before he could finish the sentence, Ugo's fangs were in his neck, sending waves of pain through his body. He was taken by such surprise that he had no time to set himself, no time to react. So he merely writhed there, pinned at the throat by Ugo's needle-teeth, as the Vampire's formidable hands roamed his wriggling body—taking pleasure, inflicting pain, teaching Josh this ancient, malignant lesson.

* * *

Paula climbed the ladder of braided seaweed up the slimy cave wall, through an opening in the ceiling, to a still darker room. She made her way quickly to an almost invisible hole in the wall, through which she squeezed, then nimbly navigated a precarious ledge that overhung a sheer drop into eternity, and finally emerged in a long, windy tunnel.

She loved this tunnel. Its ceiling was ribbed like the inside of a great animal, the wind its warm respirations. It always made her think of the story of Jonah, one of her earliest book memories; it made her feel safe. Protected, in the belly of the beast.

At its blind end was a pool of still water, which Paula dove into: she swam to the rocky bottom, pulled herself along twenty feet of curving wall, floated to the surface, and crawled ashore to a thick rug in a cozy, well-lit cave. There were towels hanging on a rack in the stone wall. Paula took one, wrapped herself in it, walked to a door in the opposite wall, and knocked. It was opened by Candlefire.

Candlefire was a Nine-prong Plugger. There were Three-prong, Nine-prong, and Twenty-seven-prong Pluggers—so named, not surprisingly, for the number of prongs in the plugs that had once connected to the outlets in their heads. When they had all been in-circuit in the City, they formed a great crisscrossing network in the Communion Room.

Generally speaking, more prongs signified greater complexities of information being transferred along those cables. But the distinctions were, in fact, far more subtle than this, though they were distinctions only Pluggers could appreciate.

The Pluggers had their own idiomatic nomenclature for themselves and the myriad states of consciousness, or "modes," of the plugged-in condition they had once shared and to which they now aspired. Themselves, they called *Primes, Squares,* or *Cubes* (Three, Nine, or Twenty-seven prongs). The four major modes they called *Light, Nolight, Singularity,* and *Fusion.* There were colors and levels to each mode; but these were concepts the Pluggers could not easily articulate to anyone who had never been plugged in.

They had chosen personal names for themselves that they each felt most intuitively described the color, level, and mode at which they usually operated when plugged in. Candlefire took his name with great care, to resonate with the several discrete elements in a candle flame, the motions of these elements, their colors, their heats, their various natures, and their unity. The meaning of this in relation to Candlefire's preferred state of consciousness didn't have to be explained to any other Plugger—and it *couldn't* be explained to anyone who was not a Plugger.

Twenty-six Pluggers lived in the labyrinthine catacombs beneath the cliffs south of The City With No Name. They had come years before—immediately following their escape from the City—after discovering a tunnel that twisted for miles, leading from one of the sewage tunnels beneath the City, south to the catacombs they now occupied. They had remained ever since, afraid to go farther, afraid to return. For they hated the thought of going back to that imprisonment: lying side by side on their backs, motionless until the day they died, their brains plugged in to the thing that used, stored, played with, augmented, mixed, fused, and stole their thoughts. Hated the memory of that slavery. And yet it had been the peak experience of their lives.

Light, Nolight, Singularity, Fusion. These were the states Humans occupied during the plugged-in Communion: presences of such moment, they could be neither replaced nor approximated. They were ultimate states.

Eighty-three had escaped to the tunnels, freed by Josh after he had freed Rose. Some were lost on the march to the catacombs, some later left to wander on their own. Fourteen killed themselves within two years, because the prospect of ever again plugging-in to one another seemed so remote.

Now twenty-six remained, hovering near enough the City to nurture the dream that they would one day capture the castle, capture the plugs and cables, and once again enter into Communion.

Some of the Pluggers had been Scribes before they had

been caught for the Queen's Great Experiment; and some of these Scribes knew of the Bookery. So three years after the escape, they made contact with the Book people and brought them into the catacombs to join forces and plot the overthrow of the City. They had been planning ever since.

It was an imperfect marriage. The Books wanted to destroy the City without quarter, though they couldn't decide the best way to do it; the Pluggers wanted desperately to preserve the network of wires that had once united them. Each group clung to its own fervor. They divided into two distinct encampments, separated by a lattice of suspicion, of tunnels and caves. Yet there were also basic bonds between the Books and the Pluggers. They were all Human.

"Please, come in," Candlefire said to Paula. She pulled the damp towel more closely around herself and entered. He closed the door behind her.

The room was large, but toasty, with two bonfires crackling on either side of an underground spring. Several people cooked at the blazes. Candlefire walked Paula to the other so she could warm herself in its breath.

In spite of their conflicting allegiances, Paula and Candlefire were friends. Paula never understood Fusion, and Candlefire would not grasp the mystical aspects of the Word; but they knew each other. They liked what they knew.

"I saw a Human kidnapped today," Paula said quietly. "He was having convulsions, and they took him to the City."

"May he reach Communion," Candlefire responded sympathetically, meshing his fingers in the Sign of the Plug.

"I knew him," she continued. "At least, I think I did. I think he was a Scribe who came to us years ago in Ma'gas' looking for his family. He wanted our help. We asked him to join us on our crusade, instead. No, he said, he had to find his people first—his wife, his brother."

"What happened?" Candlefire's voice was quiet as a low flame.

She shrugged in the whisper of the orange fire. "We were raided. Lewis was captured and no more seen. The rest of us fled. The Scribe—his name was Joshua—escaped, to . . . who knows what. So he could be captured and taken to the City five years later, for me to watch."

Candlefire put his arm around his friend, to warm her body and spirit. "It is our wretched lot on this Earth to be alone."

Paula smiled back a tear. "Unless we could fuse," she chided him softly.

"*Except* when we fuse." He nodded, gently laughing at her jibe.

She propped her head on his shoulder. He felt the shadow of her pain. She thought, It's not true, then. We are all of us islands.

He stroked her hair. "So alone, little Scribe. I'd plug you in if I could—then we could truly *be* with each other."

She hugged him silently, and wished it were so. We're like random words, she thought. We try to make sense of ourselves, but there is *no* sense, *we* have no definition. We try to stand together, to order ourselves into coherent sentences and meaningful wholes—but it comes out garbled. Single words we are born, and single words we die.

She whispered to him, "*Nouns are we, in search of a verb.*"

"Sounds like poetry from one of your books," Candlefire mused.

" 'Tis." She nodded dreamily. It was, in the end, her last refuge.

"I don't exactly understand your poetry, but it brings me to mind of plugging. They both seek to touch." He wrapped his long arms around her. In the background, the other Pluggers cooked Eel and recalled the days of the Plug.

"Perhaps," she conceded. "I don't know, I think I've just tired of living in the shadow of that castle."

"Its shadow covers the compass," Candlefire nodded.

"It used to give us unity—we shared the darkness, we looked for the light together. Now we wander each one alone, in this eclipse that never ends, bumping into one another and walking away."

"Some of us still hold hands in the darkness." He sighed, and pulled her closer.

"I used to hold hands with my brother," she reminisced. "We were orphans in Ma'gas', I was ten and he was seven. We lived in the alleys, on the run. Our days we hid, stole, and fought the smaller animals for foods. Our parents were killed by a drunken Harpie, and all we had was each other. And that's just what we did—we held hands. Sitting under the docks waiting for sundown is what I remember best— holding hands and waiting for the night to come hide us."

She paused to fix the memory, trying to hold it still, to fasten on it, to study it. Behind her, the fire cast shadows on the wall, like the ghosts of her story.

"Where's your brother now?"

"Gone. Kidnapped by pirates—Russian Lupinos. Probably dead by now, I imagine."

"But you Scribes write down the histories of your loved ones, I thought—so they never die, as long as they're read about by other Scribes. You told me this once."

Tears filled Paula's eyes. "Nathan asked me never to set down his record. He was afraid if he died and it was set down on paper, that made it final . . . but if no one ever wrote of the death, he still might figure out a way to come back—if it wasn't written down, maybe it never happened." She sighed deeply, to keep from crying. "So he's gone forever."

Candlefire took her hand in his. "Then we shall hold hands, you and I, in the hiding-night of these caves, under the shadow of the castle on the river."

The caves seemed to grow deeper around them, as if given sustenance by their despair. They held hands tightly; yet for all their nearness, they remained two, alone.

CHAPTER 4

In Which Three More Join
the Search,
and Share Their First Regret

BEAUTY was graced among Centaurs. He was born with the gift of balance, a sense that kept his keel even, even in the most turbulent waters. He had a fine, strong body, and a spirit deep as the ocean's cradle. He loved, and was loved.

For two years after he had rescued Rose from her bondage in the City, they lived in careless peace near Monterey. They withstood the Coming of Ice at first, then bent under it; then, like everyone else, moved south. Forest to town, river to valley, they migrated for three years, reaching finally as far south as the Saddlebacks—as far south as they dared, without actually entering the Terrarium. It was during this meandering emigration that Rose had begun to grow distant.

Beauty hadn't noticed at first. He was preoccupied with the climate, the winds; with what he sensed as an increasing unpredictability in the behavior of all the animals. He kept his eye intent on the horizon, so he didn't notice that the tiny boat in his safe harbor was starting to drift away. By the time he did notice, Rose was at sea, and shipping water fast.

She was prone to cry. Aimless, forceless weeping, for no apparent reason. She could never say exactly why she was crying; or, when she stopped, why she stopped. Only that it had something to do with loss.

When Beauty finally caught on that this was no passing melancholy, he could find no way to help. He was kind with her, or stern. He was a rock. He was a beacon in the night storm, yet his light gave her no comfort: she was disconsolate.

Until she met Blackwind. He was a wild-eyed wanderer

Rose and Beauty met in the North Saddlebacks, with whom they shared a cave during a two-day hail shower. A bleak little man, Beauty thought; on the edge and on the run. As it turned out, Blackwind was a Plugger.

There was almost instant recognition between Blackwind and Rose. Their shared experience in the City had left them with a kind of radar for people of their own kind. They talked in whispers, continuously, for the two days of the storm. When it finally cleared, Blackwind stole away without a word to Beauty; and Rose was left with the bottomless stare gone from her eye.

They worked their way east for a few weeks, Beauty increasingly concerned. For where Rose had been lost, she now seemed trapped; before baffled, now morose. He caught her gazing at him with a defeated resolve.

Then one day she told him she was going to see Josh. She had to speak with their old friend. Beauty was reluctant to let her go alone at first, but she insisted; and he came to feel that, somehow, maybe Josh would be able to help where he obviously could not.

So she left. And did not return.

Through it all, Beauty never lost his sense of balance. For every thing there was a season, Jasmine had once told him, and those words felt right with him. All things in their time. This didn't mean some things didn't upset him, or put him on guard—simply that he wasn't easily derailed or swamped.

So when Rose didn't come back on time, Beauty tracked her to Joshua's camp. He looked forward to seeing Josh as well—they had had little contact for two years, and Beauty missed his comrade sorely. It was a double shock, then, to find both Josh and Rose missing. Double, but not entirely unexpected—Beauty had had an uneasy feeling about the events all along. The feeling was confirmed when he found Joshua's note.

The note was addressed to Beauty on the outside, but directed to Ollie and Jasmine in the text. He assumed one of them had left the note for him to find, for him to follow and join them all at the pit of his greatest fear—The City With No Name.

He had suspected matters were heading in this direction; he didn't know why. Somehow, it almost seemed inevitable, as if the unfinished business there demanded resolution.

"Damned City," he muttered to himself wearily. He rarely swore—it brought one too close to teetering. He regained his equilibrium quickly, though, and sat down to plot his course.

He would need help. The City would be much better protected against assault than it had been the first time he had violated its armor. He needed someone he could trust; he soon thought of D'Ursu Magna.

D'Ursu was an old, dear friend, a Bear-Chieftain and first lieutenant to Jarl, the Bear-King. Jarl's forces were in nearby Newport, Beauty had heard—waiting for the Doge to make his move. So Beauty went to Newport.

On a crisp, cold morning in January, Beauty cantered into Newport's central square, his Dragon-rib bow slung across his shoulder. He asked after D'Ursu Magna, and was directed to the old Bear's favorite den—a place called Owl's—two steps down into the cellar of a stone building in the old section of town.

There were no windows in the place; it looked like a cave. Several Bears lolled on the dirt floor in various stages of hibernation, some of them chewing poppies, some chewing rye mold. A couple of Trolls lay, wasted, in a corner hollow, while a bat fluttered uselessly on its back near the door. From a side room, the sounds and smells of unventilated sex bubbled thick as tar in a fetid pool.

Sitting on a log beside the connecting door was D'Ursu Magna. The great brown Bear's eyes were glazed with loveless satisfactions, his fur matted with sour sweat. Beauty walked over to him, put a hand on his Bear friend's shoulder.

"D'Ursu Magna," said the Centaur, "I came for your help. But Bear, you look like the sorriest of Bears."

D'Ursu looked up at him as if awakened from a long dream. "Beauté Centauri," he growled. "You have come to save me again. My claws bleed from clutching at this drain

in this sink of contaminated refuse. Beauté Centauri, deliver me."

Beauty helped D'Ursu up and guided him out the front
door. He walked the great Bear slowly to the edge of the
city, sat him beside a clear pool in a deep meadow, and
gently washed him with handfuls of cold, winter-pond water. Gradually D'Ursu's eyes focused as he let the Centaur
clean him. He looked around, saw where he was, and let
out a long basso profundo roar to the day.

"Feel better?" asked Beauty, whisking the last of the water from the Bear's back.

"Beauté Centauri, I am shamed to have you see me so.
Stinking like a Human." He spat.

"You stink like a Bear who has forgotten the forest and
thinks perhaps he can remember it chewing jimson weed."

"I have not forgotten!" he growled. Then, softer: "I have
not forgotten." He licked his paw. "Only, this city is making me crazy with citysickness. We sit and we wait for the
Doge to attack, and still we wait. We live crowded together
in houses and huts so the Doge can't guess our numbers
from his spy ships on the sea. Can you believe it, Beauté?
In a house it isn't possible to see the sky, or smell the forest, or roll in muddy grass. But still we sit. We are behav-
ing like the Doge's Humans so we can destroy them, and
instead we are *becoming* them. How is it possible, Beauté
Centauri?"

Beauty smiled, sensing the old Bear's spirit returning.
"It is not only possible but inevitable, D'Ursu Magna. We
all become as we behave. So it is important to behave properly."

The Bear-Chieftain wagged his head. "I can't abide this
city, and I can't leave Jarl, our King . . ." He stopped and
looked at Beauty as if seeing him for the first time. "Ah,
Beauté Centauri," he roared, and gave the Centaur a long
Bear hug.

Beauty returned the fond embrace, then sat beside the
old Bear. D'Ursu spoke again.

"What a vile old Bear I've become. It's the stinking city,
I tell you—but that's no excuse, I know. You need help, I
can see it in your eye. How can I help you?"

"I will come quickly to the point, for I have not time, old friend. My wife, Rose, has gone. I track her south—to The City With No Name. I need help getting into that city."

"Your wife, Rose." The Bear scratched at the fur on his cheek with his huge paw. "A Human, is she not? As I recall, you were trailing her south last time we met. Have you not found her yet? Or is she forever wandering off?"

"Do not jest with me, ugly Bear. Her absence has torn a piece from my heart." He went on to tell D'Ursu about how the shadow of earlier times had overtaken him and Rose.

"But why?" D'Ursu squinted, unable to comprehend.

"I believe to regain something of herself she felt she had lost."

It was beyond the Bear. "How Human," he said, somewhat baffled.

"Yes," responded Beauty, "how very Human." In his voice was love.

"And this other Human, this Plugger," D'Ursu went on, "what was his measure?"

"I liked him not." Beauty closed his eyes to blot out the man's image, but this only brought it out more clearly, so he opened them again. "He said everything he had to say as if it were a conspiracy, to be kept from everyone to whom he was not speaking. It pleased me no more to be included than excluded. Still, he shared much with Rose that I could not share." This clearly pained the Centaur. "His name was Blackwind. I liked him not."

D'Ursu dangled his legs in the pond. "So now you want to get back inside the City and search for Rose once again. Beauté, don't think me harsh, but this has the smell of a dry hunt. She left you of her own will, in her own time. What if you find her and she doesn't wish to return?"

This was a hard question for Beauty, but one he had already faced. "If she wants to stay there, I will leave her and find my own place. First, though, I must find her to ask."

D'Ursu Magna rolled into the water, swam down twenty feet to snap up a dozing fish he had had his eye on, then floated to the surface and lumbered back onto the bank. "I think I can help you," he said around a mouthful of fish. "And free myself from this stinking city as well." He stood up and wiped his snout with the back of his paw. "You wait here, Beauté Centauri. I have things to do. I'll be back by sunfall." So saying, he waddled back into Newport.

Beauty watched him with affection, and tried to suppress the spark of hope the grizzled old Bear had ignited.

Jarl, the Bear-King, looked out over the sea. It shattered the sunlight in its churning stillness, like the face of a highly cut gem.

"It's cold, even this far south," said D'Ursu. "Newport was never this cold before."

"I like the cold," growled Jarl.

D'Ursu remained silent. He carefully chose the issues over which he argued with his King.

Jarl spoke again, his nose to the seawind. "My counselors tell me the Doge will attack from the water—he will send an Armada. I disagree, D'Ursu. What say you?"

"My Bear," said D'Ursu Magna, "I wish to leave."

Jarl looked down on his lieutenant. "The Doge frightens you?"

"No, my King. I wish to accompany our old friend Beauté Centauri on a quest of his. He has asked my help."

"Who is this Centaur, and what is his quest?" The old King looked skeptical.

"You remember him, your Animal Honor. He came through our forest many seasons ago with his Human comrade, seeking his Human wife. It was decided their quest was with justice."

Jarl nodded, straining to remember. Long memory was not an animal virtue. "Humans, by and large, are the lowest form of animal," he cautioned. "I think you would do better to remain here."

"I don't mark many Humans as friend," D'Ursu agreed. "But this Human who rode with Beauté Centauri—we learned from him. For this reason I would help Beauté find him now. Also that Beauté Centauri is my great friend and an animal of virtue, and he has asked my help. Also that I fear to lose my spirit if I stay too long in this city."

Jarl squinted at the sun's reflection off the water. "I do recall something of this Human who came through our forest. A Scribe, I believe. He smelled not of deceit or Human-sickness. He had virtue, for a Human. Perhaps it is that a Human in the forest is more animal than an animal in the city. So you fear losing your spirit, eh? I fear we're *all* becoming peevish cloistered here so. We used to be free animals, D'Ursu Magna, one with the Great Forest. Now to guard our freedom, I am become a tyrant, and my animals slaves to an idea. How Human we're becoming. Yes, go, D'Ursu. Go with your friend. Friendship is the only good idea a Human ever had. Only, come back soon, and bring us a piece of the forest, that we not forget who we are."

D'Ursu lumbered in the side door of the Vampire brothel. Every city had a stable population of Vampires; and consequently, most had brothels where Humans of both sexes sold warm draughts of their blood to any thirsty Vampire with the coin to buy. D'Ursu tipped the concierge, and was directed toward the end of the hall. Slowly, he walked up the dark corridor.

Along the length of the hallway, most of the doors were open, and D'Ursu Magna threw a glance into each room as he passed. Some were empty. In one, a naked young man slept peacefully, blood crusted around his neck. In another, a jaundiced Vampire sucked lasciviously from the femoral vein of a muscular woman who moaned and swore.

D'Ursu shook his head and walked on. "Humans," he grumbled.

The door to the end room was closed. He knocked, and the weight of his paw swung it open. Inside sat two figures. On a chair in the corner was a brawny young man bandaging a small gash on his left wrist. On the bed sat a lean, handsome, pale Vampire, a cup of blood at his lips. The cup steamed a little in the unheated room.

D'Ursu spoke. "Aba—excuse me—" He started to back out, but the Vampire on the bed raised his hand.

"No, please come in, D'Ursu Magna. I was just finishing." The Vampire downed the cup in a few long swallows, turning his back somewhat to the door, for modesty's sake. D'Ursu, likewise, looked away, seeing the Vampire was a bit embarrassed. The Vampire put down the empty glass and motioned to the young man on the chair, who stood and left the room without a word.

D'Ursu entered and shut the door. He and the Vampire bared necks to each other. "Forgive me, Aba, I meant only to knock and—"

"Speak no more of it, D'Ursu. How can I help you?"

They sat on the bed facing each other. "Something for both of us, perhaps. I go to The City With No Name on a mission with a friend—Beauté Centauri. He is the same Centaur who was befriended by your tutor."

Aba's pupils dilated. "He knew Sire Lon well, this Centaur?"

"Lon died saving Beauté Centauri's best friend—a Human—on the walls of the City, to which we now journey."

Aba wrapped himself in his wings against the chill in the air. "And why does he return there now, this Beauté Centauri? And why do you join him? And why do you tell me?" There was no suspicion in his voice, no challenge; only a desire to know, as if clarity were the key to all things.

"He returns to find his wife, and to find this Human for whom Lon died. I go with him because he is my friend and he asked me to help. Also, this Human interests me—virtuous animals feel a passion for him that is like what I feel for the Heart of the Forest. And I remember him a little myself—he was not like these greedy Humans who will sell their own blood for . . ." He stopped in mid-sentence, then dismissed what he had just been saying, with a sweep of his paw. "I meant no insult to you, Aba. It's this city. It makes me say things I—"

"No offense taken," the Vampire assured him. "Please go on." He coughed and covered his mouth with a wing tip; but they both knew he did it to obscure the shame that had fleetingly passed across his flushed face at D'Ursu's uncensored remarks.

D'Ursu continued, in a gentler tone. "I tell you this because I know you loved Lon. He was your tutor in life, and I think you are his student still. I think you might still learn from him, at the place of his death." He paused, then went on more gruffly. "And I tell you too because I think you may be of some help to us in the city of Vampires and runaway Humans."

Aba stood and smiled. "Just so," he said.

When D'Ursu returned to the pond near dusk, accompanied by a lean, pale Vampire, Beauty was napping under a cluster of birches. At the first smell of the Vampire, though, he jumped awake, nostrils flaring, feet pawing the ground.

"Be calm," growled D'Ursu. "This Vampire is friend. His name is Aba."

Beauty and Aba bared their necks to each other in the ritual sign of friendship and honor.

Aba spoke with a shyness of manner that pleased the Centaur. "D'Ursu Magna tells me you were a friend of Lon-Sire, noblest of Vampires."

"Noblest of all creatures of the Earth," answered Beauty. "You also called him friend?"

"News of his death left me friendless."

"Then *we* are friends," avowed Beauty.

"D'Ursu tells me you're returning now to the place of his death—to see those, perhaps, who killed him."

"Those responsible, perhaps. Are you claiming Venge right?"

The Vampire shook his head. "Vengeance is an act of noise without light. Its echo is hollow, and never ends. No, I want no Venge right. But I would accompany you on your journey if I may—I dearly wish to see the where and the why of Sire Lon's death. I wish to understand it—that I may leave it behind. For it hasn't left me yet."

"Then welcome," Beauty said softly.

"Then let's be off," rasped D'Ursu. "I have a plan that Shoshoroo herself will sing songs about."

"And what is this plan?" the Centaur inquired with the thinnest trace of skepticism.

"To Ma'gas' by foot, along the shore. There we get a boat, and sail to The City With No Name."

"And when we reach the City?" Beauty pressed politely.

"Why, we walk in the front door, impudent Horse!" he bellowed, and began lumbering south. Beauty smiled and followed, Aba close behind. Neither noticed, at first, the rolled paper D'Ursu had tied deep into the fur of his belly.

They walked south along the coast all that first day, between the foothills and the sea, keeping silent for the most part. D'Ursu sang simple, growly songs when moved to do so—once by the radiance of a red poppintail bush; once by a cloud in the shape of a fish—and once, he took off in merry pursuit of a giant Jack Rabbit that looked particularly tasty.

As the sun went lower, though, and they all became easier with one another and the journey, they ventured a little conversation. For while they were each taciturn by nature, they were none of them unfriendly.

"Tell me, Aba," said Beauty, "how came you to live so far north."

"My father, may his blood run red, kept an estate near Newport. He loved the clear air and cold winds, unlike most of our race. I don't live there myself, I only visit now. I call no place home."

"Nor do I, so much the worse."

"Few can rest their bones for long in one den any more," D'Ursu interjected. "If it isn't the Ice, it's the Ice Madness. Not a soul isn't chased or chasing."

"If I could just see the why of it, I should be happy," Aba said, a little sadly.

"Things no longer have a reason, I fear." The golden Centaur shook his head. "Ice Madness, citysickness—the world lacks reason, and there is the whole of it. It is no wonder so many have lost their balance . . ." He spoke in general terms, but his thoughts were still of Rose.

The day lost its last light, and they headed inland a bit,

to look for shelter from the wind, to make their camp. The mountains were a mile offshore and separated from the sea by a marshy woodland, where they soon found a high dry area in a holly grove.

Aba spent the next hour gathering firewood, while Beauty shot Catfish in a nearby pond with his bow and arrow. D'Ursu discovered a string of animal traps that had been recently laid in the tall grass by some Human trapper. One trap had a wounded Fox in it, which D'Ursu set free. The other traps were unsprung. He triggered each one with a holly branch, and then urinated on the closed device, both as an aesthetic judgment and to warn away other curious animals with his smell.

He lumbered back into camp as the fish were being cooked, and told the others what he had done. "It was a good trick," he laughed.

Aba said softly, "Humans must live, too, D'Ursu Magna. They, also, must eat."

D'Ursu's eyes narrowed. "Humans always take more than they need to live—that's just the Human way. They lay waste to the Earth, by trickery and discontent—only sometimes, we trick them back. Eh, Beauté Centauri?" The old Bear rumbled and nudged Beauty, who didn't respond. Only then did D'Ursu remember the Centaur's wife was Human, and his best friend as well. "Beauté Centauri, forgive me, I've been stupid and tactless again. Of course, it goes without saying, not all Humans are this way. Else I wouldn't be with you now." He roared ingenuously.

Beauty couldn't take offense from his old friend—the Bear was loyal and without guile. "Humans are a much-maligned race, I think," he said.

"I agree," said Aba. "They have much to offer."

"They've offered too much by half, as far as I'm concerned," spat D'Ursu. "And if they'd but leave us alone, I'd be content to do the same to them."

Night was full now, as were their stomachs; as had been the day. The ocean breeze not far away was sweet, the company good. So without further discussion, they put the fire out and went to sleep.

* * *

Aba's eyes were most sensitive in the dark, so he was awakened first. His movement aroused the other two.

"What is it?" whispered Beauty.

"A faint glow—over there." Aba pointed into the marshland. D'Ursu nodded. Beauty couldn't see it at first, and finally could only barely detect it out of the corner of his eye if he looked in another direction.

"Split up," growled D'Ursu. They fanned out slowly, to approach the glowing area from three different directions.

Beauty walked directly toward the light, which was strong enough for him to follow by the time he had gone twenty paces. It was easy to move silently, for the ground cover was mostly moss and soft dirt. The trees became thicker at one point, then thinned again; then got very close. Beyond this break, the light was fairly bright, and Beauty was able to peer around one of the larger trunks to see into an expansive clearing.

Fifty feet away, a gathering of small, Humanoid creatures was holding some kind of ritual. Beauty couldn't name them all, but among the beasts he could identify were Trolls, Dark Elves, Grendels, Spriggans, and Goblins, all standing in a circle around a ten-foot-tall cone-shaped object. They were mumbling, and passed from hand to hand some kind of bundle, which activity caused their gold bracelets and necklaces of gems to clack and glitter in the light. It was difficult to discern much detail, however, for the only illumination afforded was by numerous jars full of fireflies flickering on and off, a cool, eerie green. Beauty silently observed.

After the bundle had been passed all around, the mumbling stopped. The covey walked in ever smaller circles around the tall, dark cone; then one by one, each member seemed to disappear into the ground, somewhere near the base of the obelisk. Soon the clearing was empty.

Beauty waited five minutes. When nothing further happened, he softly entered the arena. He saw D'Ursu and Aba do the same. Quietly, they walked toward the center, until they met near the cone.

"What was that?" Beauty whispered.

"I've seen one before," growled D'Ursu. "A Changeling ceremony of the Unseelie Court."

Aba nodded. "I've heard of them, but never seen one."

D'Ursu continued to Beauty. "It was a Human baby they were passing—the stinking trapper's, I don't doubt. They've just stolen it, and exchanged one of their own into the Human infant's crib. In this way, one of their own race will be raised by Humans, to spy and to learn."

"And what happens to the Human child they have taken?" Beauty wondered.

D'Ursu shrugged. "No one knows. It is the secret of the Unseelie."

"We must save the babe—" Beauty began, moving toward the upright cone.

D'Ursu stopped him, though. "It is not your concern, Beauté Centauri. Other matters press us this day."

"It's difficult to fathom how they can be so cruel," said Aba. "To steal an infant from its mother, in such a calculated—"

D'Ursu raised his paw. "Both of you, hold. It is an act of self-preservation these small people have devised, to protect themselves from the blind fears and hatred of the Human. Also, we know not what is done with these Human cubs—they mayhap live in great peace beneath the Earth. Also, this is not our affair, nor ever was it. I bid you, come back to our camp, that we may continue our own search."

Beauty was reluctant to leave. He approached the large cone, to examine it. Long before he reached it, however, his hoof knocked against a lip of stone in the dirt. He looked down to see a continuous ring of gray stone, about two feet wide, jagged, completely encircling the cone, which seemed to rise from the Earth at the center of this ring.

The cone itself was circular at its base, having a diameter of about six feet and sides that sloped gently to meet at a point ten feet in the air. Beauty walked up to view it closely. It seemed to be made of iron, or steel, and had a dull, frosty sheen in the light of the fireflies. He touched it: cold, hard. Down one side was a seared, feathery crack filled with moss, as if lightning had struck here once.

Aba joined him. They walked its perimeter. "What is their religion?" asked Beauty.

They stopped at the opposite curve of the object to notice a cluster of runic symbols etched in the metal. First there was a small rectangle, with thirteen lines running its length and a lot of stars grouped inside a small square inset into its upper left corner. Below this were different lines, which looked like writing to Beauty; Aba held up a jar of fireflies and read aloud: "United States of America. USAF." And then, below it: "MX Missile. Group F. Silo 47."

"You can read." Beauty stared at Aba with some surprise. Then: "What does it mean?"

"I'm not certain," Aba shook his head. "When I studied with Lon, he mentioned this United States of America once. It was an ancient kingdom, I think. Before the birth of the animals."

Beauty winced. It wasn't until some years ago that he had found out—from Jasmine—that most of the creatures who now roamed the Earth were the result of experiments in genetic engineering, only a couple of centuries old. Prior to that he had always believed—and part of him still believed—that the Centauri were an ancient race, older than Humans, as old as the trees. It still pained him to deny this history, though he knew he must.

D'Ursu padded over. "I've found where they went into the ground. Here." He showed them a line of scratched rock just inside the ring of solid stone that encircled the cone. It demarcated the edge of a massive door into the Earth. "If you want to chase them, here is where to start. As for me, I'm going to finish sleeping." So saying, the old Bear waddled toward their camp.

Beauty hesitated a minute; Aba stood behind him. Finally they, too, walked away, toward the sea in the graying night.

They set out early the next morning, Beauty glum, Aba contemplative, D'Ursu boisterous. The brown Bear romped along the beach, making loud noises at the Sandpipers to scare them, and then laughing ferociously at the magnitude of his wonderful trick.

Around noon they came upon an overturned cart; behind it were three wary Humans, two of them hefting spears. The third stayed partially hidden from view.

"Come no closer," shouted one of the men, raising his weapon.

"We mean you no harm," Beauty called back. "We journey to the south. Can we help you?"

"You nor your kind. Leave us be!" yelled the other man.

"Let's away," gruffed D'Ursu. "I need no further invitation."

"I know some healing," Aba called out. "If any of you are sick—"

"Begone, vile thing," the first man bellowed.

Aba flinched, hurt far more than if the man had loosed his spear. He knew how Humans felt toward his kind; he internalized their hatred, and atoned for the sins of his race daily, in act and thought. "Truly, we only wish you well," he said to the man.

The third Human stood up now, and they could see she was a woman. She whispered something to the man; both men shook their heads. She whispered more urgently, and again the men refused. Finally she turned toward Aba, and it was suddenly clear she was holding an infant in her arms—it could hardly have been a week old.

"It's my baby," she cried out. "He used to be so happy and noisy—he was all the time laughin'. Now suddenly he's turned all pale, and he won't eat, and quiet as the grave, it's almost like he's not the same baby—he's so changed." One of the men tried to pull her back, but she tore her arm from his grip, and spoke again to Aba. "Can you do anything?" she pleaded.

Aba, Beauty, and D'Ursu shot sidelong glances at one another; but none knew what to say. Beauty could not look at the woman. D'Ursu Magna pawed the sand, scratched his ear, then let out a huge roar to heaven, which frightened the poor Humans even more.

Finally Aba spoke. "Yes, I'll tell you what to do," he said evenly, like a healer. "Make a pap of fish roe, bread crumbs, and milk, and dip your finger in it and the child will suck your finger. Give him love, and he will return it."

They were all silent, looking at one another. Finally Beauty set off around the overturned cart, and continued south toward Ma'gas', with D'Ursu and Aba close behind, as the woman wept, and thanked them.

CHAPTER 5

In Which D'Ursu Tricks Himself; And the Insatiable City Almost Takes Some Country Cousins for a Ride

"ALL right, so I was wrong," D'Ursu grumbled when they were well away. "How was I to know the Changeling's family would assault us with tears? I swear that is the cruelest weapon a Human ever invented."

"Seeing the mother did not make it wrong." Beauty spoke with deep regret. "We had it in our power to save her child last night, and we did not."

"Perhaps," said Aba, "but had we been killed last night, we'd never have finished this journey to save your people." He said it to convince himself as much as Beauty.

"Then we acted selfishly if that was our motive—and not merely out of ignorance."

"Don't berate yourself, Centaur. A choice was made, for better or worse. We make choices every day, and we live with them. I think it's time to leave this one behind."

Beauty agreed there was sense in that doctrine.

"Beauté Centauri," D'Ursu said, laying his great paw on the Centaur's back, "you were my captain once, and you are my captain still. From this time on, whatever is your wish, it is my mission."

"My wish, ugly Bear, is to move faster and speak less."

At this, D'Ursu Magna snapped his snout shut and lumbered down the beach at a trot. Aba jumped on Beauty's back to ride, as the Centaur geared up to a canter. The Bear stayed several hundred yards ahead, playing in the surf, running up the dunes, lying in the sand grass, then taking off again. He was so glad to be out of the city he could barely contain his spirit. Periodically, he would roar for no reason in particular; and this gay abandon, inevitably, lifted Beauty's mood.

As evening neared again, D'Ursu went up into the hills to scout a campsite, while Aba flew out over the water and south, to see how far they were from Ma'gas'. Beauty lay on the warm sand and looked for the first star.

He was glad for his companions. Their hearts were strong, that was the main thing; it would have been a lonely search without them. Lonely and uncertain: this was the legacy of Rose's disappearance. Beauty felt, for the first time, cut loose from his moorings. Nothing seemed as certain as it once had.

The first star of the evening winked dimly, high above the sea. He wondered what it was telling him. He wondered if it shone now on Rose or Josh.

A shadow passed over the star, then momentarily obscured half the sky, before the sound of wind snapping leather told Beauty that Aba was flying overhead. The Vampire landed a few yards away, his great wings blowing the sand in swirling gusts around for several seconds. As the sand settled, he walked over to Beauty and sat down.

"Ma'gas' is very near," he said. "If we leave at dawn, we should arrive before noon."

Beauty nodded. "What brings you with us now, truly?" he asked suddenly.

"Truly, for clarity," Aba replied. "To understand the world, I must understand myself. And part of my self died with Sire Lon."

"What was he to you? How did you know him?"

"When my father died, he was my father. He was teacher and guide, and friend when I wasn't friend to myself."

"I knew him only briefly, but his honor and loyalty made me richer in the knowing," Beauty attested.

"And this friend of yours for whom he died—Joshua— what is *his* measure?"

"Joshua . . ." pondered Beauty. "He is a man much like other men. He is a Scribe, which I essay not to hold too heavily against him; and he is a hunter, for his food. He is simple and unexceptional, and a hero only to those who love him."

Aba smiled warmly. "And a lucky man, withall, to have so steady a friend."

Beauty smiled back with his eyes only. "Friend I may be; but steady, I fear not—the legs of my spirit shake with doubts."

"Doubt is no reason for shame. Doubt is only the sense with which we smell death. You pick up the scent of your mortality, you shiver from its thrill; you call it unsteadiness, but it's not: it is your perception that this life is shimmering beneath your feet, and will momentarily dissolve."

"Like faltering on early spring's thin ice over deep water," Beauty answered with his eyes closed, trying to see the image Aba described.

"Just so." Aba nodded. "And to call that unsteadiness is to ignore the fact that it touches the nature of the ice, and remarks the nature of that which lies beneath."

"So you would have me applaud my doubts?"

"At least the existence of the sense. As to the specifics of your doubts, I cannot say—I scarcely know you."

Beauty smiled with his entire face now. "I think I begin to know Lon better through you."

There was a rustling in the grasses up the dune, and suddenly D'Ursu came rolling down the sandy slope, wheezing and breathless with laughter.

"What's happened, old Bear?" Aba began laughing with him.

"I found two nests, not forty paces apart," D'Ursu choked out when he had quieted down a bit. "Green-tailed Runyon, and Green-breasted Emu. Both full of eggs, both unguarded." He lay down on his back to collect himself.

"Slow down, Bear." Beauty smiled. "What of these bird nests?"

"I slipped an Emu egg in the Runyon nest, is what! When the silly hen hatches her children, she'll find three green tails and a green breast! What a good trick!" He coughed and cackled.

Beauty became quickly sober. "D'Ursu Magna, that was not a good trick. The poor birds will be terribly confused and frightened when the eggs hatch. How could you do this after the grief we have seen at the Human child taken from its nest?"

D'Ursu was suddenly incensed. "It's not the same thing at all! These birds aren't even born yet. And besides, when they do hatch, no harm will come. It's a prank, no more! It's done all the time." His anger was quickly turning to guilt.

"D'Ursu Magna," said Aba, "where is the sport in confusing a poor bird?" His tone was curious; he merely wanted to understand.

"It's not sport!" D'Ursu roared. "It's a joke, a simple trick." He was feeling worse and worse. They all hung their heads in silence. The stars were in full blossom now, like diamonds on a cape of black velvet. D'Ursu spoke again, finally. "It's only . . . I'm so happy to play at my forest games again, I . . . got carried away. Yes, that's what happened, and it won't happen again. You're right, Beauté Centauri—it was a bad trick."

Beauty grabbed the Bear's ears and shook his head vigorously.

The Bear growled, then said, "Here. I will die of remorse on this very spot." With which he tumbled back and lay still.

"Get up, lazy Bear, and gather us some wood, for all our trouble in putting up with you."

D'Ursu jumped up. "No! First I will go and put the egg back nicely in its proper nest, so the poor stinking greenbrain won't die of confusion in the spring." He lumbered back up the dune and disappeared over the hill.

Beauty found a turnip patch, and roasted some of its bounty with a lot of acorns over a small fire Aba had put together. When, an hour later, D'Ursu hadn't returned, they began to worry. Aba flew over the area, but returned in ten minutes shaking his head.

"D'Ursu!" Beauty shouted, but without response.

Alert and deliberate, they walked up into the hills. They hadn't been gone five minutes before they heard it: a mad fluttering sound, followed by silence; then, again, the fluttering. They moved cautiously toward the noise, crouched down in the grass, until finally they came upon the scene:

D'Ursu lay motionless beside the Emu nest; beside him the Emu fluttered in its death throes, then stiffened and died as Beauty and Aba stood there. They quickly ran up to the inanimate Bear.

The head—and only the head—of a Quetzal Viper had locked itself in D'Ursu's foot, its fangs buried deep into the meat of the Bear's hind paw, its body torn off at the neck. Beauty kneeled beside D'Ursu Magna's face: the powerful Bear still breathed, and his pulse was strong; yet he remained unresponsive to all prodding.

"He lives," said Beauty.

With great effort, Aba pulled open the snake-head mouth, extracting the fangs from D'Ursu's foot. Beauty tore a handful of vine grass from the earth and made a tourniquet high on the Bear's leg. Aba then slit open D'Ursu's swollen foot with his razor-sharp nails, and bent down to suck out whatever poison was still in the wound.

Beauty examined the Emu—dead, a Viper bite in its chest. The nest beside the mother bird had only one egg in it now, pale green in the moonlight. Nearby, Beauty finally found the body of the serpent, still writhing slowly in its own death dance. Its neck was ragged where it had been torn from the head; and just distal to it were three egg-shaped lumps all in a row, inside the snake's midsection.

It was clear to Beauty, now, what had happened. D'Ursu had brought back the Emu egg he had taken, only to find that a Quetzal Viper had, in the meantime, killed the mother Emu and was now probably dozing after a three-egg feast. D'Ursu had replaced his poached egg, stomped on the Viper's head, and yanked its body off at the neck while he stood on the skull. As he moved to throw the decapitated body in the brush, the half-crushed head had reflexively clamped down on his foot, sending its deadly venom coursing through the poor Bear.

Aba stood. "No more poison, we'll just let it bleed, though. Help me get him on your back, Beauty."

Together they struggled with the Bear's weight, until the limp carcass was slumped across Beauty's back. Aba tied him in place with lengths of vine. "I know a doctor in

Ma'gas' who has antidotes for many things," the Vampire panted. "If we hurry, he may be able to help."

Beauty nodded, and stepped carefully down the hill. Aba started to follow, then paused to look back. He ran over to the Emu nest, removed the solitary egg, walked forty paces into the brush, and in a few moments found the Runyon nest, its three hazel eggs clustered still as a long pause. Quickly he placed the Emu egg in their midst; then ran down to join Beauty, thinking all the while that poor D'Ursu was right: it had been a good trick, after all, to put the Emu egg in another nest.

They reached Ma'gas' in the peach-gray of the hour before dawn, when a city sleeps its deepest. Beauty's hooves clattered over the boardwalk under the weight on his back, while Aba flitted from alley to street looking for a place he remembered.

Light seeped into the sky; the city stirred. Sailors hoisted rigging, or stumbled out of the taverns. Vendors opened their windows, swept their walks, laid out their stocks, and sang and coughed and spat. And suddenly, a new day was rising.

Aba found the door he wanted, halfway up a narrow alley. He banged on it repeatedly, joining in the morning noises, as Beauty clopped slowly up beside him. After a minute of this, the door finally opened, and a grizzled old man stood blinking in his nightgown.

"What the hell do you want?" he croaked. This set off a coughing spell that threatened not to stop, until a large glob of phlegm struggled free into his mouth, which he expectorated at Aba's feet.

"Our Bear friend is near death—bitten by a snake last night."

"Did you bring the snake?" the old man demanded. His hair was wild, his body twisted with arthritis. He smelled like an old man.

"The snake?" Beauty asked stupidly. He was exhausted—from the physical burden, the sleeplessness, the emotional strain—so his thinking was slow.

"The snake, yes, the snake!" screeched the old man.

"What did you think I said? The rake? The cake? The flake, maybe? Idiots. Well, come in, come in, we can sit around the kitchen table and guess what bit him."

This brought forth a laugh from the aged doctor, which gave way to another coughing fit, which was punctuated, finally, with another huge glob of sputum, spat into the street. This concluded, the old man ushered them into his apartments and shut the door.

The place was filthy. Beauty was instantly sorry he had come, and was about to leave when the old man tore off D'Ursu's bindings and tipped the unconscious Bear over onto his back on a long table. He then pulled open the window shades, and in the bright glare of daylight, through clouds of settling dust, Beauty saw it was the kitchen table.

"I'm Dr. Jerome," the crotchety old physician stated as he rattled through a pile of greasy, crusted pans in the sink, looking for something. "Do you have any money?"

"Yes . . ." Beauty hesitated. "We—"

"Give it to me, then. How the hell do you think I live here—on the charity of my neighbors? I'll tell you how, you mangy myth. They suffer me to live here even though I'm a Human and a grouch and a well-known Scribe, 'cause I fix 'em when they get sick, and I pay my rent. So give me your money!" He stamped his foot; Beauty reached into the leather purse he wore slung around his neck, and handed over most of his coin. The doctor grunted. "Not much here," he mumbled.

"About the Bear . . ." Aba suggested.

"And you didn't bring the snake!" Jerome ranted, pounding his fists on the sink.

"It was a Quetzal Viper," Aba pressed on. "With short yellow feathers, and—"

"A Quetzal?" Dr. Jerome's eyes twinkled. "You saw it? You know what it was? Why the hell didn't you say so? *Now* we're having a conver*sa*tion!" He hopped all around the room, madly opening and closing cupboards, coughing, talking to himself. D'Ursu breathed in fits and starts on the table.

They followed the doctor into the next room, his study, which was even filthier than the kitchen. Shabby, faded books lined three walls from floor to ceiling. The dust on the bindings looked at least a century thick. The floor was strewn everywhere with papers, leaves, ropes, tools, dirt, tiles, and pencils; it was impossible to actually see it, let alone walk on it. Against the fourth wall was a great desk, containing a microscope, more papers, more papers still, jars, glasses, powders, prisms, and a sleeping kitten. Dr. Jerome rummaged through the mess for several minutes before he realized Beauty and Aba were standing behind him.

"You still here? What the hell are you still doing here?"

"We just—" Beauty began.

"Out, get out! How the hell can I get any work done when I'm bothered by visitors at all hours. Idiots! Visiting hours are over! Get out!" He pointed to the door.

"When should we—"

"Don't even think about coming back until tomorrow morning. By then, we'll know one way or the other—hoo-hah's or boo-hoo's. For right now . . ." But his sentence sputtered out in a paroxysm of coughing, during which the two friends slipped out the front door. On their way, they saw into a large back room: five mats were lined up on the floor; on one, a young female Centaur slept peacefully, her hind legs swathed in bandages; on another, a Wolfman tossed in torment, his body coated head to foot with some kind of blue ointment.

"Odd sort," said Beauty when they reached the wharf. "You . . . are confident in his abilities?"

"Oh, he's good, he knows what he's doing," replied Aba. "Little crankier than I remember . . ."

"Well. We are here now. I need some food and a bed. You know a place?"

Aba knew a place. It was a two-story boardinghouse, set back from the oceanfront—which meant it was less noisy than the dock area; more conducive to rest. They couldn't find it at first, but kept asking directions until finally they were steered to a building more or less similar to the one in Aba's childhood memory; and so he was satisfied.

The concierge was a jolly, Oriental, cloven-hoofed woman who seemed immediately smitten with Aba. She winked, and asked if he would like a Human sent to his room to warm his blood. When he declined, she appeared hurt; but quickly regained her spirits, took his coin, pinched him on the bottom, and went to ready their rooms.

"But you *must* be hungry by now," Beauty suggested to the Vampire as they stood in the lobby, waiting.

"A bit," Aba admitted. "But I wouldn't drink anyone in a city like this unless I were starving—they'd almost certainly be poxy or jaundiced."

Beauty nodded at the wisdom of this view, and said no more. The concierge came back presently and showed them to their rooms—small and adjoining, off the main corridor, with mats on the floor. Beside each mat was a candle and a bottle of wine.

"First drink's on the house!" The concierge beamed, pinched Aba again, and left.

They went into Aba's room. The Vampire lay down on his mat and opened the wine. "I wouldn't mind a sip of this to relax me, though—I'm tense as a new clot." He took a swallow and offered the bottle to Beauty.

The Centaur shook his head. "I'm tired enough now to sleep standing up." He opened the connecting door and walked into his own room. "We can check about boats to rent later this afternoon. For now, dream well." He closed the door.

"Go in good blood," Aba called after him. He heard Beauty answer, "Until soon," but was already getting too sleepy to hear more.

It was Beauty who couldn't sleep. He was too exhausted; so he just lay on the floor of his room, staring at the shredded curtain that flapped listlessly in the shallow breath of the window. After an hour, he realized Mistress Sleep was being shy, and he knew from experience that at such times it was wisest not to pursue her.

He rose, slipped his longbow across his back, and opened the connecting door to see if Aba was similarly spurned. The Vampire was sound asleep in the corner, though, so Beauty exited quietly and made for the docks, in search of food.

The waterfront was churning with creatures. The sounds of their clash and intercourse rose and fell, almost musically; and for the first time in his life, Beauty was able to appreciate the love some beasts had for city life.

He strolled leisurely down the main wharf, sampling the smells of the street vendors as he passed each stand: hibachi Lizard bits, skewered and smoking; boiling candied taffies, with fresh fruits to dip in them; roasting litchi nuts, almonds, boro seeds, ksili nuts; plantanos sautéeing in tamari and brown sugar; pickled Dove heads; honey-fried jungle Beetles. Each vendor called out his fare to Beauty, attesting to the unsurpassed flavor of the particular delicacy being sold. The Centaur bought a stickful of Lizard, two plantanos, and a cup of bamboo wine, then sat, greatly contented, on one of the piers, enjoying the tasty meal.

A faint beating of drums caught his ear. He traced it to the middle distance of the cove, where a grand ship could be seen slowly making its way toward the harbor. He asked a passing sailor what it was, and was told it had to be the fabulous Chinese ship *Tai-Phung*, making its annual stop in the port. It generally stayed a week, making repairs, trading slaves, brocades, spices, and the like, then set off again, for points south.

Beauty finished eating and felt much better. A Hermaphrodite approached him, sat down, and made him a proposition that ordinarily would have offended or embarrassed him. Now, though, he merely declined with a hearty laugh, and even felt slightly flattered. The combination of the general vitality of the city, a pleasantly full stomach, and the dry bamboo wine had made him quite optimistic about almost everything. He took a deep breath of sweet sea air, reared up on his hind legs for a long stretch, and set out to walk down the docks once more.

Fifty paces along, he paused to watch a shell game. A Sphinx nimbly moved three walnut half shells back and forth atop a small stand, challenging all comers to discover which one hid the pearl. Beauty watched for ten minutes— of course, he never bet money—and never once guessed right. He laughed, shook his head, and continued meandering.

The sights were endless. A dancer with feathers enticed a crowd of onlookers to delirious cheers, then kissed each and every one who threw money. He watched a round-robin knife fight between an Accident and two Satyrs—whenever one animal was cut, he would sit down and the other would enter the fight. All three were bleeding, laughing, and drinking.

There was a slave auction at one end of the docks. Buyers inspected the merchandise while sellers extolled the virtues of their stock. Beauty didn't stay there long. It occurred to him, sadly, that even when he was full and sleepy, the city was hungry still.

The rhythmic drums on the water had been growing progressively louder, until, suddenly, they stopped. Beauty looked up to see the enormous Chinese ship anchoring in the middle of the harbor. And giant it was. Slowly, he walked back along the docks, to get a closer look.

The *Tai-Phung* was a sailing ship, but the strangest one Beauty had ever seen. For it had seven masts, each a hundred feet tall, spaced along the hundred yards of deck; and chained to each mast were thirteen Vampires, one above the other, many with wings outstretched and manacled to the crosspieces.

Beauty was incredulous. The harbor master had sailed out and was shouting to the Monkey mate that the ship had to anchor farther south in the harbor, because of the reef. The mate, in turn, shouted orders to the Vampires chained to the masts. The Vampires whose wings were free began vigorously flapping; those whose wings were bound out oriented themselves at various angles on command; and slowly the huge vessel sailed to its new mooring.

Some of the Vampires simply hung, unmoving, suspended from chains that strapped their chests and legs to the mast, their heads lolling limply upon their sternums. Two crimson Dragonflies, four feet long, flitted up and back and hovered in front of each of these seemingly unconscious Vampires, offering cups of blood to the silent lips with what appeared to be small Human hands. Some of the Vampires responded, drank the sustenant liquid, roused themselves; others remained motionless.

There was a bustle of activity on the deck. The crew busied themselves running lines all around, opening hatches, securing battlements. Large, opulent Peacocks strode along the bow, curious about the new surroundings. At the tiller stood an eight-armed Shiva; a six-foot-tall Parrot shouted orders from the quarter-deck. Three Elephant-headed men dropped a long, wide float overboard; rope ladders quickly went over the side, and soon dozens of crew—men with antlered Elk heads, Rat heads, or Elephant heads—were off-loading crates onto the floating barge. Monkeys ran up the masts, unchained the Vampires who still weren't moving, and heaved them into the water, chains and all, where they sank without a trace.

For a time, Beauty watched all this with intense fascination. The afternoon was getting on, though, and he had business of his own. He wondered, briefly, at the variety of animal experience, and what it signified; but it was beyond his understanding. So without further delay, he set out to hire a small boat.

There were none for hire. The arrival of the *Tai-Phung* was such an event, it turned out, such a massive appearance of scarce and exotic treasures, that not a single boat-owner was willing to miss the unveiling. Absolutely everyone wanted to be around to buy *something* from the winged sailing vessel. And not only were they unwilling to leave the city to ferry Beauty to his destination, they were unwilling to rent their boats at all, afraid of losing their only means of carrying off whatever strange and wondrous goods they might happen to buy. The Centaur was frustrated at first, then angry, until finally, deciding they would just have to walk to The City With No Name, he fell asleep on the pier, as the great ship from the west sent ripples through the harbor.

He awoke at dusk to a huge commotion. Looking down toward the water he saw a medium-sized skiff just leaving the pier. In it, four of the *Tai-Phung's* Elk-headed sailors pinned down a struggling captive with their hands and antlers. Beauty rubbed his eyes and stared hard at the scene:

the raging prisoner was a Vampire: moreover, it looked like Aba.

Beauty stood up and ran to the end of the pier. "Aba?" he shouted.

The Vampire victim in the skiff twisted and roared: "Beauty!" But to no avail. His captors held him firm.

Beauty scanned the *Tai-Phung*. Other Vampires were already being shackled to the masts—at the empty spaces where, earlier, the dead had been. Those being cuffed into place now screamed and fought and shrieked the supersonic Vampire calls of distress. Useless. Their wings were pulled into taut extension and wired to the crosspieces.

Beauty's mind cleared swiftly, and he looked back to the skiff—too late, for it was rounding the stern of the the ship, going behind it, out of sight.

The Centaur was quietly frantic, with rage and fear. For a few minutes he lost his sense of internal balance entirely, straining to focus on the whole ship at once, uncertain whether to swim out to it, start shooting flaming arrows into its side, or run for help. Then he saw Aba again, and in the space of moment, became calm, his balance restored. He knew what to do.

Planking had been erected beside each mast. Up this latticework the Elk-headed sailors climbed, clutching the weakened Aba, carrying him to the top of the second mast. Evenly, Beauty pulled an arrow out of his quiver; serenely, he strung it on his Dragon-rib bow.

It was a sensationally long shot under any circumstances—over a hundred yards distance from Beauty's position on the ground to the top of the mast. Add to this distance the thickening dark, the ocean wind, the wild movement of the obscured figures. An impossible shot by most accounts. Yet Beauty was a remarkable archer.

He pulled back the tense bowstring, aimed but a moment, let the arrow fly, drew a second arrow, and strung it while the first was still in the air. The first went two feet high and wide, and sailed on free into the night; the second hit one Elken sailor in the armpit; the third hit another in the neck; the fourth clipped Aba's arm, the fifth hit the mast, the sixth hit another sailor in the thigh. The three sailors who had been hit fell a hundred feet to the deck; the fourth jumped into the harbor. Aba was left standing, shaken but whole, on the top plank beside the masthead.

There were shouts all around, now; running, clattering, on ship and on shore. Beauty felt himself jumped from behind, spun around twice, and pulled violently down by many hands. He threw someone into the water, but others beat him viciously about the head and flanks, and he felt himself starting to sink.

Suddenly there was a dark swirling whoosh, and Aba was in the fray. He killed two of the attackers rapidly, slashing their necks with his talons. Beauty mortally wounded another, thrusting one of his loose arrows hard through the beast's ear. A Python got in the melee, winding up Aba's left arm, twisting it over, dislocating his shoulder. He groaned in pain. Three more Monkeys ran up, and then a boatload of Elk-men piled on. Soon Beauty and Aba slid into unconsciousness, to the myriad blows of fist and bludgeon.

They awoke with a start on the foredeck of the *Tai-Phung,* doused with cold water. Angry faces surrounded them. Someone kicked Beauty in the stomach, and he threw up.

The eight-armed Shiva spoke: "*Sun you, tao li ch'yeng no loo. Chao rama no ling see.*"

The giant Parrot looked down at the crumpled figures of Beauty and Aba and translated the Shiva's remarks: "She say you very unwise. She say tomorrow at noon she make example of you to rest of city."

"*Oan liao ch'i soong lo,*" the Shiva added.

The parrot threw back his head in delight. "She say you be very sorry then." Whereupon he screeched gaily: "*Rawhk!*"

Fat, foot-long Glowworms squirmed slowly all around the deck, shedding a whitish light. Beauty watched the faces of his captors in the glimmering and thought how like stories of the Underworld it looked.

He was dragged down into the hold with Aba, brutally tied up, and dumped into a small cargo room. They sat back to back in an inch of water. Two of the large sluglike Glowworms writhed together in one corner, a milky excreta oozing from the end of one, clouding the water at that end of the room.

Aba leaned forward and peered through a crack in the wall he faced: in the next room, close to a hundred gaunt, naked Humans crouched, slept, stared, their wrists all cut, bruised, or bleeding: the food supply for the Vampire slaves tied to the masts. Aba hissed. He leaned back, tried to work his bonds free, and gasped in pain: his shoulder was still dislocated.

"Are you badly hurt?" Beauty asked.

Aba closed his eyes and sighed. "They drugged me at the hotel—the concierge, I imagine. The wine."

"And then?"

"And then they were on me when I awoke. And then you saved me, and then I didn't save you." He was trying to close his mind to the pain in his arm.

"There must be a way out of this abominable ship." Beauty squirmed fiercely, but the ropes cut into his wrists and ankles. The Glowworms began giving off an odd odor.

"There must be reason to this," Aba muttered. "If only the reason were clear . . ."

"What is clear is that there is no reason . . ." Beauty shook his head.

"But we can't just give up."

"When there is nothing to do, you must do nothing." Beauty smiled, recalling Jasmine's words. For a moment, he had almost lost his equilibrium again; but now he once more felt cool.

"There is much to do," Aba whispered. He rolled over, in great pain, and kicked a crate to the floor from its perch. It hit with a splash and split open, spilling its contents in the shallow water: more Glowworms, twelve of them, each one to two feet long, all plump and squirmy.

Beauty almost gagged, but Aba started to laugh. He laughed and laughed so hard he almost cried from the pain in his jiggling shoulder, but he kept laughing, until Beauty started laughing, too, and then neither could stop. Finally, wheezing and panting, they petered out. Then Aba began to sing, in a booming bass voice, old Vampire ballads and spirituals.

> Oh, I love thee,
> Bloody Mary,
> Your ruby lips, lass,
> The sweetest sherry;
> Your pulse against my
> Tremblin' lips, dear,
> I take you gently,
> In gentle sips, dear.

and:

> White is the blush of my true love's skin,
> And red the blue vein it beholds,
> But sleep, now, my darlin',
> We'll weep in the mornin',
> For you've gotten so stiff and so cold,
> Oh, you've gotten so stiff and so cold.

He sang this last one over and over, and soon Beauty was joining in, harmonizing, singing slower at the sad parts. There was rustling at the other side of the wall, and Aba could see the Human slaves crowding around the peep-hole, watching them, hearing them sing so movingly.

There was suddenly a loud crash, and parts of the outer wall—the sea-side wall of the little room, which was, in fact, the hull of the ship—caved explosively into the room several times in rapid succession, leaving first a small hole, then a large hole, and finally a splintered, gaping hole in the wall—the bottom edge of which was actually below the water line, so that now a gusher of sea water was roaring in. With unrestrained amazement, Beauty stared through the opening at the small sailboat that bobbed just outside the shattered hull; and standing in it, the grinning figure of D'Ursu Magna, holding the biggest sledge hammer Beauty had ever seen.

D'Ursu jumped into the flooding cargo room, fell in the rising frothing water, then stood and quickly cut Beauty's and Aba's ropes. Jumping out again was harder—against the incoming rush—but somehow all three of them made it. In the opaque darkness, nobody from the ship could see where or who to shoot at, and in any case, they were all more than occupied trying to evacuate that part of the hold, seal off that section, repair the startling breach in the planking. By the time D'Ursu's little craft had sailed thirty yards toward the mouth of the harbor, the *Tai-Phung* was already beginning to list a bit.

By the time the small sailboat had reached the mouth of the harbor, Beauty had put Aba's arm back into its socket. And by the time the little sailboat was out on the open sea, the three comrades had calmed down enough to tell one another their stories.

"This doctor was crazy," grumbled D'Ursu. "So I had to leave. He wouldn't tell me where you'd gone—Humans love secrets, you know—but you left a trail of smells even the stinking city couldn't cover. Then, by evening, of course, absolutely everyone was jabbering about the Centaur and the Vampire who'd been captured by the *Tai-Phung*, so I knew I had to help you out of trouble again."

"But how did you ever get this boat?" Beauty demanded. "I looked for hours—no one was renting."

"Renting?" D'Ursu looked askance. "Another Human invention. I just took the damn boat. That terrible singing told me where to find you—and smashing the bottom of the ship in with that iron hammer was the greatest trick I ever played. And that's my story!" D'Ursu roared, laughing.

The others laughed, too, then tended their wounds in the sea water, in the cool night air, in the laughter of the dancing stars, as the little boat sailed gently south, toward the darkness at the mouth of the Sticks River.

CHAPTER 6

Queen Takes Knight; Knight Mates

JOSHUA tensed as the door to his cell swung open. His neck was black and blue from repeated Vampire bites; his skin had the pallor of blood loss mixed with fear. But no Vampire entered this time, and no Neuroman. This was a Human.

A girl. Naked, frail, her head shaved. A thick black cable plugged into the back of her skull trailed down to the floor and out the door. She held a silver bowl filled with liquid.

Josh tried to stand, but he was shaky from anemia.

"Don't get up," said the girl. "You must be awful weak." Her voice was thin, as if it got little use.

"Yes, I am," he replied. She understood. She was like him. "Who are you?" he asked.

"Oh, I'm just a little bit." She began unbuttoning his shirt.

"A little bit of what?" He was too tired to resist her, whatever it was she wanted, so he just lay back.

"A little bit of the Queen. She's all of me, of course." She pulled off his shirt, untied his pants.

"But there is no queen," he protested weakly. "It's just you pitiful slaves, wired like animals to the Neuromans' computer."

She took off his pants, pushed him flat on the bed. She was stronger than her atrophic arms made her appear. "Well I happen to be in direct communication with the Queen—the Queen in me, anyway—and we laugh at your innocence. Ha, ha, ha."

She took a sponge from her silver bowl and began gently

81

washing him with the clear, perfumed liquid. It was cool and soporific, and Josh relaxed in spite of himself.

"What do you want of me?" he asked.

"To be open, and tranquil, and ready."

The lavage seemed to give him strength, its sweet aroma to arouse him. She brought the engorged sponge to his loins, where her silky fingers stroked tensions out, warmth in.

"Ready for what?" he murmured. It was long since he had been with a woman.

"For your time with the Queen," she whispered. Her own body was responding now, hard and soft and flushed.

"The Queen in you?" he suggested. He was getting light-headed. His hand had fallen into the silver bowl. He raised it, dripping the slippery perfume, and drew his fingers along the line of her breast, weighed its mass in his palm.

She quivered. "No, the Queen without," she sighed, and pulled away.

"Wait," he pleaded, but she withdrew quickly, backed out the door, and was gone.

He stood to catch her, but his knees melted, and he collapsed to the floor. For many minutes, he sat sobbing.

When the door opened again, it was Ugo, the Vampire, who stood there.

"The Queen will see you now," he snarled, picking the young man up and supporting him out the door.

Josh was terrified his blood was to be drained again; but that was not what happened. Instead, he was led by Ugo down half a dozen empty corridors, up two flights of stairs, into a laboratory. Here lights of various wavelengths were shone on him; his body was soaped, steamed, scrubbed, and blown dry; sound-generation devices buffeted him with vibration. This was Final Decontamination.

He suspected the end was near, and in his mind prepared himself for the Dark Journey.

He was pointed down a red-lit hallway; at its end, three doors: LIMBO, NIRVANA, COMMUNION. The titles jerked him out of his half-trance—he had been here before. Five years before. He tried to turn back, but the door behind him was

closed. There was nothing he could do but walk ahead, into
his past.

He crossed the corridor, opened the door labeled COM-
MUNION, and entered. It was as he remembered. Row after
row of Human beings, lying still as Earth, their heads
shaved and trailing black cables that twisted down the
aisles like serpentine thoughts crawling from the brains of
the eternal sleepers.

It tightened the pit of Joshua's stomach. He stepped forward—to free them, as he had done once before—but was
stopped by an electrified wire grid that now separated the
walkway from the room. He hadn't noticed it at first, his
attention was so focused on the bodies; but when he walked
into it, it sparked and jolted him, and he jumped back.

There were four unmarked doors at the end of the hall.
Three were locked; one was ajar. He pushed it open and
entered the next room.

The space was large, dark, muffled. Drawers and
shelves lined the nearest wall. In the corner by the door
was the large cylindrical trash receptacle that Josh knew
formed a continuous vertical shaft to the underground tunnels, conduits of the underground river. In the far corner,
Joshua's eye was immediately drawn to a dim light, and
beneath it what seemed to be a large chair; and in the
chair, a figure.

Josh walked toward the light.

As he approached, he saw the chair was in fact a
throne—oversized, of marble and teak, inset with jewels,
veined with gold, littered with cushions—and the figure that
reclined there, a woman.

When he was twenty feet away, she spoke, and he
stopped. "Welcome, Joshua, Human and Scribe."

She was beautiful, he could see—at least, what he could
see was beautiful. She sprawled in the throne, half-covered
in the sheerest silk veil, her pale body limp with suggestion.
Yet from the ceiling above, several feet out from the wall,
hung a brocade curtain. It stopped six feet from the floor,
but since it came down in front of the throne, it acted as an
opaque screen to the Queen's face, obscuring both her head

and the entire back wall. In the dimly lit room, Josh had the unsettling impression he was being addressed by a headless ghost.

He took two more steps toward the dais on which the throne sat; then halted again in the recoil of his crosscurrent emotions. Her sultry posture aroused all his bottled sexuality, so recently uncorked by the girl-Human's visit to his cell. The fact that her face was hidden from view by the brocade curtain was both seductive and disturbing. The situation was dreadful; he was weak from loss of blood, his mind dulled from loss of Human contact, his senses disoriented by the loss of time. He reeled a little.

The Queen spoke again, through the thick curtain. "I am Queen of The City With No Name." Her voice was deep and layered and almost sounded like many voices in unison.

"There is no queen," Josh insisted. "Gabriel told me it was all computers, it's—"

"Gabriel lied to protect me. There is a Queen, and I am she, as you can see, as you can see. But let us not quibble, let us go then, you and I, for I have sought you these five years and more."

"You've sought me? Why? What do you mean?" This somehow scared Josh more than anything else that had happened—hearing from this mysterious woman that she had been looking for him for five years.

"I will tell you, since you ask, and since you are mine now, for me, for me, and may not flee, as you can see." She laughed then, a raspy laugh, a whispering of laughter, the sere laughter of dead leaves. "These ANGELs, these Neuroman Genetic Engineers, engineered me. That is the story of my species, of which I am the only member. A memberless member. Dismembered before my time; time remembered. Or is it re-membered? Misremembered? I misremember. I, Miss Remember—soon to be Miss Remember. Yet a member is but a part, and I am many parts, and today we have naming of parts, the parting such sweet sorrow. But I digress. Is it perfume from a dress that makes me so digress?"

Surely she was mad. Josh had never heard such rambling, spoken with such meaning. "I don't . . ." he began.

She stopped him. "You needn't apologize. My story is not always easy to follow, for I am the Kingdom and the Power and the glorious euphorious victorious storious. So they engineered me, these Genetic Engineers, engineered this unique creature you see before you, or almost see, as you can see, to have unique cerebral powers, to rule, to fool, to implement their goals, to realize their dreams. Yet they control me. For they engineered me such that I am dependent on a single, synthetic nutritional source which they alone can make and dole to me. Goal, dole, control. Sole. Soul. Souls.

"Many souls. I have become many souls. He and she and me and we, as you can see, as you can see. Our mind is great, we shall not want, the Word is One. I learned, you see, to join my substantial brain, substantia nigra, locus ceruleus, bluer than blueleus, to other, lesser brains. So less is more. We kissed, these other brains and I, these less substantial ether others, touched our dura maters, pia maters, grayer matters, fused with wires, used a fuse or two to fuse, confuse, refuse, defuse, infuse, suffuse. As you can see."

She rested a moment here. Again, the hoarse laugh.

A certain rhythm to her speech was beginning to hold Joshua's attention, even though he understood barely half of what she said. Her cadence held him still, though, and pulled him along.

"I know things now," she began again. "Things I cannot explain, to your shrunken brain, shrunken brain. I am not the addition of all the minds with which I am in communion: I am their multiplication, I am the sum of their powers to the power of their sum. I—can see!

"Yet still these feeble ANGELs hold the reins, for they control my food. Angels of Mercilessness, I must do as they bid. But soft! What light through yonder circuit breaks! For lo! one day, and I discovered, while scanning some adrenergic connections in the area between my red nucleus and median longitudinal fasciculus, I discovered a recessive trait which the engineers had inadvently engineered. An electromagnetic trait, to be sure, which they couldn't have been expected to expect, let alone to defuse. A trait, a magnificent trait, don't you see, which can never never never be fully expressed in me. Traits which are recessive can hardly be expressive when others more repressive dominate.

"For this trait I am hemizygous: alas the gentle gene is masked by her coarser brother, indomitable sibling calling all the tunes, dancing the electron dance . . . this gentle gene in the ion mask asleep in her neuronal dungeon. But if . . . but if . . . but if she should wake, what trumpets would sound! If she were joined by her true and proper twin, homozygous then, this panting pair, these lurid ladies, mirror sisters of the chromosome, well, then, oh, then what gyral matters would obtain, would obtain, in my brain, swelling brain! No, but wait, stay with me, listen, I'll explain to you the pain and the pain and the pain . . ."

She stopped, panting, sweating, her chest heaving deeply; and though her face remained hidden, Josh could see a languid stream of clear saliva curl hotly down her neck, until it slowed and feathered between her breasts. After a moment of stillness, she continued speaking.

"The pain. The pain of this single isolated recessive gene of mine is the pain of seeing but being unable to touch, of knowing but being unable to act. Because, Joshua, this pretty gene codes for a small, dense section of my brain, a gem of latticed neurons that kens the universe, that understands it All. And had this gene its identical mate, the twain would code for such a brain that would not merely comprehend but would *command*—would *be* the universe. Yes! The beast with the piece of pontine matter coded for by two of my one gene would know the heart of time and beat as one with it.

"But how to find this other gene, another creature with the chemistry of my soul? I couldn't tell the ANGELs of my self-discovery—Angels of death, they wish me no greater power than that which I have, the power to see, and to tell. As you can see, as you can see. But see, this jewel of special nerves in special relays sparking their synaptic humors to connect with other special nerves in special ways—these patterns are a brief electric symphony, reflected by a certain type of brain wave, of a certain frequency and amplitude and shape and timbre, which waves are dulcet sometimes, sometimes crashing, ever-steady rhythmic waves of variable intensity, ever generated by the auld electron dance of that peculiar chip of brain encoded by my special gene. The nature of the *gene* was neither here nor there to me: it was the *brain* I craved—the just-so configuration of neurons, which happened to make a just-so brain wave, gentle wave, crystal wave. This wave I worshiped. I analyzed this wave, computerized it, isolated, synthesized. And when I knew its nuances precisely, I put its purest form down on magnetic tape, and transmitted it from megawatt transmitting towers, throughout the land. And you responded, Human flea, as you can see, as you can see."

This last remark was obviously directed specifically at Josh. He replied, "What do you mean? How did I respond?"

"Something there is, in your brain, that resonated to the frequencies I transmitted. You had your 'spells,' and you came, my errant knight."

"My spells!"

"Quite right. When an epileptic with a certain cerebral focus of activity is exposed to lights which flash at the frequency of his firing nerves, this cerebral focus resonates with the lights, begins its rhythmic firing, generates the automaticity of pulsing discharges that is a seizure. So! A boat passes through a rippling pond, its waves swell, impose themselves upon the surface, obliterate the ripples, then recede and fade and let the million random ripples that are the pond's waking and sleeping thoughts return. Such was the magnitude of my electromagnetically transmitted waves: they washed away the wind ripples and fish currents of your placid brain, gave you spells and trances and convulsions, and drew you, finally, to the source, as you can see, as you can see."

Josh was dumbfounded. Here, then, was the real cause of his spells. This mad Queen, sending signals his mind responded to. Because of a wave she worshiped? It was beyond all reason. He couldn't sense its implications. She seemed lucid at times, incoherent at times, yet somehow he knew she was leading somewhere. If he could only find her thread.

The Queen went on. "So you came, you came, are yet to come. Others came, with minor spells, their waves were close, but none just like yours: only yours were mine. But still, what means this pulling wave, this tidal force? No less than this: The rolling waves, the medullary waves your wee brain generates share unity with those I send, and hence, and hence! that piece of brain of yours, that cubic-centimeter section is identical to its counterpart in me, and thus it likewise must be coded for by the identical gene! It must! My sister gene, long lost twins, your pauper to my prince, the regent's maskèd Doppelgänger unmasked. It's you! You are my sun gene, my only sun gene, you make me happy when matters gray have fallen black enough that not-to-bè is less a question than an answer. But now you are here! You are here!"

She was sweating again, and laughing that troubling laughter of the edge. "I've studied your waves carefully since you've been here, Joshua—integrated potentials, wave slopes and peaks, feedback loops, cycles per second—and yes, there is no doubt, our waves are one, we are of a kind, we are of a mind, there is a crucial cube at the stem of your thinker identical to one at mine. We must, perforce, share that shred of DNA responsible. There, by the by, the similarity ends; but oh, the correspondence!"

"But . . . so what?" Josh wanted to know. For all of that, he felt no particular kinship to this madwoman—only ambiguous fear, sexual tension, and claustrophobia. His eyes darted left and right, seeking a door.

"So what," she echoed. "So this. Any child of our union will have a one-in-four chance of being homozygous for that gene—of having this recessive trait fully expressed. Think of it, dream on it, by the second fertilization the chances will swell, the chance of swelling my belly, producing a child with this transcendental trait, this golden power, this—"

"What do you mean, producing a child," Josh gasped. "What are you talking about?"

Her body shifted slightly in the throne. "Come, make love to me."

He felt a simultaneous thrill and physical horror at the thought of touching that body. "No," he choked out, backing away.

"You cannot resist," she whispered in a lower voice. "My pheromones are potent, I blossom at will. And well we know that your more primal wave forms are synchronous with mine. As you can see, I send them now, I send my waves, my smells, my heat, my ch'i, I send my love, as you can see."

Her legs fell apart as she slipped down slightly, the weight of her buttocks pressing flat on the edge of the seat. The downward movement brought her mouth and nose into view below the level of the curtain. The mouth was soft, full, open, moist; the nose, royal.

Josh took a step forward, his palms sweating. He had never seen such a beautiful form—waiting, wanting him. The air smelled perfumed; the floor felt cool beneath his bare feet. He wasn't used to feeling so heady, though, and it confused him, frightened him, tightened his stomach like wet twine. He walked closer.

Her lips smiled. She rubbed her hands along her flanks, smoothing the perspiration into an even gloss. His lust was becoming overpowering, yet still, below the surface was a sick loathing—of the situation, of the compulsion. Briefly, his ambivalence held him back; then quickly, he approached.

When he was three feet from the dais, the angle of his vision allowed him to see up under the curtain, to just above her eyes. Stark, round eyes, purple, violent, seductive, destructive. Compelling. Transfixing. She licked her lips, held out her hands. He stepped up to the throne. He wanted to lie beside her, he wanted to run, he wanted to freeze the searing moment and never draw breath again.

She pulled him to her, drooling heavily. The touch of her flesh burned. Molten ecstasy. He closed his eyes against the fire. He pressed his palms against her swollen breasts, pushing sounds from deep within her throat. She gripped his hips, drew him fast between her legs, pulled him in, deeper in. His body swam in rhythms, he opened his eyes. Her head—

He saw the top of her head for the first time. There was no skull, only puffy gray brain emerging from the topless cranium, ballooning out the head from a point just above the eyebrows. And huge. Maybe ten times the size of a normal brain, maybe more—it was hard to tell. Hard to tell because of all the cables inserted deep and shallow into the substance of the brain, thick black wires streaming out in all directions, coiling to the floor like a hundred sleeping serpents, writhing along the floor behind the throne until they came together again and exited in a bundle through a port in the wall.

For an eternal moment, Joshua felt frozen to stone.

Then everything came alive again, the horror, the horribleness, the flesh, and the heat. She laughed a rasping moan as he exploded inside her, over and over, spasms of release.

When it was done she pushed him to the ground. He lay there, unmoving. It had been like no other experience for Joshua. Intense, surreal, transcending, abhorrent. And now he wanted to be alone for a thousand years.

This was hell, surely. How often would she force him to do this? Surely, he couldn't again. He had never wanted to die, and he didn't now, really. He only wanted never to do this thing again, and there seemed to be only one way to achieve that.

Quickly, before she could arouse herself to act, he stood up, staggered twenty steps to one of the waste disposal chutes, opened the lid, and threw himself in.

It was deadfall thirty feet before he hit the electrified grid. The shock knocked him unconscious as he crashed through, and set him spinning so he careened from wall to wall of the rough shaft, breaking his fall enough so he broke only his legs when he hit bottom.

Bottom was a tunnel a foot deep with rushing water that carried his unconscious body through dozens of branching turns until it finally dumped him out its mouth, over a tumbling falls, and into the ocean.

He was jolted half-conscious by the cold-water plunge

but hadn't nearly the wherewithal to fight the riptide, which dragged him miles out. By this time he had inhaled enough water that he started going down. He woke briefly, sensing he was drowning. As he was. He sank completely underwater, though, too weak to struggle, too disoriented to know which way was up. He stopped trying to resist.

He thought calmly of his friends, how he loved them. Beauty, Jasmine, Rose. His brother, Ollie; his dead bride, Dicey; his dead friend, Lon, patient and wise. Life had been good, death would not be bad. He faced it with a sense of profound peace, faintly curious. We are words in the wind, he thought. The Word is One.

He saw before him a beautiful Mermaid, floating calmly, holding out her hands to him. She looked like Dicey; Dicey, waiting for him on the other side of death, waiting to guide him. He smiled. She understood death was no fearful thing, she was to help him, to lead him through its dark gates into the dark land. His eyes were closed, but open. He held out his hands to her, and died.

CHAPTER 7

In Which Joshua Plumbs the Depths

THE next consciousness Joshua had was of a gentle breeze, a vague suffusion of light, a pleasant, weightless warmth. This was the journey, then: good. It was good.

He opened his eyes. A dazzling blue panorama surrounded him; he rocked calmly within it. Was this the inside of the Great Word? Had he become part of its light? He breathed in deeply. The smell was sweet.

A face appeared before him. His Lady of Death, the Mermaid, the one with Dicey's eyes. Where had he seen her before? She looked so kind and concerned. Nurturing, yet vulnerable. He smiled at her.

"Is this death, then?" he whispered. He expected it was necessary to whisper in the Dark Land; there were no loud noises. But this place wasn't dark at all. It was endlessly bright.

"Thou wert dead, but not now," said the Mermaid. "My people have much knowledge of pulling life from the sea."

Josh felt a little disappointed that this wasn't the Other Side—but this emotion was quickly replaced with curiosity. "Where am I, then? And who are you?"

"I am Kshro," laughed the water creature. "Thou art in the sea of my people, the Selkies. Thou hast rescued me when I was caught in the net in Ma'gas'; and when thou wert netted, I followed thy boat. I waited in the bay for thee, outside the great castle on the cliff—and finally, thou camest. Only, thou wert broken, and breathing water. So I brought thee here, to my sea, and my people blew the water from thy lungs, and revived thy spirit, and began the mending of thy legs. And now thou art with me."

She laughed again, joyously, her laughter like a summer

93

fountain. Slowly, Josh looked up and down, to try to take in his surroundings, focusing through this new perspective.

He was floating in the ocean, he now saw, on a huge bed of kelp. The day was cloudlessly, blindingly azure. Beside him floated this Mermaid, this Selkie. She was beautiful.

He remembered her now, the creature he had freed from the fishnet in Ma'gas' during one of his post-ictal half trances. She had been suffering abuse by Vampires, and she had reminded him, somehow, of his dead wife, and he had cut her loose. And the next thing he knew, he was in the castle.

He viewed her closely, now, delicately. She looked to be about nineteen. Her hair fell in dark-gold waves around her wide, strong shoulders. Her skin was the color of creamy coffee, her eyes green. The line of her nose was straight and long, her cheekbones high. Her clavicles gracefully curved out of the line of the long, thin neck, and mimicked the curve of the supple breasts on the well-muscled rib cage. Her belly was covered with fine, downy hair that glistened in the sun and grew thick over her sleek hips until it was a full coat of soft tan fur over her entire lower extremity—a trim, muscular, dolphinlike fishtail.

She lay beside him, smiling angelically, supporting his head above the pontoon of floating kelp on which they rested so he could peruse his domain. About a hundred yards distant he saw an island that ran a mile across and half as deep. The shoreline was sandy beach at one end, becoming rocky at the other, pocked with grottos and blowholes. The meager interior of the island was thick with palm trees, birds-of-paradise, tropical vines, and jacaranda. Gulls circled lazily overhead.

Beyond this island was a second island—foreshortened to Joshua, he couldn't decide exactly how far, but it seemed only another hundred yards or so beyond. That island was smaller, more barren. It was too long a distance for Josh to make out any real detail.

He looked to his sides and, arching, to his rear: nothing but sea, and sky, and sea again. He looked down at his legs —and jumped in dismay: his two legs were now one thick, brownish limb, slightly tapered, and fluted at the end. He

gaped in morbid astonishment at the transformation. "You've turned me into a Merman," he cried, twisting away.

She laughed her bright laugh. "No, no—would that it were so. We've only wrapped thy legs together in a binding weed that grows in the bay—so that thy fractures may heal—and wound into the weed an old Selkie tail to cover thy feet, that thou might get around better in the water— though, truly, thou shouldst not move thy legs to mention, but let the sea support them full, and rock them tenderly, as one does a child. Then as they heal, thou mayest swim; and then in time walk like a man. But for now, be a child."

She smiled, bent over, and kissed him on the mouth. He was too surprised either to respond or to pull away; but she ended it herself in a moment and, beaming, rolled over twice in the water. She came up under him—behind him— put her arm around his chest, and began smoothly pulling him backward through the water. When they were out of the kelp bed and in open water, she came around 180 degrees, so that now they were heading for the island.

"Anyway," she spoke again, her head behind his, her mouth near his ear, "thou wouldst not be a Merman; thou wouldst be a Selkie, which is what we are. But thou are not. Thou art Human."

He thought he detected a note of sadness in her voice, but was far too preoccupied with other questions to ask her about it at the moment.

As they rounded the point of landfall, Josh could see it was not simply elliptical; the end turned up, forming a deep natural bay on the side that faced the second island. They drew even with this bay area that separated the two land masses. Josh saw it was close to three hundred yards across and appeared to be calm as a small lake. Kshro turned again, pulling him directly between the two islands.

The small one was, in fact, nothing but a profusion of rocks on rocks, beside rocks, between rocks; piled high, strung out to form a microarchipelago. And sprawled out, sunning themselves, or playing like seasoned porpoises, were the Selkies. Dozens of them, male and female: pushing each other off rocks, diving deep, then jumping in the spray of a thundering wave; or just sleeping carelessly in the sun's warm caress, the tide's gentle lull. To see them so gave Josh a feeling of exhilaration mixed with longing he had not experienced before.

He turned his head in the opposite direction to view the bay of the larger island, the bay they were now entering. Here he received a still greater surprise. For the entire concavity of land that encompassed the bay—almost a mile from arm to arm—was strewn with ships along its shore. More precisely, shipwrecks. Some looked recent, some looked as if they had rested there since antiquity. Ships of every time and culture: broken-masted clipper ships, Chinese junks with crushed hulls, great flat barges and balsa-log rafts, fragments of schooners, splinters of bowsprits, weather-faded figureheads, cast-iron shells, burned-out spines of hulking warships, up-ended steamship wheels, half-submerged cargo ships, the razor keel of an old luxury liner wedged deep in the sand: nuzzling one another, crunched into one another, rising and falling in the shallows on the quiet respirations of the tide.

As they drew closer, Josh saw that here, too, the Selkies gamboled—swimming circles around the bobbing debris, hiding in overturned wrecks only to spring out, surprising one another amid billows of splash and laughter. Kshro pulled him effortlessly along this sunken, beached, and reefed flotilla to the other end of the cove, at the west side of the island, where the caves and grottos seemed to bubble out of the sea.

Just as they neared a precarious-looking igneous outcrop that hung like a canopy over the water, Kshro giggled into Joshua's ear, "Before thou meetest Luashra, it would be luck to take a turn around the Wheel."

"Who's Luashra?" Josh coughed. Trying to talk as a wave slapped his face, he had aspirated a little water. "And what's the Wheel?"

Instead of answering, Kshro smiled and swam straight toward the center of the bay, toward a point somewhere between the two islands. Halfway there Josh felt himself first subtly tugged, then quickly dragged by the tail of a whirling subsurface undertow—and flung like a skimming stone into the arms of another whirlpool, which spun him twice around its vortex before spewing him, in Kshro's gentle grip, into the invisible clutches of yet another swirling eddy. They were tumbled all around the bay in this manner until, shooting toward the very center of the cove, Josh shouted, a touch of hysteria in his voice, "Does this merry-go-round ever end?"

Kshro replied softly, "Hold thy tongue, Human—and thy breath."

Josh obeyed none too soon, for they were instantly sucked straight down into the silent green ocean. Kshro held Joshua tightly. He kept his arms around her waist, his head on her breast, and was comforted by her reassuring strength. They continued to plummet together, sunlight diffusing through the cool water, until gradually they slowed, stopped, floated weightlessly, and finally began to drift upward once more. Josh looked up. Kshro was smiling down on him.

They rose faster and faster, breaking the surface at last with a gasp from Josh. He looked around to see they floated right where they had begun, near the canopy of stone at the west end of the island.

Josh looked up. Kshro was smiling down on him.

"A perfect Wheel," Kshro nodded with some solemnity. "Now we can go see Luashra."

She pulled Josh under the overhang and into a large open-ended cavern—filled with sea from both ends, filled with sunlight that poured in through a thousand holes perforating the ceiling. The waves sloshed against the walls of the grotto with a continuous slapping echo, while the gusty breezes blew through the holes in the roof like an orchestra of woodwinds, flooding the cave with the music of time.

Near one wall, on a bed of kelp, floated an old Selkie, flanked by two younger ones. Kshro swam quickly over to them, with Josh in tow. As he approached, Josh saw that a shelf of stone ringed the cavern at water level behind the Selkies; and on this rim of floor sat treasure: casks of jewels, chests full of coin overflowing, golden chalices—all dripping wet, washed with every swell that sloshed over the edge, glistening in the sunshine that sifted through the porous arched ceiling.

The Selkie in the middle was an old man. His nails were long, his fur thin, his chest too full. Seaweed twined his beard. And though he looked tired, yet mischief sparkled still, somewhere behind his cataracts.

Kshro spoke to him. "Grandfather, this is the Human who saved my life from the pirates' net before they had their way with me. I have brought him to thee. Chrodeesh bound his legs, for they were broken—so if it is thy pleasure, he could stay with us until he heals." She bowed her head.

The old Selkie spoke to Josh. His voice rumbled like a subterranean rockslide. "What is thy name, boy?"

Josh pulled himself up in the water as well as he could. "I'm Joshua, Human and Scribe."

"Then welcome," smiled the old Selkie. "I am Luashra, the Old One, and I am dying." When he said this, the other Selkies beat their flukes softly upon the water and lowered their heads. The Old One raised his hand. "Kshro is the last of my line. My children, my other grandchildren—they are all dead. Kidnapped by pirates, plagued by Remora, eaten by Nessies. Our colony grows smaller year by year. We are a fading jewel. But now thou hast returned to us one of our prized gems; and see, her luster shines in thy presence."

"Grandfather!" Kshro scolded, but Luashra only smiled.

"Tact is a disease of the middle years," he said to no one in particular. "It fortunately does not afflict the elderly—as everything else seems to—"

"Now thou art being melodramatic," she scolded again.

"Nor does it greatly burden the young, who know nothing of mortality, and so to whom all drama appears as melodrama." His aides, who supported him in the kelp, laughed silently. Kshro shook her head with great patience. Finally the Old One looked at Joshua again. "Yes, it is my pleasure that thou stayest with us until thy body mends. I will appoint—let me think, whom shall I appoint—ah, yes, I will assign Kshro, she of tender years, to be thy tutor in matters Selkish. Now, away, please. I am tired."

He closed his eyes, lowered his head. Kshro swam Josh out of the grotto and back along the necklace of shattered vessels. She moved like a sea snake, slithering over rotting timber and through dangling portholes, trailing Josh along like a favorite rag doll. Halfway up the coast she pulled him into the once plush, algae-soggy captain's cabin of a diplomatic frigate capsized before the Race War. Its deck sloped out of the water at a thirty-degree angle; its brass fittings were tarnished and green. Kshro and Joshua pulled themselves half up onto the crumbled planks, letting their fins trail into the water.

"Well," said Josh, having begun to assimilate his situation somewhat. "Thank you. For saving my life, and letting me stay until I'm better. It's very kind of you, and I won't—"

She put her fingers to his lips. " 'Tis thee I thank. A Human was ne'er so kind to a poor Selkie maiden."

"There are good Humans and bad ones—like everything else," he averred, deflecting the compliment.

"See, there," she pointed through a jagged rent in the hull of the section on which they rested. He followed her gaze to the sandy shore, on which were scattered the bleached and broken bones of a thousand sailors. "Human, most of them," Kshro went on. "They sailed near here and saw us playing, and thought to capture us, to make us their slaves. Every one had this in his mind. And every ship that tried was caught in the Wheel and pulled down to bed and thrown aground here in Mother's Arms. And all who lived we killed, for what they had tried, and wished. But thou . . ." she whispered, as if unable to understand. "But thou."

So he stayed, and began to learn their ways. He made friends quickly; they were the friendliest of peoples. He met Kourr and Kshro's best friend, Yhrsh, who was expecting a child in a few weeks. The pregnancy raised an issue in Joshua's mind.

"Why haven't I seen any babies?" he asked them, sunning on a rock one day.

"It is our nature that the colony shares but one birth each season," explained Yhrsh. She was older than Kshro, and darker, with black hair that was longer than her body. Everything about her seemed deep—her intellect, her compassion, her intuition. She let Josh put his hand on her belly, big with child. "This is my time," she went on. "With only one infant in the group, there is no competition, no vying for attention. The child receives the affection of the entire community—from birth, it knows only love, the giving and the receiving. In this way, we engender a nurturing society."

"And a narcissistic one," laughed Kourr, pulling the looking-glass from Kshro's hand, to straighten his own blond curls in its reflection.

"But that still doesn't explain why there aren't any babies around now," Josh insisted.

"No; we've just had bad seasons, thou," answered Kshro. "Last year Oshar died in childbirth, and her pup, too. The year before that pirates kidnapped several young ones; and before that it was Nessie got past the coral reef."

"But shouldn't you make more babies for the next few years? If more die than are born, your whole colony will sink of old age."

"Perhaps," Yhrsh said, nodding, "but more than one child at a time would foster competition. It would be better for our race to die than to embrace that demon."

"But you wouldn't have to—"

"That is our way, Josh." Kshro smiled. "I see it is not thine."

But he did begin to make their ways his. With the soft seaweed cast wrapping his legs, he not only looked like a Selkie, he began to feel like one. He swam more and more every day—mostly in the shallows surrounding the shipwrecks, but sometimes in the deep water at the island's backside. Once or twice he even rode the Wheel alone.

They were a tremendously playful culture, and Josh hadn't played in a long time. He was ripe to join them. Most of their days were spent lazing on the rocks of the smaller island, warmed by the sun and cooled by the sea spray. The only interruptions to this blissful inactivity were the games: deep-diving games and jumping-through-crashing-waves games; tag games around the island and mid-air acrobatics, underwater ballet, shipwreck obstacle-course events, and scavenger hunts; group singalongs, sponge-throwing, stone-skipping, octopus wrestling, spinning the Wheel, floating, racing, leaping, and laughing. And whenever he could, Josh joined in. It was a balm for him, too, such playfulness—not only was his spirit salved, even the pains in his broken legs seemed to disappear. The energy of this place healed much in him that had been torn.

He was accepted and encouraged wherever he went, for the Selkies were also a loving people. And he felt this sentiment no more strongly than when he was with Kshro. Kshro, for her part, grew daily more in love with the kind, odd Human, so unlike the others of his species. He was eager to learn, easy to laugh; proud, yet unassuming. Happy to take on the role of Selkie, still he never forgot who he was: a Human, and Scribe.

In fact, after a number of days, he discovered a shelf of books and some corroding writing utensils in one of the old wrecks. He cleaned them, dried them, made ink from what he found in a dead Squid bladder, sun-baked a roll of paper he scavenged from a crumbling sea chest—and set down the record. The Selkies were fascinated. In short order, he was teaching them to read, and write, draw, and doodle. They were delighted with the strange activity; it was a new game.

Josh and Kshro became each other's best pupils. She taught him the importance of play and intuition, the beauty of the sea, the peace of living without a goal. He taught her how to be transported to any world by reading of it; how to make whatever she loved live forever by writing of it; how to share each other's old, sleeping thoughts by reading each other's old, forgotten writings.

It made Josh a little homesick, to speak of Scribery again. But the Selkies were so kind and warm, and they lent such a new, wondrous perspective to the art of scripture, that he was, overall, well content. His legs seemed to be healing; if slowly, yet surely. He was gaining valuable insights not only into this tender society but into his own. He was, inevitably, falling in love.

One evening, they lay side by side in a whispering grotto, as the setting sun turned the water to wine.

"After thy legs heal, wilt thou stay with us?" asked Kshro.

"I . . . don't know," he answered. Truly, he didn't. There was so much he had to do at home—his friends, his obligations. Yet, here . . .

"I love thee," she vowed. She pulled him closer, her hand on his breast.

"I haven't known love for a long time," he said. Was this love? Surely he was content, even greatly at peace. And this Selkie who had saved his life—she was beautiful, her people were beautiful. This was life as life should be. He stroked the soft fur of her hip, then the exquisitely soft fur of her thighs.

She leaned over, brought her mouth down on his, her breast pressing his breast, the swell of her hips pinning his bound legs to the smooth sea-washed stone. He caressed her cheek; their kiss became passionate. She reached down, below his waist, and gently spread the thick strands of seaweed that encircled his hips, releasing him; they slid into the water. She rolled onto her back and pulled him atop her slippery body, opening herself to receive him. He kissed her as if he had become a creature of the sea, she, his beast of wild dreams. Rolling there, in the cobalt water, they made love.

The wedding ceremony was traditional Selkie. As the first bands of dawn light crossed the channel between the islands, two rows of Selkies formed at the west end of the island, near Luashra's grotto. These were the Witnesses. Kshro and Josh swam in stately fashion between them, as they lightly splashed water at the passing couple. Everyone was decorated in water flowers, braised kelp shawls, and jewelry taken from the ruined ships. At the end of the line, Luashra was to meet them and say a few words. They never made it that far, though. Midway down the column of Witnesses, Joshua had a seizure.

It didn't last long. Everyone crowded around to keep his head above water; when it was over, they rushed him to the grotto of Whsh, who had certain medical abilities. But Whsh was baffled.

Josh lay on the watery stone for an hour, trying to collect his senses, as Kshro sat beside him, holding his hand, never looking away from his face. The others huddled in dismay at the mouth of the cave.

Finally, though he was still somewhat post-ictal, he hadn't yet become totally disoriented by the hammer of repeated convulsions—so he knew, shaky as he was, what had happened and why.

"The Queen," he whispered to Kshro. "The spells . . . my helmet . . ." He couldn't say what he wanted to say. He stared intently at Kshro, to make her understand. But she only mopped his brow, as a tear inched down her cheek.

"How can I help thee?" she implored, bringing her face close to his.

"My head . . . inside helmet. Need steel helmet. Inside steel helmet. Put me inside. Inside steel." But the effort was too much for him; he lay back panting, and rambling under his breath.

She didn't know what he was talking about, but she thought he had said something about putting him inside something steel. So she picked him up and carried him through the water to a smallish, ancient warship, listing and aground, whose hull was rusting through. She thought steel didn't rust, but someone had once told her that this boat was of a metal *like* steel, so she swam inside the open hold with Josh and propped him up on a detached, floating stairway.

He quickly recovered. And as long as he remained within the confines of the iron hull, he stayed well. If ever he ventured out, though, he immediately got the heady feeling that forewarned of a spell—so he quickly had himself taken back inside.

It was a great shock. He had managed largely to forget all that had come before—this was a different life, he had told himself. Now suddenly reality had boxed him in once more.

He told Kshro more about his past—about Beauty, Dicey, Rose, Ollie; about the Queen, and her transmissions that gave him spells in order to draw him back to her. The vile Queen.

"But that was another time, thou," she told him. "Thou art here, now, and safe with me. We are thy people now."

"Am I to live in this ship forever?"

"We will fashion a small cap, as thou hast described to me—fashion it of things from this ship, that it will protect thee from this Queen's devices."

He shook his head in great sadness. "I must leave, Kshro. This Queen must be destroyed—she cannot be suffered life. I've got to return home—to my friends who are dear to me—they're probably looking all over for me. I've got to go help them."

Kshro looked near tears, but loved him too much to intrude on his wishes. At that moment, though, old Luashra entered, buoyed up by his two steady companions.

"I beg thy pardon for overhearing, Joshua. It was not my intention to eavesdrop. And I will beg thy pardon again before the day sleeps."

"Grandfather, what dost thee—"

"Be silent, thou, and I will be brief. Only this: thou mayst not leave these islands. Thou knowest too much of our where and our ways, now, to be free to wander among pirates and worse."

Josh looked hurt and offended. "I'd *never* tell anyone about—"

"Torture is not unknown to the greedy of the Earth. Nor canst thou be responsible for thy mutterings during thy spells—thou hast said so thyself."

Josh looked from face to face, aghast and confused. Kshro had feelings so mixed that she could look at no one. She didn't know whether to laugh or cry.

Luashra continued. "I sleep with great sorrow for telling this to thee, but there is no other way. Know that we love thee as our own. Know that thy life here will be full with happiness. But know that thou mayst never leave the sea."

With that, Luashra left.

Never leave the sea! The very thought put Josh into a state of acute despair. Never to run across meadows, or see the ragged teeth of the Saddleback Mountains rise out of the distance as he approached. Never to walk side by side with another Human being. No! But what could he do? Tears came to his eyes, and he looked helplessly at Kshro.

She began to cry in sympathy, and held him to her—though, in fact, at least a few of her tears were joyous.

"Do not think of it, thou, not yet," she whispered, trying to soothe him. "Thou canst do nothing until thy legs heal anyway—by then thou mayst have found great peace with us. With me. By then, anything could happen."

Many things did happen.

The next day Josh was awakened by a cooing, wailing sound. He looked out of his iron cage to see all the Selkies of the colony clustered around something fifty yards away. Soon Kshro came racing back to him and embraced him powerfully, too upset to talk.

"What is it, Kshro? What's happening?"

"Kourr has fallen prey to a Remora," she wept. "Now he must go."

"A Remora? What's that?" He had never seen Kshro so upset, and it jarred him. He held her at arm's length.

"A foul fish," the breath whistled through her teeth. "It hath a sucking thing for a mouth that attaches itself to our skin and cannot be pulled off. It saps our strength, and we die two years later—die in shame, for it makes us ugly, and alone."

"Can't you kill it?"

"When it is killed it immediately releases its eggs into the water. Ten million of them, we could never kill them all."

"But why does Kourr have to go now? He has to be cared for—I know some remedies . . ."

"No, no," she cried, "the Remora hath put its eggs into his blood now. He must swim as far from us as he can—before a week's time, when the larvae will spew from his mouth and infest whoever is near. From this hour on, Kourr must shun all creatures." She shuddered, and hugged Joshua closely.

He held her for a while, stroking her quiet, thinking to himself. Finally he said, "Ask Kourr to come to me."

She looked at him without comprehension, then swam off. In a minute, Kourr had returned in her place. Stuck directly to the center of his back by a slimy suction-cup mouth was the Remora. It was plump, eelish, sticky, and gray. Kourr looked distraught.

"Does it hurt?" asked Josh.

Kourr wouldn't look directly at Josh, but only shook his head. It was a great shame.

"Take me with you," Josh said.

For a moment, Kourr's eyes flashed at the Human, thinking he was being goaded. Then he saw Josh was serious, and his simple anguish returned. "I cannot," he choked.

"I'm needed by my own people," Josh went on. "You're being turned out by yours. Some of my friends know strong magic. Take me back to them, and perhaps they can find a cure for this . . . this—"

"Thou wouldst leave Kshro—?" Kourr questioned.

"I would come back to her—but for now, if I can, I must go."

"No, I cannot—the thing would infect thee. And besides, Luashra said thou mayst never leave the sea."

"Luashra is old."

"We are his thoughts; he is our voice. But no more of

this. Fare well, Human brother. I thank thee for the game of writing. Fare well, for we shall ne'er meet again."

So saying, he swam out past the coral reef and north toward the black waters of the Ice. Josh bared his neck to the vanishing Selkie.

Later that week, Luashra died. The colony was unprepared for a second great sadness so soon, but there was nothing to be done.

That night they held the ceremony under the white light of a half-moon. All the Selkies formed a circle, its diameter extending from island to island. For an hour they whimpered and slapped the calm water softly with the flat of their flukes. When the keening stopped, Luashra's body was floated out into the bay, where it was picked up by the tail of the Wheel and spun quickly around several circuits, until at last it was pulled under by the maelstrom, not to be seen again.

Kshro found an old greenish metal spiked helmet in one of the sunken galleons near the east Arm. Josh tried it on out in the open, and it seemed to block transmissions, though it was rather bulky and kept slipping.

He began to swim again, exercising his legs as much as he dared without disturbing the setting. Kshro doted on him. He was overpowered alternately by affection for her and longing to return home. All about them, life went on.

The next week, Yhrsh had her baby. Josh watched it squirt out into the warm water of the tide pool and immediately wriggle its way to its mother's breast. Only twelve inches long. It was a baby boy.

All the others crowded around, and soon more attention was being lavished on the infant than it knew what to do with. Josh smiled at the scene, glad for the appearance of new life; then swam off by himself, suddenly depressed.

For this was Joshua's last straw—it made him acutely homesick; he was desperate to return to his own Human kind. All the births, the losses, the joy, the pain, of his own—it was all going on without him, back on land, back home.

"Thou art empty, thou," said Kshro. She had swum up behind him.

"I love thee, Kshro," he answered. "But never to run again, and never to see a child of mine born to run with me . . . they are hard thoughts to hold."

She looked down. "Perhaps there *is* a way . . . only, I said nothing before, that I hoped thou wouldst want to stay."

Hope brought his heart to the edge. "What? What are you saying?"

"I could never keep thee prisoner for long—I love thee too well. Still, Luashra said we must keep thee in the sea—"

"Kshro, tell me!" he begged.

" 'Tis a ship, a special ship. Come, I will show thee."

They swam among shadowy plants and broken shapes that had once been ships, coming eventually to a small grotto. Floating there was a bubble of glass.

An oblong bubble, actually; twelve feet long and eight feet high. Inside were two chairs and numerous strange implements of impossible description.

"A ship," Kshro said in answer to Joshua's thought. "It arrived, with its two-man crew, over ninety years ago—when I was just a child."

Josh stared at her. Could it be she was a hundred years old? He said nothing.

She continued. "They stayed here with us for a time, before they died. They had been lost, and then they got sick. They were Humans, but they lived not on the land. They lived in the sea. Beneath the sea."

"Beneath the sea?" Josh couldn't make out her meaning.

"Yes, thou. In bubbles like this, only giant. I know where—they told my mother, and she told me. I could take thee there. It would not be against Luashra, for thou wouldst still be in the sea. Also, they possess medicines and great magic for healing thy legs—and truly, thy swimming has improved, but I fear thou will never fully mend with us, nor ever be able to walk on land again. Down there, in this land below us—'tis true that thou wouldst not see thy old friends; but at least thou couldst run with other Humans, and so be happy."

He just stared at her. He didn't know what to say, or think, or do. She saw this, and helped him.

"Get thee in," she whispered, opening the airtight hatch at the side of the clear, glassy vessel.

In a daze, he obeyed; he felt hypnotized by the force of her will, the power in her eyes, the touch of her hand. With muscular arms, she helped him over the edge, into the craft, then snapped the door shut. She pulled the little ship out of the grotto, along the shore. She dislodged two anchors she found there and tied them both to the propeller of the glass boat. When the boat began to sink, she guided it out into the bay and held on tightly as it was sucked down the center of the Wheel.

Josh wasn't at all certain he was doing the proper thing. He was leaving the island, but abandoning his dear Kshro. And going to what? A place of rumors beneath the sea? To a land he didn't know, populated by hostile creatures? No creatures at all? But Kshro wouldn't leave him there, then.

He looked for her, but couldn't see her: they were too deep, now, the ocean was too black. Slowly, the little boat continued sinking, tilted somewhat astern due to the added weight of the anchors. Josh was becoming frightened.

He felt his momentum shift several times as Kshro pushed the bubble forward or laterally. Once, he fell, and had to grab onto one of the fixed chairs to avoid tumbling wildly. He was growing claustrophobic. Eyes wide open, he could see nothing. Moreover, the air was getting thick. He had no idea how long they had been floating, but the increasing stuffiness in the closed space told him suffocation was not impossible. If they had to return to the top, he knew he wouldn't last.

The blackness became denser. Josh felt himself getting dizzy. Would this be his end, then? Why hadn't he stayed with the Selkies? Life would have been simple, free. No, not free. He wanted to see Kshro once more. Bringing his face up to the edge of the glass, he stared out into the watery night. Nothing. He tapped weakly. His vision blurred. It seemed to be getting lighter, now. Was he dreaming? Just another spell, perhaps. His breath was coming shorter.

A form appeared in the water a few feet from him. Kshro. She approached, brought her face to the glass, stared inward. Josh brought his mouth up to hers, and they kissed, separated by this crystal barrier—lips, hands, cheeks, almost touching. He saw her chin quiver; she cried, he knew, her tears one with the ocean. His eyes rolled back, and the blackness closed in.

Josh had little recollection of the following days—it might have been hours, or weeks—except in the way febrile hallucinations are recalled: distorted images, overpowering sensations, flashes of lucidity.

The texture of this dreamscape glittered with bizarre visions and apprehensions: a bearded old man kissed his lips, blew air into his body until he floated above the ground; a woman of glass caressed his legs, sending electric blue jolts through him, excruciating, sensual; crushing, suffocating darkness; an army of skeletons and dancing bones surrounded him, chased him, jostled him, buried him; giant insects needled him with poison, sucked his blood; a presence, lonelier than any absence, laid its hollow hand upon his brow; he tried to squirm free, he could not stop squirming, he grew small, there were fires, it was cold, he wept, someone touched him; a great silence.

When he finally awoke, it was upon the softest bed he had ever felt. His eyes came open slowly, and he looked around; a room, like any other room—some simple chairs, a table, artificial lights of a type Josh had never seen before.

He stood up and walked over to the table; his legs felt weak as a kitten's—his legs!

With a shocked excitement he pulled up the robe he found himself wearing and looked at his legs. They were no longer broken. They bore his weight without pain, without buckling. How long could he have been asleep, then? And where was he now?

On the table was a sheet of paper; and on the paper, writing. Josh sat down in the chair and began to read the page before him.

Visitor—

I know not who you be, or even if you can read—but this, I vow, be the only communication you will ever get from me.

You have come to the city of Atlantis. We be a city in a bubble of polymer, fashioned by our ancestors and anchored here at five thousand fathoms over two hundred years ago, by the reckoning of the sun we no longer know. Our machines be powered by generators that take their energy from the ocean currents around us. With these machines we extract oxygen from the sea to breathe, and salt that we may drink the water. And light, and heat, and &.

We made this descent to escape the insanities of the upper world. But in this respect there was no escape. For like our namesake island before us, we have died. Only I am left, alone. I am the city.

The specifics matter not. Patterns cannot learn from themselves, and we are naught but whirls in the pattern. Yet even so I try to deny this my deepest belief—for if you come here that I might tell you what befell us, if that is your purpose in the pattern, then I say to you only this: I Will Not Tell! Yet even as I write I know the pattern is not for me to view, and mayhap my fillip is the very thing I thought to confound, and were I to perceive the true pattern, I would see my role is Not To Tell.

But I weary of this commerce.

The vessel you returned in was lost on an expeditionary journey over a century ere. Our sea locks were programmed to admit it back inside, and will ever remain so. I revived you easily, for we were advanced in the medical arts. It took but a few days to heal your fractures electromagnetically.

The city be as much yours as mine now. Yet try not to seek me out, for I will shun you—and will I harm you if you press me in this matter. For I like not the company of men, or talk, or aid.

There be a manual of instruction in the submarine, where it sits in the sea lock. If it be that you can read, so will you learn to operate the craft, and also how to open the sea lock, to sail from the city. If the matter of reading be otherwise with you, then none of this has bearing in any event.

Know also that if you leave and try later to return

here with others, I will kill you all in the sea lock with the
hammer of the ocean.
Nor Will I Tell!

I welcome you without joy or rancor, for we are but
lines in the pattern.

My name is nothing extra.

Josh read the extraordinary document over twice. Then
he set out to explore the city.

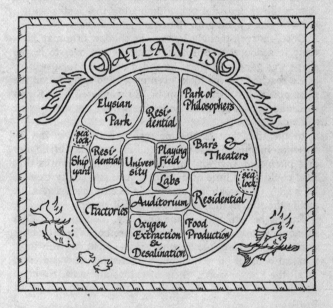

Under a glasslike dome, it was about one mile in diameter.
Glass buildings rose up many stories, sparkling in the light
of a thousand incandescent bulbs that cast a hazy glow into
the crushing ocean beyond. A city of palaces, stunning and
jeweled. And not a living soul to be seen.

Yet everywhere Josh walked were strewn bones. Skulls,
vertebrae, clustered carpales. Sometimes entire disarticu-
lated skeletons—some embracing, in struggle or in ecstasy,
it was impossible to discern; some alone.

Josh came across them in the streets, in the houses, in assembly halls; in the garden. One whole section of the city was a garden—overgrown now, choked with weed and fruit, under the undimming radiance of special violet lights, fed by an ever flowing artificial spring. Josh picked some fruit and ate. It was good. But here, too, bones lay, half-hidden, half-smiling.

He explored for hours, discovering all manner of wonderful things: a fountain of flame that never died; a beacon shining down into the sea, illuminating the depths with a knife of green light; a machine that made music.

Once, he even thought he saw the shadow of a man hovering in a doorway. But by the time he ran over to it, the shape was gone, and when he called out, no one answered.

He reached the sea locks eventually, and there found the glass pod Kshro had put him in. He wondered how Kshro was, and her people. He hoped he would see them again some day.

In the ship, just as the message had said, was the instruction manual. But it was so full of *propulsion dynamics* and *pitch and yaw* and myriad other baffling words that Josh could make little of it. With a grim and empty tremor, he began to despair of ever again seeing his friends, or seeing the sun. In this dark mood he fell asleep.

During his explorations the next day, though, he made a miraculous discovery: the library. More books here than he ever imagined possible in one place—including the most magical book of all, a dictionary. Incredibly, it was a book of all the known words, their meanings and uses. He cried just to hold it in his hand; his tears tasted the pages of words.

Here, too, was something called an *encyclopedia*, which told about *things*; and an *index*, which told where the things were told about.

And there were other manuals, and textbooks, and essays and novels, and thin yellowing picture-books called *monthlies*, and . . .

There was great power here.

With trembling resolve he began looking up some of the mysterious instruction-manual words in the dictionary. He found their meaning. Later, he even found whole books about some of the critical words, like *guidance systems*; but that was later. For now, he was content to learn the simple meanings.

He spent many weeks in Atlantis and learned many things. But he never met the man who would not tell, so he never learned why.

CHAPTER 8

In Which the Trackers Get
Very Close

JASMINE and Ollie left Ma'gas' late in the afternoon, heading south by foot. The Saddlebacks weren't exceptionally high here, but they rose abruptly, making habitation or concealment difficult. The land to the west, on the other hand, was studded with small woods, ravines, and marshes: it was there that trouble lay.

Ollie and Jasmine stuck close to the hills. This area formed a fairly clear corridor, which was both good and bad for them. It allowed them to make good time; and it was open enough that they could see in advance if danger was approaching. But it left them exposed; others would know they were here. As the sun ebbed, they set a faster pace.

Once, in the dwindling twilight, a flapping sound accosted their ears from above. They crouched immediately, and looked up, weapons poised, breathing stilled.

They saw two Pegasi, soaring together, nuzzling each other, fluttering around and around in a wind-whipped courting dance high in the air where the light of day still hovered. The Pegasus stallion was a palomino. He whinnied and pawed the air about his roan lover as if he were trying to break through some ethereal barrier to reach her. She pranced before him, wings billowing. Something in his color reminded Jasmine of Beauty.

She had not thought of Beauty, physically, until this moment. Even as she had left the note for him in Joshua's camp, he had been only an abstraction to her, the abstraction of a memory. Now, watching the magnificent flying horse rise and dive for his lady, Jasmine closed her eyes: the memory of Beauty was thick, almost palpable.

117

His smell, his touch, his voice, his sometimes ridiculous sense of propriety—these things were suddenly real again for Jasmine, as if the Centaur were actually standing before her. Tenderly, she reached out to touch him—but the memory was elusive, and refused to show its face for long.

Jasmine sighed. She had managed to keep Beauty submerged, for the most part. Rarely, events like this would call him to the surface. She knew she must push him back, though: he had chosen another woman, Jasmine had chosen another life. Still, it was nice, sometimes, to bring him out, touch the memory, savor it, then put it back. It made her feel vulnerable, though—an indulgence she could ill afford on this journey. She sighed again, and opened her eyes.

The palomino was just mounting the roan. Behind her, atop her, his forelegs straddling her shoulders, their necks stretching, heads into the wind, wings pounding in unison, they rose and fell, turning great circles through the air, roaring their passion . . . when suddenly another form flew toward them from out of the woods—a smaller creature, with a bestial body, and talons, and the head of a man.

"Mantichore," whispered Ollie, shaking his head in foreknowledge.

The Mantichore tore into the palomino Pegasus, literally ripping him off the back of his lover. They tumbled out of control, as the evil little beast sunk its gnashing teeth into the Pegasus's face, twisted the palomino's arching neck, lashed at his wings with its hind claws. In a few moments they had careened back to Earth, somewhere into the nether woods, and were lost to sight.

The roan Pegasus fluttered around desperately for a minute, trying to see where her beloved had fallen; but the last of the sun was passing now, and little could be seen. Her fear and confusion were obvious, her flight erratic. After a minute of this, she swooped low over the trees to the southwest, and disappeared.

Ollie looked at Jasmine questioningly. But there was nothing to say. Or do. Jasmine suppressed the feelings for Beauty it had aroused; furthermore, she was a scientist, and so dismissed any notion that this might be an omen.

Ollie rose slowly, his breathing controlled by tension. To himself he nodded, for this was an old, and endlessly repeated lesson to him: in the moment of deepest love are we most open to attack, and nearest to death; and in that moment the attack inevitably comes, and inevitably we die, alone and in pain. This much seemed empirical to Ollie; these were the facts. The lesson to be learned, of course, was that to survive it was necessary to form a shell against love. Therein was shelter. Otherwise, one might just as well lie belly-up in a pit full of Accidents; that's what love was like.

They stood back to back, listening for sounds; but none came. After a few minutes, they set off south again, into the night.

The storm was violent almost from the outset. The rain crashed down in drenching sheets, the wind approached hurricane velocity.

"With these mountains so close, it's like a wind tunnel along here," Jasmine shouted. "We'll have to move down into the forest!"

Ollie nodded, and they ran west quickly, into the windbreak of bhong trees that skirted this forest. The rain, too, pelted them less.

They headed south once more, though at a decidedly slower pace. Bushes and mudholes slowed them, branches scratched their faces, they stumbled over roots. And the blackness was impenetrable. Except when the lightning flashed, turning everything blue-white for a few seconds, pounding the Earth with thunder. But the shadows cast by the low-hanging branches were even more ominous than the opaque night; so Jasmine and Ollie unconsciously drew closer together.

"How much farther, do you think?" Ollie asked.

"Halfway, maybe. Want to rest?"

"In this?"

"Just asking. You tired yet?"

"Should I be?" He sounded defensive.

"You know, you're a hard kid to pin down," she smiled.

"Afraid someone might get a handle on one of your few weaknesses?"

"What's a weakness?" He returned her smile.

"See? There *is* something I can still teach you." She laughed, the rainwater streaming down her face. "Weaknesses are something I can give you a lot of firsthand information about. Now take notes . . ."

He made an elaborate charade of holding a notepad in one hand, moistening a quill point in his mouth, and poising it over the imaginary paper, as they walked. Suddenly he threw down the illusory articles, hit his forehead with the heel of his hand, and said, "I forgot—I *do* have a weakness! I know how to read and write!"

The rain continued. In the distance to the west, they could see flashing yellow lights crackling and jumping beyond a wooded glen.

"What's that?" Ollie whispered.

"Looks like neon." She squinted at the indistinct light show.

"What's neon?" He took a step toward the display.

"Forget it," she held him back. A spear of lightning traced through the sky to the glowing grove, producing a surge of incandescence, followed by a thunderous *Crack*, followed by a long, animal scream.

They ran the hundred yards to a large clearing. There at its center was a huge jumble of debris—buckled over the ground, sticking up into the air, twisting around in a hopeless tangle of steel rods and rotting wood crossties—with jolts of electricity violently sparking at every crossing, the slithery charges running up and down the lengths of rail.

"Railroad tracks," Jasmine marveled.

Another bolt of lightning crashed into the tallest rod, and the charge raced down the steel and around the clackering circuit, accompanied by elemental sound and light. Off to the side, several ancient engines lay half-buried and decomposing in the mud, a great half-moon of iron plate sunk at an acute angle into the earth beside them.

"It must have been a terminal or roundhouse once," she went on.

"What's that?" asked Ollie. Another of Jasmine's wisdoms, out of another age.

"A railroad; it was a railroad," she said absently. Sparks flew all about.

There was another scream, behind a massive upturned engine. They ran around to look, daggers drawn; and momentarily stopped. The roan female Pegasus stood there, uselessly flapping her mud-sodden wings. Straddling her from behind was a Night-Mare.

It was a giant Horse—easily twice as big as the Pegasus—black as death, with reflective red eyes and rows of dripping, jagged, carnivorous teeth. Its hooves were spiked, its tail barbed. Its breath, like a Dragon's, was bacterial methane, which ignited into blue flame whenever it gnashed its flinty incisors. It was a terrifying beast. It was raping the roan.

Its colossal size drove her to her fore knees as it mounted her from behind, pressing its tuburous redness between her hind legs, beneath her tail. Lightning splashed and danced; the Night-Mare's demented eyes flashed with carmine fire.

The roan's nostrils flared, her mouth foamed, her eyes stared wildly in all directions. "Nay!" she screamed. "Naaay!" And the wind shrieked with her.

Chest heaving in exhaustion and terror, she beat her wings again, but to no avail; they were soaked. She wailed once more, as another bolt of lightning coursed through the steel rails that twisted into the air around them. "Naaaay!"

The Night-Mare forced itself grossly in her, roared its lust, ground its teeth, and blew gaseous fire from its throat, singeing the Pegasus's mane. Her tongue flopped from the corner of her mouth, her beautiful head lolled to the side. The Night-Mare clamped its sharp drooling teeth into the base of her neck, at the shoulder blade. The rain poured down.

This was all a long moment. In the next moment, Ollie was flying through the air; and the moment after that he was on the giant's back, his left hand clutching the raging mane, his right hand on his dagger, which he plunged to the hilt into the creature's right eye.

It screeched and reared. Ollie stabbed it twice more—

through the eye, into the brain. The beast bellowed, louder than thunder, and fell backward, almost crushing Ollie. He jumped clear, though—only to be attacked by the Mantichore they had seen earlier.

He grappled with the creature, rolling in the mud, getting clawed and kicked—until Jasmine jumped in to the fray and neatly cut the Mantichore's throat.

It rolled off Ollie, and stared at Jasmine for a second. Its head was Human, with several rows of Shark-like teeth; its eyes were crossed. It tried to speak. Only a gurgle came.

Weakly, it pulled itself over to the huge body of the dead Night-Mare, dragging its hind legs through the mud. When it got to the Horse's head, it licked and kissed the animal's bloody face a few times, whimpered, and died. Apparently they had been friends.

Jasmine and Ollie walked over to the roan Pegasus, who lay shivering in the mud. She shrank from them and whinnied abjectly when they tried to examine her for wounds; but they soothed her, put her to rest, and tended her through the night. Jasmine, in particular, set her at ease; for she had a way with Horses.

Ollie, too, rested in the old trainyard as the storm gradually passed through the night. He was cut and bruised, but had no serious injuries.

In the morning, the sky was clear. The Pegasus seemed much improved—in fact, she quickly flew off, then quickly returned. She spoke no language that Jasmine knew, but somehow they made themselves understood. Jasmine and Ollie climbed up on her back, and she flew them the rest of the way south, letting them down on the mountain ridge overlooking the jungle caves Jasmine was seeking—the hiding-caves.

They bared necks and waved good-bye, and the Pegasus flew west into the nebulous grief and freedom of her own future. Jasmine and Ollie turned east and began the cloudy descent into Dundee's Terrarium—toward the dark cavernous channels of their past.

Jasmine sat on her haunches, staring into the ashes of the long-dead fire. Five years dead. The pitted walls of the cave had absorbed the intervening time like a vacuum, leaving the artifacts strewn about virtually untouched and unaged.

Empty tins of food, still-good Gila jerky, candles, flints, three cobweb-covered bottles of wine, some faded blankets, a few tools. Maps—the sanitation maps. The torn, yellowed maps outlining the sewage disposal system that tunneled like a maze beneath The City With No Name. The maps Jasmine and Josh had used to effect their escape from the City. The maps Jasmine had hidden in this cave.

This was the cave upriver where they had all rendez-voused then—Jasmine, Josh, Beauty, Rose, Ollie, the orphans from Bal's harem, the Flutterby—hid out here for days into weeks, until they had recovered enough to disperse to the rest of their own lives, their separate and varied paths.

Ollie sat by the spring that cut across one corner of the cave, watching Jasmine stare into the ashes of her memory. He had his own dark feelings tied up here. The last time he had sat beside this stream, he had been ten years old, and catatonic. He had seen his parents murdered by mutants, his cousin raped by Vampires. He had been kidnapped and put in the harem of a Vampire named Bal, who had jewels sewn into Ollie's frail young skin. His skin was scarred and tough now. He fingered the ruby in his chest: *memento mori.*

Jasmine opened the brittle maps one by one in the light of the candles. So familiar. Each shaft labeled according to the surface room to which it connected. Laboratories, offices, suites. The Final Decontamination Room. The Communion Room. Nirvana. The Queen's Chambers. Her mind trembled with the same excited fear she had felt five years before, going over the maps to plan the attack route, and the escape route. Jasmine was a Neuroman who savored her passions—they were all creative tensions to her, and she relished experiencing them, regardless of whether the core of the experience was pleasure, fear, rage, or tenderness. They were all, for her, colors in the sensorium of life.

She went over every inch of the maps again, now, stretching her mind over the geography of the past.

No sign of Tunnel Twenty-two.

"Don't move. You're covered!" The strange voice leapt out of the shadows like a vicious Cat. Jasmine and Ollie both froze, eyes dilating with intention.

A small flat object skimmed through the dark, heading straight for Jasmine's neck. She flattened to the ground, and the thing hit the stones just beyond her with a *Smack*. She lifted her head high enough to see it, to decide whether to grab it or run. It was a book.

"Read it!" shouted the voice in the shadow. Jasmine almost laughed with relief, but the voice still had the edge of death.

Slowly she picked it up, opened it, and read out loud, her eyes straining in the candlelight: "It was the best of times, it was the worst of times—"

"That's enough," snapped the invisible voice, relenting a little. "Toss it to your pal crouchin' by the water there."

She threw the book to Ollie, who caught it one-handed, his other hand still on the stiletto in his belt.

"The last page," intoned another voice, from another shadow.

Ollie opened to the last page. He hadn't been able to speak since entering the cave, but in the book, he found his words: "It is a far, far better thing I do, than I have ever done. It is a far—"

"That's enough, that's enough. I'm so sick of that line I could puke," rang a third voice. "What's the Word?"

Ollie shouted out, "The Word is One." It was the Scribes' responsive call to one another since the beginning of Time, since the first Word. And though Ollie didn't consider himself a Scribe, he knew their ways well.

And suddenly, the cave was alight with the flames of six torches. Four men and two women climbed down the rocks to ground level. Each carried a torch and a cocked crossbow. The leader was a robust young man with silver hair and a bold voice. He extended his hand to Jasmine as she stood.

"Delaney," he barked jovially.

She could see he was still sizing her up as his comrades hung back, so she didn't want to get up his guard with too many questions. "Jasmine," she replied. "And that's my friend, Ollie." Ollie nodded warily. Jasmine continued. "We're here revisiting our past, you might say." She had an ear for the vernacular of whomever she was speaking to, and unconsciously fell into it as a sort of disarming camouflage. She went on: "But as often as I used to come here, I never knew of any other entrances like the ones you came out of."

Delaney laughed. "Well darlin', whether you used to come here or not, these are our caves now, and if you'll just give us your weapons, there won't be any room for misunderstandin's."

Ollie tensed again, but it was too late: the intruders were close now, all with crossbows trained. Reluctantly, he and Jasmine divested themselves of their knives.

Delaney went on. "Not that I don't trust you, mind. Anybody who can read is all right in my book. It's just that we'll be takin' you through some sensitive areas, and it's best no one *else* gets the wrong idea. Right?" He started steering Jasmine toward Ollie, and then both of them toward a small hole in the wall that she had never seen before. Delaney kept up his chatter as, one by one, the captors and captives entered the constricted tunnel mouth. "Well, come on, then. Nothin' to cry about. You're just in the hands of a few good Books."

"What were you doing in our cave?" demanded David. He stared at Ollie.

"We didn't know it was yours," the boy responded. His voice was slow, and quiet as a sheathed knife. Jasmine sat beside him, and around them stood six Books. An oil lamp illuminated the eight figures; beyond, all was darkness, crossed with the echoes of lapping water.

"The ownership of the cave is not an issue," said Paula. "The question remains, What were you doing there?"

"The ownership of the cave, it seems to me, is very much relevant to its occupancy," Jasmine replied. "I discovered that hideout a hundred years ago. I provisioned it, I secured it. What we were doing there is our affair. More to the point is, who the hell are you?"

Delaney laughed. The others remained impassive.

"A comic Book, she is," muttered Michael.

There was a silence, and then Jasmine spoke again, her tone more accommodating. "Look, we're wasting time. Here's the truth—"

"Jasmine," Ollie cautioned.

"This is getting us nowhere." She shook her head. "We're here, and that's that, Ollie. Besides, these people might even help us."

Addie nodded.

"Ollie trusts no one," Jasmine added.

"A frequently necessary but nonetheless always corrosive virtue," commented Delaney.

"But our time is at a premium," Jasmine went on, "and I've seen enough to trust you with this much. Ollie's brother, Joshua—my friend—we believe to be under the influence of the rulers of The City With No Name. We think he's there now—a prisoner. We intend to infiltrate the City and free him."

David began picking at his writing-callus. "Impossible," he scoffed.

"Hear her out." At the mention of Joshua's name, Paula's interest grew.

"Oh, it's quite possible," Jasmine assured them. "In fact, the cave you found us in was the same cave we hid in five years ago after a similar mission, when we freed Ollie, here. I'm still baffled how *you* found the cave."

"Your presence there triggered an alarm in our guardroom. We know all the caves under these cliffs, for miles around," Paula explained. "They all connect—"

"Paula . . ." David warned.

"These people are friends, David. Are you too dense to feel that?"

Michael whispered to Ellen, "Delaney *said* they were Bookish."

"They don't look Bookish." Ellen remained skeptical.

Paula resumed her explanation to Jasmine and Ollie. "The caves all connect through underground tributaries of the river. These catacombs go on for miles. We haven't really even begun to explore them all."

"It could take years," David appended.

"So how'd you do it, sport?" Michael asked Jasmine. "Last time, I mean—get into the City and find your people."

"The tunnels, of course. And these maps." She pointed to the sanitation maps Delaney had confiscated in the hiding-cave. "They mark every room in the City, with its disposal chute to the tributaries belowground that are used as sewage ducts."

Michael studied them more closely now. "Look, she's right. With maps like this we could put a few Bookworms right on the money. Look, here, here's the Queen's Chambers marked clear as day."

"There is no queen, though," Jasmine said. "That's just made up . . ."

"There is a queen," Paula corrected. "And it's she who must die."

"No, the queen is a hoax, it's the Neuroman Engineers who—"

"But the Pluggers say there's a queen," Paula insisted. "They say they were connected to her brain. They knew her. They—"

"You're in contact with Pluggers?" Jasmine interrupted. This was an unexpected note, indeed—possibly with great bearing on Joshua's letter.

"Yes, they live down in these caves, too. They first discovered the caves, in fact, when they escaped from the City . . . five years ago." Paula stopped, caught short by a sudden suspicion. "That couldn't be coincidence—"

"No coincidence," Jasmine nodded. "When Joshua freed Ollie from the City, he liberated as many others as he could—many were those whose heads he unplugged from . . . whatever it was they were plugged into. They fled down the disposal chutes to the tunnels below, as did Josh and the rest of us."

Paula smiled thinly. "Our friend Joshua holds a rather interesting place in the history the Pluggers have written of their exodus—some Pluggers were Scribes, you know, and still set the record from time to time. He's a legend to them now—almost mythological. He's regarded as more than a liberator. Almost a messiah. But at the same time, a devil, a great destroyer of the peace they knew in Communion. He delivered them to a freedom they hate for all they lost. They call him 'The Serpent.' Apparently the act of being unplugged was accompanied by an all-consuming hissing sound."

"They interest me, these Pluggers," Jasmine mused. "We're trailing one of them as well—Rose. She's also a friend, but she may be involved in Joshua's recent disappearance. You wouldn't know if she's . . . here?"

Paula shrugged. "She may be. There's a nucleus of about twenty of them. Others come and go. We don't know more—they stay to themselves, mostly, in a section of caves they never let us very far into."

"Can we go see them? They may be able to give us some information."

"Yes, I think so," said Paula.

"There's a lot of things they know that would be useful to us," David interjected, nibbling at his callus. "I think this is information we can barter with. It's something they'd like to know—that their savior-Serpent has slithered back to the castle."

"You'll be sleeping here," said Paula. It was a dry, warm cave, with two blankets and a candle. "The lower levels are actually warmer in this area—because of the hot springs."

"It's appreciated," said Jasmine. "We spent last night cold and drenched."

"How many levels are there?" Ollie asked.

"No one is certain." Paula shrugged. "We're mapping it slowly, but . . ." She tipped her head at the enormity of the task. There was a brief shifting of Earth: the caverns growled; nameless fears rustled, then settled back to ground.

"Very interesting," mused Jasmine. "An entire city of spelunkers."

"What's a spelunker?" Paula asked suspiciously.

"It's just an old word for cave-explorer—you know, mapping tunnels; like what you're doing."

A light filled Paula's eyes. "You mean . . . it's a new word? A real word?"

"Well, it's pretty old, actually. But yes, it's real."

"You'd better come with me," said Paula. She took them up a long curving ledge to an opening in the roof of the adjacent cave. They emerged into a cavern a hundred feet high, whose ceiling and floor were connected by dozens of long columns of touching stalactites and stalagmites. Paula led the others across the bumpy ground, through a series of winding corridors that ended in a gradual upgrade. The slope was a dead end, and the three had to drop down a narrow hole by rope before exiting, finally, one level lower, into a huge room filled with people.

Scores of Humans sat hunched over long tables, writing. Paula took Jasmine and Ollie past them all to the far corner, where old Addie was bent over a ream of finely lettered paper, deep in thought.

"Addie," Paula said quietly.

The old woman seemed confused for a moment, then looked up and smiled. "Oh," she murmured, "for a short, sweet second I thought the page was calling me. But it's only you, sweet as you are."

Paula smiled back at the old master Scribe. "Addie, I think Jasmine has a new word. *Spelunker*. It means 'cave-explorer,' she says."

Addie closed her eyes against distraction, scanning her memory. "Yes," she said, "I think I remember something of the sort. I believe that is correct." She opened her eyes and grinned. "A rediscovered word! How exciting!"

Paula was pleased. "We'll record it at once." She wasn't all that keen on dredging up old esoteric words; but she had taken a liking to Jasmine and was happy the Neuroman was lexiphilic.

Jasmine wrote down the word and its definition, and handed it to one of the recording Scribes.

Ollie, in spite of himself, was just a little jealous. "Oh, Jasmine's very good at parties," he deadpanned.

Jasmine laughed out loud, putting her arm around the boy's shoulder. "I thought you didn't value the Scriptic arts."

"I don't." He almost smiled. "And I don't like the word *spelunker*, either."

"Neither do I, actually," said Paula. "Sounds rather like an animal I'd rather not step on. But a word's a word, I suppose. Still, it doesn't have much poetic force."

They were walking again, down more convolutions of the cave system.

Jasmine improvised: "*There was a spelunker named Jasmine, a rude and notorious has-been . . .*"

"What's that?" asked Paula.

"Part of an old poem I just made up." The Neuroman smiled.

They reached a rim of rock overhanging a large underground lake eighty yards directly below them, then sat on the ledge and dangled their legs over the sheer drop. Floating candles barely moved on the water—flickering reflections in the still surface, points of breathing light.

"This is one of my jobs," Paula said. "Making certain the candles stay lit." She liked these people, but wasn't entirely certain how far she could trust them—so she was starting out with small trusts, like what her duties were, or where some of the prettier caves could be found. Presently, she would reveal more of her views on Joshua—how she had seen him save the Mermaid in Ma'gas', how heroic and sad he had seemed, as if he were a living poem depicting the Human race. But they would have to show her a little more of themselves before she opened up that much to them.

"What's the purpose of the candles?" Ollie asked. They appeared quite lovely, like twinkling stars in an upside-down sky.

"To look beautiful," said Paula. "Only that. There is so little beauty in our lives—and beauty is truth, it has been written . . ." Her voice trailed off. The hollowness of these caves, their infinite capacity for emptiness, overwhelmed her at times.

Jasmine remained silent, just watching. Ollie took his flute from his belt and began to play. The longing melody wandered from niche to crevice down the walls of the cave, until it lingered over the water below, where the candle-lights danced to its tune. The three people closed their eyes; and in a moment, each was transported to an eternal, private land of nuance and dream, where no one else could go.

Five figures stood darkly outside the stone door to the Pluggers' section of the catacombs: Jasmine, Ollie, Paula, David, Michael. Moody, tense, they clipped one another with somber glances. The door in the rock opened, and they entered.

They were led silently through a maze of tunnels to a small, warm room with pillows over the floor. They sat and waited. These caves knew waiting and other formless dissatisfactions.

Presently three Pluggers came in, bowed slightly, meshed their fingers in the Sign of the Plug, and sat down. One was Candlefire, Paula's friend, the Nine-prong Plugger; one was Starcore, a Three-prong Plugger who was one of the group's leaders; one was Blackwind, a Twenty-seven-prong Plugger whose face was bleak and hollow as his name.

Paula began. "These are travelers from the north. Jasmine and Ollie. Candlefire, Blackwind, Starcore." Everyone nodded. Paula went on. "They are here to raid the City, to rescue a friend of theirs whom they have reason to believe is now there. A friend . . . of interest to us all."

"Of interest to you is no interest to me," whispered Blackwind. He never spoke above a whisper.

"Be still, Blackwind," said Candlefire. "Go on, Paula, who is it they seek?"

David spoke up, smirking. "The Serpent. Your Serpent of Disconnections is alive and well in the City."

"Liar!" rasped Blackwind, his eyes seeming to sink even deeper into the pits under his brow.

"What are you saying?" Starcore interrupted.

"Blasphemy!" Blackwind took a step toward David, who stood with clenched fists.

Michael quickly stood between them. "What he's saying is, sport, maybe we all have reason to pierce the castle's veil now. Maybe this tips the scales. Maybe we can join forces, fight the good fight, and all that."

"Bring Pluggers in the Bookery and get buggery," David spat.

Jasmine spoke now, her voice quiet, calming everyone back to their places. "Please, I don't want to cause conflict among you. Our mission here is simple, and private. My friend Joshua—Ollie's brother—is being drawn to the City by powerful forces, against his will. He's probably there by now. We intend to enter the City by tunnel, steal him back, and leave. We welcome your help, but will happily act without it." She could see she had walked in on a tense alliance in delicate balance, and wanted to be sure she wasn't contributing to the imbroglio. Above all, she wanted to avoid a situation in which one faction supported her mission while the other sought to undermine it.

There was a long, considered silence. Finally Starcore spoke. "It's not that simple, unfortunately. Let me explain some of our facts of life to you, Jasmine. May I call you Jasmine? Good, then here's the situation. Our comrades in the Bookery wish to enter and destroy the City—by cunning, since they aren't strong enough to do it by force. We Pluggers are ambivalent about that prospect and, for the time being, have vetoed the Book project. Now, there's only one tunnel that connects us from here to the inner sanctums of the castle—and that's a secret we keep from everyone, including the Books."

"But it's easy to get access," Jasmine said. "You can float down the Sticks River and follow any of the tributaries that dip into the tunnels under the City. Or you can go directly into the tunnels through their exit in the cliff face under the City, at the outflow. That's how we got in last time."

Paula shook her head. "We've tried that. There are electrified wire grids over every port of entry to the City."

"Except our secret tunnel," Starcore added.

Jasmine was taken aback. "That's something new, then. They must've gotten wise after our last invasion." She had suspected there might be additional defenses up now, though, and was glad to know what they were.

Starcore nodded. "Not so simple for you then, either. And now there's the matter of The Serpent. First of all, how do we know this person you seek *is* The Serpent?"

"All I know is it's my friend Josh. It was he who freed his family from bondage in the castle five years ago—and at that time, along with his friend Rose, unplugged as many Humans as he could from their cables and showed them the way down the chute to the tunnels below."

Blackwind jumped at mention of Rose's name, but said nothing.

"It *is* The Serpent," whispered Candlefire. His eyes became watery.

"And even if it is," Starcore proceeded, "we don't know that he's actually in the City."

"Yes, we do," said Paula. "I saw him."

"You saw The Serpent?" Blackwind was incredulous. "You saw The Serpent?"

Jasmine eyed Paula suspiciously, for she hadn't mentioned anything of the kind earlier. Ollie, too, took note—though he revealed nothing of his interest. He sat as much in shadow as courtesy permitted, remembering everything being said, who responded; who would be a friend, and who would not.

Paula went on to tell her story of seeing Josh kidnapped in Ma'gas', her pursuit of the pirate ship with Michael and Ellen, and the unloading of the hostages in The City With No Name.

Jasmine's eyes glowed. "He *is* in the City, then."

"*He's* in the *City*," Blackwind echoed.

"You must understand," Starcore said to Jasmine, "our feelings about The Serpent. Most of us have never seen him. We hold him in special reverence—fear, love, hate. We curse him and worship him. His return now will have a profound effect upon our order. Where it will lead, I can't say."

"We must save him," said Candlefire.

"Perhaps," said Starcore. "The whole tribe will have to discuss it."

Ollie spoke, for the first time. "With or without you, we will save him."

"Whatever these Pluggers decide," David spoke to his group, "we'll make our own decision. Wouldn't do to rush things now, with success so clear if our preparation is sound." He looked pointedly at Jasmine. "Wouldn't do for *any* of us to rush things."

"You talk a big word, sport," Michael mocked.

"When it's time to do, I'll do," David said quietly.

"I wouldn't make Book on it," Michael muttered.

Paula stood, ending the squabble. "We'll go now. Tell your people, and tell us their decision. We'll await word."

Candlefire returned to his own cave and sat in the dark, trying to assimilate the new information.

The Serpent had returned.

Something was going to happen.

He didn't know what, but something. Perhaps The Serpent would release them in some way, release them now as he had before; release them from this inexquisite life they now walked, floated through—floated through like ghosts.

That's what they were, ghosts of their former being, of the consciousness they once shared. Half-alive wraiths. He could no longer think as clearly as he did in-circuit; his feelings were no longer as dense or complex; his perceptions apprehended the world in shadow, now. He felt like a lower form of life; algae on a cave floor.

What relief to be freed from this condition. But how would The Serpent do it? Destroy the castle, perhaps, and with it the cables; and with them, all hope of ever plugging again. Without hope there could be no grief; no waiting, no more agony. No more emptiness: like a bottomless pit, these catacombs had swallowed his soul. Yet now, such terrible rumors of light . . .

Perhaps The Serpent would simply kill the Pluggers, his poor lost children. Candlefire hoped this was truly why The Serpent had returned—for death would be the only true rest, the only real release from the shackles that locked his brain to his body, held it within the confines of his own skull.

Or would The Serpent return his orphans to the castle, actually rejoin them to the Plug? Could Candlefire possibly hope to know Fusion again, to be in-circuit with the Queen and all the others? His mouth went dry just to think of it. What if he was given a choice between the freedom of following his own mind down here in the caves—or wherever he wanted to let it lead him—or the Circuit, lying captive, naked, degraded. And ecstatic.

To his deep shame, with a desperate craving, he knew he would pick the Plug.

Perhaps The Serpent was here only to raise these questions, to force his children to come to terms with their lives and *act*.

Silently, Candlefire wept, and beat his fists against the wall of the black cave.

Blackwind raced to the deepest cave he knew of and wedged himself in its tapering blind crack. Here he felt safe. Huddled in the darkest, lowest, most inaccessible corner of the catacombs, he could not be reached without his knowing, and few could find him at all.

The Serpent! What did it mean? Almost certainly he was in the castle to unplug more Humans from where they lay in-circuit. More lost souls loose in the world.

Oh, God, to have seen Heaven and then be thrown out into these wormholes . . .

And Rose! Her name was Rose, the Plugger he had met in the north and convinced to come here. Rose, who was *with* The Serpent when he unplugged the rest, Rose who went with The Serpent during the first years.

Maybe The Serpent was here for her! Maybe he had come for *her*, to take her back. Maybe Blackwind could strike a deal with The Serpent—give him Rose in return for a Plug, or a chance to get back in-circuit, in the Queen's good graces.

Yes, that was it. He would make a deal. He laughed his hoarse, whispery laugh in the bottom of the stone crevice, but soon the laughter turned to tears, tears that wouldn't stop, tears of desolation for something that once was but was no more. His sobs echoed off the stone, his hollow eyes reflected the blackness of these tombs his life had become.

* * *

Starcore sat staring into the coals of the blazing stove fire; so close, his face flushed from heat and pain. He circled the core of the fire, probed the white-red center with his eyes, with his soul.

Come, Serpent. Come, O living deathless cable. Join us, Dragontail of Connections, he thought to the flame.

His heart was beating rapidly, almost fluttering; his breaths came quick and shallow. He salivated.

Come, I bid you, suck my swollen brain and sting me with your burning venom, Serpent! You have come to save us, Serpent! I am yours.

Starcore called a meeting of all the Pluggers an hour later, in the great meeting-cave. He told them The Serpent had returned to the City. There was disbelief, outrage, swooning, sobbing, and ecstasy. Even the unblind caves themselves seemed momentarily to raise their heavy lids, and snarl uncertainly into the depths.

Only the newcomer, Rose, now called Windlight, silently sat in a dark corner, shedding the dry tears of guilt and the dense heat of constrained passion.

CHAPTER 9

The Brevity and Understatement of Feline Wit

Isis twitched her ears, opened her eyes, raised her nose. Something. What was it? A sound? No. A smell. Well, nearly a smell. A presence. Joshua. It was Joshua. She stood quickly, sniffed every direction. Her eyes dilated.

After the flood in the tunnels that had separated her from her friends five years before, she had waited. Certainly, Josh would come to get her. But hunger had overcome her patience finally, and she had ventured out for food, still staying close to where she had become lost. That was the beginning of her subterranean life.

She had become a tunnel Cat. She preyed on Rats, Fish, occasionally eggs. She hated the water but learned to develop a sort of stalemated adversary relationship with it, even learned to swim, after a fashion. And she waited for Joshua.

For the entire first year, she consciously waited for him. Gradually, during that period, she explored more and more of the network of wet and dry tunnels beneath the City. There was much activity during that time—Vampires and Neuromans abounded, trying to track the commandos who had violated their impregnable fortress, looking for hideaways, access routes. All without success. Finally, they retreated back up to their lairs, and Isis was left alone once again. She continued to wait.

After Josh failed to show for the better part of that year, she twice tried to ascend the stone shafts that connected the tunnel system to the City above. Both times the chute was blocked by an electrified wire grid that knocked her, semiconscious, back down into the running water below, and would likely have killed her outright but for her feline resilience.

She continued to live in the dark corridors after that, continued to wait—though what she was waiting for became less and less clear. She remembered Josh intermittently for another year; then simply continued to wait—for what, she knew not; then simply continued to live down here, since this seemed to be where she lived.

Now, in an instant, that was all changed. Now she smelled Joshua, and remembered.

She walked up and down the watery ducts for an hour before she picked up his true scent. There was no doubt, now: it was Joshua, returned for her.

She made her way slowly against the current—chest-deep on her—staying close to the walls, where the footholds were better and the stream less rapid. At every turn the smell got a little stronger, a little more insistent. Isis licked her nose.

Finally the presence became so great that she stopped and looked around wildly, expecting to see him at any moment. Nowhere. Only the shaft above, where Joshua's odor was heavy. She crawled out of the water, shook herself dry, dug her claws into the pocketed stone, and began the vertical climb up the black, windy chute.

The hairs on her back stood up at the memory of her previous encounters in these shafts—the electric shocks, the battering falls to the water. She took a long pause with each step, sniffing, listening, half of her wanting to run ahead, the other half wanting to run back. Her eyes were wide and wild.

She reached the place where an electrified screen had been—the screen Josh had crashed through on his plunge out of the Queen's chambers—and stopped. A few ends of singed wire remained, sticking out of the stone. Isis sniffed. They reeked of ozone and Joshua.

She climbed carefully here, to avoid the remaining wires, then ran up the last stretch without stopping. When she reached the top, she jumped over the lip of the bin and landed in a four-footed crouch on the floor.

It was dark, but less so than the tunnel had been. Joshua's smells were strong, but now mingled with others. Predominantly one other. Isis looked around. There, in the far corner, sat a lone figure.

Isis padded casually but directly toward the seated woman. As Isis approached, she noted both Joshua's and this woman's smells intensify. These were soon mingled with dozens of other presences—not exactly smells—which Isis couldn't see, or identify in any other way.

By the time she was within a few feet of the throne, Isis was heady with Joshua's recent proximity—his smells were all over the strange woman in the chair. The little Cat jumped into the Queen's lap, curled up, and began to lick the back of her left paw in a manner she felt was dignified and touched with enough noblesse oblige so that the strange woman in the chair would know she had been royally graced by Isis's choice of her lap.

Isis decided she would wait there for Josh: without dramatics, without anticipation, without the barest betrayal of her truest feelings: she would wait, like a Cat.

The Queen looked down in surprise at the sudden appearance of the small furry beast in her lap. She stroked Isis's head a few times and smiled. Isis ignored her.

"Hello, little kitten. To what do I owe this honor? And wherever did you come from? The tunnels, by your look. Well, go on, then, give yourself a good bath, you need it very well, we can tell, we can tell, by your smell, fishy smell. A tunnel Cat in the Queen's chambers, that's a step up in the world for one such as you, that's what I call sweetening the kitty, pulling up your own puss-'n'-bootstraps, coming to me, as you can see."

Isis ignored her, continued licking her own paw.

"What then, Cat and Mouse with me, is it? Cat got your tongue, foul little Ratcatcher?"

Isis licked the Queen's leg once, almost accidentally as she licked the side of her own paw; then, without breaking stride, without acknowledging the Queen in the least, lifted her paw to lick its underside.

The Queen was briefly miffed, then quickly relented. "Well, clean yourself, then. Cat as Cat can, I suppose! I'll have my sterile Neuromans give you a proper cleaning in a bit, little twit, little kit, you're likely seething with bacteria. I'll have to have my royal self decontaminated after such a redolent visit—but not degerminated, no, not that, by my seed, indeed. Ah, you don't *mind* my scratching your neck here, do you? There. I need something to comfort me these days—just something soft to touch. I suppose you knew that, though; else why would you've come? It's those placental hormones, I don't doubt, have made me so needy, and drawn you here. I wish you could talk to me, though. We could plot the new world together, you and me, and baby makes three, as you can see, as you can see."

Isis ignored her, and went to sleep.

CHAPTER 10

The City With No Name

BEAUTY, D'Ursu, and Aba approached the drawbridge over the moat that surrounded the outer wall of The City With No Name. Beauty couldn't suppress a shudder at being so near the place again, but D'Ursu scolded him under his breath, and warned him to breathe normally and wipe the smell of tension from under his arms. Quickly, Beauty regained his composure.

D'Ursu himself seemed wary but at ease. The days out in the open had done much to calm his spirit. Aba maintained an outward sense of equanimity, though excitement sharpened his eyes and ears to every nuance in the air. A Vampire culture was being developed here, it was said; a Vampire destiny being shaped. Aba was anxious to find out just what these rumors meant. And then, of course, he had his other reason for being there—to search for Lon's last lesson.

He stood behind D'Ursu as they approached the gate, Beauty off to the side. Near a bush by the gate, a movement caught Aba's eye. Inconspicuously, he placed his hand on D'Ursu's back—lightly, briefly, just to get the Bear's attention. "Walk easy, old Bear. We're watched, from the copse."

Suddenly a Cerberus leapt out of the bush and planted itself directly in their path. It twitched its ears, salivated, assumed a posture of attack, and growled. The three pilgrims bared their necks; then D'Ursu took another step forward and spoke.

"We are emissaries from Jarl, the Bear-King, and would have diplomatic audience with your Queen."

The three heads of the Cerberus growled louder. D'Ursu

"Nay!" she screamed. "Naaay!" And the wind shrieked with her.

took one giant step forward and backhanded the creature so hard it flew ten feet and landed on its seat.

"Insolent Dog," D'Ursu growled, "didn't you hear me use Jarl's name? Now go fetch your master and tell him we've arrived, before I chew off your middle head and feed it to the others."

The Cerberus inched away, then jumped up and ran inside the portico. In a few moments he returned with three Vampires and two Neuromans.

"That's better," growled D'Ursu. "An escort."

They all introduced themselves, and again D'Ursu stated he had King's business with the ruler of The City With No Name.

"Of course," the captain of the entourage, a supercilious Vampire named Lec, said, with a haughtiness he had no interest in suppressing. "I'm certain it's important business, too. If you'll just follow me, I'll see you're settled in until the Queen has time for you."

With that he turned—without awaiting a reply—and walked through the front gates and into the City, followed closely by Beauty, D'Ursu, and Aba.

As they marched through the roiling Outer City, only D'Ursu managed to remain unimpressed. Beauty had strong and complicated feelings about what he saw, based partly on his shadowed memories of the night he floated down the river that cut through the City, to snatch Rose back to freedom. Aba, too, had his senses jostled. His nostrils flared in resonance with the throngs of Vampires and the rich odors of their Human chattel.

It was like a throbbing organism, this city without name.

A profusion of houses and stores had filled up most of the outer section over the years. They jumbled up and intersected one another without regard for street or structure. To the right of the main gate a great open-air market remained, and the noise level from the bartering there drowned out even Beauty's thoughts.

They were taken over a bridge that crossed the major tributary of the Sticks River, then marched west again, toward the castle. The castle itself was overwhelming. Monstrous, made of stone, with turrets and towers, it lorded over everything that could see it. Thousands of fine, electrified wires radiated from the castle, crisscrossing to the outer wall like the strands of a complex spider web, preventing aerial attack or escape from the City. The spider, seemingly, was asleep.

And everywhere, Vampires. Hundreds of them, dressed in flowing, wildly exotic colors; more in one place than even Aba had ever seen. They strutted the twisting avenues, many walking their Humans on leashes—a social activity known as harem-strolling. At one point the group walked near a pit where harem members bred for fighting were matched against one another by their owners. The Human who lost was passed from Vampire to Vampire, for their pleasure and drink. Aba felt sick at the sight of the spectacle, and had to turn his head.

Presently they came to the inner wall, were passed on through by the guard, and entered the Inner City. Nothing could have been more different.

There were almost no Vampires here—it was virtually a Neuroman enclave. In contrast to the Outer City, this inner compartment was quiet, orderly, clean, and colorless. Neat rows of barracks lined spotless streets that met at right angles. The Neuromans were all in uniform, rarely spoke with one another, and all seemed to have someplace to go.

D'Ursu Magna had no use for either sector. "Stinking cities," he grumbled, and spat.

At the castle gates, the Vampire guard turned back, and the three friends were escorted by the Neuromans into the grand foyer. It was cool inside, surrounded everywhere by stone. Here, too, Neuromans seemed to glide by with quiet efficiency; few other creatures were visible.

They were marched down the main corridor, up one flight of stairs, and down two more halls before being deposited, finally, in a large, bare room, where they were left alone with the only door shut and locked. D'Ursu Magna looked as if he was on the verge of smashing the door down with a single blow of his paw; Aba, seeing this inclination in the Bear's mind, shook his head no, half-pleading, half-parental.

"This is a fine welcome for visiting dignitaries," gruffed D'Ursu. He immediately lumbered over to a corner and urinated.

"Is this the way it was?" Aba asked Beauty. "When Lon was here?"

"I never saw the inside of the castle then," Beauty said, thinking back to that desperate time, "but the City outside is the same." He paused. "I never thought I would come back."

"Not through the front door, anyway, eh, Beauté Centauri?" laughed D'Ursu, scratching his back on the doorknob.

"Do you fear recognition?" asked Aba.

Beauty shook his head. "None saw me then; I was only in the river and tunnels. It is for Rose I fear, and Joshua. She was known here; and his spells are a constant threat to his safety."

"How will you find them?"

"As the King's emissaries, how else?" rasped D'Ursu. "They'll give us the run of the castle."

Aba looked dubious.

Beauty said quietly, "I memorized the room locations on those maps many years ago. If we can steal a little solitary time here, I think I know where to look."

"The keys to the stinking City, that's what they'll give us," D'Ursu assured them.

"Little use if we don't get the keys to this room," commented Aba.

There was the clicking of a latch and the door suddenly opened, knocking D'Ursu to the floor. In walked a stocky, powerful Neuroman covered with reptilian scales from head to foot. He pulled D'Ursu to his feet with a single easy motion, then stood facing the group.

"I am Ninjus," he said, his voice like a file over rusted iron. "I am chief of security. Please state your business."

"Multitudinous amenities to your Queen!" D'Ursu bowed with a trace of farce. "I am D'Ursu Magna, chief captain to Jarl, the Bear-King. These are my escorts, Beauté Centauri and Aba. Here is our paper." He handed Ninjus the rolled-up document he had kept tied deep in his fur since the outset. Ninjus broke the seal, opened the scroll, looked at it briefly, then sniffed it for a long time.

"Smelling is believing, eh?" chuckled D'Ursu. The paper had Jarl's scent all over it.

"All right," rasped Ninjus. "What do you want?"

"We wish to propose an alliance between your Queen and our King. In general terms, you would help us now in our fight against the stinking Doge, and we would help you collect his stinking Humans for your harems and experiments. We would have to discuss the specifics of our proposal with the Queen herself, of course."

"Of course," Ninjus said, more to himself than the others. Then, louder: "What is your fight about with the people of Venice?"

D'Ursu became less jovial. "The Doge is like the Ice: cold, blind, and without virtue."

"I see," said Ninjus. "Well, we'll have to discuss this at our council. You will be our welcome guests until a decision is made. Osi will show you to your rooms."

Before anything further could be said, he turned and left, and immediately a tall, dark, muscular Vampire entered. "I am Osi," said the Vampire. "You will please accompany me."

Two ramps and three corridors later they found themselves situated in a plush four-room suite—a bedroom for each of them, with connecting doors linking all three to a spacious, comfortable study.

Osi paused in the doorway before leaving them. "Please forgive the brisk reception you have experienced thus far. It's only that . . . we seldom receive visitors." He seemed to be looking more at Aba than the other two, even though D'Ursu was obviously the leader of the delegation.

Aba returned Osi's stare. The Sire had a commanding presence—nearly seven feet tall, bald head, violet eyes—and seemed to be in total control. Aba unconsciously bared his neck a few millimeters to the dominance of Osi's power; then replied to the Vampire host. "I assure you, as a humble guest, we intend to keep the lowest of profiles."

Osi bowed. "Honored guests, feel free to use this castle as if it were your own." Again, his look spoke to Aba.

D'Ursu yawned loudly. "At the moment, I am hungry." he said.

Osi replied to the Bear, though his eyes never left Aba. "All your needs will be seen to. Please ring the cords by your beds if you want for anything." He bowed again, and left.

When they were alone again, they sat in the study and discussed developments.

"Is it true?" Aba asked his Bear friend. "Your proposition?"

"No," whispered D'Ursu, "but much can be gained by the ruse, I think. The document, I put on Jarl's stump, just before he sat there, so his smell on it is strong. It was a good trick, I think." He beamed.

"What if they send someone to check the story?"

"It will take time to do so. In a few days we will know if Beauty's friends are here, and what the position of this Queen is on Jarl and the Doge."

"Unless we're still prisoners here," Aba cautioned. He walked to the door, tested the handle. It opened.

"What did I tell you, child. We are honored guests now."

"We had best not test that assumption yet. The longer we stay here free of suspicion, the freer rein they will give us."

"For the moment, I'm content to rest," agreed D'Ursu. "We would all do well to rest, we may yet have to fight our way out of here." He padded heavily into the middle bedroom and was soon asleep. The others quickly followed suit.

Aba awakened an hour later with the feeling he was being watched. He opened his eyes and looked down at the end of the bed. He was being watched.

Sitting there was a brace of Humans, a strong young man and woman, both naked save for the glittering jewels sewn into their skin.

"What do you want?" Aba asked.

"We're here for your sustenance and pleasure, Sire. We're from the harem of Sire Osi."

"No, no, please, I—"

"Please don't reject us, Sire. It would mean great shame if we returned without the mark of your tooth."

"But I don't want . . ." Aba felt himself caught in several binds. The most important, for him, was his own ongoing crisis of identity: he had to drink blood to live, usually Human blood—this was a genetic imperative—yet it was an activity he loathed, esthetically, morally, historically. He hated the suffering it brought, at the expense of his own unsuppressable thrill. The smell of Human blood simultaneously excited and tortured him. At those moments of exquisite delight when ecstatic life itself danced between his teeth, he was most shamed to be a member of his species. So he drank Human twice a week, when hunger forced him; the delicacy of his appetite a matter of will and discretion.

There were now other factors to be considered, as well. It would be a great insult to turn these prizes away—an insult to Osi as well as to the Humans. Osi was showing him honor by such a gift; to reject the gift was, for purely social reasons, unthinkable.

It was further complicated by the fact that these Humans were probably spies, with instructions to eavesdrop, watch, and remember everything Aba said, in his sleep, or surrounding moments of passion. To turn them away might mean he had something to hide—which he did.

And finally, there was the impalpable sense that Osi could be kind, even a friend, under other circumstances. Aba couldn't say why; he only knew he liked the older Vampire—without cause, but without serious cause for alarm either. He found himself wondering if Osi had been there when Lon died, if he could ask him about it at some point. Better to wait.

He looked at the two hopeful faces at the end of the bed.

"We're for complementary tastes," said the girl. "My blood is cool; my brother's, spicy." She bared her smooth, pale neck to him. There was not a mark on it—she hadn't been touched in weeks—and her silvery-blue jugular was plump with blood. Her brother leaned over and licked the spot on her throat where the jugular crossed the carotid artery, leaving that faintly pulsing bulge in her skin a little moist, a little glistening.

Aba wiped his lips between thumb and forefinger. "For my sustenance, perhaps," he whispered. "Though it gives me little pleasure. I'll drink some from each, that neither of you suffers in excess of the other."

The boy smiled tentatively and, like his sister, bared his neck to the helpless Vampire.

The next morning, D'Ursu mentioned that the thing he disliked most about cities was the absence of light and openness; so he was taken, the next day, on a tour of the sunrooms.

These were in the topmost turrets of the castle, without ceiling, with walls of glass. In the center of each room was an enormous green crystal—it looked like a many-faceted emerald ten feet in diameter.

D'Ursu was finally impressed. "I've never seen a jewel that big," he growled.

"It's not a jewel, actually," his guide told him. His guide was a Neuroman named Moira. She was polite and fastidious. "It's a solar collector—partly organic, with chlorophyll-based photovoltaics in a crystalline matrix. We'll be powering the whole city this way soon."

D'Ursu looked past the glittering green to the horizon. "You can see for miles up here," he said.

"We'll power all of it someday with these," said Moira proudly.

D'Ursu became irate. "Is that all you can say when you see that view? How good it will be to control it? Will you Humans never learn?"

"I am *not* Human," Moira replied archly.

"You sure act it." The Bear shook his head. "You're going to try to collect the sun with these things, eh?"

"We are, even as we stand here, so doing."

"But what's the point?" D'Ursu roared. "The sun is lovely where it is! I can walk to the stream and eat a fish and the sun will dry me nicely!"

"You needn't shout," Moira said cooly. "I don't see what your breakfast has to do with our energy supply."

"My breakfast *is* my energy supply!" he bellowed. "What more would I need? What more should anyone need?"

"We need much more." She nodded sincerely. "We have our experiments to consider—"

"What experiments?" he grumbled.

"Well . . . like this one, in solar collection, for example—"

"*Rowwwwrwwwr!*" D'Ursu growled imploringly to the sun through the green haze of the light-hoarding crystal, leaving Moira quite perplexed.

Osi entered his harem. The gifts had returned home. In the soft morning light, the tall Vampire examined the newly bruised necks of the siblings. "Well?" he said at length.

"He seems kind, this Sire Aba," began the girl.

"And quite complimentary to you, Sire," added the boy.

"How's that? How do you mean?" asked Osi.

"Well, he told us repeatedly what a noble master we must have, to look and behave as we do." The girl nodded.

"He did, did he?" Osi rubbed the boy's thigh.

"Did he not," the boy concurred.

"And as he slept," the girl went on, "he asked for more."

"So we gave him more, which woke him up." The boy smiled.

"But when he woke, he bade us stop, and save our marrow's blood for our 'thunder-eyed prince.' "

Osi raised his eyebrows. "Thunder-eyed prince?"

"So he called you, Sire."

"Go, then; *laissez-moi*," said Osi.

The two pale Humans stood, bowed, and left the room. Osi lay back on his couch.

He was intrigued by the mysterious young Sire. Imagine—a Vampire in the company of a Bear and a Centaur! How amusing. He seemed well bred—quite charming, really. "Thunder-eyed prince," indeed. Osi laughed.

He rang a crystal bell on the table. Presently a sultry woman entered, carrying a tray of early-morning cuisine.

"Breakfast so soon, Sire?" she smiled. Strands of pearls,

loosely wrapping her entire body, delicately clicked as she walked.

"Apéritif only, Vera," he mumbled.

She sat beside him, taking a decanter of golden liquid from the tray and pouring it into a thin glass. Then in a single movement, she pricked her ear lobe with a beautiful needle ring and tipped her head slightly away from Osi. He leaned over, licked the blood from her ear, then took a sip from the glass. He repeated this several times. When the glass was empty, he applied pressure to her ear lobe until the bleeding stopped, dismissed her, licked his fingers, and looked out the window. The rising sun caught his image in the glass at an angle, causing the transparent reflection of his violet eyes to glint as he turned. In his throat, softly, he made a sound like thunder.

It was going to be a beautiful day.

Beauty expressed an interest in the educational system provided for the inhabitants, hoping that, as one thing led to another, he would eventually be shown the research facilities, where Josh might now be. The guide, a Neuroman named Ondine, was impressed with Beauty's clear, pithy questions, and on the second morning showed him a day school for Vampire children.

There were four Vampire students: three boys and a girl ranging in age from six to sixteen. They sat in a small classroom, books open before them, as the teacher read aloud some passage. The teacher herself was a Vampire, about twenty months pregnant—which was almost full-term for a Vampire. She paused in her reading as Beauty and Ondine entered.

"Please continue," Ondine said to her. "We're here only to observe."

"We were just finishing," said the teacher, closing her book. The four young pupils stared at the Centaur and Neuroman intruders. "But we're on our way now to Gol's confirmation ceremony. You're welcome to watch if you like."

"Quite, quite," said Ondine. "Lead on."

"We must get ready first," said the teacher. "You go

ahead. It's to start in ten minutes, in the Temple. Class?" The students rose, and followed her out a side door.

Ondine smiled at Beauty. "This way," he said. He spoke as they walked around a long, spiral corridor that sloped gently upward. "We maintain a Vampire temple in the west wing, for just such functions. Of course, we'd like eventually to get away from these primitive rituals, but for the time being the confirmation ceremony helps the Vampire children maintain a sense of identity—cultural heritage, that sort of thing."

"We had racial customs among the Centauri," said Beauty, "but none religious, as such. We had no temples but the sky."

"Quite, quite," nodded Ondine. "I believe these Vampire species are rather older than the Centaurs, though, so their rites of passage tend to be more Human."

Beauty flinched at this reference to the genetic novelty of his species. His aloofness increased. "What is the nature of the service we are to witness?"

"The most ancient Vampire transition ritual, the Coming of Tooth. Every Vampire child performs the ceremony at the age of ten, when the last baby teeth are gone and the adult fangs begin coming in. It's quite a beautiful ritual, really— I think, sometimes, that what I miss most about being Neuroman are rites of passage like this. Ah, here we are . . ."

They came to an arched doorway and entered. Inside was a circular room, perhaps forty feet across, with an altar at one end and half-filled with pews. The four Vampire children stood at the altar, dressed in red robes. Several adults sat in the front row. Standing at the head of the altar was a large scarfaced Vampire in sacramental dress— Beauty was struck by the fact that he was neither clean nor pretty, like most members of his race, but instead rather vile, despite the splendiferous garments he wore. This was Ugo.

Beauty and Ondine stood at the back of the tabernacle, while Ondine continued in a whisper. "These Vampire children are the privileged ones, actually—being allowed to live and study in the castle. Generally, only Neuromans are allowed in here, you know."

Beauty wasn't sure whether this was meant as an insult or a compliment, though he felt certain it was directed at him. He simply said, "Quite."

Ondine went on. "They're being specially groomed, you see, to be the Queen's representatives in various Neuroman-animal affairs, as they develop in the New World. So they're given special training in these matters here—as well as being allowed to go on with their traditional Vampire teachings, of course."

"What does this New World training consist of?" Beauty asked. "Little is known of it in the northern provinces."

"That is not for me to say to an outsider. We have—"

One of the older Vampires in the front row—the pregnant instructor they had briefly spoken to earlier—turned in her seat and looked at them. "Sshhh," she said. Beauty and Ondine hushed. The ceremony began.

A fifth Vampire child entered by a door behind the altar. This was Gol, the ten-year-old boy. Naked, he was trying to repress a grin, which turned into a giggle at the sight of one of his little friends. He got a stern look from Ugo, though, and quickly became appropriately solemn.

He climbed onto a gold marble slab that formed the center of the altar, and lay down flat upon it. At this point Ugo and the four robed children commenced singing—a sequence of crescendoing high-frequency beeps that seemed to please the adults in the front row, but which only hurt Beauty's ears.

Finally the singing stopped. Ugo spoke some sonorous words, then bent over and placed his neck against the young boy's open mouth. The four other children chanted:

> Long of tooth
> Long of life
> Song of truth arise!
> Sing, little wing,
> Now in blood you are wise.

Ugo motioned to the girl Vampire—she appeared to Beauty to be about twelve—and she walked up to the marble altar. Ugo untied her robe, and it fell to the floor—whereupon she climbed onto the altar, mounted the little boy, and they began copulating.

Beauty was a bit shocked by this behavior, ritual or no. He had a strong sense of propriety, and Centaurs simply didn't do such things—not at that age or in public. Nobody else in the chapel seemed offended, though—they all watched with unabashed enjoyment, in fact—so Beauty swallowed his distaste and tried to avert his eyes. There was just no way he could avoid watching, though. The two children were fornicating rambunctiously, rolling all over the marble slab, their little wings fluttering, hips grinding. Still, with all that exuberance, it was over rather quickly, and they lay panting, half-fallen over one end of the stone.

Ugo lifted the girl back to the floor and tied her robe back on her. The boy got up and stood facing the others. There was more supersonic singing, during which a Human was carried in and bound down to the altar on his back.

Beauty tensed. His nostrils flared as he strained to see the face of the Human.

"What is it?" Ondine whispered to him.

"Nothing, I—just wanted a better view," Beauty whispered back. They got a cold look from the lady in the first row, and kept quiet again.

The singing stopped. Ugo stood beside the altar and said something to the Human, who turned his head wildly from side to side. Beauty relaxed a little now: he could see the man wasn't Joshua.

Suddenly Ugo plunged his razor-edged talons into the center of the Human's chest, and drew them haltingly down along the underside of the man's left fourth rib, opening his chest cavity like a ripe pod.

The man screamed and fainted, his breathing immediately becoming shallow. The children surrounded the altar. Ugo moaned in what looked to Beauty like an ecstasy of base desires, dipped his knobbly hand into the Human's chest, then raised it slowly, the dying man's still-beating heart pumping desperately in the Vampire's palm.

Blood foamed over the lip of the thoracic cavity, although

the heart still maintained connections to its major vessels. For some minutes, Ugo carried on what appeared to be a conversation with the valiantly contracting organ, then said a brief, reverent prayer, then bent down to take a large, ravenous bite from its meaty, pulsing apex. Blood rushed down his chin like a flood. The boy, Gol, took the next bite. Ugo and Gol took a succession of such mouthfuls, alternately, until they had eaten the entire heart. The bleeding stopped. No one moved. The ceremony was over.

Suddenly everyone was talking merrily—the children squealing and pushing, the adults congratulating and toasting, the confirmation boy, flushed and triumphant, wriggling from under his father's hand so he could sneak off to play with his friends.

The sacrificial Human lay pale and gutted and still.

Beauty exited quietly with Ondine by the back door.

"Rousing service, don't you think?" Ondine smiled paternally as they walked back down the hallway.

"Quite," Beauty replied. He tried to say more, but couldn't.

"Come in, Sire. Osi-Sire is expecting you."

The ancient liveried butler showed Aba into Osi's suite and had him sit in a great, overstuffed chair. Behind him, in an alcove, a young girl played the zither—a quiet, classical piece from the Orient. The lighting was amber, the time was evening. Osi glided in like a soft wind, draped in silks, smelling of perfume and tobacco and casein.

"Please, don't get up," he said touching Aba's shoulder, and lowered his massive body into the chair opposite. He was wiping a blue stain from his hands with a chamois. "You must excuse me—I've been painting."

"Oh? What kind?" Aba asked.

Osi shrugged. "Just dabbling. Oils, for the most part." He dropped the blue-stained rag on the floor.

"I'd like to see one."

"Would you? Well, yes, in a bit, that would be nice. Something to drink, first, I think." He rang a crystal bell that sat on the marble table beside his chair, and almost immediately a naked boy-servant entered, carrying a tray with two glasses. He handed each Vampire a goblet, picked the crumpled paint rag off the floor, and left.

Aba sniffed the aroma of his drink: blood, brandy, and cinnamon, with a twist of orange peel.

Osi raised his glass. "To vein-glorious life," he toasted.

"Vein-glorious life." Aba lifted his glass in return.

They drank.

They ate a light dinner—raw lamb marinated in hemolyzed red blood cells, stripped veins in a delicate marrow-and-serum sauce—then retired to the study, where Osi's half-finished painting still rested in its easel. The picture portrayed a female Human weeping over the limp body of a man who was exsanguinating from a gash in his neck, their faces clouded by the shadow of a Vampire wing.

Aba was impressed. "You have a sensitive palette," he commented.

"I'm not insensitive to the implications of my existence—to the contradictions inherent in being 'civilized.' "

"They're contradictions that can be diminished, I think, by a truly civilized Vampire."

"*Au contraire*," Osi wagged his finger. "The more highly developed one's civilization—one's sense of civilization—the more acute these contradictions become . . . must become."

"How so?"

"When all Humans are consigned to being either the Queen's experimental subjects or Sired harem slaves, we will enter the period of our highest degree of civilization—yet the Human pain I tried to embody in my painting will assume its most concentrated form. The contradictions are not only obvious, they are inevitable."

"Then perhaps we should celebrate them," Aba replied.

"You're being sarcastic, but I forgive you. Sarcasm is the first step toward real introspection."

"Ah, the end of an evening is in sight when philosophy degenerates into aphorism."

"If it's degeneracy you perceive, it is—more correctly, right now—due to intellect, sodomized by digestion."

Aba laughed, strolled to the window, let his vision linger in the starry night outside. "Tell me, what is this new world your Queen is trying to create?"

"A world of peace and achievement, nothing less," said Osi. His voice grew quiet with feeling. "All Humans placed either in harem or laboratory. All other animals kept in huge preserves where they can roam freely, without fear or constraint. The world culture a partnership between the clever, passionless Neuroman and the wise yet sensual Vampire. A model world, by all accounts."

"It has a certain allure," Aba maintained. "Yet it is, at inception, coercive."

"And what is not coercive, Aba-Sire? Does not the sun coerce the Nightowl into hiding? Are we not merely giving direction and purpose to the coercion that is Nature's hand?"

Aba turned and looked into Osi's compelling eyes, trying to plumb their depths. "It's all very well to philosophize great issues. It's moment to moment that I have trouble reconciling. Sating lusts I can't control, at the expense of lives I can't help but empathize with—"

"Sire Aba, you must never deny who you are. Accept your genetic imperative: Vampires need Humanoid blood to live. There is no shame in ecology. We're all integral parts of the carbon cycle."

"Natural cycles and nutritional requirements do not give free license. We should be creatures of reason, not compulsion."

"To be sure. Nonetheless, all creatures live because something else dies. This tension is the passion of life. For every Human that dies to your palate, a fish goes into a Human stomach. And how many leaves of clover die screaming every day to the sinister munchings of the Rabbits?"

"We all eat to live. Just so." Aba shrugged. "Perhaps my problem is that I commune too much with my supper."

Osi chuckled. "It is, finally, a question of identity. I know who I am. I know being a Vampire is neither good nor bad—it just *is*. There are good and bad Vampires, to be sure—*that* is a question for individual will and conscience. But once you're made that decision, you must delight in what you are—else what is the point in being?"

"And how to delight in the suffering we cause?"

"This isn't, of course, to say we shouldn't *sympathize* with the Human condition—though I would caution you never to forget: it was Humans made us. We are a product of their technology and their dreamwork. We're their creations. Well, they made their own bed, and by my blood, the Vampire need not assume a drop of guilt for that." His voice rose toward the end, imbued with feeling. The outburst embarrassed him, though, and he sipped at his drink to quiet himself.

Aba felt Osi's chagrin, and kept silent a moment to give the air time to recompose itself. Looking out the window again, he said softly, "It's the strength of my lust I can't abide."

"Rejoice in your lusts, Sire. They are your destiny."

Aba tapped his temple with the long nail of his index finger. "*This* is my destiny," he smiled, more rueful than triumphant.

Osi's gaze fell on the almost suede softness of his young guest's wings. Impulsively, he reached out and touched the warm, downy leather along the shaft of Aba's tall, main strut, then withdrew his hand quickly, as if caught in the act.

Aba smiled uncertainly. He took two slow steps in the general direction of the door.

Osi rang a silver bell near the easel. "There, I've been rattling on too much. If you leave now, I shall feel quite humiliated."

"No, please, I must leave, really. It's very late, I think."

A harem girl entered, naked except for the hundred emeralds and single diamond sewn, in fluid design, into her skin. She knelt between them, her neck bared. Osi said to Aba: "Won't you stay a little longer? Just for a nightcap."

Aba licked his teeth. "No. Thank you. You've been most gracious, Osi-Sire." He averted his eyes.

"Well, then, the pleasure has been mine. Go in good blood."

"Go in good blood, Osi-Sire."

They bared their necks to each other, and Aba left.

Osi stood leaning against the closed door. His hand trembled slightly. "Who is this pretty Sire that makes me hold my breath?" he whispered.

The harem girl crept forward and wrapped herself around Osi's leg. "Would that I could hold it for you, Sire, to leave your hands free to pursue other matters."

He stroked her head. "He is not unconscious of me—yet how cool he remained. I confess, Denise, I am quite taken."

Denise pulled herself up and opened the Vampire's robes. "Then stand erect where you are, Osi-Sire, and you'll soon be twice-taken."

He closed his eyes to her caress as, across his field of vision, the fluttering of soft leather wings turned the velvet blackness red.

CHAPTER 11

In Which There Are Two Daring Escapes

OLLIE sat in the dark corner of a Bookery cave, teasing melancholy strains from his bamboo flute.

Jasmine sat twenty feet away, alone beside a small fire. She brooded.

Addie crouched at a low table near one entrance, setting the record. In the next room, Michael and Ellen nattered at each other about some obscure footnote in a recently unearthed, revised edition. All the other Books were either in conference or out scouting; or scribbling in the Great Lexicon; or tending the Bookery winery on the first level; or sleeping, or reading, or eating.

Jasmine brooded over the fact that she couldn't find a way out of this morass. There was so much internecine bickering among the Books and Pluggers that she couldn't rely on them for anything. They had been waiting two days now for the Pluggers to make a decision, and as far as Jasmine was concerned, it might have been two years. Furthermore, she had little hope of finding the connecting tunnel without help, and the news of electric screens covering all the other openings was particularly frustrating. Josh was in the castle, Paula had said. Every hour brought him closer to Final Decontamination.

It was the caves. Jasmine didn't know exactly how, but she felt them: sinister, suffocating, miring. Evil, almost. As if, in their endless, shadowed inturnings, the tunnels had devised a power for stifling lesser wills, smothering all hope. She felt it almost as an external consciousness, engulfing—or, perhaps, seducing—them.

She looked at Ollie, absorbed in his somber melody. His

feelings were too distorted for her to analyze, his mask too thick.

Footsteps approached from another entrance. A shadow jumped, then lay still between Jasmine and the fire. She looked up at the figure who stood before her.

"Rose," she whispered.

"Hello, Jasmine," said Rose.

In the corner, the music stopped. Ollie stood, dropping his flute, with a clatter, onto the stone. He ran over, paused; and for a long second, they looked into each other's eyes. Then they fell together in a powerful embrace that took away their breaths and held at bay their demons. They had been prisoners together five years before, herded south by Vampires and Accidents, tortured, humiliated, and intimidated. This was a bond of fire that would never break.

When finally they pulled apart, they were weak with cumulative tension. Jasmine stood, and also hugged Rose, somewhat less desperately.

"Rose," Jasmine said again.

"Yes, it's good to see you, too," she answered.

"Tell us what's happened." Jasmine's voice was tender.

All three sat before the fire. "I'm a Plugger now," Rose began. "Nine prongs. I pulled the cap off my outlet back in the Saddlebacks, so I can receive again now."

"Receive what?" Ollie asked. So many emotions skittered through the boy's heart, he was near collapse. Joy at seeing Rose, who had helped him so much to endure their first ordeal together; fear at her tone; hope and despair about Joshua's plight; rage at such a world—

"I could never explain to any of you what it was like, what it felt to be . . . plugged in. How I hate that expression. Plugging is like being something else, it's like . . . stepping up another level."

"But—receive what?" Ollie repeated.

"Maybe if you just told us how you got here . . ." Jasmine suggested. She, too, picked up something in the tone of Rose's voice that was different, edgy.

"Why, I walked," Rose said, a bit surprised. "Blackwind showed me the way."

"And Josh? What of Josh?"

Rose looked down before answering. "I showed *him* the way." She shuddered imperceptibly, trying to hold all the loose ends of her life in one hand. "It's so good to see you again," she looked from one to the other. "I'm so glad you're here."

"Does Beauty know you're here?" Jasmine asked.

Rose squeezed away the brief but searing pain with a long blink of the eye. "Beauty will come. He'll know where I've gone."

"You didn't tell him."

"He would have talked me out of it."

"What about Josh?" Ollie intruded. "Where's Josh?"

"Josh listened to me, but he couldn't understand. I told him everything, but it's not something you can explain. So I took off his helmet while he slept."

Ollie sank like a deflated toy. "You took it."

"I knew that without that helmet to protect him from the Queen's transmissions, he'd begin having spells again. Remember: it was I who fashioned that helmet for Josh in the first place, I who realized the wire screen would shield him from the Queen's call. Mine to give, and mine to take back."

"But why? What did you gain?"

"I knew that without the helmet, he would have his spells, he would be drawn to the City. There they will operate on him, and he, too, will get plugged in. He'll have the experience I had, he'll understand, he'll . . . then we'll free him, and we'll get control of the cables and connections, and then we can plug in to each other, and be one, or two, or light, or lightless, or . . ."

Jasmine and Ollie looked at her as if she had gone over the edge. Rose stopped, laughed a short desperate laugh. "That's why we're here," she said breathily, "to get our connections back, and Josh, too—to get him back, he's The Serpent, you know, and now he'll be a Plugger too, so we can all have communion with The Serpent, we can—"

"What are you talking about?" yelled Ollie. The outburst stopped her as hard as if he had hit her. Even Addie looked up briefly from her writing in the corner, then returned to it. "This is Josh you're talking about, not some cult myth!" His voice crescendoed. "What are you talking about?"

Tears filled Rose's eyes, and she pulled back, shivering. "You don't understand," she muttered. "Even I don't understand." Her tears overflowed.

Truly, she didn't understand. She had gone to Josh in the mountains to try to explain it, but she couldn't, even to him. And she had always been able to explain everything to him. And then, when he didn't understand, she began having all sorts of strange thoughts and feelings—feelings she had never been aware of having before but which nonetheless seemed to be part of her. Compulsive feelings, almost obsessions: Josh *must* come to the castle, he *must* meld with the Queen, Rose *must* get him there whatever way possible. She felt these things absolutely; yet another part of her knew that these thoughts, though now part of her own brain, belonged to the Queen—the Queen's sensibilities and ideas, stored in Rose's brain during the period in which they were joined by cable; information now fragmented by time and neuronal degeneration and Rose's own internal circuitry.

So Rose was a jumble now. Her skull encased not only her own sweet mind but bits and pieces of the Queen's, not to mention shards of how many other Pluggers with whom she had been in-circuit in the castle. This was what Rose was, and this was what she felt—A harmony of selves sometimes; more usually a cacophony. She struggled for a unity of expression that never came any more, though sorely she strived—except, in one thing did she feel single-mindedly unconflicted: in her driving, craving need for the Plug.

If it was the Queen in her that had taken Joshua's helmet, it was the Rose in her that tried to explain the complexity of her psyche to Jasmine and Ollie; tried, but could not.

Yet Jasmine sensed the twisting of Rose's spirit, the darkness looking for light. Jasmine had a fine, intuitive sensitivity, and she hadn't lived over three hundred years without learning a thing or two; and what she was thinking now was that Rose looked like a person whose mask had cracked; and who was desperately trying to hide the fact that several of the faces that lurked behind it were not pretty; and who was trying to plug the crack before these faces poured out into the world. Jasmine called this torment *Face Pressure*, and felt great tenderness for any who suffered its pain.

Ollie did not feel so tenderly. "Rose, you sound crazy," he fumed.

Rose squeezed her eyes closed.

To keep the mask from bursting open, Jasmine thought. "Rose," she began, extending her hand.

Rose pulled away. "My name is Windlight," she hissed, and ran into the darkness.

Beauty shook his head. "They are not here. At least, I cannot find them."

"Do you think you've looked everywhere?" asked Aba.

"He's had a week," growled D'Ursu. "He's looked everywhere twice. And now they won't *let* us leave. Stinking city."

"They'll let us soon enough," Aba said, trying to calm the Bear. "I've been talking to Sire Osi—"

"On several occasions." Beauty spoke in a monotone.

Aba was somewhat taken aback by the Centaur's manner. "And what of that?" he asked politely.

Beauty began to tense. "The way you carry on with that Sire, knowing he is one of the chief architects of these vile Human experiments, is enough to—"

"Who said he was a chief architect?"

"It is said."

"Then how better to learn what the place is about?" Aba was angered by Beauty's supercilious tone.

"By looking in the architect's cellar, perhaps."

"I find cellars beneath me."

They glared at each other a moment; then Aba relented. "Beauty, don't look to blame me for your dead ends here. I came to help you find your people, and perhaps part of my past. We've found neither, so far—you needn't grudge me because I find Osi's company interesting. He's a complex

Sire, he is light and dark, and I learn from him. So let it rest, and we'll make our peace, you and I. Otherwise, I cannot help you further."

Beauty listened in silence, then hung his head. "I apologize, Aba. You have reason. I . . . am distracted by our confinement here, and by our lack of success. And in my unbalance, I clutch at those who look more steady. Forgive me."

"There's nothing to forgive. We all seek clarity."

Beauty finally relaxed into a smile. "When I was young, everything was clear. Now I am older, my clarity has matured into confusion and uncertainty."

Aba laughed. "Perhaps when you're very old, you'll have evolved to the view that breathing is a cause for dilemma—and then you'll die, your maturation complete."

"Then I am wise before my time, for eating already perplexes me." He put his arm around Aba's shoulder. "But not so wise as you, who can confound my despair by joking of my death."

"You can joke of death," D'Ursu spat. "I've seen enough here."

"As have I, unfortunately," Beauty sighed. He feared Joshua was lost to time; and Rose, dear Rose. He knew he wasn't responsible for the loss of his two greatest friends—yet his sorrow was so deep, it felt like guilt, which is, of course, the most deeply buried emotion. He almost hoped he would be held in the City forever, as a prisoner, that he might keep his vigil for his lost friends indefinitely. He didn't know what else to do.

"I've seen enough, too, I suppose," Aba agreed. He, too, had a profound feeling of dissatisfaction about his inquiries. No one he had spoken to had ever heard of Lon—though he had had to keep his questions discreet, and some people he still hadn't asked at all. "I only wish I'd seen the Queen herself," he said.

Beauty smiled. "I wish I'd never heard of her."

Isis sat regally in the Queen's lap and allowed herself to be stroked as she thought of other things.

She had been smelling Beauty for several days now and

had expected, along with that smell, Joshua's scent to blossom full for her to follow. But Joshua's scent remained stronger here on the Queen than anywhere else; so here she stayed.

Still, she thought, the Centaur might know where Josh had gotten to. They had been pretty close once, Isis remembered—Josh and Beauty. Not as close, of course, as Josh and Isis; but still, Beauty might know something.

She remembered liking Beauty, more or less. He was a bit pompous, she thought; apt to make pronouncements, prone to believe they came from a higher authority. But overall, a good sort. Loyal. Self-sufficient. Clean. And Josh liked him.

So maybe she would go see him now, in any case. Even if he didn't know where Josh was, he would be more fun than this boring Queen, with her unsubtle fingers and endless chatter.

She jumped precipitously from the Queen's lap.

"Oh," the Queen said—rather stupidly, Isis thought— "Through being petted, are you?"

Brilliant, thought Isis, and padded out the door without hurry or hesitation.

She ambled down a curving corridor, then up a gentle ramp to a stairwell. She stood beside the door patiently, until someone opened it, then walked through in a manner both stately and matter-of-fact, as if the door had been opened expressly for her. She trotted down two flights of steps, then slithered through another door just as it was closing, and raced along the hall like the wind, just for fun.

When she got to the door that was strong with Beauty's odor, she sat down, licked her paw, drew it over her ear and across the back of her head. Repeating this motion several times, she stopped just long enough to scratch a few times at the crack where the door met the jamb, then quickly went back to assiduously cleaning her head.

Beauty looked up. "What was that?" he said.

"I didn't hear anything," grumbled D'Ursu, half-asleep in the corner.

"Something scratching at the door, it sounded like."

He walked quietly over and pulled open the door. No one there—until he looked down.

"Isis," he gasped. He had been certain she died in the tunnels years before.

"*Mrow*," she purred, arching her back, going up on her toes and walking slowly against his leg.

"Isis!" he repeated, as if trying to convince himself. He picked her up in disbelief, stared at her a few long seconds with growing joy, then brought her to his chest, hugged her, stroked her, scratched her ears, jostled her.

She bore this display quite patiently for five or six seconds, then pushed off Beauty's chest, out of his gentle grip, and onto the floor, where she began sniffing seriously at a dust ball.

Beauty laughed. "So you are alive."

"Surrre," she answered, a little put off by his surprise.

Suddenly another thought came to him. "Joshua! You know where Joshua is!"

She looked disappointed. "Nooo. You?"

"No," he shook his head. "I hoped you might have."

"He was herrre," she nodded. "Not nowww."

Beauty's stomach jumped. "He was here? When? Where is he now?"

"Don' knowww." She brought her left hind paw up to her chin and scratched frantically ten times.

"Well, is he coming back?"

The little Cat shrugged. "I'll be herrre."

Beauty caught his balance, smiled slowly, and picked Isis up once more, cradling her to his chest. She hung limply in his grip this time, purring. "Anyway," said the Centaur, "it is good to see you again."

She licked her shoulder twice, then fell asleep in his hands.

After their meeting with Rose, Jasmine and Ollie came to the same conclusion: they had to act quickly if they were ever going to save Josh. They slipped unobtrusively into a dark side tunnel and began discussing specific plans of attack for that night. Within minutes, though, Blackwind appeared before them.

"What do you want?" Ollie demanded quietly. His words had the sound of a poised blade.

"I heard you," Blackwind whispered. The air tightened. "I want to go with you."

"Impossible."

"I can show you Tunnel Twenty-two," he promised slyly. "It's the only safe way in."

They all paused.

"Why," said Jasmine.

"The Serpent . . ." he almost hissed the word. "We must bring him down here . . . he won't know where we are . . . we have his Windlight . . . he has our future . . ." His voice trickled off, at the end, into vision.

Jasmine and Ollie looked at each other in tentative agreement. The zealot couldn't be trusted, but he might be used.

Unconsciously, Jasmine looked over her shoulder—expecting the caves to thunder a denial of such precipitous action. But their silence was even more ominous, as if protest were unnecessary.

Jasmine was awakened by a slight pressure on her arm. She opened her eyes in the darkness. Beside her crouched Blackwind.

"Come," he whispered.

She rose silently and immediately, and saw that Ollie already stood near the Plugger. They exchanged looks, but no words.

Like wraiths, the three scurried across the cave floor, Blackwind in the lead. He took them down tunnels, up shafts, through crevices. Twice they had to swim under water, once for an extended period. Once they crouched in a damp hollow for ten minutes to avoid being seen by a small band of Pluggers, before slipping furtively into a hole in the rock.

From this point they followed a series of descending corridors until they stopped, finally, in a shallow stream at the mouth of a large tunnel that ran knee-deep with fast water. The tunnel opening was covered with a wire screen, which Blackwind easily pushed aside, allowing them all to pass. A light bulb hanging from the stone ceiling glowed. Blackwind faced the others and whispered his raspy whisper.

"This is Tunnel Twenty-two. This way lies Queen and Serpent." He nodded once, and stepped upriver into the main tunnel. Ollie and Jasmine followed closely.

At each successive tunnel crossing, they turned at the crossing branch; left, then right, left, right. Each intersection was lighted by a dim bulb, each shaft marked by a scrawl of numbers or letters. A rush of memories flooded Jasmine and Ollie, full of undercurrents threatening to suck them into the past. But they pushed on. Silently, they counted off each turn.

Beyond the decussation of the tenth branching, the water became much deeper, so that they had to wade chest-deep against the current. It was slow going. At the eighteenth turn, it shallowed again, though, and they paused to rest. It was there Jasmine first heard the noises.

Ollie heard them too, and looked around. "Minotaur?" he murmured.

Jasmine shook her head. "Smaller than that. Blackwind, what are the Queen's Tunnel Guards composed of now?"

"Minotaurs, mostly," he nodded. "Some Lizards, some Gators, some Ghouls."

"Ghouls," echoed Ollie.

The sounds splashed to a halt down some nether tunnel. Only the engulfing burble of the running water remained.

"Move on." Jasmine spoke low. "But make no sound."

They walked slowly to avoid making noise. The nineteenth and twentieth turns took as long to reach as had the prior five. In addition, some of the light bulbs were out in that area, making the shadows darker, the echoes louder. They stood flat against a slippery wall, waiting. The skitterings that haunted them came closer. They separated, crouched, drew weapons. From the near tunnel a form emerged. Ollie coiled to pounce.

"I've come to join you," said the figure as it stepped into the half-light. It was Starcore.

Ollie relaxed. Jasmine stood up, angry. "You might've been killed, following us like that."

"I heard you sneaking off, and I wanted to help. I agree

with what you're doing," the Plugger leader whispered. "I can't ask the others to go, but something must be done." He smiled timidly at Blackwind, and they made the Sign of the Plug, both flushed with the first dim glimmers of hope.

"Come on, then," said Jasmine, and moved forward.

Before she had taken a step, a massive shape knocked her over and mashed Starcore into the rock. It was a Dragon's tail. Twenty feet of it had been half-submerged beside them, but now the sleeping lizard, disturbed from slumber, slithered up its tunnel and was gone. Only Starcore was left in the tail's wake, his chest crushed.

Blackwind shivered, unable to take his eyes away.

Jasmine shook her head. "This is a bad beginning."

"Let's go," said Ollie. He had to pull at Blackwind to get the Plugger to show them the way.

Soon they had gone the full twenty-two tunnels and stood at the base of a narrow vertical shaft.

"This is it," whispered Blackwind. "The chute we all came down, out of the Communion Room." He licked his lips with a dry tongue.

"Will there be guards up there?" Jasmine wanted to know.

"There never were. The Queen felt the presence of others would destroy the harmony of Communion. There was rarely anybody in this wing, except when needed." He suddenly trembled all over and sat down hard in the water. "Starcore . . ." he rasped.

Jasmine propped him up against a wall, patted his forehead with cool water. "Take it easy," she said. "It wasn't pretty, but it was too fast for it to have been painful."

Ollie looked impatient. "Let's go. Leave him here—he can guide us back."

"No, no," Blackwind protested, "I want to go up. I can go." On wobbly legs, he stood. Jasmine steadied him. "I'm fine," he said. "I'll go first, I know the way."

He pushed her back and glanced with not a little triumph at Ollie. Slowly, he put his foot on the first rung of the shaft and began the vertical climb. Jasmine waited thirty seconds, then began to follow, but hadn't pulled herself ten rungs up before Blackwind ran into her coming down again. They both dropped down to the main tunnel, where Ollie waited.

"What?" Ollie demanded.

"As I feared," Blackwind's breath came rapidly. "An electrified grid across the chute halfway up. Strong enough to knock a man out, or almost."

"You have tools to cut it?" Ollie looked at Jasmine.

"Yes, but there might be an alarm system to detect breaks in the circuit. Is there another way?"

"As far as we know, all conduits leading anywhere have the electric grids—except Tunnel Twenty-two."

"What's that?" Ollie pointed fifty feet up the tunnel to the next vertical shaft. Something could be seen hanging out the bottom, an irregular shape clicking against the stone. They walked up to it with care.

It was a broken mesh grid, dangling down the end of the shaft by a few remaining strands of wire that trailed back up the tube to where the grid had been connected.

"Looks like it fell out of this one," Blackwind said quietly.

"Looks like it was torn out," commented Jasmine. "In any case, this looks like the shaft with the access. Let's go."

Blackwind held her arm. "This one leads to the Queen's Chambers." He spoke with reverence and fear.

"Will she see us come up?" Jasmine asked.

"I—I don't know. She'll be alone, unless she's holding audience, which is rare."

"Can we rush her?" Ollie asked.

"The Queen!" Blackwind couldn't comprehend it.

"If we can sneak past her, so much the better," Jasmine advised. "We have other things to do right now."

Ollie agreed.

"Can you take us directly into the Communion Room from up there?" Jasmine looked above them.

Blackwind nodded uncertainly. His face was darker than ever, but with a thin-lipped smile he climbed around the hanging screen and up the chute. Jasmine and Ollie quickly followed.

It was a long climb. Fifty yards up, they found the shelf

from which the broken grid hung and gingerly hoisted themselves over it. Fifty yards beyond that, Blackwind stealthily raised his head over the top lip of the shaft that rose out of the floor as the refuse bin in the Queen's chamber. Jasmine and Ollie held the rungs inside the shaft just below him.

With a strange mixture of cunning and awe, Blackwind looked around the darkened room until his gaze fell upon the sleeping Queen forty feet away. And there his gaze froze.

He had never seen his Queen before. His brain had been plugged into hers, his being as one with hers, but he had never seen her. He stared at the shadowy form as if this were God herself. God and the Devil. It made him tremble.

The Queen never truly slept, of course—as Blackwind well knew—but her attention was now directed inward, so she was unaware of his half-hidden presence. Gently he lifted himself over the edge of the bin and dropped to the floor without a sound. Immediately the other two followed him.

For a long moment, they all stared intently at the Queen to see if they had wakened her clouded, shrouded being. Then, in single file, like ghosts they tiptoed ten paces to the side door and exited.

They found themselves in the Communion Room: row upon row of Humans, lying in dense quasi coma, black cables trailing from their heads. Jasmine and Ollie stared, incredulous, powerless to move, mesmerized by this vision. Blackwind couldn't contain himself.

He gazed, weeping, at his comrades-in-circuit. He fell to his knees, distractedly pulling tufts of hair from his head. He gulped air between sobs. He fell forward into the electrified screen that separated the corridor in which they stood from the rest of the room. There was a brief buzzing of electricity before Jasmine kicked him off the wires, unconscious.

She checked his pulse. "Alive and well." They pulled him into a dark corner.

"Leave him here," whispered Ollie.

Jasmine nodded. She pointed her head toward the room of wired bodies. "He's not there." Meaning Josh.

Ollie nodded, then inclined his head toward the next door. They moved into the next room.

They quickly went through *Limbo* and *Nirvana*—the first consisting of Humans, encased in glass boxes, in a state of diminished metabolism; the second, similar, except that the Humans were without brains. The brains were revealed to them in a third room, a room of bottles and shelves. But nowhere, Joshua.

The next room was a large lab. It offered no clues to anything, but Jasmine stocked up on numerous items she thought might be of use at some future date: syringes, wires, batteries, an all-purpose biokit that included microtome, wax, lenses, forceps, autoincubator, culture tubes, agar patches, scalpels, transistors, plugs and cables, copper tubing. All this she stuffed into her secret abdominal compartment, then reclosed it with a snap. Ollie, meanwhile, was trying other doors, other rooms. And still, no Joshua.

At length, he returned. "I've found the Human Quarters," he whispered.

Two doors, two halls, another door. He opened it a crack, and Jasmine looked inside. Cages, floor to ceiling; Humans filling every cage. Twenty feet away, in the center of the room, sat two Neuromans and two Vampires. One Neuroman dozed; his three cohorts rolled bones. Ollie shut the door again.

"Fast and straight," he said.

She thought a moment. "All right. I can't think of a better way."

They opened the door and were two steps into the room before the nearest Vampire looked up. Ollie raced at the creatures as they stood, off-balance, their wings half-furled. With a syringe in her hand, Jasmine ran toward the startled Neuroman.

With unbelievable speed, Ollie was on the Vampires. In passing, he slit one's throat. This gave the other one time to come alert, though, and in a moment, he and Ollie were locked in a death grip—Ollie's knife in the Vampire's side,

the Vampire's teeth in Ollie's neck. In two seconds the air
reeked with bloody vapor.

Isis snapped her head up out of a deep sleep, ears twitching, pupils wide, nares flared. Joshua? No, but close. Like
Joshua. Kin, perhaps. She jumped out of the curl of Beauty's belly and stretched.

Her neck hairs were on end as she slipped out the door
Beauty had left open for her. She smelled excitement. Out
in the darkened corridor she put her nose up and sniffed
the air for several seconds, then turned left and began
briskly walking in the direction of the smell.

So, more of Joshua. First his own smell, his very smell,
on the boring Queen. Then the appearance of the old comrade, the Centaur. Now this brother smell—and it was a
blood smell. It was bringing her closer to Josh, she just
knew it. Soon they would be together again, and he would
love her and take care of her, as she would him.

The blood smell grew stronger. She ran, Cat-fast, up the
next stairway.

Jasmine and Ollie sat on the floor, back to back, recovering
their energies. Strewn beside them, two dead Vampires lay,
thick with new blood; and beyond them, two dead Neuromans. Jasmine had killed them—the last one with Ollie's
assistance—by flipping open the Hemolube valves on the
back of their heads, and injecting 50 cc of air into the
valve spiggot with a syringe she had just stolen from the
lab.

Jasmine was unhurt. Ollie was bleeding, slowly now,
from the neck and arm. They looked at the hundreds of
Humans who stared at them from the cages along the
walls. Gaunt, scared, hollow, the prisoners gazed from the
squalor of their cells like repressed nightmares. Ollie
couldn't look at them long. They reminded him too much
of himself.

Jasmine looked them over, grim and hard; Josh wasn't
among them.

She searched the bodies of the guards but couldn't find

keys to the cells anywhere. Some of the prisoners stuck their arms through the bars; none of them spoke.

"We haven't much time left," said Jasmine. "We're sure to be—"

"We have to find Josh."

"I don't think he's here, Ollie. I think we should leave. We can make a new plan later."

He looked at her bitterly: it was good to kill Vampires, but he still needed to find his brother. They ran into the hall, closed the door behind them, and sidled around toward their point of origin.

They made it back to the labs without incident. Not until they were almost to the Communion Room did they hear the Vampire patrol.

"Somewhere in Q Sector," came one burly voice in the adjacent hallway. "Electrical discharge."

"Probably a short circuit," said another.

"Or a lost sewer Rat."

Ollie looked at Jasmine. "They're heading toward Communion," he whispered.

"Blackwind," she said.

They quickened their step. The door to the Communion Room was ajar, and through it they could see a squad of four Vampires and two Neuromans just discovering Blackwind's still-unconscious body. Ollie whispered to Jasmine, "You must escape. To bring help."

She nodded. Before she could say another word, he leapt into the room. He killed two Vampires before anyone knew what was happening. Jasmine was right behind him, breaking the head valve on the nearest Neuroman.

The commotion woke up Blackwind. With a shudder, he threw his arms around the knees of the other Neuroman, and began wailing: "Plug me, I beg of you." He cried openly, tangling himself in almost everyone's feet.

Ollie was in a clinch with one Vampire, while the other was beating him from behind. He was beginning to sink. Jasmine finally killed her opponent, but saw the other Neuroman was dragging Blackwind off into another room.

Jasmine saw Ollie go down. But she couldn't let Blackwind be taken alive: they had only to plug his brain into the Queen's to gain total access to all the information stored there—the location of Tunnel Twenty-two, the location of the Bookery and the Pluggers, all their plans and secrets. She couldn't let that knowledge into these hands.

She pointed her finger at the Neuroman and triggered the small napalm flare inside it. The flame danced across the room and ignited the plastic skin of the Neuroman guard, who dropped Blackwind to the floor. Jasmine swung her hand around and pointed what was left of the flare at the Vampires throttling Ollie. The fire drove one back but made the other one only madder.

Jasmine slung the swooning Blackwind over her shoulder, ran through the Queen's door and shut it behind her. The noise aroused the Queen, fifty feet away.

"What is that?" mumbled the disoriented monarch.

Jasmine ignored her and ran to the bin. Balancing Blackwind precariously, she climbed over the lip and began the long descent down the shaft. Just as she reached bottom, the guards began throwing things down at her from above.

In the Communion Room, two Vampires held Ollie to the wall, while a third beat and bit him.

In a corner crouched Isis, watching, invisible as a shadow on the dark side of time.

Beauty awoke with the dawning sun in his eyes and Isis's tongue on his cheek.

"Good morning, small Cat. And what is our lot today?"

"Ollie herrre."

Beauty squinted awake, sat up. "What do you mean? Ollie is here? In the castle?"

The Cat nodded.

"Since when?" the Centaur pressed. "You know where he is?"

"Caught last night, sneaking innn. Caught harrrd."

Beauty brought his head down to Cat-level. "Where is he now, Isis? Where are they keeping him?"

Isis shrugged. "Joshua still not herrre."

She rubbed her side against his beard. He scratched her neck, but his thoughts were elsewhere.

Suddenly Aba came in through the connecting door, from his bedroom. "Good luck," he said with a smile. "They're letting us leave today."

Beauty looked at him. "Now we must stay." He looked past the young Vampire, into the near future.

Jasmine sat on the stone floor of the cave, surrounded by a few Books and a crowd of Pluggers. Blackwind lay beside her. He was dying.

Glass thrown from above had pierced his belly just before he cleared the shaft. The wound wouldn't stop bleeding. By the time Jasmine got him back to camp, he had lost too much blood, and too much heart.

Jasmine was finishing her story: telling the others the tale of the adventure, what they had gained and what they had lost. The assembled listened in rapt silence, their fingers meshed in Plug-sign. When she was done, no one spoke for several minutes, digesting the implications.

Finally, Candlefire shook his head sadly. "So much suffering. Starcore dead, and Blackwind dying before our eyes. Was it worth all that? What have we to show for it?"

Jasmine, still numb from the effort and the pain, stared into the fire that warmed them. These people seemed to have no will to act—or perhaps too many wills, so that action was suffocated by the fits and starts of a million indecisions. The caves. Slowly, she opened and reached into her abdominal cavity, extracting the cables and plugs she had stolen from the lab. "This, for one thing."

There was a collective gasp from the Pluggers. Candlefire took the connectors from her as if they were sacred artifacts. Blackwind sensed something of the kind and, with great effort, opened his eyes. When he saw the cables in Candlefire's hands, he reached out with trembling fingers. "Plug me," he whispered.

Candlefire sorted through the tangle and found a cable with plugs at both ends having the right number of prongs. Gently, he lifted Blackwind's head and plugged one end of the cable into the occipital socket. Then he lay down beside Blackwind and plugged the other end of the cable into his own head. For many minutes they lay there, side by side, unconscious to the world, barely breathing, surrounded by an audience in awe. Then, in a single moment, Blackwind sighed, Candlefire opened his mouth in a grimace of pain or ecstasy, and it was over.

Candlefire sat up and pulled the plug from his head. "It's over," he said to the group. "He's dead."

Rose sat beside Jasmine and put her arms around the Neuroman. "We'll have to think about this," she said. "But I'm glad you're safe." She felt close to Jasmine once more. Partly because Jasmine was now her last link to the past, a past as fondly remembered as a childhood before some great loss of innocence; partly because she knew Jasmine was trying to understand her plight as a Plugger—the Neuroman was attempting to reach out across the chasm that had come between them: the breach was too wide, yet Rose still felt touched. She hugged Jasmine again and whispered, "Forgive me."

Again, Jasmine saw the pain and confusion in her old friend; but she had already given so much that, at the moment, she had nothing left to give. She merely let herself be embraced, and nodded tiredly. Finally she stood, and spoke. "I'm going to the other side now. To tell the Books." She walked over to the few Books who had been present. "Come on," she said.

Rose accompanied them to the door. "We have cables now," she wept, dumbfounded. "You gave us cables."

"But now Ollie is trapped again, and Josh is still missing. I think it was a bad trade."

"You think this will work?" growled D'Ursu.

"Yes," said Beauty, with more conviction than he felt. Then, to Aba: "I am not proud of exploiting your friendship with this Vampire."

Aba waved it aside. "To save a Human life is a rare privilege."

Beauty bared his neck to the Vampire, and Aba bowed low.

D'Ursu grumbled, "I would save a hundred Humans if I could leave this stinking city."

Aba smiled nervously and left, walking elegantly toward Osi's suite.

"Tell Sire Osi it is Sire Aba," said Aba, standing at the door.

The old manservant waved him in. "Yes, Sire. On my Blood, he will be pleased."

Aba stepped in, and the old man closed the door. "This way, Sire."

Aba followed him into the study and sat down, while the old servant went to get his master. The painting on the easel was almost finished now: the anguish in the weeping woman's face was almost palpable; the blood on the dying man's neck, almost wet; the shadow of the Vampire's beating wing, almost audible. Osi walked in, sipping a Bloody Mary.

"Good morning, Sire Aba. Can I offer you anything?"

"Thank you Osi-Sire, no. I've just been told we are to leave within the hour. Without audience."

"So I have been told."

"I wish . . . to say good-bye. To you."

"I have enjoyed our conversations a great deal. It pains me to see you go. These Neuromans are bloodless company."

"But we will see each other again, we—"

"Lie to me not."

"Hope is not a lie."

"Hope is a passionate lie. And its greatest evil is that it occasionally comes true."

"Then think of me as the passionate liar I am." Aba spoke in secret warning.

Osi replied, "Then go in good blood, friend."

There was an awkward silence for several moments, until Aba found the voice to say what he had come to say. "Before I go, Sire Osi, I would ask a favor. I would buy one of your harem—a girl, I think—a gift for my youngest harem boy. For his birthday."

Osi's violet eyes seemed to flame. "Buy her, you say? You insult me so? You call me friend and offer to pay me for such a—"

Aba laughed. "*Sois gentil*, calm yourself, Sire, and *give* me the wench."

Osi bowed. "Now *that* is more to the point. A gift, then, between friends. Now, whom did you have in mind?"

"Well, he's a young slave, fifteen summers this week, so the female I bring him should be experienced enough to be able to educate him, but not too old to play child's games. Say, thirty years."

"I have several such," nodded Osi. "What of coloring?"

"Well, his hair is dark and his skin light, though sunned. In his chest I've had sewn a giant ruby—it is his pride. Perhaps you have someone with red coloring to complement the jewel."

"Yes," nodded Osi hesitantly, suddenly thoughtful, suddenly alert.

Aba went on, half to himself. "Ollie is his name. He's the most temperamental boy I've ever had. And totally devoted to me. Why, do you know, he swore the day I left that if I wasn't back in time for his birthday party, he'd come find me? Such insolence, but he knows how strongly I feel about him—I let him get away with so much. He's even a bit addled, I think. He goes quite wild at times. Maybe if you could find someone with a heavier hand than I've got with him, someone who could teach him a little restraint—"

Osi held up his hand, then scratched his cheek. "I think . . . I think I may have a surprise for you when you leave, Sire Aba."

It worked, then. Aba felt simultaneously elated and ashamed at the success of his ruse. Still, no meanness was intended; only a bit of guile, for a greater good.

"Well, we both have things to do, I'm sure," Osi said as he walked Aba to the door. "I shan't detain you. Your gift will be ready as you leave."

"I hope you will remember me without much rancor, Osi-Sire." They stood in the foyer.

"I will remember you not at all, young Sire."

They looked at each other a long, curious moment, mixing emotions with their respirations. Then Osi pulled Aba to him in a powerful embrace; kissed him open-mouthed, sensuously, seriously. Aba gave himself to the moment. When it passed, they parted gently; Aba stepped into the hall, and Osi closed the door behind him.

"Wait here," croaked Ninjus.

Beauty, Aba, and D'Ursu stood in a large, bare room, facing the only door. Surrounding them were Elspeth, Fleur, Osi, Ninjus, and three other Vampire guards. Ninjus left and came back a moment later. With him were two more Neuroman guards, and between them walked a badly beaten Human—Ollie.

He recognized Beauty instantly, but held his tongue at an imperceptible sign from the Centaur.

Aba saw the sign, too. He leaped forward, shock pulling his features tight. "Ollie, what are you doing here! What have they done to you?"

Ollie caught Beauty's wink a second time, and immediately fell on his knees before Aba, hysterically weeping.

Aba turned to the ANGELs in a fury. "What is the meaning of this?" he screamed. He was letting himself play on his real feelings, now, for truly, the sight of such a badly beaten Human upset him greatly.

Ninjus stepped forward. "This one belongs to you?"

"He is my favorite," Aba hissed.

"He snuck in last night—he would not say how. He was with two others who escaped—he would not say who. Between them they killed seven of our citizens—he would not say why."

Aba turned back to Ollie. "Is this true?" he whispered fiercely.

Ollie threw himself prostrate at Aba's feet. "I didn't k-kill anyone, I s-swear I didn't," he choked out between sobs.

Aba turned back to the guards. "He's my youngest steward. He begged me not to leave him alone. I fear in my absence he fell into bad company and came looking for me. What his companions were after, I cannot say." His voice was a mixture of confusion, anger, and fear.

Ollie picked up his cue. "Y-you promised you wouldn't l-leave me, Sire. I paid them to h-help me find you. From

Ma'gas' they were, plain pirates. It was the riches of the castle they w-wanted, and made me help them once we was inside. It was you I wanted, Sire, only y-you." He grabbed Aba's ankles pitifully.

"Tell us how you got in the castle," said Osi, sternly but softly. "Tell Sire Aba."

"Tunnels, Sire. We came through the tunnels."

"The tunnels are all electrified," Ninjus said evenly. "How did you get past the wire screens?"

"They said they h-had a friend on the inside, Sire. They s-said the electricity was turned off for a few minutes, just when they cut their way through. They took me up as a hostage, Sire, in case they got cornered. They thought y-you wouldn't hurt me, because I told them about—about us. Sire, forgive me." He wept uncontrollably.

Aba shook his head in shame and dismay. "It is not mine to forgive," he said to the boy.

The ANGELs and Vampires conferred briefly. Ninjus looked repugnantly annoyed; Osi, bemused; Fleur, nonplused; Elspeth, dubious.

"Kill them all," growled Ninjus, "and throw 'em down the tubes."

"We should question them, really." Fleur raised the objection rather mildly.

"Let them go. All of them." Osi spoke with quiet force.

"Why?" grumbled Ninjus.

"It wouldn't be worth our while to antagonize Jarl at present. If he sent a force down on us now, it would be . . . too distracting. Besides, no harm had been done."

"No harm!" Ninjus boiled. "Seven dead and our security breached!"

"Then the intruders did us a favor to point up our weak spots without really compromising our projects. As for the dead, they've been properly punished, I think, for their stupidity." Osi smiled thinly at Ninjus, whom he disliked not only on general principles but on specifics of character as well.

Fleur said, "You're certain there's no other reason you're being so lenient, Osi? You're not having an affair with that gangly, awkward Vampire, are you?"

"He's not—" Osi hissed, then stopped himself. Calmly, he said, "I don't know to whom you refer."

Fleur displayed a sickly smile.

Elspeth muttered, "*Glunog Osi dentak, nef Aba loroi, Jarl elesku orogro dor.*"

Fleur nodded. "Well, it's your decision, Osi. I'm sure the Queen will understand."

Osi raised his lip imperceptibly, the barest hint of ritual grin.

Ninjus turned to Aba. "This is neither forgiven nor forgotten. It is recorded and remarked." He made a fist. "And by Quark's Charm, under the ephemeral auspices of diplomatic immunity and the good graces of this council, it is reluctantly dismissed."

He turned on his heel and strode out the door, followed by the other council members. When only the four interlopers were left, D'Ursu turned to Beauty and said, "I think that means we can leave this stinking city."

And so, late in the morning, D'Ursu Magna, Beauty, Aba, with Ollie on Beauty's back, walked slowly out the main gates of The City With No Name and headed south along the coast.

CHAPTER 12

A Gathering of Clouds

FLEUR, Elspeth, Osi, Ugo, and Ninjus sat at a small round table, looking grim.

"We have much to discuss," said Ninjus. "Something is happening."

"There's only one item of importance," Fleur said petulantly. "And that is surely the Queen."

"There are a multitude of items," corrected Ninjus, "which I will list." The others sat quietly listening. The Chief Security ANGEL proceeded. "There is the arrival of a Human, probably involved in the attack on the City five years ago, a Human sought by the Queen these five years. There is this Human's escape—"

"And likely death," added Fleur.

"—His escape down a disposal shaft, which was subsequently not repaired."

"Not repaired because the Queen would not permit a repair crew into her chambers."

"One of her moods?"

"Possibly. Or possibly she suspected reentry by that route. In any case, there is then the convenient arrival of a delegation from Jarl, proposing an alliance. There is the announcement by the Queen that she is pregnant—undoubtedly by the Human who escaped. Then there is another invasion of the castle—this time by three creatures who kill our guards and steal some spare parts. Two of these escape—one, we think, is an escaped Plugger; the other we don't know. The third is caught—obviously a runaway harem slave, as the jewel in his chest so brands him—and we are told he belongs to the Vampire who happens to be here on a diplomatic mission. This slave tells us

185

that we have a castle spy, who cut electricity on our security system long enough to permit the thieves' entrance. Now, this is a lot to digest. Comments?"

"You think this is all part of a unified plot, do you?"

"There are too many coincidences to think otherwise."

"Perhaps." Osi spoke now. "But I trusted Aba, the Sire from Jarl. I thought his story—and his slave's—were self-corroborating, and perfectly believable. For the rest, you may be right."

"You're blinded by your infatuation with this young Sire," snorted Ugo.

"There is a castle conspiracy at the base of this," rasped Ninjus. "Mark my words. These breaches of security—"

"Stuff," said Fleur. "You see conspiracies between the day and the night."

"Do you deny—"

"I deny nothing. And by all means, brace up your security, ferret out your traitors, do whatever. We have but one problem, as far as I am concerned."

"Which is?"

"The Queen's child, of course. These other things, be they related or not—the appearance of the Human, the infiltration by a few scruffy saboteurs, a diplomatic mission that is either sincere or bogus—they are things easily dealt with and easily forgotten. They are minutiae. They are too insignificant to matter in the sweep of what we will achieve in the next five years with the grace of our Queen. But this child—this is an unknown quantity. We don't know what it will be, how it will think, how it will affect our Queen's commitment to our goals. And we may well not have the control over it that we have over our Queen— we don't know what the nutritional requirements of the child will be. We are so close, now, to reaching total and virtually unheralded domination of this sector that we cannot afford any new, uncontrolled genotypes to enter the gene pool at this point. I tell you flatly, we have but one urgent problem: this child must not be."

There was silence as the others nodded.

* * *

Immediately upon walking out the gates of the City, D'Ursu, Aba, Beauty, and Ollie walked south down the cliff path, found D'Ursu's boat still anchored in the south harbor, and sailed it first north, then west, to lull suspicious eyes from the castle. When it was dark, they turned again, this time south, and Ollie guided them, with some difficulty, to the Bookery caves.

There followed two days of rejoicing. The reunion of Jasmine, Beauty, Ollie, and Rose—after all the horror of the previous nights—was just the kernel of joy the little underground community needed, around which to coalesce and warm.

Beauty and Rose stayed more or less to themselves the first day. They had much to discuss. Rose wept a good deal of the time—for causing her beloved Centaur such pain, for separating herself so inexorably from him by her flight, for having feelings he couldn't understand.

Beauty was confused and frustrated. Now that Blackwind was dead, the object of much of his anger was gone, leaving the Centaur with a sort of helpless, empty love for Rose—the love he had always felt, but tempered now. He was painfully happy to see her; but now that he found she *had* left of her own will, his heart was a thing without substance. He could not but wish her well; yet for himself, he could find no direction. Still, he maintained his balance throughout, and it was well known—among the Centauri, at any rate—that balance without direction is always preferable to direction without balance.

Ollie, not quite so selflessly disposed to Rose, spent his time actively ignoring her.

Rose wished she could explain to Beauty the convolutions of her soul—her yearnings, her bleak apprehensions, her gray dawns: dark corners that kept emerging under the light of the Plug. She could no longer keep her emotions sorted or the universe at bay.

Candlefire came to stand beside her the morning of the second day. "Join me," he said. He took a four-foot cable, plugged one end into his head, the other into Rose's. They quivered momentarily—almost fell—then walked, in perfect step, like reflections, into the darkness.

As soon as the Plug made contact, Rose was aware of a tingle, like an internal flush. She walked beside Candlefire, yet she felt as if she were walking inside him—she saw with his eyes, felt the ground with his feet. Their senses were one; they functioned in perfect unison. They went into a black cave and lay down.

Flashes of light, like distant exploding novae, in a black space that twisted on itself. Rose soared along the curve, then turned, broke through the curve, into—

A deeper blackness. Lights no longer sparked here, they flowed. Rather, the photons flowed, in concentric waves that interfered with one another, settling into troughs of void, crests of sublime intensity. Intense brilliance. She moved into the light.

The light had a texture that enveloped her and filled her at the same time, a moving texture like a hum, the sound of glowing. All other light was stationary to her, fixed forever in time, as space tumbled and curled around her in a series of interlocking doughnuts, helices, knots, and bowls. She was the light.

The light was a wind, she was the wind-light blowing down the spiral corridors of space, through echoing time, once more into a void.

The Void. No Thing. No light. No sense; only the No Sense. Perfect, an eternal moment. Again. Again. Again. The moment rebounded, then hovered between the two consciousnesses, in the cable, in the humming electrons, spinning packets of energy; buzz, the moment, vibrating, humming, No-Thing humming softer and softer, dissipating into a fine, final sigh, like a soul passing dead lips and disappearing into the wilderness.

So the caves sheltered a great orgy of self-indulgence: Pluggers plugging, Books reading to one another, old friends coming together, coming apart, breaking hard, in and on one another in great splashes of emotion. The caves seemed not so hollow. Yet still, Paula felt very alone.

"You seem lonely," a voice behind her said on the afternoon of the second day.

She turned. A young, thin Vampire sat near her in a

shadow. It might have been an ominous vision, but Paula didn't feel scared. "Not lonely," she said. "I am alone."

"You seem alone," he amended. "And lonely."

She drew herself up defiantly. "I am a rock. I am an island."

He smiled affectionately in the darkness at her, though she could not see. He said, softly, " 'I have my books, and my poetry to protect me.' "

She caught her breath. "You—you know the Old Words!"

He shrugged modestly. "I've read many old books and papers. Some are quite beautiful."

"But you're a Vampire. There are no Vampire Scribes."

"I'm not a Scribe. I merely like to read."

She walked closer to him, interested. "How are you called?"

"I am Aba."

"I am Paula."

Tentatively—with no more than a whisper of movement—they bared their necks to each other. "How is it that a Vampire reads?" she asked uncertainly.

"The same way he bleeds—from the heart."

"My Word, but you have a poetic turn, for a savage. We must read together sometime."

He winced, as if stung. "If my wings make me savage in your eye, I would rather read alone." He turned away.

She came up to him, touched his arm, stopped herself. "Wait," she mouthed. He looked at her. She studied his face closely. He looked kind. She said, "You're lonely, too."

"I am alone," he shrugged.

"I heard the story of how you rescued Ollie from the castle. It was a noble act."

"It was an ignoble and deceitful act . . . in an honorable cause."

She regarded him thoughtfully. "You are a creature of some layers, it would seem."

"Like a Book . . . of many pages." He bowed his head to her to lay the compliment at her feet. He liked her quiet way, her solemn forthrightness. He thought: She's proud, without being arrogant.

She thought: How like a book he is, and how unlike a Vampire—he gives, and doesn't take.

He thought: She's hard on the outside, to insulate a center that easily shatters.

Beauty called to Aba just then. The Vampire excused himself, with the hope that he and Paula would talk again soon, and walked over to the Centaur, who was saying good-bye to D'Ursu Magna. The great Bear had rejuvenated his spirit in the caves; but now, with winter nearing an end, exhaustion had finally overcome him. He needed to hibernate for at least a few weeks before returning to his King.

"I'm not certain what I've learned on this journey," D'Ursu said, scratching behind his ear, "but I hope I've been of some help."

"You have been of great help," Beauty assured him.

"Even so," the Bear scowled, "your woman is happy where she is, and your man is still not found. Furthermore, my King will receive no help from this stinking city on the Sticks. It all seems to have been a waste of time."

"Time is never wasted, D'Ursu Magna. Only put aside for later consideration."

The Bear squinted. "You've been with Humans too long, Beauté Centauri, if that's what you believe. In any case, good-bye for now. I'll be curled up at the end of this tunnel. If I sleep longer than one moon, please wake me, for I must go help my King once I'm rested."

"Dream well, old Bear."

"And dream up some new tricks," added Aba.

"Then, till we meet again, in the Great Forest, and may the cities all burn." He gave Beauty and Aba a great Bear hug and loosed a roar that resounded through all the caverns and echoed for a full minute. Then D'Ursu lumbered groggily down into his sleeping-cave for a short winter's nap.

Jasmine and Beauty hadn't seen each other for some years now, and their last parting had been underlaid with so many ambiguities, sexual tensions and demientendres that on meeting again, now, neither knew quite how to behave.

"It's good to see you again." She spoke softly to him, as if it were their secret, "to see you're safe."

"I am glad you are here," he nodded.

"Your face is a cloud," she whispered.

"An apt description. We are like gathering clouds, here, waiting for thunder."

They could all feel it; and a wild storm it would be.

"How are you feeling?" asked Paula.

"Fine. I'm fine," said Aba. He wasn't. His skin was gray, and he lay alone in a corner, too weak to move. In other corners of the cave, lovers whispered, Pluggers plugged, Scribes wrote exalted scribbles, and dreamers dreamed. It was dusk outside—historically a time of moment for the Vampire—and Aba had leaving on his mind, though leaving was not in his heart.

"I brought a book of poems to read to you," Paula said. She opened the book before he could respond. "You're a creature of great sorrow, I think," she continued, then read: *"Come to me, Sorrow—the darkening night/ Wraps me in peace by your side."* She smiled. "It's an old poem: I copied this book over last year—that's how I knew of it. The original was crumbling. It . . . reminded me of you."

"Crumbling?"

"No, no. The poem." She reached out her hand to stop his self-deprecatory thought, and touched his chest—the first time she had touched him so. It startled them both. She left her hand there, resting lightly. "You remind me of Sorrow," she whispered.

He kept his eyes focused on her face, and nodded. "The 'darkening night,' indeed, brings no peace to me."

"And why, pray?"

"It's the time of day that brings me most to mind of my own compulsive desires."

"I've never seen you compulsive," she said; but it was almost a question.

Ever so slightly, he lifted his chest to the pressure of her hand, as he spoke a poem of his own:

Perfumed, velvet black night,
Shadow in dark flight, I have come,
In the starlight, I will come;

Secret, furtive hunger
Seems to linger in the night.
I see you turning to my light.
Slow, now, dance to my tune,
It will end, love, pale and wan,
In the ice light of the dawn,
Now we mingle, now we swoon,
I'm the night ride of the sun,
I'm the midnight of your noon,
I'm the dark side of the moon.

The slow force of his words compelled her to move closer and closer to him as he spoke, so that by the time he finished, her face was only inches from his own.

"Those are powerful words," she whispered.

"They're from an ancient Vampire love song," he whispered in return. He brought his face closer still.

She tipped her head back: in fear, in desire; in anguish. She caught her breath. "Come to me, my Sorrow."

Tentatively, passionately, he brought his mouth to her throat. The smell of her body heat under the dark musty overhanging cave wall revived him. He submerged himself in the perfume of her flesh; and in her blood, which called him at his deepest center.

She tensed, then relaxed, as the hard whiteness of his tooth dented, then perforated the tender skin of her neck. She felt a warm flush spread from that point, as at the moment of a first kiss, until it changed into the vortex of a black maelstrom, which carried her to its core in great sucking waves, as if she herself were the very substance of this funneling, foaming sea.

In the distance, the wind picked up; storm coming in.

CHAPTER 13

An Almost Bloodless Coup

Isis sat purring in the Queen's lap. The Queen petted her with a stroke Isis considered inept but tolerable.

The little Cat kept her nose near the Queen's belly, which was becoming rounder daily. Something was growing in there, Isis knew—something that had a piece of Josh in it. It wasn't the brother smell, and it wasn't Josh himself; it was something similar, though. It had Josh about it.

She licked the Queen's bare belly twice at its greatest girth. The Queen smiled and patted Isis's head. Isis only smiled.

"It's ready," said Fleur, holding the vial of amber liquid up to the light. "*We're* ready."

"*Delio nulong abortion gloan tog*," Elspeth replied, nodding. "*Osi gelendis*. The Queen suspects." She sat in an overstuffed chair, clenching her jaw.

"She must," Fleur agreed. "She's refusing to let any of the inner circle of ANGELs near her. You're right, of course. Osi will have to do it." He walked around behind Elspeth, placed his spindly pink fingers on her shoulders, and began massaging tenderly. "We're sailing troubled waters, my dear."

"*Logress*," Elspeth grunted, leaning into the neck rub. She held her deformed hand up behind her and stroked Fleur's side.

"Lie down and let me walk on your back," Fleur suggested. "Then I'll go coerce that Vampire into involving himself. He's just like the others, the pompous ass. Lots of rhetoric, but when something needs to be done, it's *Let Fleur do it*."

193

Elspeth lay on her belly on the floor. Fleur walked up and down her back. Elspeth groaned with pleasure. "*Olientog*," she muttered. "Tell *that* to Sire Osi. *Olientog orogro dos.*"

Isis lay sleeping in the crook of the Queen's arm as the Queen spoke softly to her.

"Sleep, little kitten, sleep as my fetus sleeps, fetus keeps, grows in me, as you can see, as you can see. Beautiful fetus, dream unto me, beautiful embryo sleeping in utero, beauty wilt thou be, not ugly like me unapproachable me. Only kittens and embryos could love such a one as me. Unfit for Human consumption, untouched by Human hands—except once! Yes, one time was I touched, by hands and heart, little sewer Cat, once for a moment I was beautiful, as the Rose in me knows, so my embryo grows, for a Human felt warm toward me once. Joshua his name, his fetus fills me, ontogeny recapitulating the moment in Time and Space when I wasn't the isolated hated fated sublimated overweighted ugly lonely used abused insanely grand and horribly unseemly Queen I've always been and likely e'er will be, as you can see, as you can see."

At Joshua's name, Isis briefly opened her eyes and raised her head; but as she didn't see him anywhere, she put her head back down and returned to sleep.

The Queen laughed a raspy laugh and continued talking to the dozing Cat, in her voice of many voices. "Lonely we are, my little black familiar, familiar to the rotting witch I am, which I am, which I am familiar with, as you are familiar, too. Lonely in this house of rubble, rubble, schemes and trouble in this cold and homeless house, this homely mother soon will be alone no more—this borning will release me from my lifelong night to the morning of my motherhood, the mourning of my long and barren, fruitless early years. Be still, the blossom ripens even now; the fruits of this labor shall sweeten our dry and tasteless life, as pomegranate to the sun-parched wanderer, our birthing fetus shall sustenance be, as you can see, as you can see, as you can see, as you can see."

Isis yawned, and settled herself a bit more comfortably.

* * *

"You called me, Highness?"

"Fleur, I am in labor."

"But that isn't possible, Majesty, you're only three months—"

"I'm having contractions, every three, as you can see, as you can see, do not quibble with me, I want this child!"

Her last word was almost a scream as she winced from the twist of another spasm. Isis sat hunched like a Sphinx on the dais at the Queen's feet, staring curiously, unmoving, at the monarch's face clotted with pain.

The Queen relaxed again.

"A miscarriage, perhaps—" Fleur began.

"There will be no miscarriage, of justice or embryo. You will retard the contractions if you can, and if you can't, you will recant, and operate, and section me in Caesar's way, take a page from Caesar's book that which is Caesar's, do the C-section, amniotic sea section, snatch the bloody baby from this spastic womb before it is a tomb, but save this baby!"

"My Liege, as for saving the life of a three-month fetus—"

"This is no mere fetus, you detritus, this is a Princess, and powerful enough to hold her own in this airless, fetid place if you will but deliver her. And I as well will be well pleased if you deliver me from this pain." The last words a whisper, now, as a sweat broke over her grimaced lip.

"Yes, my Queen." Fleur smiled. "We'll do what we can. I'll get the anesthetist—"

"No," she choked, "no, nay, no, nn, nn, no, there will be no anesthesia, no pain medication, no drugs or tubes or needles of any kind!"

"But my Queen—"

"I am ruler here still, and master of my own body as well as all others. I am expert at the autoregulatory control of all my body's functions, autonomic or otherwise. Give me but a moment to compose myself. I will control my pain. I will control my respirations. I will even control my bleeding as you put the knife to me. I am in control. I am master, without peer, without fear, I am mistress, without distress over this stress, or any. I am she with the power, and my time is near to be a mother, and you will help me now as I ask."

"Yes, my Queen. At once."

The Queen lay flat on the marble dais, her eyes closed, her breathing regular. Her belly was big; bigger than a three-month gestation would have promised.

Ten forms stood around her, gowned and gloved. All were Neuromans: doctors, nurses, technicians for any contingency. Isis sat watching from the throne. Fleur held a scapel. He looked around. All was ready.

Firmly he placed the edge of the blade on the Queen's belly, stretched hard and tight by the fetus within. Meticulously he drew the blade in a downward arc, slicing the skin from xiphoid to pubis. It made a yellowish, vertical wedge, dotted with points of red where the bleeders oozed. Once again he drew his knife down the first incision; deeper this time, to the fibrous peritoneal sheath; and one last time, through the peritoneum, into the abdominal-pelvic cavity, exposing the swollen uterus.

Fleur next took a few minutes to tie off bleeding vessels, though there was little need: true to her word, the Queen had shunted blood away from this area to minimize blood loss at the incision. When the way was clear, Fleur put his scapel at the top of the uterus, and made two quick cuts into it, extending the second cut down vertically to the base of the womb, opening it wide.

And then, out of the uterus jumped the fetus. Only, it wasn't exactly a fetus. Rather, it was a fully developed child, a girl child, appearing nearer three years, in age, than three months. She looked almost Human. The immediate apparent differences consisted of a head somewhat more elongated than one of normal Human proportion; strange, hollow, reflective, discoid eyes; a beaklike sort of nose; a long, oval, red birthmark flaming at each temple; dry, spindly, pointed fingers; and a thin, pink, fleshy tail.

She leapt to the throne like an agile monkey and immediately chewed apart the umbilical cord that connected her

to the placenta, still attached to the lining of the Queen's
uterus.

She looked from face to astonished face, turning her
head with the short, jerky movements of a bird. Her eyes
finally rested on the small Cat who sat beside her on the
throne, and she smiled, and petted the creature. Isis purred
and licked the child's hand: the hand smelled faintly of
Joshua, and Isis was unafraid.

The child's gaze went again to the faces of the terrified
Neuromans, stopping at Fleur's. She cocked her head to the
side, her smile vanishing. Fleur was suddenly aware of the
child's thought, projected to him telepathically. The thought
said: *You bad. Don't like you.*

Involuntarily, he took a step back. He felt chilled. The
child continued staring at him with a kind of raw, un-
formed anger. Fleur felt it as a physical pressure, pushing
him back, probing him, squeezing harsh, nonverbal thought
into his brain, holding it there like a cold steel ball: *Bad.
Don't like you.* He was unable to close his mind to it. He
took two more steps backward.

The child smiled again. She looked down at her mother,
the Queen, still gutted on the floor. The Queen opened her
eyes and looked at the child.

"My baby . . ." she murmured.

The child spoke to her telepathically: *Mother, give me.*

The Queen closed her eyes again and opened up her
mind to the girl, letting flow, in synchronous progression,
the layers of electromagnetic field that were her thoughts
and perceptions, mixed and woven with those of the
hundred Humans that lay in the room beyond, connected
by head cables electronically—umbilically, in their own
way. The child absorbed it all; received the transference,
stored it in a thick, proton-rich metafield created by the
cube of midbrain the Queen had foreseen the child would
possess, that configuration of gray matter she had engineered through the art of copulation.

When the transference was complete, the child said to
the Queen, in the thought-voice that was already louder
than it had been at first, *Mother too. Must no. No no no.*

No no no. Child yes yes. Yes yes yes. Yes yes no. Yes yes. Yes no. Yes yes. No. No. No." Whereupon the strange and birdlike little creature jumped from the throne and landed, on all fours, in the Queen's still-gaping belly; and tore open the monarch's abdominal aorta with her delicate, clawlike little hands. The onlookers gasped and retreated, as the Queen quickly bled her life out onto the dais. The child hopped back up on the throne—beside Isis, who watched with unperturbed interest—and said to the incredulous gathering, without making a sound: *Queen dead.*

Long live the Queen.

CHAPTER 14

A Father-and-Child Reunion

IT was at the depths of a night late in April of the year 127 Age of Ice, toward the end of four days and nights of violent, continuous storming—an expected occurrence for the season; typical, in fact, following a brief false spring—that the good ship *Atlantis* popped to the surface of the ocean some twenty miles south and west of The City With No Name. The series of events surrounding this emergence is difficult to interpret without invoking popular fallacies like divine intervention, coincidence, fate, Providence, synchronicity. The circumstances were, however, neither more nor less than a click in the ratchet of Time's wheel; they therefore are opaque to analysis.

First of all, there were none of the frequent Vampire reconnaissance flights from the City—this because of the turbulent and generally dangerous flying conditions, and because Vampires hate rain (and water, for that matter) more than most creatures. So no spies saw Joshua's craft when it surfaced—which was all the more remarkable since, almost immediately after it broke the waves into the churning night, the craft was struck by lightning.

The lightning bolt had three effects: it rocked the small vessel's sailor into a state of deaf, shaking semiconsciousness; it damaged the ship's electrical system sufficiently to make it impossible, temporarily, to resubmerge; and it caused the elliptical crystal bubble to glow the eeriest of gossamer-green glows.

St. Elmo's Fire, it used to be called; the ungrounded static electricity built up on a ship during a storm. Only this was no ordinary ship. This was a floating bubble of polymer-silica glass, and one of its probably less remark-

able properties was that it could efficiently store a charge—
even a great charge—for considerable periods. So the lightning bolt was in the glass, now giving it a crackling, green
incandescence that all but blinded the voyager within.

It was a long ordeal. The ship was tumbled about every
axis, dragged up swells and down troughs, heaved upside-
down into the torrential air, then swallowed with a belly-
sucking *Thud* under the next wave. Josh was tossed reck-
lessly from crate to wall, until, in a flurry of sustained will
before losing consciousness, he managed to tie himself
firmly in place to the steering shaft.

He revived momentarily several times—only to think he
was about to die each time. Once, there was a horrible gut-
wrenching *Crunch*, and Josh was certain the hull had burst
open; but it was strong stuff, this polymer.

It was like a difficult birth. This little embryo, a light,
tentative, radiant egg, pushed out of its black, fluid womb
into all the raging chaos. And truly, the Earth wailed that
night.

Until slowly—it's tempting to say inevitably, though that
would, of course, be untrue—the crystal ship was drawn by
the currents toward the yawning of cave-mouths in the
cliffs south of the City that formed the entrance to the
Bookery tunnels. Not so surprising a destination, really—
for it was the sweep of the continental shelf, the inexorable
tectonic nudgings, and the endless lapping of these very
same currents that had hollowed out this meandering cove
in the first place; and to this cove would these currents
ever return.

The ship was about two miles out when it was first seen
by a Bookery lookout as a speck of light sometimes altogether obscured, moving up and down in the darkness. By
the time the craft was a mile offshore, most Books and
Pluggers had been told of its approach, and stared silently
at the apparition from numerous crevices and caches that
dotted the cliffs around the cave mouths. It hovered there
about an hour, as the storm began to break, then somehow
swirled out of its crosscurrents and headed directly for the
main cavern entrance, swept forward on huge swells that
pounded the cliff rock and echoed through all the tunnels.

The waiting Humans were all armed, though they little knew what to expect. No one had ever seen a floating, glowing ball such as this; not even the aged, worldly Jasmine; not even Ollie, who had once been a pirate; or Aba, who had proved to be a Vampire of great learning, in spite of his misbegotten heritage.

When the iridescent pod was fifty yards away, it was picked up by a mammoth wave and hurled at the cliff. There was a great crash as some of the cliff face crumbled into rocks, accompanied by a loud hiss as some of the stored electricity in the boat's shell passed to ground, with a dimming of its glow. The Pluggers cowered at the sound, for it was the sound of The Serpent.

The vessel battered the rocks all around the caves for some minutes—each time it touched ground the hiss and crackle of escaping electrons were heard, with a correspondent dimming of the glow in the ship's hull. All the onlookers—especially the Pluggers, who remembered so vividly the whisper of the Serpent-God who had unplugged them—stared, transfixed, at this bobbing, gleaming marble. Until finally the static electricity was drained and they could see the craft for the hollow glass ball it was; until finally a wave pulled the vessel *into* a cave mouth, and all the Books and Pluggers ran down to see what it was.

There was a great hubbub of murmurs as they shone their lights all around, through the glass, and realized a Human was inside—a stunned, unconscious, possibly dead Human, lashed to a piece of strange machinery.

"What is it?" asked a Plugger.

"Who is he?" demanded a Book.

"Weapons for the Queen, I'm sure of it."

"Looks like a message in a bottle." Jasmine smiled as she lowered herself to the lip of rock that acted as a natural pier to the pool in which the small ship bobbed.

Ollie came down next, and then Rose. Perhaps forty people were craning their necks beside the glass vessel, and the small cave was quite packed. Rose wormed her way to the front and looked into the crystalline cabin just as Josh began to stir. He lifted his head, and the crowd outside gasped. He looked blankly at the frightened faces that stared at him through the glass; until his eyes came to rest on three in front: Jasmine, Ollie, Rose. His mouth opened and closed.

Jasmine whispered, "Joshua."

Ollie's heart jumped; his eye even moistened; he had to sit down hard.

"Dear Joshua," Rose whispered. After a moment, she turned to the crowd behind her and spoke in a somewhat louder voice: "It's The Serpent."

Perhaps, after all, it *was* Providence.

The next days were such a mixture of emotion that they are difficult to describe in discrete terms. To the Pluggers, it was a profound religious experience—the return of The Serpent: their deliverer, savior, destroyer, messiah. They meshed their fingers in the Sign of the Plug to him at every opportunity. To the Books, it was the emergence of a truly heroic Scribe—all the more wonderful because he brought with him his journals: detailed written records of all his exploits and adventures, replete with footnotes, dates, and maps, compiled during his weeks in Atlantis. Furthermore, he brought many Atlantan books, including the dictionary—the profoundest list of old and new words any Book had ever seen; a book that would serve as source for the Great Lexicon for years to come.

To Aba, it was the appearance of the man for whom Lon had died—that special Human who was actually with the old master Vampire at his death on the walls of the City.

To Jasmine, Beauty, Ollie, Rose, and Joshua, it was a weaving of past and present; a miraculous recrossing of paths. It was the coming together of old friends.

But to the caves, Josh was anathema—for he was the focus around which everyone now rallied: a magnet that gave direction, and escape. So there followed, upon his arrival, several days of sentient rumblings, angry tremors. Yet nothing of greater moment resulted—for the power of the catacombs came from their embodiment of bleak, bottomless despair; and once that pit was filled, its hollowness was only a memory.

As soon as Josh had a chance to recover from his journey of rebirth—sometime the next evening—they had a dinner together, just the five old friends.

Rose began weeping immediately upon joining the others in the small, warm room. She hugged Josh fiercely, and they held each other. "Joshua, Joshua," she muttered between sobs.

He soothed her. "Why do you cry when we're all here again at last?"

"She cries for herself," said Ollie, not completely unkindly.

"She weeps for us all," amended Beauty, his great sadness of recent weeks tempered now by Joshua's return.

"For her joy at seeing you, Josh," said Jasmine. "For all we can share now, that we haven't in so long."

Beauty raised his wine glass. "Six winters ago, in a cave not far from here, we drank to one another this toast—'To all we have lost, and all we have found.'" He drank.

They all drank, and the dinner began.

First, they caught one another up on the facts of their lives. It was a history of laughter and tears.

Rose couldn't find the words to speak of the act which had brought them all here: her removal of Joshua's protective helmet. "'I pray you understand.'" She wept as she spoke to him. "I did it from love—that you would know what I had known—that we might someday know it together."

"I've never seen you act with malice," Josh answered softly, unconsciously adjusting the new helmet that Kshro had found for him. "I'm safe now, and we're all together here—richer for it, by the way. You can stop chastising yourself for our bruises."

Jasmine thought to herself, He's grown into a man since last we met. Beauty caught the thought in her eye, and nodded agreement. They smiled a secret smile at each other—for they had grown very close these past weeks, waiting for this night, though nobody had known it until now.

Finally, Josh told his extraordinary tales: the spells, the Queen, the Selkies, the city beneath the sea.

Which brought them up to the moment. With a single impulse, they stood and hugged one another all at once, fused into a single, great groping creature by the gravity of their love.

They vowed, that night, to fuse their efforts as well—and put an end to this strange and noxious Queen, who seemed so intent on the controlled destruction of the Human race.

For a moment, the caves grew darker, trying to extinguish the light in their eyes; but the light was too strong, and in the end the caves could only twist inward on themselves to look for darkness.

The child sat on her throne, surveying her chambers. Beside her, Isis crouched, sphinxlike, eyes slits. Before her stood all the ANGELs, Vampire, Neuroman captains, tacticians, and group leaders that constituted the governors of the castle and The City With No Name.

In the brief week of her existence, the child had already grown and changed. Her tail was longer, her hands and feet more clawlike. She was six inches taller, and while her nose remained beaklike, her head had taken on more human proportion. Her face had even developed a certain allure, the flame birthmarks at her temples having mellowed into a subtle wine color, matched by her reflecting eyes.

She spoke in a child's voice to the assembled minions. Her inflections were odd, though, almost animal noises at times. And periodically one of her words would surge forward as if telepathically impelled into the minds of the listeners.

"I am your new *ruler*. Your *Queen*, my mother, is *dead*. Things are different now. *You* will *follow* my rule."

There was absolute silence. Some of the Vampires looked at one another. Elspeth, standing behind Fleur, glowered steadily at the throne. Isis yawned. A soft wave of generalized muttering crossed the room, then quieted against the walls. Osi closed his eyes in concentration. Ugo and another Vampire traded whispers.

Ninjus stepped forward and spoke loudly, like a warrior. "I say the Queen is dead. I say long live the Queen." He dropped to his knees and bared his neck to the child-monarch.

She had no eyelids, this bird-child Queen. And as her eyes were burgundy reflective disks, wherever she turned her head, the creature at whom she stared saw himself reflected.

Back and forth she flashed her gaze across the room; the short, jerky head movements of a raven. The silence in the room turned into trance—like an ancient magus, the child could hypnotize, probe, subliminally suggest. There were none who didn't at least feel the power. Some submitted to it gladly; some bridled; some broke under it. By the time she had finished her entrancing surveillance, six ANGELs and four Vampires, pale, sweating, terrified, had run from the room.

"Don't be afraid," the new Queen said to those still standing. "Those ones were having *bad thoughts. Bad thoughts.* They will be killed. Bad thoughts kill."

The Neuromans and Vampires remaining all bared their necks in unison. "Long live the Queen!" they shouted.

"Good," she said to them. "Now *leave* me. If you don't want to join me, *leave* the City before I hear a bad thought from you. I don't like *bad thoughts.*" She paused a moment. Nobody moved.

Suddenly she screamed: "I said *leave!*"

There was a restrained push for the door, and in less than a minute, the child-Queen was alone, with only Isis beside her. The little Cat licked her paw twice, licked the child-Queen's leg twice; then curled up and slept. She had no fear of this bizarre new animal that had something of Joshua's smell about it. She was barely curious. She only knew she liked the new animal's scent; and then and there seemed like a good time and place to sleep.

The child-Queen looked at the sleeping Cat, then growled in her mind. She jumped off the throne onto the dais, ran like a brachiator into a dark corner—her knuckles touching the ground every other step—and sat there facing the wall, rocking, holding her knees to her chest, brooding and silent.

* * *

Beauty ran over the hill at a gallop, Josh and Rose riding double on his bare back. It was a fine, brisk April morning, cloudless and new, and for the first time in many months they thought of nothing but the moment and the wind on their faces.

Beauty ran through the tall grass, jumped logs, splashed through ponds and mudholes. It was wonderfully, carelessly dangerous being this open so near the City. But for too long their spirits had been poor of exhilaration; so they took this time now with great, whooping glee.

They came to rest, finally, in an apple orchard inland from the cliffs above the caves. Josh and Rose dismounted, and the three of them walked hand in hand in silence, until Beauty was cool and dry. Josh found his two old friends distant from each other, but comfortable with that distance, as if they had reached a peace with themselves. They walked without speaking for some time, until eventually they reached the large oak grove where the feast was ready to begin.

The feast was for the entire encampment, and everyone was there—Books, Pluggers, Jasmine, Ollie, Aba, Rose, Beauty—for today was a day of speeches, games, toasts, oaths, promises, and plans: for Joshua was here to guide them and tell them what to do. And their hearts all dared whisper: No more, the caves. Yet Paula and Aba hung back—if only a little—from the festivities. Their love for each other had grown over the weeks—the blue and yellow marks of Aba's passion streaked down Paula's neck. That they were so absorbed in each other protected them somewhat—though not entirely—from the dismay, the chill glances, and the frank disgust with which many of the Books regarded them: for it was considered the worst kind of degradation for a Scribe—for any Human—to willingly submit to the sanguinary abuses of a Vampire. Yet to Paula it was not abuse: it was love. And to Aba, Paula was no mere object of his blood lust; she was the fountain that sustained him, body and spirit. They read poetry to each other; they shared their isolation.

Ollie shared his isolation with no one. He felt relief that Josh was home and safe; great relief. Still, by and large, he remained at the outskirts, looking in. He played his flute, and from time to time little groups would even dance to his music; but the music was meant for no one save himself.

Ollie had only two other competing emotions at the moment. The first was hatred of The City With No Name. Twice in his life he had been nearly destroyed by the creatures in that place. That the place still existed was no longer tenable to him. He greatly looked forward to impending assault. He would kill many Vampires.

Which brought him to his other emotional focal point: Aba. He had been fixating on the gentle Vampire's presence, and finding that presence increasingly intolerable. But even more intolerable was Aba's refusal to justify any such hatred—the real rub was that Aba was too good.

Ollie had taken to insulting him openly—to the glee of many of the Books—but Aba never rose to the bait. On the day of the feast, Ollie was feeling even more sullen than usual—this was common for him at times when others were being particularly festive or sociable, for at such times he felt even more excluded. So he wasn't any too kindly disposed toward Aba as they met unexpectedly in a quiet area of the grove; on the other hand, he did empathize somewhat with the Vampire's sense of isolation, and so was not as openly hostile as usual.

Aba was sitting on the ground, pen and paper in hand, his back against a tree, when Ollie strolled up.

"What are you doing, Vampire?" he asked quietly.

Aba smiled. "Writing a poem," he replied.

Ollie held out his hand.

Aba considered the request, then handed Ollie the sheet of paper. Ollie read it out loud:

> Black Stone sitting in the black night,
> Cries to the fading stars:
> "Answer me!"

"It's called haiku," added Aba.

Ollie just looked at him, then back at the poem, as the wind shuffled through the trees. Very softly, the boy said, "I feel this way sometimes."

Aba smiled sadly. "You must never stop waiting for the fading stars to answer."

Paula walked up just then, suspiciously. She hated Ollie for his treatment of Aba. "What's going on here?" she demanded in a voice full of quiet anger.

Ollie handed the poem back to Aba, then looked at Paula. "If it isn't the Vamp tramp," he sneered.

"At least I haven't forgotten how to be Human," she said with disgust.

"No, you prove to yourself just how Human you are by bleeding half to death for anyone with a big mouth."

She slapped him hard in the face—so hard it took his breath away for a moment. Then he smiled with trembling lips and stalked away.

Paula turned on Aba. "Why do you let him talk to us that way? When will you stop his vile insults?" She was livid with anger, and there were tears in her eyes.

Aba stood and held her. "He can't help himself, Paula. He's just scared and lonely, as are we all."

She put her head on his chest. "Do you have to be so inhumanly understanding?" she said, weeping.

He looked a bit baffled as he comforted her. "I don't understand anything," he whispered.

Fastidious Ellen spent the morning of the feast with dictionary and knife in hand, walking painstakingly from tree to tree, carving ancient, rarely used words of great power, as totems to protect the gathering: *hoyden, dysbulia, Kleenex, ottoman, ref, quincunx, zarf, Bogart, $E=mc^2$, Lancelot, Om, Canaveral, wa', pi, ergo, DNA, Cinemascope, syntax, oxymoron, wol, eloi, fab, muon, carburetor, pez, doubloon.*

Others wrote words in the leaves, that disappeared with the wind—these were called Raku poems, and it was said they were read by the sky. Wine was passed freely, as Pluggers told exotic stories about lands and adventures they had learned of while in-circuit in the castle, from Pluggers who had once lived in other parts of the world: lands where giants lived, where sorcery was commonplace, where

Humans were kings and animals had lost the power of speech, where giant Lizards ruled the land.

And Josh listened to all the stories and read all the words, and felt great love for this congregation of renegades and misfits celebrating his return from a watery grave.

He stood before them and proclaimed in a loud voice: "You here today—all of you—you're my family!"

The crowd cheered wildly, and repeated the word back to him like a litany: "Family—family—"

Family. Family. The word repeated itself over and over in Joshua's mind until it was just sounds, made no sense. Family family family family family famil famil famil fami fami fam fam fam fam fam fam fam fa fa fa fa fa fa fa fa faaa faaaa faaaaaaa faaaaaaaaaaaaaaaaaaaa-ther. Faaaather. Faather. Father. Father. Father.

Father.

The word suddenly sat in his brain and would not move. Father. He jerked his head right and looked to the north. Father. Father, come.

"What is it?" Jasmine asked him. "You look so odd. You're not going to have another spell, are you?"

Father, come.

Josh stood up, holding his head, facing north.

Father, come.

Josh began walking north, but hadn't taken two steps before Jasmine stopped him. "Josh, what are you doing? What's going on?"

Suddenly the entire camp was aware that something was amiss. The joyous din withered quickly to a hush.

Josh looked confused, intent. "She calls," he muttered.

Jasmine and Beauty moved around in front of him. "Who calls?" questioned the golden Centaur. "The Queen?"

Josh shook his head. "My daughter," he said.

Father, come.

Josh started walking north again; again, Jasmine stopped him. "You can't go there," she said.

Father, come.

"I have to," he answered. There was an edge in his voice.

"We will go with you, then," Beauty declared.

"I have to go alone," Josh insisted.

"We won't let you," Jasmine said quietly.

Father, come.

"There's no other way," he answered her just as quietly. Then, turning to the attentive crowd, he shouted: "I'm going to the castle, now. Alone. You're all to wait for me here."

There was a dense silence. Even the spring wind died in the trees. This was The Serpent speaking. The hunter. The master Scribe, and friend. Not a soul breathed.

Gently, Josh lifted Jasmine's hand from his shoulder. Uncertainly, she stepped aside.

Father, come.

With pounding heart, Josh walked, alone, toward The City With No Name.

The storm was at hand.

It took him over an hour to reach the main gates, but long before that, he could see strange events were underway.

First, there were the Great White Birds. Flocks of them passed overhead, flying low, flying north. They had thirty-foot wingspans, huge, scaly talons, and heads like Albatrosses. Even singly, they were rarely seen this far north; they were never seen in flocks. Except now.

There was the sky, sparkling bright only minutes before, now purple-black.

As he approached the City, caravans of Neuromans were making a disorganized exodus north, or east. And droves of Vampires swooped out the main gates and away, over the sea, screaming in a cacophony of high-frequency beeps.

And of course, there was the voice in his head.

Father, come.

He walked right through the door to the Outer City, past the outpouring of citizens, without anyone paying him much heed. Inside, the City was chaos.

There were large clusters of Vampires and Neuromans talking and shouting. Others ran here and there, like ants in a burning box. Humans were in the streets, too, wandering, dashing, wailing. Occasional stragglers were run over by hysterical packs; or pulled, screaming, into empty houses.

Father, come.

Black smoke rose from some corners of the fortress. Josh crossed a bridge and walked steadfastly into the Inner City. Here all was quiet. Deserted, even. It was eerie, like a dreamscape, devoid of color or movement. Somewhere, an animal cried. Josh entered the castle.

Father, come.

The castle, too, was in turmoil. Smoke and the acrid odor of chemical fires filled the air. Dimly outlined creatures flapped and crawled up and down the corridors—carrying objects, fighting, gasping, curling up in corners. Distant explosions rumbled the stone. Somehow, unerringly, hall after hall, Josh knew exactly where to go.

Father, come. Father, come.

A flaming door blocked his entrance to a stairwell at one juncture. Without losing a step he retraced his route until he found a more accessible path; and went on.

Father, come.

Up stairs, through burning rooms, over crumbling arches. He felt entranced. Finally into a room he knew: the laboratory. Beakers broken on the floor; steam hissing from a twisted valve. He stepped gingerly around the debris, into the next room. Communion. Row upon row of Humans, in-circuit. All dead.

Josh did not look at them long. He went on to the next room. The Queen's Chamber. He approached the throne: on it sat two small isolated figures. One of them instantly jumped down, ran across the floor and leapt at Josh. The furry little creature hit him full in the chest; he caught, and held it there.

"Rowr!" Isis purred, trying to burrow into his breast. She flipped completely upside-down in his hands, rubbed her head hard against his arm, licked him ferociously, and said again, emphatically: *"Rowr!"*

"Hello, Fur-face," whispered Josh. He rocked her softly a moment, holding her soft black face to his face, stroking her tenderly behind the ear, just the way she liked. Then he dropped her to the floor and approached the throne. Isis remained where she had landed, purring and preening herself.

When Josh was ten feet from the throne, he stopped and studied the child-Queen—as, poised, she studied him. He was surprised to see she seemed to be near ten or twelve years old. Nor was she exactly Human. Her head was elliptical, and port-wine feathers sprouted from her temples. Her eyes and nose together looked more like a mirrored beak-mask than anything else, though her lips were full and red. Her naked body was Human enough, and female, certainly—though markedly androgynous. Her hands had fingers that were both delicate and clawlike; her feet resembled velvety talons. She had a downy, prehensile tail. And along the back of the length of both arms ran an array of short feather buds, mostly gold and green.

Josh felt his heart beating faster. This was his child.

After a long silence of mutual examination, she spoke to him—though he sensed that even if she hadn't spoken, he would have understood her meaning. As it was, certain words or thoughts clearly rang through telepathically.

"*You* are my *father*. Do *not* be *afraid*. I will not hurt you."

"Where is your mother?" Josh asked her. He didn't feel afraid.

"In my infancy *I killed* her, which act *I regret*. I have grown since then. You have *no*thing to *fear*, father-creator."

"What are you about?" Josh asked. His immediate sense was of her vulnerability.

"I am yet to learn. I have *powers*. But I *change* daily. Each day I get new *visions* of the Ether-Mother. She is ever *changing*, ever sly. And each day my *powers* grow. I can *change* things. And I *change*. You see, I am in metamorphosis."

"How do you do these things?"

"A powerful mind generates a powerful energy field. When this field is strong enough, it can *bend* the substance of *space-time*—like a great star, a black hole. All minds do this to a small extent—it is usually undetectable, though, as is the *force* of small masses, or the effect of small veloci-

ties. But just as *time* slows and matter contracts at veloci-
ties near the speed of *light*, and just as space, light, and
time *curve* around the densest of masses, so are space-time
distortions created by the energy field of the megamind.
Do you understand?"

"No," said Josh. "I understand you're very powerful."

"Understand also this: you have *nothing* to *fear* from me.
You or your people. You are my father-creator, you have
manifested *me*. *I am* the twist in the Ether-Mother produced by the spasm of you and my mother-creator, whom I
have killed in ignorance and entropy. But *you are* safe."

"And the rest of Earth's creatures?" He felt he could
take her at her word—at least, her intentions. What she
actually might do, he felt just as surely, was beyond even
her control.

"I cannot say. My *powers* are untrained, my *visions* incomplete. I can*not see* what *will* come."

"What do you wish?" He felt hopeful. He felt strangely
powerful in her presence, though he suspected she could
extinguish his life with a blink.

"*I* wish for harmony. Yet *I* cannot *grasp* the scale. Still,
it will come. *I* could wish for *your help*."

"Why mine?"

"*I* am your manifestation. *You* are my progenitor. *Help*
is the theta field of that relationship. *Love* is the Electro-
Motive Force. *Balance* is the wave-form. Wavelength is the
passion. Do *you* understand?"

"No."

"No matter. Time is our *grace*. Go, now. I will call
again—you must help me. I can send thoughts, yet I receive them still only imperfectly—at close distances of
space or time, in the absence of interference by other
fields. But the simple wavelengths are simple—for trans-
mission and reception: *Come*; *go*; *help*; *love*; *hate*. Do you
understand?"

"No."

"No matter. *I* am your child. Will *you help* me?"

"You're my child; I'm your witness."

"*Go* now."

Josh turned and left. Isis padded along beside him.

Together they weaved their way through the smoking castle, the desolate Inner City, the thrashing Outer City, and south, beyond the walls, to the tense, waiting Bookery camp.

CHAPTER 15

In Which the Gentleness of Friends Does Not Always Suffice

JOSH arrived back at camp in the frosty shadow of evening. His friends were huddled around small fires; silent, tense. There was a palpable sense of relief on everyone's face as he strode into the oak grove, accompanied by the proudly strutting Isis. They all converged on him, wrapped him in blankets, sat him down before the central fire, and even dared the night's black forces by putting another log on the tenuous flames.

He told them of his meeting with the child; and for a long minute after he finished, nobody spoke.

Finally Jasmine said, "And you're certain she said the Queen was dead?"

"Positive," answered Josh. "Said she killed her."

"And the City? . . ." ventured Beauty. "It was in ruins?"

"Not completely. But on its way."

There was another long silence. The group was totally mystified—they could not quickly assimilate this confusing new data, and were at a loss for response. After several minutes, Jasmine spoke again: "Joshua, what do you think?" Her look was pensive.

The crowd edged closer, hanging on his words.

"I'm not sure what to think." His tone was measured. "I know we personally have nothing to fear from this new being. The old Queen's experiments are over now—the City is coming apart, most of its inhabitants are fleeing, the harems are dispersing. Our vigil is over . . ."

"But?" said Rose.

"But the child is strange beyond understanding. She has

215

powers I don't grasp. But she is my daughter. But she murdered her mother. I believe she means well . . ."

"But . . ."

"She's changing," resumed Josh. "I think we should wait and see. I think she wants to do what's right. Let's watch and see if she can find out what it is. Part of her is wondering child, part is monster, and part is darkness itself. But she's my child, and part of her is me."

They all nodded solemnly, straining for comprehension. Josh stared into the fire. Isis lay curled, asleep, in his lap. The others withdrew in groups of two or three to consider the meanings of what had been said.

That night was one of strange and chill occurrences. First, the clouds descended, lower and lower, until they hung, black and puffy, barely a hundred feet above the ground. And then it began to snow.

Fat, wet flakes sank quickly to the ground, covering everything like a shroud. Lightning ripped through the cloud bank, too—cracking loud as cannon, piercing the bloated clouds with white sparks and thunder.

Just as suddenly, the snow stopped, and a hot wind blew through the forest, melting the ice and blowing out the campfires.

Lost sounds floated on the air. As if the sky were moaning, or the Earth rolling off its orbit.

Once, a tree fell. Just one tree, in the midst of all the others, near the north edge of the encampment. It buried itself several feet underground.

The campfires relit spontaneously, but now their flames were blue, the color of burning methane, with streaks of violet, as if suffused with potassium vapor.

The clouds settled lower, and the abiding chill returned.

In the morning, the sun returned emphatically, dissolving away the ghosts of the darkness.

Jasmine had not slept at all. She had brooded darkly through the night, occasionally talking to herself. Now that Josh was awake again, she walked over to him and spoke quietly. "We should assume a friendly stance with this child; show her we're friends."

Josh nodded. "I feel hopeful."

"Good. So do I. I think you should go back and see her. Make an overture of friendship."

"You think I should go alone?"

"Well, take a couple of friends. Not so many as to be intimidating. Just some good comrades. Take Beauty. And Isis, the child likes Isis, you said. And take a good bottle of Scribe wine."

"How about Ollie? He's her uncle."

"Better wait on Ollie. He still gets moods, he's temperamental. Take Beauty—he has balance and tact."

"What will we say?"

"Pay homage. Toast her health. Offer our support."

He looked at her curiously. "Are you sincere?"

"You're our emissary. We're one and all as sincere as you'll be when you speak with her."

"When should I go?"

"Go this afternoon. Rest first." She held her palm to his cheek a moment, then stood and walked away. She spent a little time talking to Isis behind a rise, fussing affectionately with the Cat as she spoke. Josh slumped back against a tree, exhausted. He felt very childlike: vulnerable, malleable, caught in a web of unknown design; near tears. He sighed. Then he pulled the quill from his boot and wrapped himself in the comfort of his oldest habitual activity: he opened his journal and set down the record.

Paula sat in the cradle of Aba's wing. With her index finger she languidly traced lines along its metacarpal struts, around its leathern folds.

He read to her from an ancient, half-disintegrated book:

> Only the lonely can e'er defy /
> Time's bottomless thirst and roving eye.

"That's beautiful," she answered. She was pale as a white rose petal.

He closed the book. "Lonely no more," he intoned.

"Nor I." She smiled a secret smile and rolled on top of

him. They kissed. "What'll happen to us now?" she whispered.

"Fly north with me. I'll buy a harem to husband for my sustenance; and love only you."

She looked at him deeply, searchingly. He pulled her mouth down to his mouth, pressed their bodies together so tightly they seemed to fuse, wrapped his great wings around them both. And within each other, they flew.

Ollie, like everyone else, was uncertain what to do. Josh was safe, Rose seemed to be getting herself sorted out. The Queen was dead, the Vampires leaving. Ollie felt at loose ends; it appeared to be time to move on. He wanted a new adventure, a new corner of the universe to explore. No more to be learned here, no more challenge; no more views from the brink.

He was taking a short walk, wondering whether to head north into the Terrarium or east into the desert, whether to leave in the morning or wait a couple days, when he quite unexpectedly came upon Aba and Paula, blissfully lying together between two trees. The sight enraged him. He could not say why, precisely, but undoubtedly it had something to do with their happiness and togetherness against his lonely apartness, with Aba's Vampireness against Paula's Humanness, and probably, finally, with Ollie's growing liking of Aba—despite his own good judgment and his many oaths that he would never like a Vampire. With this new affection, the terrifying sense that the entire emotional structure he had erected to protect himself was being eroded so enraged him that he kicked Aba viciously in the leg, and swore, "Get up, you filthy beast! Damn your blood, I can't stand looking at you any more."

The pain seared through Aba's calf, and he reflexively jumped up and unfurled his wings. The wingtip caught Ollie on the cheek, carving a deep gash and knocking the boy over. When he saw what he had done, Aba was horrified. He pulled his wings in and extended his arm to help Ollie up. Ollie was wild, though—unappeasable, blind; mad, really. In a flash, his dagger was out: he sliced the Vampire's palm.

Aba cried out; Paula ran over, her face mottled with fear and anger. Aba squeezed his bleeding hand into a fist. Ollie touched the wound on his cheek, looked at the blood on his fingers, smiled. "You have first blood, it would seem. I will have last."

"Get out of here!" screamed Paula. As she yelled, she kicked Ollie in the groin, doubling him over.

Others came running, attracted by the shouts. Ollie grinned through his pain. "He's chosen the time and place," he whispered to Paula, referring to Aba.

"You're not Human," she spat at Ollie. "You think you're so superior because you've suffered—well, suffer this . . ." She directed a blow at his neck, but he caught her arm instantly, and with almost inhuman speed, punched her in the solar plexus. She went down, breathless, unconscious. Ollie stood facing Aba. Half the camp surrounded them now. Jasmine stepped forward.

"What's going on?" the Neuroman asked quietly.

"A duel," said Ollie. "Here and now. Barehanded." He threw his dagger into the dirt.

Aba shook his head. "I will not fight," he said.

"You have no choice." Ollie smiled maliciously. His blood was up now, and suddenly he hated the Vampire more than anything he had ever known. This Vampire *was* his hate. "You have no choice," he repeated. "You drew first blood."

"It was an accident," Aba protested slowly. "My wing struck you as I stood. I didn't intend—"

"I challenged him, and he cut me, and I cut him back," Ollie insisted. "He chose here and now. I choose the weapons: bare hands."

"Why did you challenge him?" Jasmine asked.

"What difference?" Ollie rasped. "I hate his foul Vampire breath."

From somewhere in the crowd, a Book yelled out, "That's the Word!" And a few in the back muttered slogans.

Ollie was encouraged. He said, "The beast was taking advantage of the girl. She's lost her letters. I found it intolerable, and I challenged him and he answered the challenge. There's nothing else for it but to duel."

The crowd formed a circle in a clearing, and bodily carried the duelists into it. Paula lay gasping on the ground. Josh remained asleep, exhausted from the night before. Beauty had Rose out for a ride. Most of the Pluggers were in-circuit. The Books who ringed the antagonists were keen for the fight, and the air was electric with anticipation.

Jasmine stepped into the circle. "You're sure you want to do this?" she asked them both.

"We have no choice," Ollie said, staring hard at the Vampire.

"I will not fight," Aba insisted.

"Then die," cried the boy, and lunged forward, locking his thumbs around Aba's throat.

Everyone shouted as the two of them rolled in the dirt. Jasmine backed off, reluctantly obeying the code of the duel.

Aba was turning blue as the onlookers cheered—venting all the months of tension in the sickening spectacle. Ollie's hands were gripping the Vampire's neck tightly, his legs squeezing the creature's waist in a vice lock, when suddenly he stopped—realizing with an even greater fury that Aba *wasn't* fighting: he was rolling limply, passively, in Ollie's grasp; on the verge of death.

Ollie stood up. "Fight, damn you!" he hissed.

Aba lay there, breathing heavily, shaking his head. He felt dizzy with pain and anoxia, but he had vowed not to fight back. He had already hurt these people too much, he felt, to inflict any more pain now. He was the very personification of all their dreads, real and imagined, and they were right to hate him; and even if it meant his death now, he would not abridge that right. He would shed no more Human blood against their will. And this, above all, he believed: he would never again sacrifice Human life to his passion; and if he died on this spot, he would not spill this Human's blood.

He looked at Ollie now, reeling above him. He spoke

softly, for the boy's grip had bruised his larynx. "I will not fight."

Ollie kicked him in the belly, but he only grunted and shook his head again. There were a few more shouts from the crowd, but most had become quiet, suddenly disturbed by the evident disparity in Humanity being displayed before them. Unable to control himself, Ollie pounced on the downed Vampire and began beating him in the face. Aba didn't lift a hand to protect himself. By the time he lost consciousness, some of the spectators began drifting away, too uncomfortable to watch further.

Jasmine couldn't stand it any longer. She ran into the circle and pulled Ollie off the stuporous creature, and in a voice filled with disgust said, "Stop! Stop this sick show!"

Suddenly Ollie turned on Jasmine—as if, once started thrashing, he couldn't stop—and, tears in his eyes, tore *her* to the ground, hit her a few times, snapping the cap off the valve at the back of her head. She lashed back at him with her hands for a moment—cutting his nose, and inadvertently tearing the ruby from his chest, sewn there so long before. The jewel lay in the dust, and left on Ollie's chest a ragged, bleeding scar. He didn't tangle with Jasmine long, though. He jumped up, and fled through the woods towards the desert.

Several ounces of Hemolube oozed out the valve in Jasmine's skull before she was able to reach back and recap it. Then she just sat where she was and composed herself. At last she stood and walked over to Aba, who was trying to sit up. Paula stumbled over now, too, finally able to move again; and the two women helped the bleeding Vampire to the nearby stream. The rest of the audience withdrew into the trees, variously hushed and ashamed.

Fleur, Elspeth, and Osi sat in an access room under the humming power station. They spoke in whispers, though no one else was around.

"She is unpredictable, and powerful beyond measure . . ." Fleur began.

"No longer committed to the ideals which the Queen, *orong olo glia,* embodied," Elspeth added.

" . . . Capricious, I would venture to say insane," Fleur went on. "Elspeth spoke with her yesterday—she had the attention span of a two-year-old. And she was trying to make it rain *inside* the castle."

They paused, looked around the great room. Giant machines buzzed an ancient drone, blinked their lights. Osi wondered what private jokes they winked about.

"We must kill her," Fleur intoned.

"And engineer a new Queen?" asked Osi.

"If we can. First, though, we must kill this one."

Easier said than done, thought Osi. She's the master of us all: she's decimated our harems, burned our city, made nightmares of our dreams—and still she controls us. We think we can return to what was, but we cannot; we can only tumble in these waves and hope we won't be broken on the sand. He said: "We would be wise to leave, like the others. We'll never be a power in this city again."

"We will; we will," croaked Elspeth. "But we must act quickly—and together. *Nuliento gor!*"

Osi nodded. "All right. I'll help you. Come to me this evening and we'll discuss a plan." He walked out before they could reply.

So, thought Osi, I league now with mutant machine-men against deranged children. Blood of my blood, what have we come to?

He was troubled as he walked back up smoking corridors to his suite, for his feelings about the child were complex—too complex even for his own introspective nature to piece together. On the one hand, she was destroying the City—that much was certain. Buildings crumbling to ruin, animals fleeing or going berserk—it was worse than the Ice Madness. And with this distintegration, all of his dreams were dissolving: dreams of the New World, where everything had a place, a place by design instead of rude chance. It made his fists clench to think of all their work gone, gone . . . He hated this child.

Flames leapt out at him from an open door, burning the fine hair on his arm before he could jump away. The floor beneath him rumbled with the vibrations of a distant, muted explosion. Yes, he hated her.

And yet . . . And yet, he felt drawn to her. Drawn to her power. To her insanity? he wondered. In her presence he felt dizzy, heady, almost helpless. In her absence he felt anger and frustration. Strong emotions, about such a small, new creature.

He reached his quarters and lay on the bed. He had a headache. He rang the crystal bell on the bedstand, but no one came: half his harem had left. Run away, or just disappeared. The rest came back only to sleep—otherwise they roamed the halls, explored regions of the castle previously forbidden them.

Vera walked in, eating an apple. "You call?" she asked petulantly. She was his most trusted Human, and even she was acting odd.

"You took your time," Osi snapped. "Bring your neck over here."

Vera hesitated. "Say you love me first."

Osi roared, jumped up, and pinned her against the wall. She gasped, then swooned as the Vampire clamped down on her neck, pulling her head back by the hair.

When Osi finished, he dropped the unconscious Human in the corner and stormed into his study. A fresh canvas waited upright in the easel; unopened paints sat on the table beside it. Deliberately, Osi tried to calm himself. With careful, precise strokes, he began to paint.

Maybe he should just leave, after all—take a few of his best and find a nice, quiet cave in the jungle to inhabit. This had really gone beyond the pale, down here. And yet . . . something here wanted him to stay. Perhaps he would stay . . . for just a little while.

With an angry snarl, he threw down his paintbrush and quit the room. "Vera . . ." he began apologetically. But Vera was gone. He hissed softly and headed for the harem quarters.

Ugo scratched the glossy scar on his cheek. "And you? What will you do?"

"I stay," rasped Ninjus. "There is power in the child. This is where the power lies, and by Quark's Charm, I will lie with it!"

Ugo smiled. "It's a dangerous bed."

"Be off if you're not up to it," Ninjus barked. "I want no cubs in my den."

Ugo growled uncontrollably a moment, then quieted himself. "There are plots already against the child. She will be well pleased with those who stand by her to thwart such activity."

Now it was Ninjus who smiled. "She'll be well pleased, and we will be well rewarded. She tears down now to build up later. I will be with her at the foundation, to set the cornerstone."

"And I to slit the throat of every wight that tries to stop her!" Ugo actually drooled a bit, over the scarred edge of his mouth, so excited was he with visions of new blood and wild death.

"That's the stuff," rumbled Ninjus. "We will prevail."

The two new allies huddled together, and began to draw up plans for defending the child.

Josh, Beauty, and Isis walked slowly into the Queen's chamber. Isis immediately ran up to the throne and jumped up beside the child. The others approached with more decorum.

"Who are you?" The child looked at Beauty.

Josh said, "This is my closest of all friends, Beauty, of the race Centauri."

"Welcome, then," the child nodded. She looked very like she had the day before; only now, the feathers that sprouted along the backs of her arms were longer, and she kept her tail wrapped around her left leg. Also, she spoke only words today; no telepathy.

Beauty bared his neck.

Josh began: "We come because—"

"I know why you come," the child-Queen dismissed his speech with a ruffling of her head feathers. "You come because you're frightened—you want to talk about the weather last night. Why is that the only thing anyone can ask me about today? And what's in that beaker?"

Josh put down the bottle and cups he had been carrying

in his sack. "Wine. It's an old Scribal ritual—a Human ritual, actually—to drink among friends."

"We are not friends yet."

"No." Beauty spoke for the first time. "Friends must be equals. You hold too much over us to be our friend."

"And why should I want to be your friend?"

"If you need to ask, then it is you who are not wanted."

The feathers on her arms stood straight up, and her eyes seemed to sparkle with tiny explosions of light.

Josh quickly intervened. "We don't mean to provoke you. Like you said, we're only scared—of the weather."

The child's feathers smoothed, her eyes dimmed. She extended a hand and coolly stroked Isis, who lay alert, but still, beside her. "I told you once: I will not hurt you. You have nothing to fear."

"Can you tell us—"

"Last night I was experimenting with the atmosphere. With electrical and gravitational fields, with matter and energy conversions. I was testing and flexing some of my muscles—no, I was stretching. Can you tell me what it is you do when you stretch?"

"No, but—"

"No, but you do it just the same, and feel better for it. So it was with me last night. Only I was stretching my mind."

Josh smiled. "There's not yet a word for what you were doing last night."

"Then I make new words. I am my father's daughter, after all—child of a Scribe."

"What else are you?" Beauty asked quietly.

She considered the question, weighing many answers. "I am . . . curious. About everything. Everything is new— but also old. Do you understand?"

Josh nodded, Beauty waited, Isis licked her tail.

"I saw two Vampire guards playing something called a game, today," the child went on. "Throwing bones. What is a game?"

"They throw bones to see how they land. How they land depends on chance and skill. How they land determines who wins the game." Beauty kept his tone factual, observing the child's response.

"I don't understand 'chance.'"

"Then let's play a game," Josh suggested. "Here." He gathered ten splinters of wood from the floor near a shattered window frame, and dropped them in a small pile before the child. "This is pick-up-sticks. How they fell depended on chance. Now each of us must try to lift one stick off the pile without disturbing the others." Gingerly, he lifted away a precarious stick; no others moved. Delicately, he pulled another through the center. Once more— He jarred a support, and three splinters settled. Josh laughed. "Your turn," he said to Beauty.

The Centaur prided himself on this game, for it required balance and delicacy. On his knees, he removed one stick from the pile; then another, and— A great roiling explosion somewhere in the west wing shook the entire castle, causing the little pile of sticks to move again. "Ah," smiled Beauty. "There is *chance* again. So be it. Now comes your turn, child."

The child still looked faintly puzzled by the whole thing, but jumped down from the throne and studied the sticks. After a while, she said, "See? Do you see it? What it forms?"

Beauty and Josh shook their heads.

"It is the South Wall of the Serengeti Crater. This configuration is not new. Is that the game? To recognize the pattern? To name where it has been before? Ah, I see now! What a good game. I like games. But where is the chance in this?"

Josh and Beauty exchanged a glance that was not altogether lost on the child. She looked crestfallen, and said, "I've lost the game, haven't I?"

"You make your own games," Josh replied gently.

"So. I make new words, and I make new games," she said a little defiantly.

"And you make new friends," Beauty said, bowing his head, gracious but formal.

The remark made her coy. She smiled, began to speak, then didn't.

"What you did with the weather last night," Josh interceded, "that was really something."

A smile flashed brightly across her face, followed by a vexing glower. "I cannot do as I wish, though," she admitted. "I try to turn the air into fire—instead, it rains. I try to turn the sea to stone—instead, rocks melt. I bid the moon ignite for me—and it does, only it's a moon of Saturn." She looked down; then up at Josh. "I told you pridefully I was stretching my mind, but I fear it stretches me. Father, what should I do?"

Her voice suddenly had a bleak and helpless ring. Josh was reminded of his first impression of her: vulnerable, confused.

"Go slower," he advised her. "Time is your servant. Be a little gentle with things—with the Earth and its creatures—and you'll learn much more of their nature . . ."

"And of your own nature, little curious one," Beauty added.

The child smiled a sad smile, catching the others in the prism of her reflective eyes. She shook her head slowly, and Josh was briefly seized by the sense that the lonely child was sage beyond her years. "The universe is not gentle, Father," she whispered.

"Thus with gentle friendships do we hold back the Void," breathed Beauty.

"Then let's drink to gentle friends," said Josh, uncorking his bottle and pouring three cups.

"And to new games," she added, taking a cup from him.

Beauty took the last cup. Isis suddenly had an itch, and began biting furiously between the first two claws of her left forefoot.

Josh raised his glass. "To new games, and the gentleness of friends."

They all drank. They all drank one sip, and then spat and sputtered on the floor—the wine had gone bad. The child threw her glass down. They pursed their lips and spat again, trying to rid their mouths of the sour, bitter taste.

"What filth is this?" the child screamed. The sudden commotion scared Isis, who jumped down to the floor and put her paw right into a glob of the child's red-streaked spittle. She shook her foot hurriedly, and ran into the corner.

"It's no trick," Josh apologized, trying to smile. "The wine just turned. It happens sometimes, to old wine. There's nothing to be—"

"*Leave* me," the child-Queen rumbled. Her feathers were all up; her eyes, twitching star clusters; her words, again edged with telepathy.

"No, really," Josh pursued, "it's just vinegar from—"

Beauty tried to restrain him with a surreptitious touch, but it was too late. The child screamed at them: "Leave, I say!" Sparks crackled around her head; the air pressure in the room seemed to drop.

Josh and Beauty slowly backed out the door. Isis darted out just ahead of them from the corner she had been crouching in. In a moment, they were all gone.

Leaving the child-Queen alone in the half-darkness.

For many minutes she sat there, seething. She knew there had been no malice involved, on Joshua's part, in this drink business. She had felt his mind on that account, and his mind was clear. In fact, the taste of the wine seemed to surprise them all equally. Still, she hated discomfort of any kind, and she was angry.

She sulked a while, but this just got her more pent up. She needed release; catharsis of her confusions. The darkness of her thoughts tormented her. She wanted to scream; to explode.

Osi.

Steam began to rise from her head, so much hotter was it than the surrounding air. Rhythmically, distractedly, she scratched her nails on the arm of the throne.

Osiiiiii!

Osi walked in, approached the throne. The difference in their statures was remarkable—he was over seven feet tall, she was barely four. His body was hairless from head to foot, hers was feathered. His skin was dark, her spirit was darker.

"You wanted me, Highness?" In his mind he had heard her call; and was helpless to resist. Something about this bird-child had possessed him; corrupted him, somehow. She had begun making him do . . . things. Toying with him in a way he was unable to stop—or unwilling to. So much else about his life was in tatters now, like a raveled edge. This child had become his only focus. That was the only reason he could find for why he stayed in this crumbling ruin of a city—something about the bird-child he both feared and lusted after: the same feelings members of his harem had for him, he knew. He smiled philosophically as he stood before the bird-child now. She is my Vampire, he thought. Perhaps everybody has somebody who is his Vampire.

The child nodded, as if she had heard his acknowledgment. "Kneel," she told him.

He knelt before the throne. She nodded imperceptibly. With a smile that mixed anticipation and fear, he began to lick one of her smooth thighs as he caressed the other with his brown, powerful fingers. She wrapped her prehensile tail around the back of his neck, pulling his head closer in. He let his fingers wander up her belly, linger over the delicate whiteness of her chest, dent the small rosy nipples.

A hiss poured from her mouth, like air escaping under pressure, and she dug her talons into his shoulders, so deep, deeper; an inch deep. He tensed as her razor nails punctured his skin, felt his own blood trickle down his arms.

She released her tail grip on his head, and with strength far greater than his own, pulled him up by the claw hold she maintained in his shoulder muscles. His wings unfurled. Wet all over, now, steaming and sweating, she wrapped her legs around his waist; pulled her nails from his shoulders; buried her right claw ferociously into his left breast; and with her left hand, pulled his mouth to her throat. He bit down hard on her jugular, sucking in rapt obsession.

Her feathers fanned out full, her slight body flushed all over. The air around them crackled and smoked. They writhed, and rolled to the floor, bleeding, reeling toward release.

CHAPTER 16

In Which It Is Possible, on Starry Nights, to Hear the Laughter of Time

JOSHUA, Beauty, and Isis quickly made their way out of the castle and into the City. The castle itself seemed completely deserted as they ran down its now randomly lighted corridors, stepping quickly over rubble and dead bodies—some already beginning to decompose.

The City outside the castle walls was a different matter. Dozens of creatures lined the streets of the Inner City—huddling, whimpering, waiting. Vampires, Humans, Neuromans, Lizards, Accidents. Josh and company walked by under the surveillance of this spooky assemblage, but no one came near, no one moved. Steam filled the air.

The ground began to rumble, next—a continuous, jolting shudder that made it hard to walk. It wasn't like an earthquake. There were no shocks, no shifts of land. Just an unceasing rumble, as if the land were shivering. Then the sky began to change colors: suddenly bright orange, then an intense lavender; now obsidian black, now emerald green.

Josh picked up Isis and jumped on Beauty's back. The Centaur trotted to the inner gate; when he emerged into the Outer City, he began to gallop.

All the evils of the City were fouling one another here. Vampires, Cerberus guards, Minotaurs, giant Rats, sewer Snakes, Cidons, Accidents, and mixed-breed pirates were running amok. Gangs of them would overtake some lone beast—wounded or weakened—and eat it alive. Josh saw a Rat calmly gnawing whatever parts of its own body it could reach with its mouth, until it finally lost consciousness, bleeding and mutilated. Creatures were tied to roofs, and

231

then the houses set afire. Death was everywhere, like the undertow in troubled waters.

Quickly, Beauty ran through the gates. No one followed them. There was no steam outside the walls of the City, and the sky was a normal, clear blue. Beauty reared up on his hind legs, pawed the air, and set off southeast at a dead run.

Ollie lay baking on the sand of the Ansa Blanca. The sun burned down, burned through him, parched his dry flesh, killed the budding mold within. In this cleansing desert crucible, he waited for death.

He had reached his crisis with Aba, and come through it. The putrefaction that had been growing in his soul all these years had come to a head under the heat of that Vampire—Ollie had picked at the boil and worried it until finally it had burst, spewing its purulence and bloody agony over all who came near, leaving Ollie drained, torn, released.

And now, cleansing. The purifying sun radiated down, healing the frayed edges of his wound, baking out the last vile pocket of pus. He could feel it: all the years of jungle rot necrotizing within him were burning away, searing to ash. When the process was complete, he knew there would be little left of himself, so much of his substance had rotted. Then he would die when the sun finished its business. This was his test by fire, then. If he still lived at the end of this crucible day, after all the reek of his spirit had done oozing and the sun had evaporated his evil and cauterized the wound—if he still lived then, he knew he could start over with what substance remained. Weak but clean. He doubted he would live until evening.

The sun was at its zenith now: unremitting, without anticipation or memory. The sands of the Ansa Blanca stretched out in all directions like a waterless ocean of infinite depth.

Ollie touched the hole in his chest where the ruby had been ripped out. It was sticky with a fresh clot at the center, crusted with dry flakes at the edges. Painful but clean.

He took a deep breath, filled his lungs with desert air, and waited for death.

Jasmine walked up to them as Josh slid down off Beauty's back. "How did it go?" she asked.

Josh shook his head in consternation.

Beauty said, "Badly."

They all sat around the campfire and ate as Josh and Beauty gave their impressions of the interview with the child. Isis sat quietly in Jasmine's lap.

"She has powers she does not begin to understand," concluded Beauty. "She is given to whims and tantrums. She cannot be trusted."

"She's only a child, though," Josh added. "She'll grow. She'll mature. I think, with some guidance . . ."

Jasmine, absorbed in concentration, finally spoke. "Joshua, I hope you're right. But I think we have to make some immediate contingency plans."

The whole camp was listening. Most would do whatever Josh said: but they knew his great respect for Jasmine's judgment, and they focused intently on her words.

"What do you suggest?"

She opened her hidden abdominal compartment, removed a number of tubes and implements, and laid them beside her in the grass. Next, she lifted Isis's front paw, took a scissors, and cut a slender thread that had tied a little patch of material to the foot-pad. She held the patch up for all to see.

"This is an agar cell patch," she said. "It happened to be in the box of bioengineering lab paraphernalia I stole when I raided the castle with Ollie. It's a special polymer-nutrient adhesive, designed centuries ago to hold a tissue culture for up to forty-eight hours. I tied it to the bottom of Isis's foot this morning, but left it sealed. I gave her instructions to bite off the seal—secretly—when she was safely ensconced somewhere near the child-Queen."

"But why—" began Josh.

"I didn't tell any of you of this before because we believe the child can read the minds in her immediate vicinity—if not thought for thought, at least intent and feeling. So if *you* knew what my intent was, then *she* would know. I didn't even tell Isis the real reason I wanted her to do what I asked her to do."

"Which was what?"

"Which was that when the child spat, Isis was to put her paw down on the spittle and soak it up with this agar patch. Then, if possible, she was unobtrusively to cover the patch up with another paper seal I'd stuck to the bottom of her other foot. Which it looks like she was able to do." She stroked Isis's head fondly, and Isis beamed.

"But how did you know the child was going to spit?" asked Beauty.

Jasmine laughed. "Because I knew the wine was bad. That lot turned sour years ago—bottles I'd stored in my hiding-cave."

Josh—and everyone else—looked confused. "I still don't get it."

Jasmine tore the seal off the agar patch, took a slender spatula, and scraped half the jelly off the patch. She then uncapped a silver test tube, stirred the spit-and-agar-filled spatula around in it, and finally recapped the tube. She repeated this entire process with the other half of the patch and another tube. When done, she spoke again: "I wanted the child to spit—that's why I had you offer her bitter wine. I wanted her to spit because I knew she would probably shed some cells from the inside of her cheek into her saliva, and those cells would then get adsorbed onto the agar patch when Isis made contact. The child's own cells, that's what we want. The cells were kept alive on the patch, which, thank goodness, Isis was able to seal again—"

"In the corner, when she jumped off the throne—" Josh interjected.

"Wherever. I told her only that I wanted her to get the child's saliva on her foot, so I could smell it when she got back—nothing particularly threatening about that for the child to tune in on. The second seal was crucial, too—the cells probably wouldn't have lived without it during your journey back here. In any case, I've taken the brew and divided it in two, now, half into each of the two culture tubes—tubes containing a bacteriocidal culture medium that greatly favors the growth of animal cells, promotes tissue culture. And there's enough nutrient in each tube to keep a tissue culture alive for weeks!" she ended brightly.

Most of her listeners still weren't very clear just what her purpose was. Aba had studied some of these ancient forms of magic with Lon, though, and so was more sophisticated than most. "But why would we *want* a culture of the child's buccal cells?" he asked. His throat was still bruised with Ollie's thumb prints, so he spoke slowly and without volume.

Jasmine smiled. "A good question. In fact, that's precisely the question to ask. And the answer is that I have friends in a camp in the Mosian Firecaves—Neuromans, many of them genetic engineers, the same people who reconditioned my body two years ago and gave me all these tricks up my fingers, my secret compartment here, and so on—friends, in any event, who can make use of these cells. Because I'm convinced that if we have to defend ourselves against this child—and I'm not saying we will—but if we do, her powers are beyond equal. So our only possible defense will be a molecular-biological one."

Aba nodded tentatively.

"Huh?" Josh said.

"Well," Jasmine went on, "they've got a good, isolated lab up there. They haven't got all the resources they used to, but they haven't been sitting still, either. They'll be able to isolate the genetic material from the cells that have proliferated in these tubes, analyze the genome—reconstruct it if they want, either identically or with alterations. They could clone it and get a twin identical to our child in the castle—or a twin with differences if they had enough time. Unfortunately, time may be a factor, though. There are numerous possibilities, however—they have all kinds of experiments up there that may prove fruitful when applied to our problem. So, the point is, we have to get these cells up there in a hurry. I've divided them into two parts because I think two expeditionary forces should set out by different routes; if one fails, the other may not. I suggest one group take one tube and carry it east and north, around the Terrarium. The other tube could be entrusted to another party of three or four. They could take Joshua's glass submarine straight up the coast—that would be fastest—then anchor it way north in some hidden cove and trek due east to the camp in the Firecaves. I'll give the parties going an emergency codeword known only to Mosian Neuromans, so they realize this is top priority. So that's my plan. So what do you think?"

All in all, they thought it was a good plan. At least, it gave them something to hang their hopes on, in the face of the strange, disconcerting turn of events.

As they began deciding who would go north, Aba stepped forward. His face was swollen, his right hand bandaged. "I'll take one tube," he said to the group.

There was a stunned, guilty silence. He spoke again. "It's the only sensible way—I have the best chance of getting through. Besides, I can fly there faster than anyone here can walk."

Partly it was a heroic gesture to throw in the face of all the Books who had spurned him as his relationship with Paula had grown. Partly it was just for Paula. He sensed more and more that she was—they all were—in real danger from the queer child; his proposal seemed an essential step toward their protection.

There was a long, general hesitation; no one knew quite what to say. At last, Josh spoke: "I say this is a Vampire who's won our trust. He was once the best friend of the finest Vampire I ever knew; he's never done us harm, yet we've treated him badly. And now, he offers us his life in our service. I humbly thank him; and I say he goes."

That decided it, without debate; for Josh was the leader. In any case, before more could be said, Ollie suddenly reappeared, almost out of nowhere. He was sunburned red over brown, with great areas of white, dead skin peeling off in wrinkly, thin flakes. His lips were cracked and puffy, his eyes deep-set with dehydration; yet he smiled. "And I'll take the other tube," he asserted loudly. There were murmurs and exclamations.

Paula walked up. "You've got some nerve even showing your face here again."

Ollie looked at her, then at the rest. He spoke slowly and

clearly. "I ask your pardon for my behavior—all of you; and you . . ." he briefly locked eyes with Aba, then went on: "I wish to atone for my crimes against the spirit of our humanity. I ask you to let me bear the burden of this mission for you."

Jasmine looked intensely at Ollie. "You think we can trust you?"

He bridled, then wilted, then stood his ground. "I've never broken my word. Besides, I have a better chance than anyone here—except you, maybe—of fighting my way through hostile territory to make it up there. I'm the best natural commando around. And besides that, Aba is right—*he* should take one tube, for he can fly there faster than anyone—and at this point I could hardly ask him to do anything for us I wouldn't do myself."

Ollie and Aba looked at each other. There was still a deep-rooted strain between them—but now, with the first threads of acceptance.

Ollie felt a measure of burden lifted by his *mea culpa*; and he felt lighter by half when by consensus he was granted the grave and terrible adventure. He hoped he could beat Aba to the Mosian Firecaves—for, recantations notwithstanding, Ollie was still Ollie, and he craved some kind of honorable victory over this Vampire nemesis.

Four others were decided upon to accompany him: Beauty, who knew the area round the Firecaves and how to get there; Michael, who was nearly exploding with potential energy; Ellen, whose vocabulary was great and who would try to protect the enterprise with the strength of her Scribery; and David, who pulled rank to go—probably so he could prove something to Michael.

Jasmine, Josh, and Rose, it was decided, would stay behind to monitor the child-Queen. Paula would remain to supervise continued work on the Great Lexicon.

All was concluded over the course of the evening; by midnight, good-byes were being said to the brave departing messengers.

Beauty bade farewell first to Rose, whom he loved now as an old friend with whom he had shared good times and

misery. The scarred ligaments of their love were fused forever. They hugged without words, close once again under
the specter of their obscure new peril.

Next, Beauty told Jasmine good-bye. Once more, as he
had five years before, he now felt both happy at the knowing of her and sad at the knowing so little. He wanted
more, and again circumstances had prevented any deeper
connection between them.

"You are a remarkable woman," he said to her, his
hands on her shoulders, "and I shall miss you."

"Our friendship isn't over yet," she protested; though she
knew somehow, as he did, that it would be a long time
before they saw each other again.

They hugged a hug to last until the passing of millennia.

Finally, Beauty said good-bye to Josh. They were, had
always been, would ever be, each other's friend. Through
years of separation, tests of will, trials of faith, times of
forgetting and of remembering, they were enduringly this
for each other.

"So much," Beauty whispered to Josh as they stood face
to face. His voice cracked.

Josh smiled with tears in his eyes. "And so much more,"
he whispered. They held hands tightly, each memorizing
the other's face; then separated—now, more than ever before, perhaps, forever.

Ollie's leave-taking of Josh was brief. Arm around shoulder, a quick hug—and they parted.

D'Ursu Magna chose this moment to lumber into camp,
rubbing his eyes, yawning, and scratching. "The Earth has
been groaning for days," he grumbled. "A fine trick, indeed. Where is Beauté Centauri? And what's going on?"

Beauty trotted over to his old friend and laughed. "Have
you had a good rest, then, Bear?"

"No. Who could sleep well through all that?"

"Then perhaps you were not destined to sleep this winter."

"Destiny is for Humans," the Bear spat. "I would rather
have sleep."

"Perhaps you are right," Beauty chuckled. Then he told
the Bear chieftain what was happening.

D'Ursu scratched his cheek, ruminating for a minute, then grunted. "Mhh. I have decided. I will let you take me as far as Newport in your boat. You will gain the benefit of my company, and I will join my King more quickly. A fair trade, I think."

"Fair enough," Beauty said, smiling, and took him to where Josh was watching the western horizon. "Joshua," said Beauty, "you will recall D'Ursu Magna, friend and Bear chieftain, whose aid in the Forest of Tears you remember well, and of whose more recent exploits on our quest you have been told. He has risen, and will favor us with his company until we reach Jarl's army."

"Of course I recall." Josh smiled. "Welcome, D'Ursu Magna, and thank you. Beauty's told me all you've done. Your strength is legend."

The Bear smiled, straining. "Yes, I think I remember you. You had an animal way about you, for a Human." And with no further salutation, D'Ursu ambled away toward the stream, to prepare himself for their departure.

Jasmine gave them one more piece of advice. The Mosian Firecaves were deep in glacier country. With all that intense heat in the middle of all that ice, the wind blew continuously out from the center in all directions. So if anyone got separated from Beauty, they could always find the Firecaves by walking into the wind.

And with that, the six adventurers set off.

Aba put the test tube on a thong around his neck. From another cord hung a tiny vial of Paula's blood—to remember her, to protect himself, with this token.

Finally, when there was nothing more to do but leave, he spread his wings and flew, deep into the sea of night.

She stared after his receding figure, and thought to herself. He was soon borne away by the waves, and lost in darkness and distance. And then she said, in a still, quiet voice, "And I am alone, again."

The child sat alone in the blackness of her room.
Who am I? What am I?
Her arm feathers were longer, darker. Her breast was

stained with a sticky crust of blood. She rocked on her haunches, her lanky arms around her doubled knees, and rocked, and rocked.

Will no one tell me what I am?

Her mind spun through the ether, whirling in vertiginous loops, singing the stars, dancing with infinity. Yet still, she was only a child.

Will no one tell me what I am for?

A frightened child, staring into the Void. Laughing and crying. She was taller now by a foot than she had been several hours before. And her eyes, mirrors of the universe, were darker than they had been; more recessed, in shadow. Black fire.

Mother-Ether, what am I?

She reached out to the stars for affection, which she craved deeply. But the stars were not affectionate. Gentle friends, he had said; but where were the gentle friends for such a one as her? She was alone. No one had ever been so alone.

In rage, she generated a flux against the walls that surrounded her. But only the roof exploded off into space; the walls stayed erect, unaffected. To quiet her brains, she twisted at Time, to hold it back, to stop it all. But it only speeded up for a while, and only near the eastern wall, so that the stones there rapidly crumbled with age into an archaic pile of rubble. She tried to make the sun explode, and it did. But it was a distant sun, in another eon.

She screamed, and it rained.

She knew she could effect enormous changes—it was within her power to do so—but what changes? And how? And when, and why, and for whom?

For Joshua, perhaps. Her father-creator. She felt a bond to him, not like with Osi, and not the same as with the Mother-Ether; but a bond, still. A warmth. Tenderness? What was that? A special wavelength, part of the Epsilon Field. Something in the nature of electron spin-spin interactions. Was that it? No.

Gentle friendship. What was that? She could not fathom, except in proximity to Joshua. Was that the key? No, surely not. She was the key. The lonely key.

She was alone. Bored. Waiting. Curious. Powerful. Impotent. Darkness. She was the key.

But what was the lock?

Mother-Ether, will no one tell me what I am?

The universe. The universe comes to all, in time.

Who am I?

The bright dark. Time's blinding wheel.

Will no one tell me who I am?

The node, and the key.

Mother-Ether, What am I?

The City lay crumbling, steaming in the night.

Here and there, small fires burned. Once, an entire length of stone wall collapsed and settled. Someone was crushed. It rained for a while, an icy-cold rain, but after it stopped, nothing seemed cleansed.

There was a brief meteor shower. Eighty or ninety white-hot boulders flashed from the ebony sky and sizzled like rockets into the ground inside the walls of the City.

A Vampire, wings flaming, careened into a wall, then lay still.

The air congealed, and for an hour—or maybe longer, maybe an eternity: maybe time, too, congealed—nothing moved; not a creature, not a molecule. Then the rains resumed, and things were as they had been.

Though, of course, things would never be the same again.

In the Bookery camp, the night passed slowly. Perhaps here, too, it took forever; for there was a certain thickness to the air, to the time, that seemed somehow impenetrable.

Jasmine, Josh, Rose. They lay side by side, staring at the stars. To look into such depth made Josh dizzy and afraid. Then he would touch one of the hands beside him, and be calmed.

Jasmine felt Joshua's hand touch hers, and she squeezed it reassuringly. He had gone through so much, this young man—well, they all had. But his test was yet to come, Jasmine sensed.

They would have to destroy the child, of this she was

certain. Too much power was being funneled through this one small being—the child was not up to it, whatever its source, whatever its nature.

And what of Joshua, then? Can he be counted on to help? she wondered. To help destroy his own daughter? Daughter of madness, child of the Void; the final genetic monster, out of control. Jasmine thought of the fey series of events that had led the planet to this edge: genetic engineers manufacturing the dreams and myths of a culture exploding with despair and chaos—until out of the ashes of the conflagration, the dream-animals and myth-demons had risen up, taken over the Earth, beat their chests and ranted . . . and finally had turned to manipulating the genes that defined them. They had made the strange, self-destructing Queen, who conjured and produced a child . . . *the* child. The unfathomable child, who would destroy them all if they didn't end her first. Dreams of dreams of dreams. Jasmine shook her head and held Joshua's hand tightly. It was quite beyond her.

She gazed out into the night, searching for the farthest galaxy. It was only a dim point in the western sky. Many of the suns there had died countless eons before their light first reached Earth. It made Jasmine sad to contemplate: so much meaning, trapped by Time and Space from ever being shared. Communicated randomly; approximated vaguely; but never truly shared.

They were all prisoners of this same keeper, Time; and in the hollow echoes of the echoless night, Jasmine heard him laughing.

CHAPTER 17

In Which Journeys to the City of Ice Are Undertaken, and Completed, but Not Without Loss

Aba flew north up the coastline for a long while. It was a less direct way to the Mosian Firecaves, but he could take advantage of the coastal winds—gliding for long periods to conserve his strength for the strenuous demands the Ice would make later.

He came down low when he reached Ma'gas', and circled a few times to check out the action. Everything seemed more or less status quo: ships in the harbor, creatures milling on the docks, pockets of noise, matrices of shadow. The sun was beginning to rise over the water, and the air was chill and clear. Aba caught an updraft and flew on.

It was hours before he approached Newport. It would be nice to see old friends again, if only briefly; and in any case, he needed a few minutes' rest, and a few pints of blood to stoke himself for his journey. So he flexed his hips, and set himself on a slow trajectory downward toward the seaport town where Jarl's troops were stationed.

There had apparently been a war. Carnage filled the streets; bodies floated in the surf. Corpses of Humans, Bears, Satyrs, Wolves, Griffins, Ursumen, Gorillas and Unicorns stained the ground: Jarl's soldiers, and the Doge's. Buildings burned. Ruin was the victor.

Some of the beasts still lived, but not for long. Jackals ran about, and huge upright Lizards from the contiguous jungle feasted on the wounded or dragged them back into the rain forest for another meal. Vampires flew from house to house, as well. Flocks would descend on any Human who showed signs of life, devouring the unfortunate, squabbling over remnants, shrieking and flapping.

Rats picked over the bones.

Aba was horrified by the spectacle. His first urge was to run through the city, trying to stop it all; but that was clearly impossible. So he just sat, heavy-hearted, for many minutes, staring at the bloody sea.

At length he got up and walked to the brothel he used to frequent.

"Hello," he called.

No response. He walked down the steps, kicked open the door, and entered. It was deserted. Furniture broken, carcasses strewn everywhere. Not a sign of life. Then, the noise.

It came from another room: a sound like a falling plank, and then silence. Aba slipped from room to room like a shadow, until finally he saw them: two Humans, cowering behind a cupboard, afraid even to blink as Aba approached them. They were BASSes—Born Again 'Seidon Soldiers—soldiers of the Doge.

"Leave us . . . leave us alone," one whispered. The other one passed out and slumped to the floor.

"You'll be found and eaten alive if you stay here," Aba said. "Come, I'll fly you to safety."

The Human pulled back. "Get away . . ." Her voice was desperate, parched.

Aba came closer, his hand outstretched. In a flash, the woman had drawn a knife and cut Aba's arm—the same one Ollie had slit. The startled Vampire backed off instantly, in surprise, and then in anger. Without thinking, he spread his wings, lunged at the woman with the knife, and knocked her unconscious with a beat of his hand.

The two Humans lay in an unmoving pile on the floor. Carrying one under each arm, Aba walked out the back door, and flew off.

Flying high, he managed to escape the slaughter of the city without being seen; but he didn't get very far. Just north of Newport, a storm was gathering. The icy winds forced him to keep fairly low above the ground for half an hour; and by the time the snow started, Aba was already grounded. Short of breath from the high-altitude flying, weak from his Human burden and the slight blood loss down his arm, cold, and hungry, he landed. Still carrying the unconscious Humans, he stumbled to a shelter in the lee of a rock slide just as the wind started to wail.

Snow began to fall in a fine, dry powder that barely settled before it was swirled around in frenzied eddies or whipped back up into the sky. Aba wrapped his wings tightly around the three of them against the weather's bite; but soon he was chattering, and the Humans' lips were blue. He felt their pulses: both strong. He looked at their faces: blushed under the powdery frost, they appeared angelic. He swooned, with weakness, and at the thought of what he must now do to these anonymous innocents. Gently, he placed his mouth upon the side of the man's neck; quickly he bit, his teeth like needles.

The man twitched once, at the moment of puncture, but immediately settled back into an exhausted sleep. Aba drank steadily from the man's jugular vein: his eyes closed, he savored every swallow, as a freezing straggler will let a cup of hot rum bring new life. He stopped after he had imbibed two pints, though he was still famished—he didn't want to kill the man; only save himself. He would drink equally from both so that neither should become too depleted.

He kept pressure on the man's neck for five minutes to stop the bleeding. He examined his own arm now, as well—the wound hadn't really been very deep, and its borders were already congealed. Finally, he looked closely at the woman who had cut him. Like her mate, she also slept like a soldier after the battle—the sleep of one whose body has exhausted its last drop of adrenaline.

Aba licked the snow from her neck, for the wind had diminished now, and the snow was beginning to settle over everything like a shroud. He clamped his teeth down along the big blue vein in her throat; lingered there a minute, filling his nostrils with her warm smells, running his tongue along her skin; and, finally, bit.

The woman's eyes jumped open, her body jerked, she tried to pull free. Aba held tight, sucking as quickly as he could. The woman grunted and gasped, her hands on his face, trying to push him away, to pull off his lips. He held her fast at the neck, his jaw shut hard, his large hands clasped around her head to keep it still. She flopped back and forth on the hard ground—twice, three times—then, finally, lay still. Through all of this, the man never woke up.

Aba kept siphoning the woman's blood until he felt sufficiently nourished. Then, as with the man, he applied pressure to her neck to tamponade the bleeding. For many minutes he sat there, numbly crying. The wind rose again, freezing his tears to his cheek.

He spent the next hour gathering wood and herbs, and the hour after that building a fire with his dragon-tooth flint and a bit of cloth for tinder. He found a dish-shaped rock, and boiled tea from a handful of snow and herbs; and spent the next two hours giving the Humans sips of the broth, warming their hands and feet, and generally nursing them.

When night came at last, Aba gathered them up inside his wings, and the three slept together like that, body to body in the great leather cocoon, beside the quickly dying fire.

When Aba awoke, it was a shimmering, bright early morning. He opened his wings carefully, slipped out from under his two fellow sleepers, stood, and shook off his mantle of snow.

"Arise, arise, ye drowsy sleepers," he called to the two on the ground. "I must be off, and you two to your own."

But they didn't move. He knelt and shook them, but still they didn't move. He felt for their pulses. They were dead.

Frozen to death in the night. Stiff and cold. They looked like toppled statues.

Aba stared at them, trying to suppress the wave of self-loathing that was starting to overcome him. No, he must be strong. Everything depended on him now. He fingered the two vials at his neck—the child's cells in one, Paula's blood in the other. These were his amulets. They gave him strength, and reason. They intertwined with whatever causes there were for Lon's death, and for Paula's love; to abandon reason, grieving for two lost Humans, was to abandon all.

He didn't look at the bodies again. He flew north, and east.

He flew all that day, making variable time in variable winds. First over the North Saddlebacks, then the great plains above the Forest of Tears. Toward evening, he landed at the southern edge of the Forest of Accidents, to rest, to build a fire and warm himself—for it had become brutally cold those last few hours.

Ice covered the ground in brittle sheets that crunched as he walked from tree to tree, collecting the driest of branches. He found a wind-screen, built his fire, ate some snow. He would rest there a few hours, then finish the last leg of his journey at night—it would be easiest to see the red flames of the Firecaves then. It wasn't long before he began to doze.

It wasn't long before he woke. He wasn't certain what woke him, but he was instantly alert, afraid. He crouched in the darkness, wings half-furled, listening for some sign. He heard it at the same moment he saw it: a band of Accidents, closing in on him from four directions. Without a second's hesitation, Aba grinned the ritual attack grin and flew full force into the nearest beast. He put two claws into its single eye and found the leverage to throw it headlong into two of its companions, though in falling, the Accident managed to tear a piece of the Vampire's wing.

Aba raced in the opposite direction—half-running, half-fluttering on his broken wing. Within seconds, the remaining three Accidents were giving chase. Aba immediately pulled ahead. He was faster on his feet; his wings, even crippled, gave him extra thrust; he was desperate. After a time, though, he started getting winded. The Accidents, on the other hand, were known for their brutish endurance. They ran slowly, but they could run forever. The trees were becoming thicker, too, and Aba continually bruised and battered his struts and broke his phalanges whenever he opened his wings too much. The icy wind seared his lungs with every breath.

He came upon Mirror Lake, and again lengthened his

lead, for the lake was frozen hard as glass, and when Aba stepped out onto it with his wings open wide, the wind blew him across its surface like a ghost in a dream.

Two of the Accidents ran out after him; but their combined weight was too much. The ice broke, and the lake swallowed them up and froze over again almost instantaneously. The last Accident lumbered doggedly around the shore, still on the Vampire's trail.

Aba was slowing in earnest now. He hurt, he bled. The sounds and smells of the foul creature who chased him were getting closer. Aba knew he had no strength left for a fight. He beeped the high-pitched Vampire sounds that only Vampires could scream or hear. But on this inclement night, who was there to hear him? He could only hope that not far from here friends might still exist. Indeed, that was the barren hope that had caused him to run into the forest in the first place. Yet now he could almost feel the Accident's breath on his back; and when he looked over his shoulder, the beast was reaching for him.

They tumbled in the frosted debris, clutching and tearing at each other as they rolled. The Accident was unbelievably strong. It had three arms and a lump that looked like half of a deformed second head growing out of its back. The smell of it made Aba gag.

He managed to jam a small log into its mouth just before it chomped down on his hand, but this gave the thing an extra second to gain a position advantage. It hit Aba in the the head, stunning him. And again.

The last thing Aba saw, as the world faded from his sight, was a horrible freak sitting astride him, bleeding and drooling from its mutant face, beating him senseless with mutant fists.

Ollie, Beauty, D'Ursu, and the three Books made good speed all night and into the next day. They followed the coast at first, then took to open sea, as their confidence grew, heading due north.

Keeping Joshua's written instructions in front of him, Michael did most of the actual driving—Josh had taught both him and Ollie how to use the controls, but Michael, a quick study, was able to master the instrument panel within hours. Ollie and Beauty tried to nap, or went over alternate routes to the Firecaves, as the little glass ship cut blindly through the black water of the winter night. D'Ursu tried to sing sea chanties, but somehow they all came out sounding like dirges.

Eventually, they reached Newport. What they saw of that city from a few hundred yards out to sea laid a grim silence over what had already been a rather subdued crew. Without a sound, they sailed in to shore.

Bodies everywhere; death and destruction. D'Ursu stepped onto the dock, looked around slowly, and loosed a profound wail to the sky, which reverberated to the roots of the city. Beauty jumped ashore and joined his old friend.

"Bear, I am sorry."

"Ah, Beauté Centauri, I am late, too late." He growled a keening moan.

"You could have done nothing to help, in this carnage, D'Ursu Magna. All creatures lost this battle. They only won who were not here."

"My King, my King," he rattled.

"Go seek him now," urged the Centaur. "We will wait."

The great Bear loped into the city, as if shouldering a great weight.

Ollie, Beauty, David, Ellen, and Michael waited tensely on the pier without speaking, trying to insulate themselves against the gasps and scrapings of the near-dead all around. D'Ursu returned an hour later.

"Gone. All gone," he whined.

"Gone to the Heart of the Forest," said Beauty.

"Beauté, my captain," D'Ursu said abjectly, "what shall I do?"

"Come with us on our journey, old Bear. There is nothing for you here—and we can sorely use an animal as noble as you."

D'Ursu looked around him, but his eyes were barren. Without enthusiasm, he nodded and without comment stepped back in the little plastic ship. The others rapidly followed suit—none wanted to stay on such bloody soil longer than necessary—and soon they were off again.

Michael found a northerly current and made good time riding it until evening. He hugged the coast until, just before nightfall, they arrived at the mouth of the Venus River. Docking the boat wasn't easy, but a series of ice caves just south of the delta provided wind and wave protection; so there the travelers secured the vessel.

The four Humans wore Wolf-skin jackets. They all carried dehydrated food, Dragon-tooth flints, dry tinder, knives, Bear-paw shoes, ropes, some of Jasmine's finger-flares, and a compass. Ollie kept the vial of cells in his belt. Beauty carried a quiver of arrows and his Dragon-rib bow. D'Ursu carried only his grief.

So provisioned, the six climbed up the ice rocks that blistered the shore, and began to walk northeast along the banks of the frozen Venus River, in the direction of the Mosian Firecaves below Mount Venus.

The entire area was then just within the penumbra of the Ice—so that once the journeyers were a little bit inland, away from the warming effects of the ocean, they were beset by cold worse than they had ever imagined.

They made a forced march through a stinging blizzard for hours, then finally rested and slept before dawn, by the light of a single candle, in the belly of a well-used cave near Southmarsh. Ollie and Beauty were having a bad enough time of it; Michael and Ellen looked ready to fold. In all their lives, they had never known cold or snow—or any true, prolonged privation, for that matter. Now their teeth chattered, their lips were thin blue lines, and only their hearts kept the strength of their intention. David was doing somewhat better, seeming almost to draw his animation from Michael's failure to thrive. D'Ursu seemed to have lost his heart; he moved only because the others did, and when they rested, his inertia kept him in place.

It was a long time before any of them realized there was someone else in the cave. Ollie detected it first: as the wind outside subsided a little, the hushed respirations emanated from a dark corner of the shelter. Nearly an hour had passed by the time he realized that the pattern of quiet breathing that filled the space they occupied was the syncopation not of six creatures but of seven: an invisible seventh party shared the cavern with them.

The three Books were sound asleep. D'Ursu, wide awake, sat staring out the cave mouth. Ollie nudged Beauty, and silently placed his hand behind his ear. Beauty looked around in all directions, sniffing, suddenly alert to the presence of an interloper. After a minute of head-tilting and nostril-flaring, the Centaur pointed to the light-less hollow where the soft inspirations paused before expiring. Ollie nodded; the two of them stood, separated, and approached the dark corner from opposite directions. Beauty readied his bow.

When he was twenty feet away, Ollie lit one of Jasmine's flares and tossed it toward the breathing. The dazzling red glow illuminated the entire back of the cavern, including the secret sharer: a small, white shaggy Pony stood shivering in the recess, its giant shadow dancing on the back wall in the smoky light.

Beauty lowered his bow and arrow. "A Pony," he murmured. "What is your name, Pony?"

The diminutive horse remained speechless, breathing quietly, staring straight ahead. Beauty and Ollie walked up to it. Ollie passed his hand over the animal's face and petted its head, but it neither blinked nor moved.

"She's blind," whispered Ollie.

"Are you cold?" Beauty asked, and the Pony extended her nose to him, sniffed his hand.

"What's your name, girl?" asked Ollie.

She licked Beauty's hand twice. Her eyes were like cracked quartz, translucent, slightly strabismic. They walked her back to where the Books still slept, and the seven of them huddled together for warmth the remaining hours until dawn.

In the morning when they resumed the trek, the blind Pony joined them. Nobody asked her to, or asked her not to—she simply came along, following two steps behind Beauty wherever he walked.

They struck out due east at first—no longer adhering to the river bank—toward their destination. The wind stayed low for a while, and the sun bright. There were Tortoise trails that could be followed, and the scattered fir trees gave the company markers to pass time. On the Plains of Babar-Dün, the weather got much worse.

Long acres of flat grassland, with nothing to break the wind but an occasional ice-rimed tree, tinkled madly in the blow. The ground was frozen, making every step slippery. And the snow was so thick that they had to check their compasses every hundred yards to make certain they were still walking east.

Occasionally the blind Pony would pause, break the icy snow with her front hooves, and nibble at the moss that grew on the ground below, then catch up with the others and walk, once more, behind Beauty.

Steadily, over the course of the day, the wind pressed its advantage. Ellen was so cold she began to cry; never had she known such frigid pain. Beauty told her to concentrate on something else—"Think of your footsteps. Focus on a pleasant memory." But she couldn't. She was too cold to think of anything but of how cold she was, how bitterly the freezing air tore her lungs and shook her bones. The wind bellowed the dry snow across the plains in powdery waves a foot deep: it looked like a ghost ocean on a lost planet, light-years from the nearest star. Cold, impossibly cold; impossibly.

And still it grew colder. Trees and shrubs disappeared altogether. Michael was no longer able to feel his arms or his legs. He wondered if this was absolute zero. The ground had become a flat white sheet that extended in all directions, glaring diffusely to the sky, without horizon. The sky itself was so bright that not even the sun was clearly visible. And what could be discerned of the sun looked and felt like dry ice.

Minute passed minute slower and slower, as if Time itself were slowly being frozen by the elements. Gradually, even their sluggish thoughts came to an icy halt; but still they continued walking, numb to every sense.

After several hours of this, some of the travelers were approaching an end to their inner reserves. Ollie held his arms wrapped around his body and in his pockets— uncharacteristically defenseless, should he be attacked.

Even so, he kept shivering. The three Books could barely walk, and straggled farther behind with every step. Even Beauty stumbled from time to time, his feet insensate, legs stiff. D'Ursu seemed largely unaffected—moving slowly, one step at a time; relentless, though unusually devoid of energy. Only the blind Pony showed no signs of fatigue; doggedly, she pushed Beauty on from the rear with her stoic plodding.

Night finally came, and with it the storm seemed to diminish somewhat. They slid, more than walked, into a giant circular scree-strewn depression, which further removed them from the raw wind. They lit no fire but crowded together for warmth. It was in this huddle that D'Ursu Magna spoke for the first time.

"Here on these plains Beauté Centauri first saved my life," he rumbled, a deep smile in his voice.

"During the Race War," nodded Beauty.

"There was no Ice then," the Bear continued. "Only these great craters we sit in now, where the Humans exploded their bombs."

"You would think we had done with battle by now," Beauty rasped wearily.

"I have done," whispered D'Ursu, barely audible in the gale.

They slept poorly, and rose at first light, having maintained just enough body heat, clustered together as they were, to feel somewhat rekindled. This small flame was snuffed when they tried to leave, though, for they couldn't climb out of the crater they had camped in; it was covered with ice.

Glistening, new ice, an inch thick, completely blanketed every stone, scrub, and foothold that had pocked the surface of the incline the night before. Every step they took up the slope, they slid back two. There was simply no traction.

Except in one place.

"Here's a spot!" shouted Michael. "Goes straight up, lots of grass, no ice." He started walking up what seemed to be the only ice-free path out of the crater.

"Wait!" yelled Ollie, stopping Michael where he stood. "This shouldn't be."

Beauty walked over, nodding. "I agree. Something is amiss." The others collected here. Ollie stood on Beauty's back to try to see up over the edge of the rise; but couldn't.

"What's wrong?" asked Ellen. "What is it?"

Beauty shook his head. "I know not. But this is not natural."

"Ready yourselves," said Ollie. "I'll look." With his dagger in his gloved right hand, he began crawling up the grassy slope on his belly, while the wind howled all around. Michael's teeth began to chatter. Beauty drew an arrow, and laid it on his bow. David reached into his pocket, put on his glasses.

They watched Ollie inch his way up the ravine, then peer out over the edge when he had gone as high as he dared. After a minute, he ducked down and scrambled back to the bottom. "About a dozen men, dressed in white furs," he panted. "Among them is a cart with a pile of burning coals, and over the coals is a big cauldron, steaming—one of the men is stirring it. The cart is pulled by Caribou. They wait, twenty yards beyond the crater. I could see no weapons . . ."

He paused, for all to consider.

Finally, Beauty spoke. "I like it not."

"Maybe they don't even know we're here," Ellen suggested hopefully. The cold was already settling in her bones again; she wanted to get moving.

"In any case," said Ollie, "we can't stay here."

Beauty spoke with authority. "Ollie and I will go up. The rest of you stay behind, but close. And stay ready."

Knives in their sleeves, Beauty and Ollie walked straight up the path. When they reached the top, they stopped. One of the men was pointing a nozzle directly at them.

"Come ahead, but come slow," the man said. The nozzle he pointed was at the end of a ten-yard length of hose. The hose was connected to the steaming cauldron that sat atop a large four-wheeled cart. Ten or twelve other men stood around, watching.

"We're friends," called Ollie, forcing a smile.

"You're food this morning, chum," laughed the one holding the hose. "Now come ahead quiet or we'll water you where you stand, just like we did the sides of your little cubbyhole last night." They all had a good laugh at that one. Slowly, Ollie and Beauty began walking to the right and a little forward.

Twenty Caribou were harnessed to the cart. Beauty saw that hitched to the back of the wide-wheeled rig was a sled, piled high with coal, furs . . . and frozen meat.

"No, no, you yummy critters," the man on the hose snickered, "not that way. Over here. Maybe we won't eat ya at all—maybe just hitch ya up to the team here. 'Specially you, there, big boy," he winked at Beauty. This got another big laugh from the group. Beauty and Ollie kept walking to the right, toward the back of the cart. Ollie noticed two men standing poised at a hand pump near the point where the hose entered the cauldron. A third snapped a lid on the big tub. "Hold up, there, I said!" the man with the hose yelled, suddenly angry.

At that, D'Ursu Magna leapt out of the pit like a rampaging giant. He was halfway to the cart by the time the leader swung the hose around and sprayed him full in the chest with a long gush of water. Meanwhile, Beauty and Ollie charged ahead; Michael and Ellen splayed off to the left flank; and the fight was on. Only the blind Pony stayed behind, unmoving at the bottom of the crater.

Ollie jumped on the nearest outlaw, and the two of them rolled clumsily around in the snow. Beauty got off one knife throw, hitting a man in the side, then reared up and trampled another. D'Ursu, drenched with water, had just snatched the hose from the leader's hand when he slipped on the ice. The man was on him in a second, struggling for the hose as it sprayed everyone within range. The Caribou shuffled, nervously pawing the ground.

David, soaking wet, grappled with one of the bandits. Michael and Ellen jointly attacked a group of three men who were trying to hold quiet the lead Caribou. These men turned out not to be armed, though, and the five of them rolled, brawling, at the feet of the animals.

D'Ursu knocked the hose man senseless, and stood up again—but with difficulty, for he was already beginning to freeze. The water saturating his fur was quickly turning white, cracking with each movement, slowing the Bear down. But the same thing was happening to all who had been soaked, too, so that in a few more moments, most of them were lying on the ground, stiff and blue. Of the gang members not frozen, two were wounded, and the rest, seeing the tables had rapidly turned, suddenly surrendered.

Beauty and Ollie stood, assessing the situation; Michael and Ellen quickly joined them. D'Ursu sat, shivering, against the cart, covered head to foot with tiny white icicles. Six scruffy men—two of them wounded—stood huddled by the burning coals in the wagon. Seven more men lay strewn over the ground, still and frosted as ice statues. One of them was David, a knife in his chest, his cracked rimless glasses frozen to his face.

Beauty pulled the lid off the cauldron and peered inside: water, steaming but not boiling. He reached up and dabbed a finger into it—barely warm, though it felt stinging hot to his frostbitten finger. He looked down at D'Ursu again: the Bear was freezing to death.

"All right, you there," Beauty gruffed sternly to his prisoners. "Put this Bear in that pot."

Ollie and the Books helped. With all of them pushing and pulling, they managed somehow to dump D'Ursu in the steaming, tepid water. It overflowed, almost putting out the coals; but D'Ursu came around almost immediately. He sat up in the water, his great paws on the edge of the tub, looked around, and smiled grimly. "Well, Beauté Centauri, have I saved your life again?" he roared.

"Indeed you have, D'Ursu Magna!" The Centaur smiled with great relief. "And once again on the Plains of Babar-Dün."

"If I were Human, I would call it destiny," the Bear pontificated from his elevated cauldron. "But, thank the Forest, I am not."

"No, but you are in a predicament nonetheless, old Bear. If you leave that pot of warm water, you will surely freeze to death."

D'Ursu considered the problem, but his powers of logic were, sadly, as bad as his memory. Fortunately, he was aware of this. "Then what shall I do, Beauté Centauri?"

"These four who can walk, we will bind their hands and harness them to the lead Caribou, to help pull. These two with wounds, we will tie to the sled, so they can put new coals on the fire. You, D'Ursu Magna, will stay where you are until this bunch pulls you far enough south that you will not freeze. When you are there, you can set them all free, and return to your forest. What say you?"

"The best trick ever!" D'Ursu barked, and began immediately shouting orders to everyone.

In short time, the four able Humans were bound and hitched to the Caribou team; the other two were strapped onto the sled, from which the furs, goods, and meat had first been removed.

"Start stoking!" he finally roared to the men feeding the coals. "And you'd better not try to make Bear soup, either. Away, you lovely Caribou, we're going home! And another thing . . ."

And on he shouted, as the long team slowly headed south in the swirling winds, pulling the cart and sled and the great stewing pot full of roiling Bear.

Beauty and the others watched a moment; then gathered their things and headed east. The blind Pony joined them as soon as they started off. In less than a minute, the seven frozen bodies on the ground were lost behind them in the blowing snow.

They walked in silence for an hour before Michael finally stopped them. "I'll die if I go any farther," he yelled into the wind. David's death had taken Michael's last strength—he suddenly felt numb to the very soul.

Beauty chose his words carefully. "Can you make it back yourself?" They all had to shout to be heard.

Ellen interjected. "I'll go with him. We'll make it together . . . unless you need me here?"

Beauty shook his head. "No. Go back. Go, both of you. Wait for us at the boat. If we have not returned in two weeks, go back to camp without us." He paused, looked at the blind Pony, who stood there, waiting patiently, then looked back at the Books. "Take the Pony with you," he went on. "She will give you support."

The Pony tilted her head in question, or in consternation; then unhurriedly turned around and stood facing west. Michael and Ellen stood on either side of the Pony, each grabbing a handful of its long, snowy fur. Then without another word, the three of them started walking away from Ollie and Beauty, heading west, back for the coast.

Night fell hard and fast. Ollie and Beauty walked with a slow, grudging determination. Up long slopes, around ravines, across plains. Still, they walked. Walked to reach a spot three feet away, and then three feet again. And always with the wind in their faces, the black and wheezing wind.

On and on they plodded, though with every step the wind was stronger, their resistance weaker. The night drew in around them like the Void. Beauty suggested they rest for a time, but neither could find a shelter where they wouldn't freeze; so on they trudged.

Ollie heard it first: a grating sound above—or rather, below—the wail of the wind. A rhythmic scraping that went on many seconds, then stopped, then started again. From the north. Ollie touched Beauty's side and pointed, and they both listened. Beauty strung an arrow.

Particles of ice cut at their faces as they stood there, motionless, heads cocked to the north. Suddenly they were aware of a distant rumbling, which grew louder with each passing second. And then the rumbling was on them.

By the time they could see it in the darkness, the beast was less than thirty feet away and charging. A great bull Mammoth, white and woolly and raging. Big as an elephant, its trunk shorter, its tusks meaner. The short trunk gave it a rather Boar-like snout, in fact, and this, coupled with a mouth full of teeth, made it an unequaled adversary. In fact, the species had no natural predators. The only force that kept its growth in check was the howling fierceness of these winters, and the scarcity of food. And this creature—now twenty feet away—was clearly starving.

Beauty had time to loose but a single arrow, hitting the Mammoth square in the snout, causing it to squeal in agony, lose its footing, and come crashing down on top of the Centaur's front legs. In the moment it was down, Ollie scrambled up its back, pulling himself up by the lengths of matted, stringy fleece that covered the animal. The beast quickly rose again, and screaming, tossed its head in fury; but Ollie had a firm grip in the Mammoth's fur, high on its back. He quickly took his long knife and plunged it deep into the creature's neck, at the base of the skull—in, and up, trying to pith it.

The beast bucked spasmodically once, tossing Ollie high in the air, then crumpled to the stony ground and lay there without moving as the snow swirled madly.

Five pieces, a still life: Beauty, unconscious, his legs broken horribly; Ollie, stunned, lying upside down against a large boulder; the Mammoth, an arrow in its proboscis and a knife in its neck, still breathing, lying heavily on its side; the wind, churning the snow into drifts beside each figure; and the night.

Beauty woke first. He tried to move, but the pain in his legs was so excruciating that he passed out again. The Mammoth woke next. It tried to move, but could not: it was paralyzed from the neck down by Ollie's knife thrust, which had penetrated far enough to break two cervical vertebrae, but not far enough to reach the brain. The beast opened its mouth to roar, but the arrow hurt so much that the creature only whined a bit, then lay still.

Beauty woke again to see that movement, to see the beast wasn't yet dead; and carefully, gingerly turned himself to fit another arrow in his bow, to finish off the Mammoth from where he lay.

Finally, Ollie came around. He slid off the rock he was on, examined himself briefly for damage, and finding none serious, looked up to see Beauty about to shoot the slowly breathing body of the downed behemoth. He ran over to Beauty and knocked the bow down just in time to send the arrow skittering harmlessly over the ice.

"Why—why did you stop me?" Beauty rasped. "The brute is still alive."

"Don't move," Ollie yelled. "We may need him." He stepped cautiously over to the Mammoth from behind, knife in hand, and deftly prodded the creature at key spots—sometimes with no response, sometimes eliciting wild growling and head-jerking—until he had ascertained that the Mammoth was indeed paralyzed.

He came back to examine Beauty's legs. "This looks bad," he said.

Beauty looked carefully at his own legs for the first time: they were like twigs—all angles, all in the wrong places. He looked up at Ollie, and said, "You must leave me now. Take the vial and go."

Ollie studied his old friend's blue lips and crushed legs, then shook his head.

"I will be fine," Beauty continued. "My legs do not hurt in this cold."

"Prepare yourself," said Ollie. He grabbed Beauty under the shoulders and dragged him around to the ventral side of the flaccid Mammoth. Once again, the pain was more than Beauty could bear, and he mercifully lost consciousness.

Ollie took his knife and pierced the Mammoth's abdomen just under the breastbone; then with ripping, halting cuts, he extended his incision down the entire length of the sad animal's belly. The steaming guts puffed through the seam. The spinal cord had been severed, though, so the animal felt no pain. With great difficulty—for his own hands were now blue and numb with cold—Ollie dragged and stuffed Beauty, who remained unconscious, into the belly of the beast. Soon, only the Centaur's head remained outside the huge abdominal cavity. With that, Ollie climbed in, easing himself among the warm, wet loops of intestine. When his head, too, remained alone outside in the frigid gale, he pulled together two flaps of woolly skin and closed the rent he had made, holding the incision together by sticking Beauty's barbed arrows through the opposing edges of flesh, stapling the Mammoth from the inside.

As the wind and cold increased, Ollie pulled even their heads inside, leaving only their mouths and noses exposed to the air. And so they spent the night: sleeping fitfully, sucking on the bitter-cold wind from their refuge deep in the bowels of the Mammoth. They were exhausted and bat-

tered, but finally, warm. If Beauty kept still, he felt no
pain. In the end, their only awareness of that long night
was in the sound of the baying wind without; the creature's
slow, almost serene respirations within; and its heartbeat,
the rhythmic, resonant *mmm mmp*, surrounding and filling
them, lulling them at last to sleep.

When Ollie awoke, he was first aware that the Mammoth's
heart had stopped; then, that its breathing had stopped. He
pulled apart the skin flaps that retained him, and rolled
out into two feet of snow.

The wind still blew hard, but the snow had ceased falling.
The day was sunny. Ollie washed the blood and fluids off
himself in the dry snow, then bundled up in the coat he
had left outside during the night. Still, his face was frozen
in seconds, and he broke the ice off his hands only by
moving his fingers constantly.

Beauty awoke. "Thank you," he said.

Ollie shrugged.

Beauty went on. "I will stay here. The poor beast is dead
finally, but his corpse will keep me warm another day at
least. Now, you must go."

Ollie nodded. "I'll come back," he said.

"Of course you will." Beauty stared at him hard, a farewell stare. "Now go."

Ollie walked into the wind. The few hours of sleep he
had stolen couldn't make up for the total enervation he felt,
but it was a new day, and he walked on. He walked down a
gentle grade, and then up a steep rise—which he practi-
cally had to crawl, the wind being so strong, the ice so
featureless. At the top of the rise, he looked down.

Less than a hundred yards away he saw the vision: a
vertical crystal wall of ice; inside it, a glowing red flame,
like a resistant ember deep in the iceberg. It was the Mosian Firecaves.

Ollie wept at the sight of it, fat, salty tears that froze as
soon as they formed.

Inflated by the strength of salvation, he walked toward
the glacier.

* * *

With difficulty he traversed the ice mountain's western face, coming finally to a glassy plateau, which he slid across on his backside for a hundred feet. This brought him to the lip of a sheer crevasse that looked down to a flaming volcanic pit two hundred feet below. Ollie was unsure where to go next.

But his thinking had become sluggish. Finally, remembering the handholds Jasmine had told him to look for, he discovered a series of cloth-covered rungs tracking down the northern wall of the ice shaft, toward what looked like the bottom of the fiery pit itself. Slowly, the boy made his descent.

Twice he almost fell, so weak was his grip. But the fires below warmed him as he went deeper, and soon it was hotter than he would have liked. Somewhere farther down, magma gurgled thickly. And then, just when he couldn't tolerate the heat another moment, he came to an opening in the ice. The glacier was glistening with its own melt here, and constantly refreezing—so that Ollie had to be particularly careful how he stepped, for one slip away was the pit.

He made it into the portal, though, and rested there a few minutes, trembling and weak. When he had his legs back, he stood, and found himself looking along a thin tunnel of ice. He walked the narrow channel of translucent whiteness until it turned right, and down; and so he followed it. Hall after hall of the cold aqueous crystal, ever deeper, ever colder. Sometimes pulsing orange flames could be seen indistinctly through ice walls whose thickness Ollie could hardly guess; sometimes, all was blackness.

Until he came to a well-lit chamber of cavernous dimensions, in the middle of which stood a man. Ollie approached him.

"I am Leeds," said the man. "And who might you be?" He wasn't like any man Ollie had ever seen before. His body was Human-shaped, but only roughly so—yet flowing and graceful. The flesh was clear as bubbly water, so the brain and nerves could almost be seen inside. The face was without features, the hands without fingers, the very shape without . . . definition. Like a partially melted ice sculpture.

"My name is Ollie. My friend, Beauty, a Centaur, is hiding in a dead Mammoth a hundred yards back. His legs are broken—he needs help. I have a message for your leader from my friend Jasmine, the Neuroman."

At Jasmine's name, this ice man's attention seemed to focus more, though it was difficult to say how. "And what is this message?"

Ollie took the vial from his belt. "These are the cells from a creature too dangerous to live. Jasmine instructed me to tell you a word: *Plasmid.*"

At the mention of this secret word, the creature took Ollie's hand in his mitt and led the boy to a massive, frozen wall. A few moments later the wall opened, and the two entered the City of Ice.

Leeds was a Neuroman, it turned out. They were almost all Neuromans here. A lot of them were Cognons—Neuromans with electrodes implanted in their cognitive centers, which they could stimulate at will. Most were, among other things, genetic engineers. A few robots lived here, too; but they functioned simply as manual laborers.

The city itself was a series of ice cathedrals, carved inside the gigantic frozen ocean that formed the glacier. They were great, flame-shaped rooms, etched away from the inside by the Firecaves lacing the area—volcanic holes that bubbled and hissed, and supplied all the energy the city needed to drive its generators.

Thirty or forty Neuromans lived there now, mostly working on experiments that interested them, particularly experiments in bioengineering, senescence, geophysics. They greeted Ollie's entrance with some consternation.

Visitors were few. Jasmine's stay was well remembered—they had repaired her body, and she had told them stories. And they hadn't been visited since. Ollie's appearance now, with the emergency codeword on his lips and an agar-tube tissue culture, was cause for alarm.

They immediately called a meeting of the entire city, and asked Ollie to tell his story completely—which he did, after insisting that the robots be dispatched to retrieve Beauty in the interim. Which was done.

When the tale was finished, they all debated and considered the issue for an hour, finally deciding that the matter was indeed urgent. Whereupon they took the vial from Ollie, and went to work on it in the labs that very afternoon.

Beauty was brought in, and his legs were set. Then there was nothing to do but wait.

For a week Ollie explored the City of Ice. How they had tunneled into, connected, and embellished the palaces was a glorious mystery to him. It was as if everything he saw were made of diamonds and pearls. And so big! Thousands might have lived there, instead of the few dozen who did.

There was a giant central generator, powered by the forced steam that was so readily available amidst all the fire and ice. Four great cathedrals cornered the power station, each a laboratory devoted to a different science or philosophy. At the base of each floor was a crackling fire pit, whose heat had clearly effected the hollowing out of the cathedral in which it was centered, for each ceiling was arched and peaked, some in the shape of tongues of flame, some with tiaras of exploding ice bubbles intermingled among majestic icicle stalactites. Concentric levels of smaller rooms abutted each major cathedral, serving myriad functions, from conferences to gaming to meditating to sleeping.

Ollie examined them with the curiosity of a cautious Cat. He maintained an intense interest in all new environments—primarily from a survival perspective—and the Firecaves were unlike anything he had seen before. Most of the furniture was ice—tables, divans, beds—and all the decor consisted of variations on the theme. Ice sculpture was everywhere, abstract and figurative. Stalactites were frequently cultured—sometimes into fantastic shapes, sometimes tinted like exotic jewelry. Thick ice windows looked out on orange-red lava pits that churned and boiled like the soul of the planet. Ollie slowly became entranced with the marvels and, after a couple of days, even allowed himself the luxury of wonder.

"At the base of each floor was a crackling fire-pit, whose heat had clearly effected the hollowing out of the cathedral in which it was centered–for each ceiling was arched and peaked . . ."

Beauty, meanwhile, recuperated. Slowly. The doctors told him it would be weeks before he would walk, months before he would run. Ollie spent time with him, and Leeds spent time with both, listening to stories of the outside world, its latest calamities and catastrophes. When Ollie asked about results in the laboratory, he was told only that progress was being made.

At the end of the first week, Phé arrived with news of Aba. Phé was Aba's elder sister—a giant, big-bosomed, jolly Vampire with frizzy yellow hair and a booming laugh.

The story she told was that Aba's cries for help had been heard.

"By who?" asked Ollie.

"By me bloody self, is who," she thundered, and her great breasts shook. "The Baby-Sire came down not twenty yards from the back door to Lon's den—may his spirit never clot. Me and Heart-Sire flashed right out and ended that poor Accident's tenure." Again the laugh. Heart-Sire was her name for their older brother, Lev. "So Baby-Sire, he's recovering from his injuries now. Gave me his vial of cells and told me where to go with 'em, and here I am, then." She bowed.

"What were you doing in Lon's den?" Beauty asked her.

"We live there, Blood. Me and Heart-Sire and Lon's old harem and about half of Bal's old harem. See, Bal was this bad-blood Sire who—"

"How's Aba now?" asked Ollie. He still felt guilty about his treatment of Aba, though his only conscious sensation was of a painful itch around the healing scar where the ruby had been torn from his chest. Unconsciously he scratched at it now, and winced.

"Oh, fine, fine," beamed Phé. "The boy's got red blood. The plan is now, it is, for me to fly you back to your people with whatever weapon these clever bloods devise. Baby-Sire, he'll come along directly, when he's up to heme."

"Then there's nothing to do but wait for these experiments to end."

"Wait for these thin-bloods, it is. And wait I can. I drank myself silly last night, and I wouldn't touch a gout of blood now for two weeks if you dropped a bloody hemophiliac at my feet, and that's the bloody truth!" At which she laughed and laughed until the ice halls echoed.

But she didn't have long to wait. The next day, the genetic engineers had the solution. Three solutions, actually, in aerosol spray cans.

"It's a virus," said Leeds. "It's designed to attack a very small segment of unique DNA we found in this child's cells. It's highly specific that way—pathologic only to creatures with that specific configuration of nucleic acids. And as far as we know, she's the only creature with that configuration."

"What'll it do?" asked Ollie.

"Well, it's quite virulent. Has a very short prodrome, then progresses rapidly to encephalitis and death."

"And how do we give it to her?"

"These cans produce a good airborne vector. Just spray them in her general direction. She'll get the message."

So they left. Ollie said good-bye to Beauty, telling him they would be back in four or five weeks, when Beauty was well enough to travel. Beauty nodded and wished him well. Seeing Ollie go gave him a feeling of monumental isolation such as he had never had before. The thought of being left behind, in the hollow ice caves, in the care of the cold-blooded ice-men, was overwhelming to the point of tears. To have come so far, only to become everyone else's fond memory, seemed unendurable.

"I wish us *all* well," the Centaur added in whisper. He had, at once, an oppressive sense of loss, as if his world were dissolving before and around him. He saw it all—his past, present, and future—through a darkening, reducing lens, and heard the voices of his dreams and memories as fading echoes in a twilight time. He grabbed Ollie and hugged the boy fiercely to his breast—Ollie, the messenger of Beauty's muted well-wishes, the trusted bearer of the Centaur's final touch: this, somehow, Beauty believed.

Then Phé took Ollie under her arm as lightly as if he were paper, stuck the acrosol cans in her belt, walked out onto the snow-swept ice plateau that covered the city, and roared: "Now, hold on to your bones, me blood. This is what we call a nonstop flight!"

And with that, she soared into the wind.

CHAPTER 18

Journeys into Darkness

The morning after Ollie and the others left the Bookery camp for the City of Ice with the child's cells in culture, Joshua was awakened from sleep by a voice in his brain.

Father, come.

He walked to the City. There was no gate, as such, any more. Most of the rocks that constituted the high outer wall had melted, then resolidified into an amorphous gray mass that generally surrounded what had been the City.

A city no more. Houses burned, streets in shambles. Creatures wandered aimlessly; weeping, snarling, vacant. A bank of brown fog hovered ominously over the river that coursed through the yard. Joshua crossed the teetering Bridge of Whispers, and entered the castle.

There was a snowstorm in the main hallway, turning to hail and sleet in the stairwell. All was quiet by the second floor. Quickly, he went to her chamber.

Again, she had changed. A full array of feathers spread gloriously along her arms, now, looking like wings, with her strange little clawed hands at the wingtips. Red, gold, green. Down her back, too, and up her neck to fan out over the top of her head in a bright burgundy plumage. Her beak was longer, the lips beneath it fuller. Her eyes were a black fire.

"Welcome, *creator*." She projected a new sense to him, twisting her words thickly: it made Josh feel almost drugged.

"Hello. How are you today?"

"*I* am *powerful* today. You made something very potent when *you* molded *me*. You should feel joyous. *Come, touch* your creation. *Feel what* you've made."

Josh was confused, hesitant. "What . . . what do you . . ."

269

"*Come, touch* me, creator, *see* what you . . . Wait, *why* do you shun me? You pull *away*, you . . . *What's* that? What did you . . . *You did* something to me. What was it?" Her thoughts were stern, now. Josh recoiled.

"I . . . I didn't do . . ."

She leapt to the tall back of the throne and perched there, glowering. "*What* did *you* do to *me?* You hide something, you keep it from me—what is *it?* You must tell me, *you cannot hide* it, your thoughts are murky, but your guilt is clear."

Joshua shrank under the pressure of her eyes. "I don't, I don't know, she said something about clones, I think, I don't . . ."

"*Clones!* What of clones? She *who?* Who said this, *who?*"

"Jasmine, she said she wanted your cells, in case . . ."

"Say it! Say *what* you *did!*"

"We took your cells," he whispered. "I'm not sure why."

The child looked perplexed, dark. "*Who* is this Jasmine who wants my cells?"

"A friend, she's a friend of—"

"I will *kill her.*"

"No!" Josh blurted out. "You can't harm her—you promised you wouldn't! You swore you wouldn't ever hurt me or mine. And she's mine. And I forbid you to harm her."

The child rocked on her perch, simmering. The air around her crackled. Finally: "*Why* do you want to clone *me?* Am *I* so *unloved? You* wish to do *me harm?*"

"We wish you no harm if you mean to do good in the world."

"But a *clone,* is it. To do me *battle,* do you think? That would be a battle to *burn* the planet. You would *all lose* that battle, creator."

"Perhaps to reason with you in your own language."

"Ahhh, to *speak* in the tongue of the *electron,* the language of the wave particle. How primitive your words in comparison. What *nuances* you miss, what *depths* you cannot even imagine. My clone; Mother-Ether, what a thought! I would *never* be *alone* again. My *sister*, my bride. My *self*."

"I . . . I don't know if . . ."

"I can focus better, now, you know. I know *how* . . . if I only knew on *what*."

"You need company, I think," said Josh. "Someone to talk to."

"*You see* through *me*, don't you?" she regarded him closely.

"What do you—"

"You know my *mind*."

"I know your confusion. I can feel your distress."

"Father, *what* should *I* do?"

"What do you want?"

"It's in my mind to *destroy all* things."

"Why? Why would you—"

"To be *alone*. I feel so alone now—it seems only right I should *be alone*."

"I'm your friend," he ventured.

She ruffled, then settled her feathers. "*You* . . . give *me* hope. Also with talk of this clone. My clone would know me, but . . . maybe that would be the same thing as *being alone*. I already talk to myself."

"It's different, just having another voice answer."

"And it wouldn't hate *me*, *would* it? The others all *hate me*. Because they don't understand me. Everyone is *afraid* of *me*. I frighten myself, at times. But you don't hate *me*, do *you*."

"No."

"Am *I* so *hateful?*" She fluttered off the back of the throne to the floor and stood before him, eye to eye—they were of a height now. She placed her spindly fingers on his cheek.

"No," he whispered, "I don't hate—"

She kissed him, on the mouth. Her full, soft lips pressed his; her long, thin reptilian tongue found his tongue; the cold hardness of her beak nuzzled his cheek.

Passively, he opened his mouth wider, allowed her kiss to deepen. His emotions raced wildly from fear to lust to complete disequilibrium. He felt her arm feathers ruffle down his back, her chest graze his chest. He looked into her eyes: blackness without end.

He suddenly tensed, became rigid. Her eyes flared. She ripped her talons down his side, cutting his flesh to the rib, then pushed him away.

"*I hate you*," she seethed. "Get *away* from me. *Leave me alone!*"

Josh backed off, stumbling, bleeding. A flash of lightning exploded through the ceiling and seared the brick. Josh ran from the room.

He ran through the City amidst increasing chaos—fires sprang up from the Earth. The ground itself moaned. The sky seemed to bend.

He ran out of the City and all the way back to camp, where he collapsed in a dead faint.

They couldn't revive him at first. They tried water, words, potions. Jasmine mixed together two solutions from vials hidden in her secret abdominal compartment, and poured the brew down his throat. This brought him around, but he remained largely unresponsive.

He sat huddled by the fire, shivering, staring, mute. Jasmine taped together the borders of his chest wound, but it seemed to cause him no pain. Even when an ember from the campfire sparked out and landed on his leg, he didn't flinch. Jasmine had to brush it away.

She said, "Rose, read his eyes."

Rose sat before him and looked hard into his unblinking, unseeing eyes. She searched the depths of his aqueous and vitreous humors, and beyond, but at the end, she only shook her head, and would say nothing more.

Osi stood beside the whining generator, facing Fleur and Elspeth.

"What is your plan?" The very thought of such a thing made the once proud Vampire weak with excitement, fear, disbelief.

"I've no hopes of saving this city any more. I only want to watch that bird-woman die. Two nights hence. The usurper has announced a banquet for all those who still reside in the City. To honor her," he hissed in disgust, then continued: "My plan is simple. Amidst the flood of stimuli that will be occupying her at the gala, and while you are engaging her with a riveting performance, Elspeth and I will strike. Quickly and from behind. Understood?"

Osi nodded, and left.

Osi stood before the bird-child.

"And when will this assassination attempt take place?" she whispered.

"At the banquet. Fleur will strike from behind, with Elspeth, while I am to . . . keep you occupied." He wanted to please her with his information—but also, a little, to scare her.

Her feathers ruffled. "And how will you do that?" Her tone was sarcastic.

"He suggested I start an argument." Osi's tone was belligerent, even pouty.

"I suggest you dance."

"Don't be ridiculous." What was left of his haughty racial and personal pride bridled at the suggestion.

"I insist you dance." Her tone was not ridiculous.

"And what is everyone to think?" He would not be made a fool. He would not! Yet, somewhere deep within him, even this public humiliation at her hands was somehow dreadfully seductive and arousing.

"If those who see are coconspirators, they will think you are diverting my attention; if they are not, they will think you a fool."

His teeth bared reflexively. She smiled in mock conciliation. "Ah, poor little tooth," she growled. "Come crawl over here to mother."

His wings flared momentarily, then folded as he fell to his knees. Every fiber of his being was repelled by the scene, yet her will was too strong to resist. He crawled to her.

She watched him with glee, with mastery, with lust. She reveled in dominating his spirit, while something visceral within her craved his flesh, quivered at his touch, glistened at the sight of him.

He reached the foot of the throne.

She slid down and sat astride him, her thighs lightly over his shoulders, her eyes closed, her talons in his back, her body steaming in the dark stone room.

There were, perhaps, a hundred creatures left in the City, and all were there: Vampires, Neuromans, Accidents, Cerberuses, Minotaurs, even Humans. Long tables joined end to end formed a large square, around which everyone sat. The empty space in the center of the square was for entertainments. It was a night of vile debauchery.

First came the feast itself. When all were seated, the child selected five of the guests to be cannibalized by the others for their meal. Before they could flee, a Cerberus, two Minotaurs, a Human, and a giant Rat were dismembered by Ninjus's guards. Some pieces were thrown into the great fireplace to cook, according to taste; the rest were eaten raw.

For the Vampires, Humans were passed around— dragged from Sire to Sire along the surface of the table, like sacks of grain—or, more precisely, bloated, sloshing wineskins, to be sucked on and handed along until empty. When they were dead, dry, and white, the Humans were pushed thoughtlessly to the floor, and others passed around. The air was filled with groans, shrieks, laughter and weeping, the salty spatter of blood and hilarity.

They twisted themselves further with drugs in quantity: opium, alcohol, cocaine, ginseng. The decibel level rose higher, the depravities sank lower still. This was the black heart of the City; these were the survivors, those scabrous enough to ride, screaming, at Chaos's flank.

All during the feast, entertainments erupted, mostly spontaneously, in the central clearing. An Accident dragged a swooning Human into the arena, bit a hole in the boy's belly, and performed grotesque sexual acts, even long after the boy had died. A Vampire jumped in, killed the Accident to a chorus of cheers, then cut the dead boy's heart out of his chest and ate it whole. He then called in one of his own harem slaves, whom he mounted from behind, while forcing her to stumble around the perimeter of tables, offering her neck to whomever would have her.

Fights broke out here and there around the room. The loser was inevitably set upon by several others, and added to the desserts.

The child was flamboyant. She took and dispensed favors like a heady monarch. She smoked and drank and chewed and sweat. She commanded the foulest of beasts to satisfy her desires; sometimes, at her whim, she would kill them with a stroke.

Osi sat to the child's left, remote and somber. He occasionally sipped from a filigreed cup of blood on the table before him, though he had no real thirst. His thoughts were elsewhere—on his charred hopes, frayed visions, lost loves; the oxidized empire of youth. He was feeling suddenly very aged.

Then he saw Vera. Vera, his last trusted Human, missing for so long now. She entered through a side door, into the frenzy of the banquet. He half-rose to meet her, but she didn't see him; she walked straight over to Ugo, plopped herself lasciviously down into that foul Vampire's lap, and offered her neck in the crudest manner. And in the crudest manner, Ugo took it.

Osi lowered himself back into his seat, shaken from his reverie. This was the end, then. What, after all, was he doing here?

He ordered another drink, stepped into the center of the ring of tables with it, and faced the bird-child—then lifted the goblet to his lips, and drank the mixture of blood, tears, and rum. He handed the brew to the child. She quaffed it, and dropped the glass to the floor.

Then Osi began to dance.

Slowly he turned, sweeping veils before and behind him in graceful billows. His wings opened and closed, hiding, revealing. The inebriated child watched in fascination as he touched himself, tauntingly, hauntingly, slowly turning, coming closer, holding her rapt. He rolled before her on the floor, came closer still, flexing and extending himself exquisitely before her, rhythmically undulating. Her eyes were fixed to him as he turned, teased, whispered . . .

Silently, Fleur and Elspeth climbed through the hole in the rear wall where the Queen's cables had once exited, ten feet behind the throne. Elspeth carried a short broadsword; Fleur, a knife. With desperate stealth, they approached the back of the throne, where the child sat watching Osi's diverting dance.

A foot away, Elspeth rose, raising her sword high over the bird-child's head. By the time anyone in the audience even saw her, she was bringing the sword down with all her strength.

At that moment, from a secret crawl space behind the throne, jumped Ninjus. He careened into Elspeth, and the sword crashed down on the throne itself, slicing off half the feathers on the bird-child's right arm. Elspeth was knocked to the floor.

Fleur stabbed at Ninjus, but the security chief easily knocked the knife away, and it clattered loudly along the stone floor in the sudden dense quiet.

Osi froze. The child spun around. Ninjus drew his own sword and, with a single sweep, cut off Elspeth's head: Hemolube gushed in a viscous pool behind the throne. Fleur stared in mute horror at his decapitated coconspirator; he offered no resistance as he was seized by two of Ninjus's soldiers, and dragged before the throne. Osi stood a few feet away. The rest of the crowd looked on as Ninjus stepped into the square holding Elspeth's head. The child turned to face them, alert with fear, bright-eyed with anger. The room was tense, quiet. The child looked at Ninjus, with his trophy, then at Fleur, held by the two guards; then at Osi, between them.

"*You* dance *well*," she murmured to the Vampire.

"I dance at your command," Osi replied without expression.

"You dance, I think, *too* well." Her thought pressure was icy cold.

He brought himself up to his full height. "Not well enough, I fear." His voice was barely audible, but his meaning was loud and clear. He wanted no more of such a degraded existence. He wanted the memory of his heritage to be once more a living force within him. He wanted to spread his wings and sing of the Vampire. He wanted out. He suddenly thought of Aba, the beautiful young Vampire who had so captivated him once, speaking of dreams and fears and furtive yearnings. "Go in good blood," he whispered, to the memory of Aba, and to Aba's memory of him.

Suddenly, four Neuromans rushed forward and killed the guards holding Fleur, then carried Fleur to a corner table and surrounded him. The delicate, pink Neuroman stood on the table, towering over everyone. His voice was incongruously fierce with grief and hate: "Join us!" he screamed. "Join us if you value what you value. And death to the child!"

On the spot, a pitched battle erupted. Creatures ran in all directions, shouting, swinging weapons, attacking the throne or defending it, depending on where they sensed their futures lay. A ring of guards, led by Ninjus, immediately surrounded the child, protecting her against all onslaught. The out-fighting was led by Ugo in the child's defense, by Fleur for the insurrectionists. For ten minutes, the battle raged. The child only watched, to see who would be her friend.

Osi grappled furiously with Ugo for a minute—rolling across the floor, fangs deeply inbedded in each other's neck—until he was torn away by an unseen combatant, and hurled into a far corner. He sat there a moment, bleeding, panting, watching the melee before him, gathering his strength.

The next moment, Fleur jumped on a table again, and yelled, "Retreat! Follow me!" With that, he jumped down and ran from the room, joined quickly by thirty others, running backward, fighting out the door. Without another thought, Osi stood, opened his wings, and flew out the nearest window into the congealing night.

Fifty defiant beasts—the child's army—were left in the room, along with eleven wounded prisoners, who were gathered roughly into a cluster before the throne. The child stared at them demonically, her eyes sparking, feathers on end, and screeched a long, raucous shriek to the sky: the sky answered with a shrill, gut-wrenching wail of its own:

in the next moment, the eleven captive creatures had fused into a single multi-limbed, multi-headed beast—a grotesque thing that could do nothing but snap and snarl in horror at itself while writhing, gnashing, twisting painfully on the floor.

To her minions, the child screamed, "*Go*, now! Go, and *prepare!*"

Their blood was up, their champion a black sorceress without equal. Ninjus and Ugo rallied them around the throne, and they all bowed and swore homage, then rose and left to plan for the castle's defense. For they were the black guard, the honor guard of the black magic, and soon—they could feel it, it was in the air—there would be a new world.

The child sat alone, fuming, electricity sparking around her. The fusocreature contorted in slow agony in a shadowy corner. Outside, it began to snow.

The snow fell slowly, in thick, wet globules over the Bookery camp. There was no wind, no sound. The people and animals in the camp kept a tense vigil through the night— yet it was unclear what was awaited.

The blackness was profound. Not even the campfires could thin it: they were like coalescences of light perforating a dense lightlessness; like stars in deep space. It was hard to walk more than two steps without tripping over or bumping into someone—for it was literally impossible to see anything, even inches away; and the entire camp was huddled together from fear. Only the shrunken fires were visible, sidereal and cold.

Nor did sound penetrate the void that pervaded. Animals spoke or whispered as if in a vacuum. The gentle, distant sussuration of the ocean had vanished with an alarming finality. The very substance of the air seemed dead.

The night lasted a long time.

When morning finally came, an opaque feeling seemed to linger. Everyone's movements were muffled, their senses dulled. The sky settled in a hazy film. The wind was like a shallow breath.

There was a brief hailstorm, with stones the size of fists. Once, the earth in the middle distance opened wide, creating a sudden maw, then quickly closed again—all this without a sound, like a silent scream.

Isis never left Joshua's lap. She knew he needed her silent, comforting spirit more than anything else, so she sat, sleeping, mostly; waking only to lick herself clean, or lick his hand, or purr as he stroked her without knowing he did, aware only vaguely of her watchful presence.

There he sat, straining to settle the wavering twists of Time he had glimpsed in the child's eye; there he sat, praying to the Word she didn't call him again.

Until sometime later, that long and lateless night, when he was called again.

He walked stoically into the darkness of the City. Rocks burned all around, as did the river itself, but shed no light. Into the castle he stumbled, and into the bird-child's lair. He stepped around the multibeast still writhing fitfully on the floor, and stood before the child.

Feathers covered most of her body now. Her tail was long, scaled; her eyes black ruby lights. She was six feet tall.

He felt all her thoughts as she spoke, now, like a low hum: "*Father, why have you created me?*"

He couldn't find a way to answer the question. "It was the Queen. The Queen and I, we . . ."

"*Father, why have you created me like this, the way I am?*"

"It wasn't planned, you just . . ."

"*Why me? Why what I know?*"

Josh felt his heart begin to beat like a drum. "What do you know?" he whispered over a dry tongue.

"*I know . . . all. No. Not all. I am opaque to myself. Except for this pitiable knot of stuff who speaks to you now, I know the universe.*"

"What do you know?"

"*Energy, Space, Time, it all flows through my hands— only my own self is blind to my eye, numb to my touch. This will all end, as it always has—but my own end I can-*"

not see. It confuses me, this blindness. How shall I pro-
ceed? I am the key, but I feel so sad, Father. I don't know
what to do. Why am I this way? What is the meaning?"

"What do you mean, this will all end as it always has?"

"Not always. That is, it is always different. Yet always
the same. My name is different, the circumstances unfa-
miliar, yet unmistakable. The process is unstoppable, it is
all process, we are all process. My name in this process is
Krisna. Or perhaps it is Jahweh, as it once was. Process and
precess."

"I don't understand."

"What does it mean?" she insisted harshly.

"Nothing means anything," he assured her. "Except
friends. Only friends mean anything." This he knew.

"Only the cycles mean anything. The Universe expands,
the universe contracts. Contracts into a ball the size of
. . . the universe. And then expands again, with its show-
ers of energy and twisted inspissations of light that interact
with one another to form you and me all over again and
again and again. Until we dissolve once more into the
ether, leaving only the shadow of radiation that is our echo,
our background noise, like a ghost image marking the
event that was you, the process that was me. And I am the
process; but a process cannot know itself, so I know myself
not, not my present or my future. Expand, contract, form,
unform, light, void. I am the neck of the hourglass. I begin,
I end, I return to beginning, I begin again. At the end of
the night of Time, all things return to my nature; and when
the new day of Time begins, I bring them again into light. I
bring forth all creation, and this rolls around in the circles
of Time. Thus the revolutions of the world."

Josh was transfixed. He only vaguely understood what
she was saying, yet it gripped his attention like a fist.

"Come look into my eyes," she continued, *"I will show*
you all; come, you can see the fulcrum of Time."

He walked closer, as if hypnotized, stood touching her,
his face inches from hers, now centimeters, only millimeters away. Now he stared into the infinite black fire of her
eyes.

"All things end and start here." He heard her voice as

an omnipresence. "*I am destroyer and creator, I am the fire and the phoenix; join me, come into me, come. Tell me what you see, for I see myself not.*"

He felt himself begin to fall into her eyes. Slowly at first, he floated; then deeper and deeper into the singularity, like an asteroid that first feels the tug and tingle of a star's gravitation, he fell.

"*As the axis of the Earth slowly changes direction in timely precession, describing its own inexorable circles in space, so does the axis of the galaxy precess. And so, even, does the axis of the universe wobble in nutant, stately revolution. These are the great precessions, precessions of spacial axes over the course of Time, precessions of Space, over Time; of Space, in Time. But behold now, creator, the precession of Time, in Space.*"

Josh was tumbling now, sinking into the vortex of her eyes. He felt himself fusing into her being, passing through the bounds of her substance to meld with the energy being funneled through the knot in the fabric of the ether that was the child.

"*The precession of Time nears its full cycle, now, to begin again at its beginning, to start the precession anew, to circle yet again, and again. We are at the node. And each time we pass this node, you will appear again, and your friends and their friends, and they will think, sometimes, that they knew you in a different place, a previous life, but they will be wrong—they knew you in this same place, during the last precession of the axis of Time. And every time, I will appear again, to instruct you, to mark the end of the cycle. And until you can see the way to stop it, or alter it, we will each time begin the cycle anew. Thus is the comely precession of Time in Space preserved.*"

He was vertiginous within her, gasping in the maelstrom of her eyes. He was one with her now, part of her radiant field, his electromagnetic waves like fingers laced in her waves. He whirled, he swam . . . and then, reaching out, caught himself on the lip of his sanity, on the edge of her eyes; and bloodying his fingers on this ragged edge, pulled himself out—pulled himself out and crawled across the floor, crawled away from the child; crawled, bloody and crying and shaking. Crawled out the door and didn't look back.

The child gazed inward across the measureless ether, and waited for revelation.

CHAPTER 19

The Final Battle

ALL through the night meteor showers screamed out of the sky. They struck the earth and ocean in explosions of flame that froze immediately into phosphorescent ice patterns, then melted into shimmering orange pools that danced across the horizon. No one in the Bookery camp slept.

The next morning Phé flew in, carrying Ollie and the aerosols from the City of Ice. They had made one stop, near the Forest of Tears, then flown directly over the Terrarium, with all due haste. They had flown high, for speed, and it was freezing up there—so Ollie had willingly allowed Phé to hug him closely to her breast. It was the first time he had ever been in such close, prolonged contact with a Vampire; and though he had grown tired of her endless vulgar jokes, and from time to time had to push away her boisterous, groping hands, and endure her rowdy laughter, he found he was developing, against all his better judgment, an affection for her.

The flight had exhausted them both, so after telling their stories to Jasmine and the others, they quickly fell asleep beside the campfire.

It was a day for returns, though, and shortly thereafter Aba showed up, bruised but strong. He and Paula immediately fell into each other's arms, embraced long and without words; and readied themselves for the imminent onslaught.

It was decided to attack at once, before nature could be any further subverted by the whims and spasms of the bird-child's will.

Joshua still had not returned from his meeting with the child on the previous night. Jasmine shook her head at the irony: after all that had happened, they would finally try to rescue Joshua from the castle.

Her plan was rather simple. At the Outer City, they would divide into two groups. One, led by her, would go down into the tunnels and come up in the throne room. The other group, led by Ollie, would reach the throne room through the castle itself. Jasmine and Ollie would each carry one of the aerosols. They would kill whomever tried to stop them from spraying the child.

As they were arming themselves with whatever they had—crossbows, knives, swords, torches, syringes—Osi swooped down and landed squarely in their midst.

There was a brief furor as the alien Vampire was surrounded and nearly attacked—until Aba stepped forward.

"Let him stand," Aba shouted. Then, more softly: "He is Osi-Sire, and my friend."

"Thank you, Sire Aba." The older Vampire bared his neck. "Meeting you again, here, is an unexpected joy."

"What do you want?" Ollie demanded, for he remembered Osi well from his own brief captivity in the castle.

Osi spoke to the group. "There has been a castle conspiracy and rebellion. The child is besieged by half of her own guards. I barely escaped after joining the plot—"

There were gasps and murmurs. "Let him finish," Jasmine yelled, quieting everyone.

"Thank you, Neuroman," Osi continued. "I have been flying in circles . . . for some time. I saw your camp from the air. I thought at first to steal a few of you, and set up a harem in the jungle. But on further consideration, I've decided to join you, that we might all destroy the monster in the castle."

A score of protests and accusations rose up, but Jasmine silenced them. "Hold!" she yelled; they quickly quieted.

She looked hard at Osi, as if weighing him, then said to him, "What *is* the situation in the castle now?"

"The castle is in ruins. The insurgents number half a hundred and are led by a Neuroman named Fleur. They are based, I believe, in the power station. The child is defended by fifty others, under charge of another Neuroman called Ninjus, and a Sire named Ugo—he is *sang noir*, that one. Bad blood."

Jasmine nodded slowly, then slowly spoke again: "Why *did* you come to help us?"

For a moment, Osi felt naked under her stare. He looked away—his gaze fell on Aba; their eyes met, and held. Tension, affection; question. Neither one moved. Then Paula walked up beside Aba, and put her arm around his waist . . . and the trance was broken. Aba leaned down and kissed her head. Osi looked back at Jasmine and smiled. "On my blood, Neuroman," he said, "it seemed the thing to do."

Jasmine considered a moment longer, then bowed her acceptance. Osi told what more he knew of the child's defenses and soon all was ready.

Jasmine stood on a boulder in front of the assemblage, and held a final benediction.

"What the world will be may well depend upon what we here do," she told them all. "Be strong, for we are together."

"The Word is great, the Word is One," the Books all droned responsively.

"We will take this time, too, to think on those who are *not* with us now."

All thought of Josh, trapped in the beleaguered castle—of all he had done for them, of all he meant. They would save him now, or die in the process.

Some thought of Michael and Ellen, too—lost somewhere out on the tundric wastes of the Ice; the first martyrs of this strange and final confrontation. And of David.

Ollie and Aba thought longingly of D'Ursu Magna, strongest of Bears, truest of friends. They wished him well in their hearts, wherever he was.

And Rose and Jasmine thought of Beauty, their graceful Centaur—and wondered if they would ever see him again; and hoped his world would be better for what they did today.

After several minutes of silence on these matters, Jasmine raised her voice again. "Are we ready, then?"

"The Word is great!"

"May you reach Communion, sister!"

"May we meet again in the Heart of the Forest!"

"Or turn into Scripture trying!"

And so they were off. Forty rag-tag heroes of the age, intent on storming a ruined castle.

Once through the outer gates, they split up. Jasmine took her regiment—Paula, Aba, Osi, Redsun, five Books and ten other Pluggers—down into the tunnels. Following Ollie, the other squadron—Phé, Rose, Candlefire, Isis, five Pluggers, five Books, and a few miscellaneous animals who had wandered into camp during the excitement of the preparation and had come along at the last minute—moved through the Outer City.

The Outer City looked like another planet. Purple rock formations grew in gravity-defying patterns; liquid fires trickled down the streets, emitting a vile smoke. Ollie's group stayed bunched up and low to the ground. There were no other creatures around.

The Inner City was so thick with smoke that it wasn't possible to see the castle. Ollie knew where it was, though, and kept his course true. In a few minutes, the smoke cleared, and the young man found himself on the steps of the main gate. Silently, he counted heads: all were safe. Silently, they entered.

They moved double-file behind Ollie, who took them at a crouching run up the first set of main stairs, down smoking and steaming corridors, under dangling, sparking wires. Still no other creatures.

They were making their way steadily upward, toward the third-floor center, where the throne room lay. On the second-floor landing of the maintenance stairwell, they were attacked from above and below by castle guards, ten at each end, composed primarily of Vampires and Cerberuses. The Books and Pluggers at the rear of Ollie's line were slaughtered—five of them within seconds, another five in the first minute. Ollie killed half a dozen in that time by himself, and rallied those around him to dispose of the other attackers at the head of the line.

He was bleeding, called for a retreat upward. What was left of his group followed him up another flight of stairs, pursued closely by the remainder of the child's guard.

They made it down the next hall and into the first room they came to, closing it behind them and barricading it against the pursuit. Ollie turned to his group and quickly assessed the situation: only six left!

Ollie, Phé, Rose, Candlefire, and two Books. The Vampires outside began battering in the door. Ollie looked around to see where they were. It was the Communion Room.

Only Phé looked unperturbed. "Nice fighting, little blood!" She clapped Ollie on the back. "You've got one hot knife."

Ollie ignored her and raced to the other side of the room. The place was empty now, devoid of the Humans who once lay here, plugged in to the Queen. Rose and Candlefire had lain here then, cables streaming from their heads. They stared around them mutely now, reeling as much from the shock of this memory as from the shock of the fight they had just been through.

"Over here!" Ollie called. He was standing by the hole in the wall through which all the connections once exited into the computer room. He climbed through, and the others quickly followed.

Another dead room. Huge machines lined the walls, blinking randomly, sparking, burning, smoking. The six fugitives pushed an enormous console in front of the hole they had come through. In the opposite wall was another hole, the one through which cables from the computers had traversed to connect with the Queen's brain—in the throne room.

Ollie's eyes flashed. "Come on," he whispered.

They followed him to the portal. He stuck his head through and looked around. Empty. He climbed in. The others followed suit.

Ollie approached the throne. Empty. There was a noise behind him, and he whirled just in time to see Jasmine stick her head above the lip of the disposal shaft.

"How we doing?" she whispered.

"This place is secure, but this is all that's left of us." He indicated the five near the throne.

Jasmine frowned and jumped out of the chute, followed rapidly by Aba, Paula, Osi, and a few others. "We lost some in the tunnels," she muttered. "Thought they saw Josh, and just disappeared after him . . ."

"What now?" asked Phé. "It's a big castle."

"Room by room," Paula croaked fiercely.

"There's Vampires on our tail," Ollie said.

"How many?"

"Seven, maybe eight."

"Coming which way?" asked Jasmine.

Ollie indicated the hole in the wall.

"We'll kill all but one," said the Neuroman. "Let one escape—make it look real—and we'll follow him back to his friends."

It was six Vampires, a Cerberus, and a Lizard, in fact. They reached the cable port in two minutes, then carefully entered the throne room one by one. When they were all in, Ollie fell on them with vengeance—along with Jasmine, Aba, Osi, Phé, and five Books. The combat was swift. When it was over, one wounded Vampire had escaped out the door to the Communion Room. He was soon followed.

Down the winding stairways, they tumbled and ran, over bodies and debris, chilled by dark winds. Outside, fires billowed against the dull sky, while distant explosions rumbled the stone.

Across great halls they ran, always just seeing the vanishing wings of the wounded Vampire going through the next door ahead. Rooms, doors, crumbling floors. Until finally, not so far away: a noise. A lot of noises. Shouts, clangs, and thuds. And when Jasmine, at the head of her people, burst finally into the next room, she found herself in the thick of a great battle.

Osi was right on her heels, and he looked around but a moment before he spoke: "There is Fleur, on the landing, leading his force. I don't see Ninjus, but there is Ugo, rallying the child's guard—and he is mine."

And so saying, he leapt into the fray, bent on killing the scar-faced Vampire.

Whereupon Jasmine and her entourage rushed in and joined the fighting.

It was apparent who the child's guards were—each wore one of her feathers tied at the wrist. Beyond that, little was discernible. Insanity reigned.

A hundred creatures filled what had once been the Communications Room—gnashing, clawing, slicing and stabbing one another to death amid a terrain of electrical fires, sparking generators, and dismembered parts. The floor was slippery with blood.

Ollie sought the child. He walked among the chaos almost as if he were invisible, sticking his dagger ruthlessly into backs or bellies, but never stopping to engage: he had eyes only for the child—his niece.

Jasmine, too, looked for the child, but she was attacked by a Minotaur before she had gone five steps, and was quickly rolling furiously around the floor in his clutches, battling for her life.

Nor did Osi make it far into the room before he was embroiled in a tangle with a Cerberus and a ferret-faced Neuroman he knew slightly and had always disliked.

Ugo stood at the head of a phalanx of three Vampires, fighting hand to hand with three of Fleur's best. When Osi pointed him out, though, he was rushed by several Books and Pluggers from Jasmine's party, two of whom reached him. One of these was Paula.

She threw herself on the foul beast, jamming her knife into his left flank. He screamed, and fell on top of her, his teeth tearing at her shoulder. The knife was yanked from her grip. Hissing, he brought his mouth around her neck for the kill. Paula closed her eyes.

Ugo's weight was suddenly lifted from her, and she looked up to see Aba pulling Ugo precariously to the side. A Neuroman was flung into them suddenly from another corner, knocking them both over. For a moment, they stared at each other. "You . . ." growled Ugo. Then Aba cut his neck, and he was dead.

In the next moment a blade came down over Aba's head; but he was pulled clear in time by his sister, Phé. "Watch your backside, Baby-Sire!" She laughed, and moved off in another direction.

It was then that Josh decided to enter—though decision probably had little to do with it. He was dazed, almost somnambulant. Like a wraith, or prophet, he wandered among the living and dead, seeming to distinguish little between them. The fight had thinned a good deal by now, through mortal attrition, so Joshua's entrance was clearly visible from the floor. Jasmine saw him at once.

"Joshua!" she called. He didn't seem to hear her, though his name had the effect of a rallying cry on his followers. They redoubled their efforts—though all was going against them at this stage: the child's forces were steadily winning.

Josh took no notice. Instead, his eyes were focused on a ventilation duct opening in the wall across the room, from which the mesh screen had been removed. It formed a square hole in the wall, six feet above the floor, two feet on a side. The ventilation shaft of which it was the mouth was too black to see into.

But stare into it Joshua did, from across the room, with a gaze transfixed by visions Jasmine couldn't even begin to guess at. From her own position under the window, she followed the line of his gaze to the vent on which it was fixated. And then *she* stared at the open vent, stared into its invisible blackness, could see nothing but nothing—except, wait . . . weren't there two denser spots of blackness within the ebony of the unlighted duct? Yes, two circles of black, shining black, staring back out of the blackness of the vent like . . . eyes. A child's eyes.

"Ollie!" Jasmine called out. She caught his attention, pointed to the duct, pulled out her aerosol, and started wading slowly across the room. Joshua's eyes flickered momentarily, saw what was happening, and he began walking through the melee toward the vent.

Ollie extricated himself from under the body of Redsun, who had just fallen, and began moving toward the screenless vent, aerosol can in his left hand, knife in his right. Before he had gone half the distance, though, he saw Osi downed, just a few feet away. Two Neuroman guards were on the Vampire friend, throttling him from behind. Ollie hestitated a second, then leaped onto the pile.

Ollie tumbled with one Neuroman, Osi with the other. In a minute the Neuromans were still—but in the scuffle, Ollie's aerosol had been knocked away. Now he couldn't find it.

Josh, meanwhile, was slowly nearing the focus of their attentions—he would get there just about the same time as Jasmine.

His mind was coming back, now—who he was, where he was. He could see what was happening, and guessed more or less how it had come about. But these things were beyond him—or he, beyond them. For he had spent the past night—only one night?—in places Time had taken him. Places far from there.

The center of the universe. No light there; no time. He had lost his self in that distant place for an eternal moment, spinning blindly through the hub of the wheel, without form or substance or motion.

And then suddenly from the core, through all the spokes—spokes of suns, uncountable suns, green suns, black suns, imploding and fusing suns, suckled by swirling gasses, showers of jewels, invisible planets, dimensionless creatures, organic, conscious, shimmering spokes of excruciating design, numberless patterns, waxen and glistening photon liquidities—to the edge, to the furthest racing filaments of light, each breathless to outdistance the other, to this thin, fine gossamer edge of Time and Space, where, light-headed with speed, speed-headed with light, dizzy with the momentum of the Wheel, he had gone over the edge.

Over the edge. Into nothing. Falling, falling . . . he had looked back. He had seen the Wheel. The teetering gyroscope of Time.

And now he saw the child. The child, hiding in the darkness of the ventilation duct, waiting for . . . what? For Jasmine? For the end of the world? For the universe to spin into chaos? No.

For him, surely. But who was he? He was once The Serpent, the master Scribe. Jasmine had said so. He was hunter, Selkie brother. Time-traveler. Friend. Father. Father of this child, who could see All but was helpless under the weight of her knowledge. This was the child; but who was the father? All these things? He felt like none of these things. He felt like nothing. He no longer had any sense of who, or what, he was.

A greater despair filled him. If he didn't know who he was, how could he ever know what to do? Indecision threatened to immobilize him. Dare he take another step? Dare he not?

"Joshua, thank God," Jasmine whispered, and raised the aerosol can up to the level of the duct.

Josh lifted his hand. "Stop the child," he whispered, "stop her and make this dream end . . ."

Something about his voice, or the commanding movement of his hand, arrested Jasmine, and she stared at him strangely for just a moment. The moment was long enough for Ninjus suddenly to emerge from a hidden door a few feet away. He kicked Jasmine in the head, knocking her out, knocking the cap off her Hemolube valve. He lunged at Josh in the next second. Josh reflexively jumped back to avoid the blow, and was quickly lost in the melee.

Fleur leapt forward at that—he had been looking for Ninjus from the start, looking to avenge Elspeth's death—and locked Ninjus in a vise grip with one hand, forcing a long knife down his throat with the other, trying to stick it through Ninjus's soft palate to his spinal column—his one vulnerable spot.

They wrestled against the wall, slowly turning. Ninjus had his scaly hands on Fleur's neck, trying to break it. Just as Fleur's back was to the wall, though, Ninjus lost his footing in a pool of blood, and Fleur rammed his killing dagger home. Then, before Ninjus even slumped to the floor, the child stuck her head out of the vent just over Fleur, reached out, and snapped off Fleur's valve cap. Leaning over, she put her lips to the valve and blew as hard as she could, forcing half a lungful of air into Fleur's circulatory system.

The pink, translucent Neuroman convulsed once, then settled to the ground beside Ninjus.

The child quickly retreated back into the ventilation duct.

The battle raged on, though both sides by now had few combatants; so there were signs of slowing. Carefully, the child inched backward, through the duct, until she came to a crossing of ducts in the system, an intersection and widening, where she could sit up.

What did this all mean? she wondered. What should she do? And when? And why?

Suddenly Isis trotted up to her, as if she had been waiting all along. Funny little Cat, always curled up sleeping in the middle of everything. Little spirit-Cat. The child petted Isis behind the ears; Isis purred and leaned into the child's spindly fingers.

"You've been with me since the moment of my birth," the child said to the purring Cat.

Isis bit down on the capsule Jasmine had put in her mouth earlier; a warm, bitter liquid oozed out of it, coating her tongue. She sat up and began licking the child's face.

The child giggled and cooed a moment—for the Cat's tongue was warm, soft, scratchy, tickly. Then suddenly a wave of horror washed over the bird-child's face, washed through her core like a molten star—for she sensed, all of an instant, what the little Cat was about, what it was up to, what it had done.

Starkly, she pushed Isis away, and sat back against the vertical ventilation shaft. The terror rose to her throat, began suffocating her, strangling her. She screamed: "I'm not ready! I'm not ready!"

But no one answered. Isis backed down another duct, and vanished.

"I'm not ready," the child whimpered, but already the words were sticking in her throat.

The battle ended. Wounded from both sides dragged themselves out the doors, looking for daylight.

Ollie searched Ugo's body and found the key to the Human cages. He walked, with great difficulty—for his leg was badly cut—down to the Human Quarters, and opened all the cells. Half were dead of starvation. Most of the oth-

"Funny little cat, . . ."

ers filed out disbelievingly and, dreamily, wandered toward the doors. Ollie went back to look for Josh. But Josh was nowhere to be found.

Paula, nearly dead from blood loss, managed to find Jasmine—nearly dead from Hemolube loss—and recap the Neuroman's head valve. She carried Jasmine out of the castle and halfway to the City gates before Aba saw them, picked them up, and flew them both back to the Bookery camp.

And so the others—those still alive—slowly straggled back, to lick their wounds and wonder if they had won.

CHAPTER 20

The Seven Days

JOSH was vaguely aware of a gentle tugging at the side of his chin, over and over until it became more of a coarse scratching. The next thing he was aware of was that he was wet all over—wet and cold—and there seemed to be water washing steadily across his legs. The next thing he noticed was the smell: foul, fetid, all-encompassing. Finally, there was the weight on his chest—not heavy, but insistent.

He opened his eyes. He was lying on his back in the semidarkness. Isis sat patiently on his chest, rhythmically licking first his chin, then his cheek. When he opened his eyes, she kept licking. He smiled weakly and scratched her behind the ear, just where she liked it. "Hi, Fur-face," he said in a gravelly whisper.

She stepped down beside him and sat on the damp rock as he pushed himself up to slump against the wall. He had been lying in one of the sanitation tunnels beneath the City, half in the swiftly flowing subterranean tributary, half up a moist, unlit side conduit. A dim bulb still shed some light twenty yards upstream, in the main tunnel. Josh took a deep breath, and coughed. An impossible stench filled his nostrils: he retched until his stomach twisted, empty.

Decaying matter floated by down the main tunnel—the sewage of the apocalypse: rotting torsos, grimacing heads bobbing darkly, like half-remembered fragments of a nightmare.

"What's happened?" Josh croaked. He looked like he had been thrown out death's back door. His eyes were vacant; he was broken, bleeding from the ears. Filth clung to him, matted his hair, stuck to his torn skin and shredded

297

clothes. The only clear, calm part of him was his face, which Isis had licked clean.

"Herrrrre," purred Isis, nodding her head up the direction of the dry side tunnel.

Josh followed her a few steps, then stopped. "Wait," he said. There was a humming in his brain, almost a whine.

Oooooooooooooh

Like wind blowing through deserted corridors.

"This way," said Josh. He picked Isis up and began trudging down the main tunnel, knee-deep in dirty water.

Oooooooooooooooooh

As if he knew every turn, Josh navigated the labyrinth of tunnels beneath the City, Isis perched on his shoulder.

Ooooh

He reached one of the myriad vertical shafts that pierced the underground tributaries, and began to climb the iron rungs that ran up the side. Fifty yards up, a hundred yards.

Oooooooooooh

He climbed over the lip of the shaft and stepped out into the darkened throne room. The child lay a few feet away, curled fetally on the floor.

"*Ooooooooooooooooooh,*" she whimpered.

Josh knelt beside her. He put his hand on her forehead. She was burning.

"*Ooooooooooh.*"

He looked on her with great sorrow. She was feverish, pale. Her teeth began to chatter, and almost immediately the doors in the room started rattling.

Who was this creature? He could not know. He had all but gone mad in the abyss of her eyes. He had seen things through her he could never explain, never understand. She had been demented, playful, sad, impenetrable, pitiable. He had had a part in creating her.

She seemed, now, like the saddest of all creatures.

He picked her up in his arms and carried her toward the door. Isis paused.

"Come on," said Josh, and Isis trotted along behind.

As he walked down the main staircase, still carrying her, she had shaking chills. With that, the walls began to quake, and great stones fell from the ceiling to crash and shatter all around. Josh made it out of the castle as the entire structure began to collapse into rubble, with Isis running ahead of him, her eyes wild, her ears pressed flat to her head.

The feathered bird-child hung limply in Joshua's arms, a cold, waxy sweat upon her lip.

Isis skipped merrily into camp early the next morning. A few minutes later, Josh arrived and laid his burden on the ground: the bird-child remained unconscious, breathing heavily.

In a short time, the entire community had gathered around them to watch. Josh covered the child with a blanket, adjusted her feet, mopped her forehead; Isis curled up a few feet away and fell asleep.

There were, perhaps, a hundred creatures still in camp, all straining to see the father and child: the remaining Books; the cachectic, liberated Humans; Jasmine, Rose, Aba, Paula, Phé, Ollie, Osi. Refugees from Newport had begun wandering in, as well: Bears, Elves, Satyrs. Everyone was murmuring at once, wondering what to do, how to feel. Ollie and Jasmine stepped forward from different directions.

"You should have let her die in the castle," said Ollie. "We could see the explosions from here. She would have died."

"She's dying," said Josh.

"Quick death would have been better," Jasmine suggested.

"For who?" Josh whispered pointedly.

"For her and for us," Jasmine replied.

"I . . . couldn't leave her there," Josh stammered,

"I'll kill her now," said Osi ominously, coming close. He had strong feelings still about this child who had had such a hold over him. Even seeing her alive shamed him.

Josh stood in his way, though. "No. I won't let you."

"You cannot stop me," Osi grimaced.

Josh held his ground. "Maybe. But you'll have to kill me first." He stood over the child, and spoke louder to the group. "That goes for all of you. No one will harm this child without killing me first!"

"But Joshua—" began Jasmine.

"No!" he barked. "She is blood of my blood. She's shown me things, taken me places, made me see—see what no one else has ever seen. Will ever see. Can ever know. And even if she's dying now, she may yet share something more with us—and I will not have that possibility cut short!" His eyes flamed with passion; not a creature there had, any longer, the strength to take issue with him. Most were too weak or injured to protest, in any case; and the rest simply had no interest in opposing Joshua's will.

Osi hesitated, considering the options, then finally shrugged and walked away.

Ollie shook his head once, and also drifted off. A minute later his flute could be heard playing tag with the wind.

A week of dire and unaccountable events followed.

That whole first day, the child was plagued by attacks of alternating chills and fever. During the former periods, the temperature of the air in camp would plunge to arctic levels. Animals froze to death. During the child's febrility, ambient weather conditions reversed with the speed of a dream, the temperature soaring. More animals died.

A great sense of loss began to pervade the area—for comrades lost in battle, lost in quest, lost in deceit, and to disillusion: Candlefire, Redsun, Michael, Beauty, D'Ursu, Ellen, David; most of the Pluggers and most of the Books were gone forever. And more died each day that the fading child lived.

But the survivors felt a sense of loss of themselves, as well. So much lost, so much changing. Not a one would ever be the same. The world they had known was over; the new world was not yet begun. For most of the huddling camp, it was a time of despair, or fear, or bereavement, or nostalgia—each, in its way, the experience of loss of something deep within.

The child, meanwhile, got sicker. Her eyes would open wide, sometimes, staring starkly—and at those times the sun in the sky would become blindingly, painfully bright.

Then her eyes would screw shut tight, and the sun would darken, as if eclipsed.

She had fitful dreams over the next two days, during which she would turn from side to side, whimpering, panting. On several occasions she was quite delirious. It was during this period that the new animals appeared.

Not the ordinary sort of new animals, either, as had been wandering in of late. These were *entirely* new animals, such as had never been seen *anywhere*. Some looked like patchworks of old animals. Some were simply out of whole cloth: crazy heads on strangely colored bodies, funny feet, speaking exotic, unintelligible languages. They were bizarre, or scary, or silly, or mean, or scared, or just too odd to interpret.

New flora began to appear all over as well. Surreal, fernlike things atop ridiculously tall, skinny trunks; orange, or purple fruit trees, dripping juices.

It was a true dream world, and it was frightening. Friends tended to stay near one another, for safety and comfort.

On the morning of the fifth day, Osi came forward and stood before them all. "I have given the matter much thought," he announced, "and I have decided to leave. No good can come of this—the child makes the Earth ill with her disease—and since we are disallowed by fiat from stopping this madness"—here he looked pointedly at Josh—"I will start my life anew elsewhere."

"Go, then," Paula said, without intonation.

"And so I shall," answered Osi. "But first, I would ask for volunteers to accompany me—to be the core of my new harem."

"Harem!" Paula roared.

"Volunteers!" Ollie echoed.

"That is what I said," Osi replied quietly. "To all who join me, I promise: you can leave my harem whenever you wish. As long as you stay with me, I will keep you warm and sheltered, fed and appreciated. I will protect you from the elements and from attack by any beast. I will allow no other Sires to force their attentions on you. We will grow, and be a family."

"A family!" Ollie sang, and then burst out laughing. The laughter broke the tension, and Osi responded in kind.

"A family it is, brother, and let no one tell you different. And I swear, we'll squabble and bicker and love and laugh. What say you, Sire Aba? Was my harem not a model family?"

"It was a family," nodded Aba. "And they seemed well content, all in all. Just so." Paula looked at her lover, half-aghast, half-questioningly.

Phé joined in jovially. "I'd snap his offer up quick if I was you, you runny-bloods—this Osi-Sire's a fine specimen of a Sire if ever I saw one, and he'll not soon be back this way." She laughed gleefully, and her whole body shook.

"You've got nothing to look forward to here, I can tell you," Osi went on. "Nothing but misery and privation, and a hard, short life." He smiled, waiting, looking over the crowd.

There was a long silence. Then a voice from the back said, "I'll go." It was one of the few surviving Books. "Me too," said another.

Jasmine smiled the smile of a three-hundred-year-old woman who still didn't understand a thing.

In the end, two Books and two of the freed Humans elected to accompany Osi. He gathered them all up under his powerful arms, called good-bye, and flew off into the eastern sky without one look back.

Phé became very protective of her young brother Aba. "Baby-Sire, don't you go sniffing off after that bloody pumper and get yourselves lost in these clot-sucking times."

"Phé, I'm not going anywhere," Aba responded with some annoyance. "And Paula is not a bloody pumper!"

"She's lovely, Baby-Sire, and red as the sunset—but they're all bloody pumpers under the tooth." She laughed raucously, and slapped him on the back.

"You embarrass me, Sister," he shook his head, not without love.

"Embarrassment is secret glee," she nodded broadly, and winked as Paula approached.

"Embarrassment is having a sister with yellow hair and a floppy tongue," he admonished.

"I like your sister's hair," said Paula as she joined them. "Why do you mock it?"

"It's me silver tongue he hates, but never mind. I'll take care of the Baby-Sire in spite of the bloody piss in his veins." At which she laughed and shook and pinched them both, and finally wandered off to make good-natured trouble elsewhere.

In the next forty hours, both the child and the world deteriorated rapidly. She began having paroxysms of vomiting, carpopedal spasms, increasing nuchal rigidity, and, finally, a long string of bad convulsions. Concomitant with all this was the appearance, across the land, of volcanoes spewing molten rock and sulphurous magma; firestorms that scorched the ground and burned the flesh of all who weren't tucked safely away; earthquakes that turned the plains on their sides, opening into bottomless wells, spitting geysers of flame.

At some moments the very fabric of the sky seemed to rip, letting the Void's black fluid spill out. The Earth itself began spinning faster, so nights and days lasted only a few hours, and Time rushed around like a rabid Bat, too quick to follow and all aflutter.

There was doom in the air. Some of the animals became withdrawn; but it had the opposite effect in many, inducing feelings of reckless infatuation, or deep passion. Paula and Aba became even more singularly preoccupied than usual. Desperately in love, they were virtually oblivious to the natural—or unnatural—catastrophes that crashed about them.

Josh and Rose also came together during this period. The oldest of friends, they now rediscovered sleeping passions—awakened, somehow, by their love for the Centaur whose absence they felt so acutely.

"I'm worried for him." Rose spoke softly to keep her voice from running away. "He must be so alone."

"He's safe up there—safer than us, probably. And well taken care of by the Neuromans, Ollie said."

"Will we ever see him again? There are so many things I wish I'd said . . ."

"He knows. He knows you love him. As he knows I love him. It makes no difference if we see him here again," Josh told her, looking out at a cluster of flaming trees. "We never *stopped* seeing him *here*," he went on, touching her breast.

She shook her head, crying. "But I miss him so."

He took her and held her, and they were both crying, and soon they were making love; and for brief moments over the next two days, each of them touched Beauty again, through the love the other had for that noble Centaur, dear friend.

But of all the couplings that arose during these cataclysms surrounding the child's illness, perhaps the oddest was the one between Ollie and Phé.

She came upon him playing his flute while the sea burned on the fifth day.

"Funny weather we're havin'," she noted.

"Looks like the end of the world," he observed.

She nodded. "So long as it doesn't rain. I hate the bloodless rain."

They eyed each other with guarded appreciation.

"It was a fast flight you made down here," he said to her. "I . . . meant to thank you."

She shrugged. "Keepin' warm is the main thing, with altitude flyin'. You kept me warm, is all."

"No, you've got strength and speed—I admire those things." He surprised himself a bit; he had never been so open.

She came closer to him. "And you've got some things I admire," she said, her voice somewhat huskier than she had planned.

He suddenly wanted to touch her. It was a feeling he had rarely experienced under any circumstances, and never with a Vampire. He reached out and put his fingertips against her cheek, drew them down her neck, along the cleft between her breasts; measured and fondled the tense weight of her breast in his palm.

Her eyes closed briefly, and when they opened, she

pulled him to her, drew his slight body in to the massive warmth of her own, wrapped her wings around them both, tore open his pants, pulled him deep inside her, felt his heat, his heart against her heart, his rapid respirations on her cheek, their mingling sweat, his hands all over her and urging; she put her lips along his throat, licked him there, began to shake . . . when through his teeth, he whispered, "Please . . . no blood."

This only made her tension more exquisite, though. She brought her mouth up to his mouth, kissed him hotly, grazed his inner lip against her razor tooth, and delicately lapped the drop of blood that formed there.

Around them, meteors fell and sulphur bubbled, but they were unaware of anything beyond the canopy of her wings, inside of which they lost themselves, tumbling, in timeless delight.

The liberated Humans spent the time together, constructing a large, unsinkable log raft. Wanting to get as far from the City as possible, they decided sailing south along the coast was the safest way. They were thin, wasted, bitter people. They worked together, but without speech; and somehow, without cause.

Only Jasmine kept a completely lonesome vigil—over the child. She sat beside the dwindling creature, soothing her sometimes, trying to prevent the child from biting her tongue when the seizures were bad, listening to the occasional rantings; mostly, just watching. Keeping her as comfortable as possible in what were clearly her final hours.

Once, Jasmine had a vision. She saw a woman approach—a white-haired woman who looked very like Jasmine herself, only much older, and somehow without substance. This Doppelgänger walked with broken steps from person to person in the camp, her hands outstretched, weeping, wandering. No one else seemed to be aware of her. "Help me, I beg you," the vision whimpered. "My name is Jezebel, and I've gone to hell."

She looked toward Jasmine, at last, and recognition flickered across her drawn face. "This is the end, then, for you and me—I am your death, and you are mine."

Then the alter-image hobbled off—lost, crying, aged, bereft of hope or friend. Somehow this intangible old crone unsettled Jasmine more than had any of the preceding horrors. Like a nightmare without meaning, it choked her still; like a precognition of doom, it flashed dimly in the corner of her soul's eye, and was gone.

Finally, on the seventh day the child had a long, agonal spasm of opisthotonus—her back arched, almost to breaking, in a long, taut bow; her muscles locked rock-hard in that position: her mouth stretched down in ferocious grimace; her breathing all but stopped. This was the beginning of the end.

Gravity itself increased slowly; the atmosphere became dense. The Great White Birds, which had been circling for days, fell out of the sky, suddenly unable to fly. The largest of the Earth's animals fell to their knees—their legs no longer able to support their huge frames—and could not rise again. Everyone felt newly, heavily burdened.

The sun took a long time setting, as the Earth slowed on its axis of rotation, then finally ground to a complete halt after the sun was down, to leave the huddled creatures stranded in a long, cold night.

It seemed to last for days, this longest night. The sea could be heard rushing away from the shore, leaving bare, wet beach many miles deep. The Earth roared and cracked and heaved, and almost ripped apart under the strain of sudden stillness. Mountains exploded, and the ground turned to steaming mud. The promontory of land on which the animals clustered was thrust up at an acute angle, like a shelf over the shattering world.

Then the child's pulse became thready and weak; her blood pressure fell. So the atmospheric pressure fell, and the air became lighter again—though thunderstorms speared the sky with lightning, rain, and frenzied wind, and the frothy air screamed as if it were being torn and tortured.

Until finally, the child's back broke under the opisthotonic stress, and she breathed easier for just a minute, as her respirations became shallower and shallower. And suddenly the sun rose again: only, it rose on the horizon below which it had just set; and then it continued to rise. For the Earth was rotating, now, in the opposite direction; rotating so the sun rose on the opposite horizon from that where it had always risen; and would likewise set over the opposite shore.

And so the animals stared in horrified fascination at the sun rising in the east.

In the east!

The sun, that most reliable and stately of all timepieces, which had always and ever—to every animal's memory and to every Scribe's history—risen in the west and set in the east, now was rising in the east; and would, if allowed to continue on this unholiest of courses, set in the west!

Set in the west, over the ocean.

The ocean. Josh and the others were suddenly aware of a mounting roar to the west, and looked toward the sea. In the glimmering distance, the ocean was returning—with a vengeance. A churning wall of water, hundreds of feet high, was approaching with a speed that left little time for contemplation.

Josh bent, momentarily, over the child: she was dead. At the end of this long, seventh day of her illness, she had her final rest. Before anyone could grieve or cheer over this information, the ground lurched at the first impact of the wave smashing into the cliffs to the west. Josh fell. Isis crawled into his lap and clung to him, trembling.

Suddenly Phé and Aba grabbed them up—Josh, Isis, Paula, Jasmine, Ollie, and Rose—grabbed them and flew interlocked, as high as they could, balancing this enormous, clumsy load, falling and hanging on in two huge armfuls. They were hovering at about a hundred feet, struggling to stay aloft, when the water began rushing below them, carrying the remaining survivors in all directions.

A torrential wind came with the wave, and it wrenched Phé and Aba apart. Phé was left holding only Paula. Aba carried Jasmine, Rose, Ollie and Josh, to whom Isis still clung. The Vampire siblings tried to join hands again, but the winds buffeted them and tore at their wings, and it was all they could do just to stay in the air.

The Humans' raft could be seen churning along the crest

of the wave; various creatures were variously buoyed along or dragged under by it. The noise was deafening, the winds cyclonic. Phé and Aba were tumbled farther and farther apart, until soon they were almost out of each other's sight.

Aba, in addition, was having difficulty staying airborne. The great weight he was trying to carry dragged him down, continually closer to the rushing water. And the nearer he came to the surface, the worse the winds became, which made it even more difficult to fly. Only twenty feet above the tide, his wings began to tire.

"I can't make it!" he yelled. He lost more altitude. Twelve feet over the crashing waves, the spray whipped their faces like needles.

Josh looked frantically around for the derelict raft; empty, it bobbed and plunged, too far to reach in this monster current. Isis dangled like a wet rag, her mind blank with terror. Jasmine looked for debris to cling to, and Rose was simply glad, now, that Beauty wasn't here, that he was safe and dry in a fortress of ice.

Ollie was furious. After all he had gone through—to survive, to save Josh, to learn how to feel—after all this, to die for nothing! To die in a storm, after all his years on a pirate ship, to die in a storm caused by a spoiled child! And to drag down Aba with him, Aba who had opened his eyes to gentleness and love and calm reason— No! He would not. At least he would not die for nothing. At least, after all this, he could die saving his brother Joshua, who had once risked so much saving him. He could die repaying his debt to Aba—the poet-Vampire who even now was willing to lose his life to save this ragged band of Humans.

And anyway, wasn't the raft around here somewhere?

With this thought, he pulled his hand free, fingered the raw, empty scar in his chest, and jumped into the thundering swells. He was quickly sucked under, and lost to sight.

Now lightened of his load, Aba began to climb again; and with new hope came new strength to his wings. He gained altitude slowly at first, then more rapidly as the winds loosened their grip on him. Soon he was high enough to glide, with an occasional flap to regain elevation.

He circled the area half an hour, looking for Ollie, for Phé, for Paula. Finally, his heart leaden, he gave up, and flew due east, into the rising sun.

CHAPTER 21

The Garden

THERE were major shocks and aftershocks for weeks: eventually the tide found its new level, after eating up the old coast. The weather took months to really calm down; but long before that, the air got sweet, and everything had the feel of beginnings.

Aba had landed, finally, at night, in an area of high, rumbling ground overlooking what was once the southeastern Terrarium—though the entire land mass had shifted so drastically during the cataclysm that it was impossible to say *where* in the world they were now. The five of them— Aba, Josh, Jasmine, Rose, and Isis—slept for two days without stirring. Finally, they stretched, breathed easier, and surveyed their domain.

It was an exotic garden of sorts. Strange, odoriferous blossoms filled storm-bent trees, or were strewn about the thick grass. Fruit vines sporting sweet, dripping globes of riotous color twined over mossy stumps. There were ferns, too, and nut trees; a stream that meandered to a nearby misty glen; ponds, hills; vegetables of curious description, plump tubers, leafy fronds. Most of the flora consisted of items no one had ever seen before. And it all looked somehow untarnished.

"A garden of earthly delights," said Jasmine. It was unfathomable to her, yet somehow inevitable, this turn of events. She accepted it with the equanimity she had learned, over the centuries, to accept things with; still, she knew she would puzzle over its meaning for centuries to come.

Strange, uncertain animals—creatures previously unknown—roamed here, too. They seemed for the most part

311

quite tentative about the environment, and left Joshua and the others to themselves, to spend the days exploring the wondrous new place; and the nights sleeping dreamless sleep.

Some of the new animals were terrifying, though, and put a strained, jumpy edge to existence. One day Josh came running into camp with a hot sweat on his face, whispering "Run! Under cover, quick!" Close on his heels could be heard a thundering of hoofs.

Just as they were all hidden away in the hollow of a huge broken tree, the bizarre creatures stormed into the clearing. They were unbelievably tall, thoroughly unreal. They were quadruped, their legs six or seven feet high. Short tails and short muscular bodies, with short yellow fur covered in irregular brownish blotches. And their necks! Their necks were another seven or eight feet long, sticking straight up, as if gruesomely stretched by some mad force. Their heads were triangular, bearing odd little horns. They looked around wildly, ate a few leaves from the tops of the trees, pawed the ground with dangerously sharp hoofs, and finally ran off again.

Jasmine, Josh, and Rose crawled out of hiding, shaken. "What was *that*?" whispered Rose.

Josh just shook his head.

"More of the child's dreamwork, I suppose." Jasmine sighed with relief at the departure of the scary weird creatures. "I just wish she'd been a bit less surrealistic with her inventions."

After about a week, Aba prepared to leave. He was rested, but hungry—he hadn't had any red cells for many days—so he had to get looking for a harem. He wasn't hopeful, after the flood, but he would do what he could. Also, of course, he wanted to search for Paula, and Phé.

After that, he didn't know. Maybe fly up to Lev's den to see if anyone there had survived; maybe come back. Certainly, he would visit.

Josh and Rose, after a hidden, mysterious conference, presented Aba with a two-pint flask of their blood—dripped in from cuts they had made in their wrists—to sustain him on his journey.

"It's a going-away present," said Josh.

Aba was too moved to reply. He hugged them all, and then they bared necks to each other. Without a word, he flew off to the northwest.

And then there were four.

Over the following days, Jasmine, Josh, and Rose rested, collected themselves, and marveled at the newness of their new world. Isis simply played in it. They were imbued with a combination of wonder and terror that filled every waking moment for quite a long time, pulling their emotions in flagrant disarray. It was wild, exhilarating, disorienting; hilarious, horrifying, and grandiose. It was all of this, and somehow quite sad.

They were sure they would never get used to the sun rising in the east and setting in the west—it was just too unnatural. Too unearthly. As for the rest—the bizarre new creatures and plants, all *de novo* creations of the mutant child's fevered dreams—they gradually adopted a wait-and-see attitude. Some animals seemed dangerous, of course, and these were to be avoided; others were clearly too silly to worry about.

At one point a reticent, obviously harmless, black-and-white smooth-furred, hoofed, four-legged animal with big saggy eyes and big saggy teats wandered near their camp, and said, "*Moooo.*" Josh walked toward it, but it shied away. He spoke to it, but it only answered in its odd, one-word language.

"I've never seen anything like that before," said Josh. "Look at how it cowers when I try to go near it."

"Then let's call it a Cower," said Rose.

And so they began to name all the heretofore nonexistent animals who happened through. The tiny bird with the needle beak, whose cellophane wings hummed as they vibrated, Josh called a Hummingbird. The funny little scale-plated yellow-tan long-nosed reptile Rose called Armored-yellow. Of the ridiculous four-legged, mangy, brown, braying herbivore with two humps on its back, Jasmine said: "That thing looks like it came late to its own creation." So they laughingly named it a Came-late, which later got squeezed into Camelate, and much later shortened to Camel.

All this strangeness, all this unknown. It felt like the rebirth of Time and the world. It left them balanced precariously between great swings of mood: grief, loss, emptiness, one minute; hope and awe the next. They mourned Ollie and Beauty; they rejoiced the destruction of the City. They planned expeditions to go search for their missing loved ones; yet when it came to the actual leaving of this new garden-land, they found themselves limp of spirit—somehow unable finally to pick themselves up and go.

For somehow, something always came up to make them postpone the return to the old land: one of the new pet animals would get sick; Josh would discover a hole in his pants that needed mending; Rose would find she lacked some herbs they might need on a long trip; Isis would disappear for a day.

It was Jasmine who told them finally they didn't have to leave.

"Don't go anywhere," she said to them one night as they sat drinking around a small fire. "I hereby give you permission to stay here forever."

"What do you mean?" asked Josh. "What are you talking about—permission?"

"Well," Jasmine expounded, "on the one hand, you obviously feel guilty about Ollie's sacrifice jump into the drink—about leaving him, and Beauty, to fend for themselves, all alone. On the other hand, you're understandably exhausted—emotionally, I mean. You've been on a marathon adventure, and you need to just withdraw a little now—take some time, absorb everything that's happened and seems to be still happening. There's nothing you can do for them now, anyway—either they're okay or they're not. Later on, you'll have years to find out—and to find them, if they're to be found. It's what I've always tried to teach you: when there's nothing to do, do nothing. It used to be, Joshua, when there was nothing to do, you'd do *any*thing. You've learned a lot lately, I think, but sometimes you still need someone's permission to do nothing, just to relieve you of that last little burden you're laboring under, when you feel that something *has* to be done. So listen to me now: nothing has to be done. You don't have to go anywhere. You have my permission to stay right where you are, for as long as it's good."

Josh looked uncertainly at Rose; uncertainly, she nodded.

"I feel a lot calmer, already," said Josh.

Jasmine settled back. "Peace may yet come to us all."

So the three of them and Isis spent many long weeks in peaceful contemplation in the garden. Josh later wrote extensively in his journal, describing in detail the grand adventure that had led them so variously to this sylvan place, and setting down, as he was able, the nature of his experiences and perceptions during his fusion with the child's consciousness.

Rose resumed her old love of tending plants, nurturing the land. She no longer lusted after the Plug, or even thought of Josh as The Serpent: now he was Josh, and she was Rose; and this was their garden. And for the first time in many years, she was content.

To Jasmine, this was the greatest of all adventures. New plants and animals in a new land, on a new Earth; maybe even a new universe. She read Joshua's journal and asked him hundreds of questions about the meaning of Time and Space, as seen through the child's eyes, and he answered her as he could, and they had long dialogues into the perfumed night.

Isis, meanwhile, found ten million new things to explore and play with. She naturally assumed this wondrous playground had been designed expressly for her, and graciously accepted the gift. She spent the nights prowling after shadow monsters, running rodents to ground, or giddily skittering through the branches on some enterprise of profound moment.

During the days, under the warm smile of the rolling sun, she slept.

EPILOGUE

AND SO they lived. They named all the new animals they discovered, and cultivated the plants. Gradually, some of the old animals began to appear—Horses, and Bears, and Spiders, and such—though few could speak words, as they used to. Many of the old creatures were never seen again—Satyrs, Accidents, Harpies, Elves; and only the occasional Vampire would fly by, high in the clouds, usually heading south.

Aba never returned. Whether he found Ollie, or Phé and Paula, was not known; nor was their fate learned.

And though, in the back of their minds, Josh and Rose always listened for Beauty's hoofbeats to rise in the distance, that joyous sound never came. Later it was discovered that the geography of the area was so changed that the Mosian Firecaves could no longer be located. The whereabouts of the City of Ice, and of Beauty, remained one of Time's dark secrets, until much later still.

Josh and Rose had seven children, whom they named Can, Able, Will, Dawn, Hope, Lon, and Fey. And because there was no choice but to interbreed, among them they begot grandchildren and great-grandchildren and so on—all of whom lived through their own tragedies and comedies, about which many stories have since been told.

Jasmine took long solitary trips into the wilderness, having numerous adventures, quests, crusades, and such. But she always returned to Josh and Rose, to share her experiences, and to weave tall tales around the fire to their children.

The religion of Scribery—as such—died. Josh kept his daily journal, though; and became a great storyteller. The stories of his life and struggles, passed on from generation to generation, became legendary. It was a new world, but Josh never wanted his progeny to forget the trials and conquests and friends of his youth.

The stories changed and evolved over the years, of course; but even so, long after he died, people still spoke of the time when animals could talk; of the evil snake-headed Queen who once fixed Joshua with her stony gaze; of the young bride, Eurydicey, taken across the River Sticks to the Nameless City guarded by the three-headed Dogs; of the lost city of Atlantis, dead beneath the waves; of Satyrs and Vampires, Dryads and Dragons and ANGELs and Centaurs and the island of shipwrecks where Joshua once found love with a Selkie whose name was the sound of waves crashing in a sun-filtered grotto; of the fourfold path of the Cognons, Hedons, Cidons, and Deitons, whose souls rested in their PINEAL center; of Popes and Kings and Doges and the upright trident symbols of the BASS water people; of Scribes and the Word; of meshing fingers in the Sign of the Plug, and how that symbol came to be a gesture of prayer to The Serpent; of The Serpent himself, who came to live in this garden; of the bird-child and how she died, and how what she knew lived again in Joshua, the Scribe and Serpent; and what the bird-child said, and tried to understand; and of her seven-day illness that was the creation of this new world, when it rained fire and the Earth stopped and the sky split and all the new animals appeared. And, after the deluge, how Josh and Rose came to live in the garden of Jasmine.

And had many further adventures, about which many journals were kept, many stories told.

About the Author

James Kahn lives in southern California, where he practices medicine, dallies, trifles, and broods. He is currently working on the final volume of *The New World Trilogy*.

About the Illustrator

Jill Littlewood works as a calligrapher for the County of Los Angeles. In addition, she recently received funding from the National Geographic Foundation to illustrate the anatomy of *Argentivas Magnificens*, a five-million-year-old bird that, with a wingspan of twenty-four feet, is thought to be the largest bird that ever flew.